THE UNWANTED WIFE

L. STEELE

Dear Good Girl,
does your significant other know
you're in love with
a 6' 3" billionaire
with mismatched eyes
who growls: "Mine"?

SPOTIFY PLAYLIST

All Too Well – Taylor Swift

Smells like Teen Spirit – Stevie Howie

I Wouldn't Love Me – Sam Short

Twisted Love – Ariya

Fearless (Taylor's Version) – Taylor Swift

10 20 30 – Emlyn

Pretty Distraction – SkyDxddy

Alive – 2004 Remix – Pearl Jam, Brendan O' Brien

In a Bar – Tango with Lions

It Takes a Lot to Know a Man – Damien Rice

Lovely (with Khalid) – Billie Eilish, Khalid

PRIMROSE HILL

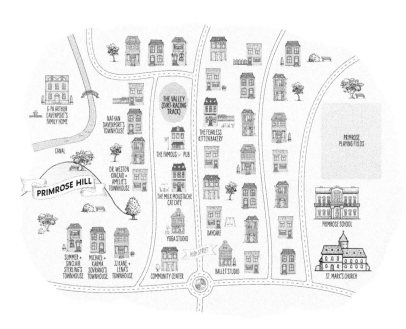

FAMILY TREE

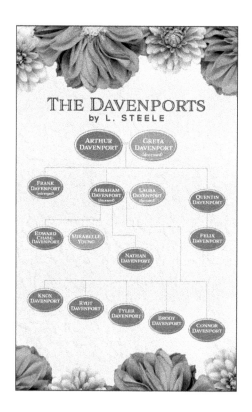

1

Skylar

"I can't do this." I lock my fingers together and narrow my gaze at my reflection. I'm in the tiny bathroom adjoining my office at the back of my bakery—my baby, my enterprise into which I've poured my life savings. And now, it's going to shut down. Unless I find the money for the rent next month... And for the utilities to keep the lights on so the sign on the shopfront continues to be lit up in pink and yellow neon... And for the supplies I need to continue baking. *The Fearless Kitten* is more than my dream; it's my whole life. What I've worked toward since I was sixteen and knew I was going to become the most phenomenal baker in the world. And now, I'm going to lose it.

"Sure, you can do it." My brother encourages me from the doorway. "You can do anything you set your mind to."

"That's what I used to think. It's why I started this pastry shop." I was twelve when I discovered I was good at baking. That, combined with my love for desserts, meant I knew what I wanted to do with my life.

Two years ago, I moved to London to work at a well-known patisserie. I began scouting for a location for my place while I saved every single penny I could.

A year ago, I found the perfect place, and my little artisan bakery with coffee shop seating was born. Of course, I work eighteen-hour workdays, which means I have almost no social life. I barely manage a few hours of sleep in my little apartment over the shop. But nothing can dampen my spirits. I'm spending my days churning out cakes and pastries. It's what I've dreamed of for so long. Only issue?

I don't have the money to advertise, and despite having a social media post go viral—which is when a lot of people look at your social media feed—and result in a surge of customers, I'm not making enough to salvage my business.

"Don't give up. You have to believe this can take off." Ben's voice is confident. If only I shared his optimism.

"Oh, trust me, I want to believe. But blind faith in yourself only takes you so far." I wish I could do better at spreading the word about the place and bringing in new customers. I seem to suck at everything outside of baking. It's why my business is on the decline.

"Success is what's beyond the dark night of the soul," my brother, ever the wise one, remarks.

"Is that a saying among you Royal Marines?" I scoff.

"It's—"

The bell over the door at the front of the shop tinkles.

"—your destiny." His lips curve in a smile.

"What?" I blink.

"The bell—it's your future calling."

I roll my eyes. "If you say so."

"Go on, your customer is waiting." My brother walks over and kisses my forehead. "Good luck. Remember, when one door closes, another one opens. Or the one I prefer, she who leaves a trail of glitter is never forgotten."

"Eh?" I stare. "What does that have to do with my situation?"

"Nothing, but it did cheer you up."

I roll my eyes, then can't stop myself from chuckling.

"That's my girl." He pats my shoulder.

Yep, that's my brother. The ever-cheerful, never-surrender person. "You'll see; it will work out." He turns me around and points me in the direction of the doorway leading to the shop. "Go on now."

"Whatever you say, big bro."

I was ten when my father passed, and Ben became the de facto father figure in my life. I'm fifteen years younger than him, an "oops baby," born when my mother was in her early forties. I hero-worshipped Ben, who, in turn, took care of me and never let me feel the loss of my father. And when my mother passed away, he took a leave of absence and came home and stayed with me, until he was assured I was ready to pick myself up and move on. He's the most important person in the world, in my life, in so many ways. And the fact that he fights wars so I can be safe is a source of the utmost pride for me. It's one of the reasons I feel terrible about being on the verge of bankruptcy. I want Ben to be proud of me.

"This is my last chance to get things right. If I can't find a way to pay off my debts, I'll have no choice but to shut down." I hear my words and realize I'm being negative. The exact opposite of my brother. I expect him to tell me off, but there's no answer. I turn to find he's left the shop. Not that I blame him. He has a two-week break before he has to ship out again. I suspect he's gone to meet his current squeeze. Ben never lacks female companionship.

As for me? I need to face whatever's in my destiny. If only my every decision didn't impact Hugo. If only I weren't running out of money to keep him in the care home that provides round-the-clock attention for him. If I can't pay next month's fees—no, I'm not going there. I will not contemplate the repercussions of what would happen if I didn't come up with the money, and fast.

With a last tug at the neckline of my blouse, which dips a little too low in the front, and which I wore to try and cheer myself up—big fail, there—I march out of the kitchen and go behind the counter. And all the air whooshes out of my lungs.

The man standing in the middle of the bakery is so big, he seems to occupy all of the space in my little bakery. He's so tall, I have to tilt my head back to meet his gaze. And his shoulders—those shoulders I once held onto—are wider than I remember. They're broad enough to block out the view of the rest of the space.

His biceps stretch the sleeves of his suit, which must cost my entire annual rent to buy, given its tailor-made finish. He's wearing a black silk tie, and his jacket is black. Wait, a suit? I've never seen him in a suit before, but OMG, does he do it justice. I take in that lean waist, and those massive thighs, which seem ready to burst the seams of his pants, and between them, the tent that was the object of my obsession for so long. He prowls over to the counter and whoa, that predatory walk of his, the way he seems to glide across the floor with the gait of a barely tamed animal turns my bones to jelly.

"There was no one at the counter when I walked in. No wonder, you need a cash infusion," a familiar voice growls.

What the—? How dare he say that! I wrench my gaze up to his face. And any remaining thoughts in my head drain away. I was prepared to give him a piece of my mind, but all of the pieces have scattered.

Those eyes—one piercing blue, the other an amber brown. Those heterochromatic eyes, which have always had the effect of reducing me to a mindless blob of need, stare into mine.

My entire body hurts. My shoulder muscles turn into cement blocks. My stomach twists. It feels like I've run into a wall. Frissons of shock reverberate down my spine, and when he rakes his gaze down to my chest, his entire body seems to tense. He brings his gaze back to my face, and it feels like I've been punched in the gut. Again.

"What are you doing here?" I manage to croak around the ball of emotion in my throat.

"What do you think I'm doing here?" His jaw tics, a muscle spasms in his jaw, and he curls his fingers into his sides. There's so much tension radiating from him, I feel faint. Apparently, he doesn't like what he sees.

That makes two of us. Nathan-bloody-Davenport. My brother's best friend. The man I've had a crush on for more than half my life. The man who turned me down when I threw myself at him the day of my eighteenth birthday party. Not before he kissed me, though.

He hauled me to him, thrust his tongue between my lips, and ravaged my mouth. He squeezed my ample butt and drew me against him, and I felt every inch of what he was packing. The kiss seemed to go on and on. My head spun. My knees gave way underneath me. I stumbled, and he straightened me. Only to tear his mouth from mine and stare into my face, his chest heaving, his breath coming in gusts that seemed to swell his shoulders. He raked his gaze across my features, like he was seeing me for the first time. Like he wanted to throw me down and mount me right there.

"Nate..." I breathed his name.

"Starling," he whispered against my lips. The sound of his voice seemed to cut through his reverie, for the next second, he released me and jumped back.

A look of confusion, then regret, then anger swept over his features. I felt his rejection even before he blanked all expression from his face. "I'm sorry, I shouldn't have done that, Skye." He turned on his heel and walked out of my birthday celebration, and our house. And my life.

That was it; he cut off all communication with me. I never saw him again. Over the last five years, I've heard about his progress in the Marines from my brother, but I never set eyes on him. Until today.

"You're the last person I want to speak to." I cross my arms over my chest, thereby pushing my breasts up higher. His eyes move down before he forces them back to my face. *It's not that I want to flaunt my double-D tits. Okay, okay, maybe I do. Maybe, I want to make him realize what he's been missing.* I'm proud of my assets. I might be a size sixteen, but I've never tried to conceal my full figure. So what if I want to run and hide right now?

"The feeling's mutual," he growls.

And the sound is so freakin' hot, so caveman like, my ovaries seem to quiver. Just because my body can't control itself doesn't mean I find him attractive. Nope, it doesn't mean anything that I haven't stopped thinking of him all these years.

I draw myself up to my full height. Not that it helps, considering I'm five-feet four-inches tall, and he's a good foot taller than me. Still, this is my space. "This is my shop, and you need to leave."

"Trust me, I wouldn't be here if I had any other option," he sneers.

"What's that supposed to mean?"

"You're looking for a bailout."

"Excuse me?" I gape at him.

"Your business is in trouble. You need money to pay off your debts."

My flush intensifies. Heat crawls up my cheeks, all the way to the roots of hair, followed closely by anger. *How dare he walk in and throw my failure in my face? How dare he not talk to me all these years, only to reappear at the worst possible moment? And right after my brother told me it was my destiny come-a-calling when the bell to the shop rang.*

"Wait, did Ben put you up this?"

"Eh?" He stares at my lips. His gaze is so intent that the frisson of awareness, which has crackled up my spine since he arrived, flares into a full-blown shiver. I shake my head, ignoring the buzz of electricity that has always hummed between us. "Are you here because Ben asked you to help me out?"

A weird look comes into his eyes. He shifts his weight from foot to foot. "I'm here because my grandfather is the chairman of the Davenport Group of companies, and he thinks your bakery would make for a good investment."

"He does?"

"I'm yet to be convinced." He crosses his arms across his chest.

So that's how it's gonna be, eh?

He glances toward the counter, taking in the various desserts on display, and his frown deepens. I follow his gaze and take in the tray of cupcakes displayed: Spicy Scene, Red Room, Velvet Ties, Purple Patches, Cave Wonder, The Vanilla Vajayjay, The Earth Moved... You have to admit, they're innovative names for the treats.

I named the first one in jest, but it proved to be a hot topic of discussion among fellow spicy book readers like me. Before I knew it, I'd ended up naming many of my desserts in a similar vein.

In fact, the dessert shaped like the backside of a woman and called Spanked is one that customers seem to love. Then there's my other hit, a chocolate cake shaped like a vibrator and called Clitasaurus. Yep, they love that one. Also, another raspberry-infused one in the shape of a peach called

Moist Goodness, not to forget the honey-glazed fruit cake in the form of a beehive called the Honey Pot, and the strawberry and cream-topped, fig-shaped shortbread I named Sweet Bits. Finally, the doughnut-shaped dark chocolate glazed treat called—you guessed it—Alphah0le, which readers love when I cater at book events.

You'd think business is booming, and I certainly have my share of loyal customers, but it's not enough to keep me in the black. I need to bring in new customers, and a lot more of them.

He stabs his forefinger at the display. "Is this a joke?"

2

Skylar

A-n-∂ that was the absolutely wrong thing to say. No one insults my baby—my bakery, my ∂ream—and gets away unscathed.

"I can assure you; they are popular amongst my customers."

He turns those searing eyes on me, and it feels like I'm looking into the depths of a frozen lake. The surface seems able to bear my weight, but one wrong step, and I'm going to fall right through and find myself trapped. I try to breathe, but all of the oxygen in the room has been sucked out by his presence. My pulse crashes in my ears, and my nerve endings are so tightly stretched, I fear they'll snap any second. And when he shoves a hand in his pocket, pulling the fabric of his pants taut over that bulge between his legs, a slow thud flares to life between mine.

I *cannot* find him attractive. Cannot risk acknowledging this chemistry that thickens the air between us. Not when I need his help to save my business. Not when I know who he is, and he's definitely out-of-bounds. Forbidden. Sirens go off in my mind. *Back away. It's not worth taking on the humungous backlog of complications that are going to come with having anything to ∂o with him.*

Then a look of boredom crosses his face. He yawns, and my pulse rate shoots up.

Strike out everything I felt earlier. It's definitely worth taking on every challenge that comes with getting him to cough up money, because by God, he needs to realize the world doesn't revolve around him. How can anyone be this full of himself? This insensitive?

Anger squeezes my chest. Adrenaline laces my blood. *And how dare he turn the most important meeting of my life into... into... something that doesn't merit even a few seconds of his attention?*

"I've seen everything I need to see. Goodbye." He turns to leave.

What the—? He's leaving? Does that mean he's decided against investing in the bakery? Think! You need to say something to stop him. You cannot afford to piss off the one guy who might be able to help save your bakery.

"Wait, don't you want to taste my wares?" I burst out.

He freezes mid-step. His shoulders seem to swell. The planes of his back rise and fall, and the jacket pulls even tighter. *Is he going to burst out of his skin and go all Hulk on me?* I swallow. And when he turns slowly and makes a growling sound at the back of his throat, I have to stop the yelp that almost spills from my mouth. Every single cell in my body has woken up and is doing the hula. *Stop that. You can't feel this drawn to this... To this arrogant beast who rejected you.*

But I also need his help. I have to save my business from going bust. And if that means swallowing my pride, then so be it. I tip up my chin and straighten my back. "I... I mean, maybe you want to taste my Honey Pot?" *Ugh. Didn't mean it to come out like that.*

His left eyelid, the one covering his blue eye, twitches, and he seems one step closer to either having a breakdown or walking away. Neither of which is desirable.

"Oh, *Fraggle Rock*. What I meant to say is, you'll definitely like the Purple Patches." I point to the range of cupcakes showcased under the counter.

"Did you use *Fraggle Rock* as a swear word?" He stares.

"I did. It's because my mother hated me swearing—being a girl, and all that." I roll my eyes. That condition had *not* applied to my brother. "So instead, I began to use names of TV series as swear words. Also, you could try the Clitasaurus?" I look at him hopefully.

"The whatasaurus?" He tilts his head. His gaze is, once again, fixed on my mouth. My thighs clench, and moisture laces the flesh between my legs. I push away the burst of awareness which seems to have stuck its claws into my skin. No way am I going to succumb to his magnetism, which has multiplied in the years since I last saw him. Especially not when his jerkhole factor hasn't reduced, either.

It's always been a mystery to me why I found his arrogance such a turn on. Now, I'm also reminded of how he always managed to get on my nerves. Not that it stopped me from throwing myself at him. A mistake I'm not going to make again. When I named that cupcake, it seemed like a stroke of genius. Having to pronounce it aloud in front of the Hulk, however, negates any laughs I've had about it so far.

"Uh, you know what I mean?" The color of my cheeks deepens and spreads to my chest. My entire body seems like it's on fire.

"No, I don't," he says in a low, hard voice.

I shiver. "You know that…that…pink pastry between the blue cakes that looks like…" I glance around, then slide open the glass door to the under-counter area. I pull on a pair of disposable gloves, reach in and, instead of the Clitasaurus, slide one of the fig-shaped desserts onto a plate. I place it on the counter. "Actually, I think you should eat my Moist Goodness, and everything will be clear to you, and—"

I hear a gnashing sound, and when I dare to peek at Mr. Grouchy Face, I see the muscles of his jaw ripple. *Oh no, at this rate, he's going to crack a molar. Or two.*

I blink rapidly. "Maybe we should start afresh?"

"Start afresh?" he asks in a tone that implies he'd rather have never met me.

Yeah, me, too. Unfortunately, I don't have that luxury. "You know, pretend we don't know each other. Pretend the last few minutes never happened?" *Pretend that kiss is not seared into my brain, and into other parts of my body I'm not going to think about.*

I pull off my gloves and hold out my hand. "Skylar Potter." Then, because I hate my life and because, apparently, the connection between my brain and my mouth has been lost under the force of his glower, I smile. "No relation to Harry, as you're aware."

"Harry?" He looks at my slim, pink-tipped fingers, then back at my face, and makes no move to shake my hand.

I set my jaw. *Oh, my god, he's so rude, I should slap one of the pies baking in my oven into his face. Only, they're too good to waste. Also, I can't risk messing up a pie when I need every sale I can get.* Every part of me wants to turn and run out of here. But I can't. I owe it to myself, to my dream, to give this one last shot. *I will not give up easily. I will not. I will stay polite, even if it kills me.* I manage to bare my teeth in the resemblance of a smile. "You know, Harry Potter? Boy wizard? *Evanesco.*" I pretend to flick my wand in his direction.

His jaw hardens further.

Ooh, he looks pissed. The tips of his ears have turned white. Also, the end of his nose. Also, the vanishing spell on him didn't work. His Royal Dickness is still here, larger than life and glowering at me.

"I'm sooo immersed in the Potterverse. Oh, and Taylor Swift. I love Taylor Swift." I beam at him.

His frown deepens.

"I'm guessing you're not a Swiftie?" I nod.

"What's that?" he asks in a contemptuous tone.

"Those of us who love Taylor Swift call ourselves Swifties."

"Sounds contagious," he sneers.

I ignore his cantankerous attitude because I need to charm him. And because I desperately need him to fork over the money I need. "I love her songs, don't you?" I chirrup.

His fingers curl into fists at his sides. Which is not a good sign. Then, because I love to go from the sublime to the surreal, I smile even wider. "Guess which Hogwarts' house Taylor Swift belongs to?" I toss my hair over my shoulder.

"Hogwhat?" He seems like he's about to have a cardiac event. Or like he went to sleep and woke up in an alternate reality. This is bad. So bad.

And I have to go and put my foot in it by prompting him, "Hogwarts."

"Hogwhat?" he snaps again.

This time, the light goes on in my brain. "Oh, you haven't heard of Hogwarts?" I titter. "That's okay. I wasn't alive when *Titanic* hit the cinemas, either…" *Don't say it, don't say it.* "Unlike you."

He blinks slowly.

"I meant the movie, not the actual event when the Titanic hit an iceberg and sank."

His jaw tics.

"Not that you were alive when the Titanic sank." I cough. "Even *I* know you're not *that* ancient."

A nerve pops at his temple. That's not a good sign, is it? *Zip your lips. Just shut up already.*

"Not that I'm implying you're old or anything." I try to contain my laughter and end up snorting—ugh, bad habit. "The grey in your hair adds to your distinguished appearance. Besides, you're only fifteen years older than me." *Oh no, I don't think that makes it better.*

The veins on his throat stand out in relief. I try to swallow, but my throat is so dry, it feels like sharp knives line my gullet. I flick out a tongue to wet my lips, and his eyes gleam. He watches my mouth with a rapacious gaze. Every part of his body seems to have turned to stone. Watching me with such intensity, he seems to have turned into a predator who's planning every possible way to jump me. If he had a tail, I think it'd be swishing from side to side.

The silence deepens. It doesn't stop me from shaking a finger at him. "You, mister, need a crash course in pop culture. Although, I suppose, I shouldn't expect someone who has grey at his temples to have a sense of the zeitgeist."

"The fuck you prattling on about?" he bites out through gritted teeth.

"Whoa, hold on, no need to show me your horns." *Although, I'd love to see the one between your legs.* "In fact, you look so angry, I'm expecting you to breathe fire at any moment." *You can turn into a dragon and carry me away anytime.* "And seriously, you should taste this." I push the plate with the moist, pink-and-white, fig-shaped shortbread in his direction. It has a button between the lips made of edible silver leaf and there's glitter around it.

"My desserts are awesome; one bite, and you'll be a convert." I nod.

He stares.

"Unless you're worried you'll get addicted to my Sweet Bits." I tip up my chin.

Did I say *my* sweet bits? I did say *my* sweet bits. "I meant the dessert that I've named Sweet Bits, not *my* sweet bits." I hear my words, and argh, didn't mean for them to sound so... provocative. But I'm not going to apologize for that. Hell no.

"Well? You going to taste it or what?" I scowl.

He must see the challenge in my eyes and, alpha male that he is, of course, he doesn't back down. Without taking his gaze off of my face, he licks the cream from the hollow in the center. A thousand little fires flare to life under my skin. I swallow; my breath grows shallow. He bites down on one of the plump lips, and a shiver grips me. I clutch at the edge of the counter. The pulse at the base of my throat speeds up. And when he pops the other lip into his mouth, I gulp. He brings his thumb and forefinger to his mouth and sucks on them, and a breathy moan leaves my lips.

"Not bad." He shrugs.

I stare. "What do you mean, *not bad?! That* is my best-seller."

"It was okay." He looks down his nose from his superior height. "I admit, the names you give your baked goods are creative, but I'm not sure that's enough for me to approve the takeover."

"Takeover?" I stiffen. "Who's talking about a takeover?"

"It's the only way I'd consider investing in your business."

"I only need help," I say through gritted teeth.

"That's putting it mildly. I reached out to the bank you took the loan from—"

"You reached out to my bank?" I burst out.

"You don't think I'd be here without due diligence—"

I cut in, "The terms of my deal with them are confidential." I lock my fingers together.

"Not when you're about to go bankrupt. When they realized the Davenport Group was considering an acquisition—"

"An investment; a loan; that's *all* I'm looking for. Something to tide me over and buy me some time until I get back on my feet."

"Keep fooling yourself. You might be a good baker—"

"So you did like my dessert," I declare in a triumphant voice.

"—but you're not a businessperson, by any stretch of the imagination."

Oh, my god! What I wouldn't give to wipe that smug look off his face.

"There are ups and downs in any business." I lock my fingers together. "Things will bounce back."

"There are ups and downs, and then, there are downs and more downs," he drawls.

Anger thuds at my temples. *I will not lose my temper. I will not.*

He slides his hand into his pocket. "Not that I don't understand your reluctance to sell out."

"You do?"

"Of course. You've invested your sweat and blood, and likely, your entire savings into the venture. Too bad you didn't have a financial person advising you."

Of course, he'd say that. Nate's always been a numbers whiz. I heard that from Ben. It's why, even when they were in the Marines together, Nate oversaw strategy. He was the person coming up with the game plan for their team. It was Nate's sharp brain which helped them both stay ahead of the enemy; or so my brother informed me over the years. Too bad his best friend's temperament leaves much to be desired.

"I would be willing to consider a merger instead of an acquisition of your little business." His gaze flicks about the place and back at me.

"*Little* business?" I curl my fingers into fists. *Breathe, count back from ten. Do not give into the impulsive need to throw a pie in his face.*

He wipes his thumb under his lip, a considering look in his eyes. "Of course, I don't have to do anything. But given you're Ben's little sister, and he wouldn't want me to leave you in the lurch, I might have a proposition that could help both of us."

"Of course you do."

My sarcasm is lost on him, for he looks me up and down. "Marry me."

3

Nathan

"You asked her to marry you?" My half-brother, Knox gapes at me.

I glare at him. He clamps his cigar between his teeth and flashes me a shark-like smile. He might be my half-sibling, but he's made it clear, when it comes to splitting the family fortune, he'll fight me on both my claim to the title of CEO and to my share of Arthur's wealth. Not that I want either, but Arthur wants me to head up his group of companies, and when I saw how royally it ticked-off Knox, I accepted the role. Just for the pleasure of watching him stew. Also, because it's rightfully mine.

"Of course, you did." Sinclair Sterling snickers. He's done business with Arthur, and over the years, my grandfather has grown to trust him and rely on his business acumen. At some point, that turned into a close friendship. Not being close to his grandsons, Arthur seems to have sought out Sinclair as a replacement. Now, Arthur likes to have him around at his weekly poker games to referee any possible run-ins the rest of us Davenports tend to favor. It helps to have someone who is not family be the neutral party. You'd think a bunch of grown-ass men could spend a few hours together without coming to blows. Sadly, our track record points to the contrary.

I take in the gleam in his eyes. "What're you cackling about, Sterling?'

"Nothing." He coughs, then slides a couple of chips forward.

I glance at my cards, then slide all my chips in.

Knox blinks. "You sure you want to do that?"

"You sure you don't want to fold?" I sneer.

Knox scowls, then, without taking his gaze off mine, moves all his chips into the pot. "Raise."

Ryot, my other half-brother who's joined the game for the first time, shows no indication he's affected by the goings on at the table. He slides his cigar between his lips, then throws down his cards. He makes a sign indicating he's out. Fucker tries not to speak unless he absolutely must.

"You're out?" Knox side-eyes his brother. "What's the matter, lost your balls?"

Ryot doesn't react. The man has a poker face—no pun intended—which reveals nothing of his thoughts. And I thought I perfected the art of being emotionless. It's the way I navigated a childhood where I was part of a one-parent home.

My mother never kept my father's identity a secret. She also made it clear she had no respect for him; not after he discarded her after finding out she was pregnant with me. They were sixteen, and he was worried his father would disinherit him. When my grandmother found out, she insisted on paying my mother enough for us to lead a comfortable life. Her only condition was my mother take me far away and not have any contact with my father or the rest of the family. She also insisted my mother not give me my family name.

My mother signed the contract, then took the money and moved to the other side of the country. She deposited the check, then promptly broke her promise by naming my father on my birth certificate and giving me the Davenport surname. She never did contact my father's family, and my grandmother never did follow up to ensure she complied with the stipulations of the contract. While I had a passing curiosity about my father's family, my mother's contempt for him and his family rubbed off on me. I had no desire to contact them. Then my mother passed away, and I enlisted. What got me through my tours of duty was my ability to lock down my emotions and focus on the task at hand.

I was very good at blocking out the world and concentrating on the job I had to do. Which is why I climbed the ladder of the military quickly. Which is why I gave orders for that last mission in which I lost my team. If not for Ben, I wouldn't have survived, either. That error in judgement is what prompted me to leave the Marines. And now, I've proposed to Ben's sister—not a real marriage, but still... It'll mean involving her in my messy family situation. What the hell was I thinking? Or *not* thinking.

The sight of little Skylar all grown up with those rosebud lips, those spectacular tits, and that voluptuous body made me want to grab handfuls of her butt and squeeze. It evoked memories of that kiss, which kept me company on many a night in my spartan quarters in whichever hellhole of the world I was serving in. I wanked off to that kiss, the feel of her flesh under my fingers, the give of her mouth against mine, that cherry blossom scent of hers, which has haunted my dreams.

And which I smelled under the aroma of her freshly baked desserts. All of it was a sensory overload. Not to mention, I looked into her features and was reminded of Ben. I remembered my promise to him to look out for his sister, and realized I could deliver on it by helping to rescue her business.

Of course, in return, she'll have to marry me. But this way, I'll be able to keep her safe. Further, it's also the incentive needed for Arthur to confirm me as the CEO of the company. I'll have the title and controlling interest and use it to have my revenge for how this family treated my mother.

I glance around at everyone, then slap my cards on the table face-up. "Royal flush."

"What the fuck?" Knox growls.

"You mean what the Royal *Flush*, don't you?" I allow myself a smirk.

He glowers at me. I lean over and slide all the notes in my direction.

"Not bad," Sinclair drawls.

Ryot does a chin jerk in my direction.

The door to the den opens, and paws patter on the wooden floor. There's a woof, then Tiny, the Great Dane who's adopted G-Pa as his dog parent, lumbers into the room. The mutt pushes his head into my shoulder. When I scratch him behind his ear, he pants happily, then drops down to the floor with his tongue lolling out of the side of his mouth.

"What are my favorite men in the world up to?" My grandfather, the reason we're all here and in one place—under one roof, despite most of us not wanting to be in this situation—saunters into the room. If there was a personification of someone having a spring in his step, then it's him. He beams at us.

Knox groans. "What have you done, old man?"

G-Pa holds up his hands. "Can't this old man be happy that his grandsons seem to be getting along?"

"*Seem,* being the operative word," I mutter.

Ryot frowns in the direction of the senior citizen. Not that it has any effect on Gramps. He bounds over to the table with the energy of someone half his age and drops into the chair between Knox and me. "Seems you won this round, my boy." He slaps me on my shoulder.

I wince. Gramps might be closing in on eighty-two, but he's strong enough for me to feel the weight of his muscles behind that tap.

"No *seems* about that." I rise to my feet. "So long, farewell, and all that."

"What, you're not giving us a chance to win back our money?" Knox growls.

I slide my cigar to the other side of my mouth. "Gotta quit when you're ahead; that's the first rule of gambling."

"But you'd gamble your life on a marriage of convenience?" Knox tilts his head. His eyes flash. I know he's trying to bait me, and I don't want to give him that satisfaction, but I can't stop myself from narrowing my gaze on him. "What I do with my life is my choice."

"Not when it affects the rest of us," he shoots back.

"It's true." Gramps bites off the edge of his cigar then reaches for a light.

"You're agreeing with him?"

"I am. What you do sets the precedent for your brothers to follow."

"Half-brothers." I tip up my chin. "And I'm not the first. Edward agreed to an arranged marriage—"

"And he's very happy," G-Pa says without any trace of smugness. For which I should, perhaps, be grateful. But I don't trust the guy. He's pretending to be uninvolved in his approach, but he knows he's steering us all on this road to marrying and settling down. A part of me resents being led in that direction. And yet, I can't help but feel admiration for his single-mindedness in having us commit ourselves.

"He might be; doesn't mean that route is the right one for the rest of us."

"Doesn't mean it's not." He blows out a puff of smoke. "All I can do is try to guide my family to find happiness."

"The way you and Greta were happy?" Knox snorts.

G-Pa lowers his cigar. "I admit, there were secrets between us. Which was my fault. I should have been more available for my sons. I should have been more open to having a conversation with my wife. I will forever regret that my oldest did not feel confident enough to approach me about having made his girlfriend pregnant or walking away from the woman who was probably the love of his life." The latter... He's referring to Edward's mother.

"Not to mention, staying married, out of duty, to our mother, and being absent as a father to the rest of us," Ryot signs.

He's a man of few words, and of late, he's taken to signing instead of speaking. And even that is rare, so when he does sign, everyone listens. Even

Tiny stops panting as the attention of the table focuses on him. Good thing, I think, I'd picked up the rudiments of sign language while coaching football for special needs children.

"It's admirable you're repentant about your past mistakes, but it hardly makes us confident about your approach to getting us hitched." Ryot's gaze narrows.

G-Pa places his cigar on the notch in the ashtray. The smoke trails into the air. His movements are careful, considered, and when he finally looks up at Ryot, his eyes are conflicted. The old man's a heartless old coot who'd do anything to ensure his company is profitable. But he's made a special attempt to study sign language so he can converse with Ryot. Likely, so he can implement whatever machinations he has in mind. I'm not ready to give my grandfather the benefit of doubt... yet.

"I'm aware of my shortcomings. I'm aware of the mistakes I made with my sons, which is why"—he looks around the table—"I'm determined to set things right. I'm determined that my grandsons will not face the challenges I or my older two sons did. I am determined all of you and your uncle, my youngest son, will find true love and happiness. The kind I had with Greta but did not cherish. It's when you have something and then lose it that you realize its importance. For you young people, life is about power and success and that malarkey—"

Knox sneers, but Arthur ignores him.

"—when really, it's about family, and relationships, and having those who care for you and those you care for around. When it's about finding the love of the right woman and having your own family to nurture and cherish. To see yourself in the faces of your children as they grow, in the happiness of your other half, without whom your life will be incomplete."

"You realize, we may not share the same sentiments?" I crack my neck.

"And you realize, the only way you can become the CEO is by getting married?" Once more, there's no smugness or sense of triumph in Arthur's voice. But damn, if the old man isn't using his condition as a way to get what he wants.

Sinclair looks between us. "Uh, perhaps it's time I left?"

"Stay," I say at the same time as Arthur.

"Your presence helps keep peace between my grandsons and I value that. It makes you family." Arthur straightens his spine. "There are no secrets from you."

I cross my arms across my chest. "You concede you manipulated events so I landed at the bakery of my best friend's little sister?"

"Oh, were you acquainted with the owner of the bakery?" His eyes are wide with innocence. In fact, the surprise on his features is almost believable. *Almost.*

"If you expect me to believe you didn't know about the relationship between me and the woman running the bakery, then you're mistaken."

"So, there *is* a relationship between the two of you?" The old man's eyes sparkle.

"There is nothing between us," I bite out.

"But there could be something in the future. After all, you did ask her to marry you?"

I glower at him. "How do you know that?'

He widens his smile. "A lucky guess?"

When I continue to stare at him, he sighs. "It was a logical conclusion, given how upset you seem, how you reacted to having met the owner of the bakery, and that I had thrown down the gauntlet of you getting married before you could confirm your position as the CEO. Also,"—he raises his hand—"I swear, I had no idea you were acquaintances."

"I've met her three times." On the first two occasions, I accompanied Ben home between our deployments. I merely saw her as my best friend's kid-sister and nothing more. The third time was when she turned eighteen, and she kissed me. And everything changed.

"That's more than enough time to know if she's the woman of your dreams." Arthur nods.

"She's not—" I begin, but with Arthur's keen gaze on me, I swallow my words.

"The bakery is a good investment," he offers.

"What do you know about bakeries?" I narrow my gaze on him.

"It was Greta's dream to run a bakery, but it was something she wanted me to be involved with, with her. I always thought it would be something we'd do together when we retired."

"You wanted to run a bakery when you retired?" Knox gapes at him.

"Indeed. I thought it would be a great way to spend time with my wife, but then Greta passed before I could find a way to slow down. Time"—he glances around the table—" has a way of getting away from you. One moment, you're getting married; the next, you're burying your wife. Then, you find you're estranged from your own children." He turns to me. "You have to believe me when I say, I only want what's best for you. I want you to have everything I didn't. Besides, as long as the owner of the bakery isn't a Whittington or a Madison—though the former is preferable to the latter—and I'm assuming she isn't either, you have my blessings."

"Not that I asked for it," I scoff. "Also, who're these Whittingtons and Madisons?"

"Only our mortal enemies."

"But you hate the Madisons more than the Whittingtons?"

"If there were degrees of hate, then yes." He glares around the table. "As long as I'm alive, there'll never be a Whittington or a Madison spouse for a Davenport, mark my words."

As if sensing the change in mood, Tiny rises from the floor. With a final bump of his head against my hip, he lumbers over to Arthur. He pushes his big head into Arthur's shoulder. G-Pa's features soften. He seems to shake off his anger and pats the mutt's head. With a sigh, Tiny plants his butt on the floor, but keeps his face pressed against Arthur's upper arm.

The old man's repentant about his past and wants to make amends for his transgressions. And I do appreciate the sentiment.

I'm cognizant that he wants the best for us. Only, he wants to maneuver us along and ensure each of us have tied the knot. The reason I'm happy to comply is because I actually want her with me. And this is the perfect opportunity to coerce her into marrying me in return for saving her business. This way, I can ensure she's by my side where I can watch over her.

Once we have wed, nothing stops Arthur from confirming me as the CEO. Then, I can use my position to steer the future of this company. I'll use my power to teach the Davenports a lesson for turning away my mother when she was pregnant and refusing to recognize her child. They may have paid her, but nothing can take away the hurt and anger that drove her to an early grave. Arthur might want to repair the damage he caused, but it's too little, too late. Only taking over the leadership role in the company, and then breaking down Arthur's life's work, will suffice. Bringing down the Davenport name is the only way my mother will be avenged.

I push away the prickle of discomfort that trickles down my spine and wave my cigar in Arthur's direction. "I don't appreciate the way you've finagled me into this arrangement, but fine."

"Fine?" He lowers his chin to his chest. "Care to elaborate?"

I blow out a breath. "Fine, I'll go through with the wedding."

4

Skylar

"What would you do if a man walked in the door and asked you to marry him?" I scowl across the table at my friend Zoey. I opened The Fearless Kitten a year ago, and a few days later, Zoey flounced in. She loved the pastries, ooh'd and aah'd about their names, then bought a bunch to take back for her office colleagues. She kept coming back, and we formed a friendship. It's thanks to her, I'm not completely alone in this town, especially after what had happened to Hugo. It's because of her, I have a small friend circle.

It's also why I didn't hesitate to close the shop early today, to accommodate the weekly meeting of the book club run by Zoey's friend Penny. Besides, given traffic to the shop trails off after six p.m., it seemed like a good idea to me.

I probably shouldn't keep it open until nine p.m. every day. I probably should also take Mondays off, but I need every penny I can make, and I've kept the shop open long hours in the hopes of bringing in more customers. The business that the viral media post brought in helped pay the bills for a few weeks, but the money ran out several weeks ago. Without another viral post, I have no choice but to agree to Nate's proposition...

No. I cannot. How can I marry him when he doesn't love me? Quite the opposite, in fact. It's clear he hates me for having thrown myself at him. Honestly, during our meeting two days ago, I got the impression he was barely listening to what I was saying. He was too busy wondering if the names I'd given my desserts were a joke. Ha. He has no idea what works and doesn't work to sell pastries. Not that *I've* had much success with it. No, correction, I have had success with it... on occasion. I haven't found a way to keep the sales consistent, is all.

"Well? Would you marry him?"

"That depends." She surveys her nails.

"On what?

"The size of his bank balance. Then the size of his dong balance."

I burst out laughing. "Dong balance?"

"Call it the Ding Dong Bell which I need for my Pussy to be well."

I snort.

"Question is, does he have a lot of money?" Her eyes gleam.

"Enough to help me save my business from going bust, yes."

"And how about his other asset?" She wiggles her eyebrows. "Does it match up?"

"I haven't seen it, but from what I've perceived? More than."

"So, what do you have to lose?" She eyes the array of goodies spread out on the table between us.

My heart, for one? Also, I don't think Ben is going to be amused when I tell him about my pact with his best friend.

"I sense a hesitation, babe." She gives me her full attention. "By which, I assume that wasn't an academic question."

"Probably not."

She scans my features and her eyebrows knit. "Want to talk about it?"

"Not yet."

She opens her mouth to protest, but I raise a hand.

"But I will. I promise. Once I've thought things through in my head."

"It's okay to share, Skylar. You don't have to try to solve everything yourself. That's what friends are for. You tell us your problems, and we try to find answers together. That's how it works."

Tears prick my eyes. I'm too damn independent. Probably comes from having to entertain myself on my own for hours once Ben joined the Marines. I'd never begrudge my brother his stellar career with the Marines, but it did mean I spent a lot of time in my head. I was never good at making friends in school, was always a bit of a loner. Then I discovered my love for baking in Home Economics and threw myself into learning everything I could about it. I practiced every recipe I found, the results of which I shared with my class. The boys, especially, would gladly eat up everything I made. But so would I.

I grew in all directions, and by the time I was eighteen, I was a size sixteen. Somehow, it consolidated my reputation as a baker. I fit the stereotype, after all—big girl who loves to make cakes and eat them. Which only isolated me further. Which meant, I gravitated toward food even more. Good thing is, it didn't eat into my confidence—pun intended. I didn't care much that the girls made fun of my size. The boys loved the food I created. They were kinder toward me. Treating me more like a pal. Not that it made any of them want to ask me out.

I went to the prom alone… and danced with myself on the dance floor. And you know what? I didn't care. I already had a scholarship to the Master Baker Program. I was on my way to fulfilling my dream, while the rest of them were too busy following the call of their hormones and getting into each other's pants. Everything was on track. After I graduated college, I worked at a well-known bakery while I saved money and searched for my own place. I was building momentum. Then, I started my own patisserie a year ago. And everything went downhill after that.

My heart squeezes in on itself. My pulse pounds at my temples. But I'm not going to give up. I can't give up. "I promise, I'll tell you when I'm ready."

To avoid looking at Zoey, I reach over, grab a C!itasaurus, and stuff the entire cupcake into my mouth. The chocolate sinks into my palate, and the gooey goodness of the cream in the icing instantly laces my blood. Endorphins fire in my brain. I feel that familiar flush of happiness invade my cells. A comforting feeling envelops me. It's as if a soft blanket has been wrapped around my shoulders.

"Mmm, this is soo good, if I do say so myself."

"It is." Zoey picks one of the Alphah0les, and bites into the doughnut. Powdered sugar coats her lips, and her eyes widen. She chews, swallows, then stuffs the rest of it into her mouth. She makes a sound of contentment, then jumps up from her chair, walks over to me and throws her arms about my shoulders. "You're a genius, babe. When it comes to baking, that is. When it comes to men, not so much."

"Umm—" I cough at the backhand compliment. "Should I say thanks."

"No, really." She straightens, then pretends to flick a tear from her eyes. "That Alphah0le almost made me orgasm with pleasure."

The bell over the doorway tinkles as it closes behind a pink-haired woman bundled up in a coat. She responds to Zoey's comment by saying, "Isn't that the main reason to put up with an alphahole? The orgasms?" She beams at me. "You must be Skylar. I'm Zoey's friend, Summer."

I rise to my feet and hold out my hand, but she repeats Zoey's performance from a few seconds ago and throws her arms about me. I confess, the last few months, I haven't been feeling very sociable or wanting to hug people—or be hugged. For some reason, it often makes me feel like crying—I don't know what that's all about. Must be the stress of trying to save my bakery. But there's another part of me that thinks it's nice to be embraced by my friends and their friends. "The pleasure is all mine."

"I'm so happy you made it." Zoey claps her hands in delight.

"So am I." Her smile widens. "This is the one time in the week that's all mine. My husband stays home with our son, and I'm here to hang out and remember what it was like to be single and have an evening out—without having to keep an eye on my child. Not that I'd change anything, but it's nice to be on my own for a change." She laughs.

"Where's Penny?" Zoey peers past Summer. "Isn't she making it?"

"Not today. Knight surprised her with a trip to Paris. Newlyweds." She chuckles. "Mind you, my husband did that on Valentine's Day. He even ensured the babysitter came along with us so she could take care of our son for the night, in a separate room, and we had an entire twelve hours to ourselves. Heaven."

The bell tinkles again, and in walks my friend Grace, who's wearing a bright yellow coat with feathers stuck to it. She's teamed it with fluorescent-purple platform boots that come over her knees. It should look ridiculous, but she manages to pull it off. She always manages to look striking in the most bizarre of combinations.

"Skylar!" She rushes toward me. "I'm so sorry I'm late. There was so much traffic getting in, it took me twenty minutes to cover that last mile. If I hadn't been wearing these heels, I might have gotten out and walked."

"When was the last time you wore flats?" I laugh.

"Umm, never?" She hugs me, and this time, I hug her back without hesitation. I'm getting back in the swing of things, despite Nate's offer hanging over my head like a looming thundercloud.

"I wanted to leave earlier, but there was a last-minute meeting with the production team on the highlights for tomorrow's program."

"You look like you need this." Zoey approaches us holding two glasses of white wine.

"Bless you." She snatches the glass of wine from Zoey and proceeds to down half of it before she takes in our stares. "What? I'm thirsty. And it's been a long day, and I have to be up at the crack of dawn again tomorrow."

"You're working long hours," I point out.

"It's competitive. There are a hundred others waiting to take my place as the host of the Morning Show on the leading TV channel in the country. I need to be on top of my game and ready to work harder than all of them."

"You were good this morning." Zoey raises her glass.

"Only good?" Grace sniffs.

"You were brilliant. Very confident. And you broke the news of that disaster in Argentina without breaking rhythm," I concede.

"It was tricky, but I have to admit, I almost enjoyed it." There's a glint in her eyes. Grace really does enjoy the challenge of hosting the leading news program in the country. She loves thinking on her feet and reporting.

"You wouldn't catch me waking up at 4 a.m. every day, not to mention getting dolled up and constantly having to perform for the cameras. And then there's you, Skylar." She turns to me. "You not only wake up at 4 a.m. to bake, but you're behind the counter selling until 9 p.m.. You two have one hell of a work ethic, and I admire it. But it's not for me." She shakes her head. "Give me my job as a book editor any day. I prefer to hide behind my computer screen and read manuscripts from the slush pile in my downtime." Zoey laughs.

"I love that all of you have such varied professions." Summer walks over carrying the tray of the goodies I set out earlier. "It makes for such interesting conversations."

A gleam comes into Zoey's eyes. "Speaking of, there's one more person who invited herself over."

5

Skylar

"There is?" I look around at the small crowd.

Zoey and I met Grace a few months ago at a club after she was stood up by her date. We ended up dancing together most of the night and hung out after. And then there's Harper. I met her when I was buying provisions for the bakery, and we hit it off right away.

She moved from New York and is working for a Michelin-starred chef in London, and like me, barely takes a day off.

She couldn't make it to the book club reading today and apologized in advance, promising she'll meet us very soon. So, it's not her.

"Who are you talking about?" "It's my—"

There's the muted roar of a motorcycle driving up. The pipes on the vehicle are loud enough for the vibrations to cause the doorframe to shudder. I exchange glances with the other girls, then walk over to the door.

Before I reach it, it's wrenched open, and a figure fills the doorway. The person is wearing a jumpsuit and has a helmet tucked under her armpit. She stomps inside, her heavy motorcycle boots making a thudding noise on the wooden floor. Her hair is shoulder length and has grey threaded through the brown strands, interspersed with streaks of blue. Tattoos adorn her throat.

Then she spots Zoey and her face splits into a big smile. "Zoey!" She reaches Zoey, throws her arms about the younger woman, and hugs her.

Zoey squeezes her shoulders, then steps back and turns to us. "Everyone, meet my Granny, Imelda."

There's silence, then I manage to pick up my jaw from where it seems to have fallen to the ground and head toward the older woman. "Hello, I'm—"

"Skylar, the owner of this cute-as-fuck bakery." She eschews my outstretched arm and hugs me. "Amazing place you've got here. Hope you don't mind my tagging along. When Zoey told me about this smutty book club, I had to join." She rubs her hands together. "Nothing like a bit of spiciness to get the blood flowing."

"I know, right?" Summer draws abreast. "I love the tattoos, by the way." She nods toward the designs that are visible around her neck.

"Thank you, dear. I always wanted a tattoo, but once I got the first one, I couldn't stop." Imelda's smile grows wider.

"Was that a Harley you drove in on?" Grace joins us.

"Indeed." Imelda nods. "To think, I never drove one until a year ago."

"Gran… I mean, Imelda's part of a motorcycle gang," Zoey chimes in.

I look at her grandmother with something like respect, as do the others.

"You girls are probably thinking, what's a seventy-year-old doing, acting like Jax Teller, huh?" She laughs.

She knows who Jax Teller is? Also, why am I not surprised by that? "Not really. I'm not—" I begin to say, but when Imelda gives me a knowing look, I nod and shut up. I'd be lying if I said the thought didn't cross my mind.

Imelda looks around at us, then nods toward the tray of pastries in Summer's hand.

"May I?"

"Of course." Summer offers her the selection.

"Why don't you come sit down? I'll get you a drink." I lead her to the table where the others are seated.

"You wouldn't happen to have a Chai Latte, would you, dear?" Imelda takes a seat, then helps herself to a Vanilla Vajayjay, and bites into it. "Oh," she moans, "this is incredible!" She closes her eyes, chews, swallows, then proceeds to demolish the rest of the pastry.

Meanwhile, I slip away and prepare her drink. Returning to the group, I slide the Chai Latte across the table before taking the chair across from her.

"Thanks, honey." She takes a sip of the piping hot liquid before looking around at our faces. "Where was I?"

"Jax Teller," Summer prompts her from the chair next to me.

"That's right. After my Joseph passed away—God rest his soul—I thought my life was also over. Until one day, he came to me in my dreams and told me it was time to do everything I'd always wanted to."

"And you were sure it was him talking to you?" I move around, trying to find a more comfortable position in my seat.

"When you love someone, you know." She inclines her head. "I woke up, realizing for the first time in my life, I was not only on my own, but I could do anything I wanted. I wasn't answerable to anyone. Not that I had to keep Joseph appraised of everything I did, but you know what I mean. I paid my dues. I could now spend my money and time on myself. Makes you wonder why I couldn't think like that when he was alive, because he wouldn't have stopped me from buying a Harley. It was my own mind that set up all the mental roadblocks." She looks into her cup. "Makes you think, huh?" She seems to get a hold of herself. "Anyway, I took his advice to heart, and the next thing I knew, I was standing in front of the local Harley dealership. Which is how I came to own Beast."

"That's what she calls her alphahole in this book." Summer holds up a paperback with flowers on the cover. "Of course, the reason she calls him Beast is not the same as the reason your Harley's called that."

"Oh, you'd be surprised. Having that massive rod between my legs has the added benefit of spontaneous O's."

I burst out laughing, as do my friends. My phone vibrates, and I look down at it to see Ben's name on the screen. "Excuse me."

I rise and walk around the counter and to my office. "Where are you, big bro?"

"Sorry, I had to head back on a mission." He sounds tired.

"I thought you'd be on shore leave for another ten days, at least?" I close the door to my office and walk over to sit down behind my desk.

"I thought so, too, but an emergency came up."

"They can't do without you, eh?" I say lightly.

"I really did want us to spend time together, but you know how it is when duty calls." He clears his throat. "I'd hoped to introduce you to my girlfriend and—"

"You have a girlfriend?" I screech.

"I was going to tell you, but uh, I only realized how I felt when I was called away so suddenly. For the first time in my life, I didn't want to go on a mission."

"OMG. You, and hesitating to take on an assignment?"

"Shut up, scamp," he chides. "It was a physical wrench to leave. I would have come by and told you the news myself, but uh… I wanted to spend every second I had with her."

"That's quite understandable." I curl a strand of hair around my finger.

"I gave her your details. She might reach out to you while I'm gone. Hope that's okay?"

"Of course. You don't have to ask." I move the phone to my other ear. "When will you be back?"

"I'm not sure. A couple of months, maybe more?"

There's something in his voice that makes me realize, he doesn't sound like my happy-go-lucky brother. His tone is more sober.

"You really didn't want to leave her, huh?" I ask softly.

"It's not every day a man realizes he's in love." I sense him begin to pace. "If anything were to happen to me..."

"Nothing's going to happen to you."

"But if it did—" Someone calls out to him. "Shit, I have to go, Skye." The phone goes dead.

I glance at the screen. It's not the first time Ben's been interrupted in the middle of a call. But it *is* the first time he's sounded so preoccupied. He needs all his wits about him when he heads into combat. And normally, he's so focused, I don't worry… but this time, there was something off in his voice. Probably just the fact that he was leaving his girlfriend. My brother's in love! OMG, I'm so happy for him. There's a knock on the door. It swings open, and Zoey pops her head around. "Skylar, you've got to get out here. My granny's a hoot." She laughs. "You're going to love her." She must see something on my features, for she frowns. "Everything okay?"

"Of course." I rise to my feet. "Shall we join the book club discussion?"

6

Nathan

"This could be something out of a smutty novel." Brody, my half-brother grunts as he lifts the barbell over his head. I spot him, and he lowers it back to his chest, his biceps bulging. The planes of his chest strain against the sleeveless T-shirt he has on. He sits up and swings his legs over the bench before grabbing the towel I hand him, and mops at the sweat beaded at his temples.

"What do you know of smutty novels?" I scowl. The man loves to read. He's never seen without a book, except for at the gym, though if I weren't here, he'd go through his routine listening to audiobooks.

"More than you, apparently." He smirks.

"Do you read them?" I scan his features.

He shrugs. "Enough to know what women enjoy."

"There's a line between fiction and real life."

"But fact is stranger than fiction." He hooks the towel around his neck, reaches for his bottle of water and chugs down half of the contents.

"Not when it comes to an arranged marriage, it's not. What you see is what you get in such a marriage of convenience." I scowl.

"Hmm, you may not have read any booktok favorites, but you sure know the language."

"The fuck you talking about? What is book talk?"

"Not book talk, book*tok*. It's a hashtag used on a popular social media platform. Perhaps, you've heard of it? TikTok?"

I roll my eyes. "Of course I've heard of it, douchebag."

"Well, what you, apparently, don't know is that it helps readers find their next read."

I rub the back of my neck. "How the fuck do you know this?"

"I make it a point to find out everything that's relevant to my target audience."

"Your target audience?"

"Hey, women make a lot of important decisions which impact the rest of us. And I've found, reading these books is the best way to understand what women want."

"I prefer to use my instincts." I scoff.

"That too... but I'll take every advantage I can get. I want to be prepared for when I meet 'the one.'"

"The *one*? Don't tell me you've bought into this fairytale notion of finding the *one*?"

"No." He shrugs. "Eh, maybe. Whatever the case, it's good to be prepared."

"Prepared?" I lower my arm to my side. "In what way?"

"I want to make sure I know exactly how to enact her favorite scenes."

"Hmm." I scratch my jaw. "There's a certain appeal in that. But how spicy are these scenes in these books."

"Enough to leave me with a massive hard-on and needing to take care of it."

"O-k-a-y?" I purse my lips. "I thought spicy books were like chick flicks, loaded with emotions and such."

"Also loaded with 'porntastic' scenes." He makes air-quotes with his fingers.

How interesting. Does Skylar read them? Based on the names she's chosen for her pastries, I think it's a safe bet that yes, she does. And if so, which are her favorite scenes? And why am I curious? Don't answer that. I know.

The arrangement I proposed will be a marriage in name only. Unless I can show her it's more than that. Meanwhile, it should be enough to confirm my position as CEO, so I can bring down Arthur and have my revenge for how he and his family turned their backs on my mother. Of course, by marrying Skylar, I'm ensuring she'll have access to the Davenport funds. Enough to pay off her debts and stop her business from going bankrupt. I promised Ben I'd take care of her, and this is my way of ensuring she'll never lack for anything.

It's a good plan. Everything will be neatly tied up, and once I make sure she has enough money in her account, I'll bring down the company and be done with this lot, once and for all. Meanwhile, I have to spend time with my half-siblings, keeping up the pretense of our family ties. It's expected. And I must do it, so I don't arouse any suspicion. Truth is, I really can't complain. Hanging out with them isn't exactly a chore. It's the old man I could do without.

"Nathan? Did you hear my question?"

"No. I'm not looking forward to getting married, if you must know." I scowl at him.

"So why do it? It's not like you don't have enough money?" There's a shrewd expression in his eyes. He might be the quietest of my brothers, but he's not to be underestimated.

"I want the role of the CEO locked down, and Arthur won't agree to it unless I get married."

"I can understand the seduction of power, but to sacrifice your personal life for it…" He raises a shoulder. "Seems a heavy price to pay."

"You grew up in privilege. You've always known what it's like to be an heir to the Davenport fortune. I grew up in a single-parent home with a mother who never missed a chance to tell me I should claim my right when I grew up. The result was, I hated the Davenports and everything to do with that name."

"It's also your surname."

"Only because I didn't have a choice."

"And you are here."

"To claim what's mine."

He searches my features. "Revenge can eat at you, and even after you get it, you'll find it doesn't satisfy you. Surely, you know the old adage: before you embark on a journey of revenge, dig two holes."

Yep, definitely astute. All of my half-brothers are. But Brody has an intensity about him that invites you to share your secrets.

"A philosopher, too, huh?" I put some space between us, then drop down and begin push-ups.

"Guess all those books I read rubbed off on me."

"Next, you'll be telling me you learned life-truths in those erotic romances."

He chuckles. "You'd be surprised. Matters of the heart and the body intersect at the gut and leave you with insights you aren't always prepared for. Of course, erotica isn't all that I read. Books have always been an escape for me, thanks to the complexity of the family I grew up in."

I grunt as I continue to flow into the push-ups. After a beat, he joins me for the rest of the hundred reps. When I sit back, so does he, and the fucker isn't even winded. He might love books, but he can match me in the gym, and that's no mean feat. I reach for my bottle to take a sip of water.

"I imagine it couldn't have been easy, having Arthur for a grandfather, not to mention, being the youngest of the lot."

"It had its moments." He hesitates, then tosses me my towel.

I wipe my face and drop it to the side, along with my bottle. Another hundred, then I switch over to sit-ups. He holds my feet as I pace myself. One-two-three — I count, until I hit a hundred. When I begin to straighten, he sits back on his haunches.

"I was bullied at school." He rolls his shoulders.

I take in his six-foot-five-inch frame, the massive chest, his thick neck, and one side of his mouth quirks. "To look at me now, you wouldn't think I was a five-foot-three-inch runt, with nerdy glasses and my nose always buried in a book until I was fifteen."

"Late developer, huh?"

"You have no idea." He rubs the back of his neck.

"Knox came to my rescue a few times when I was being bullied, but I told him to back off."

"You wanted to stand up to them on your own."

He nods. "And I paid the price. I haven't gotten as badly beaten up as I did that year, but I learned to assert myself. And then I began to grow." His lips curl. "I didn't stop until I hit my present height."

"Quite a change, then?"

He nods. "I began to work out with Knox — more like, he wouldn't take no for an answer. He shoved me into the gym and insisted I lift weights. I developed enough muscles to defend myself. Soon, my tormentors began to leave me alone. Given how strong I had become, it was logical I follow my brothers and do a stint in public service."

Four of my half-brothers did a stint in the military, or so Arthur informed me. He's proud that I, too, pursued a career in the armed forces. He used it to make the point that I'm a Davenport at heart... *Not*. But whatever helps him convince himself to trust me.

"But you didn't follow them, did you?"

"I could have, but it turned out, I had an aptitude for science." He begins to stretch out his leg muscles. "My time was better spent on medical research. I ended up studying biochemistry and started my own pharmaceutical company under the Davenport umbrella."

"Among the best performing in the Davenport Group, too."

"I've made my grandfather a very rich man—or rather, I made him richer," he says in a wry tone.

"How's that?"

"He put in the seed money for the company. He believed in me when no one else did." He continues his stretching exercises.

I narrow my gaze. "You trying to tell me the old man has a heart?"

"I wouldn't go that far, but he does believe in family."

"And the decisions he makes only make him richer," I murmur.

"It also benefits family members," he points out.

"That's why he called me up and asked me to join the board of directors? That's why he's insisting I get married before he confirms me as CEO?"

"Of course, it's good PR to show a strong, united front among family members. Not to mention, getting us to marry and settle down is one way to ensure continuity of the family line." He lowers his chin to his chest.

"Those are not the only reasons." I widen my stance.

Brody sighs. "Knowing how canny Arthur is, he's probably future-proofing the business."

I snort. "Likely, he realized it was best to bring his illegitimate grandsons under the family umbrella and give them a stake in the Davenport Group, so they wouldn't try to tarnish the family reputation with their claims later."

While Edward's mother is different from mine and Brody's, we all share a father. His only role in life seems to have been to spawn as many boys as possible, before he and Brody's mother were killed in an accident. By all accounts, he was a weakling, unable to keep it in his pants. Not to mention, he was cowed by Arthur's larger-than-life persona.

Edward was adopted by his uncle, our father's older brother, who shunned all contact with Arthur. It was only after Arthur's wife passed that Arthur became aware of Edward's and my existence. He took it upon himself to right the years of not having contact with us. He made Edward and me joint interim CEO's—no doubt, hoping we'd compete for the role. But Edward dropped out, leaving me as the only contender for CEO of the company. If you don't count Knox, who's chomping at the bit. Problem is, Arthur isn't ready to confirm me to the position of CEO until I get married. Knox is pissed off at being left out of the race, after being groomed to be Arthur's successor all these years. And honestly, I can't say I blame him.

"'Course, if our youngest uncle comes back, he'll have more claim to the role of CEO of the group," I point out.

Yep, Gramps' youngest son Quentin is estranged from him. He joined the

British Secret Service and has been busy running top-secret missions for the government. He hasn't been seen in years.

"From what I remember of him, he hates Arthur with a passion. I doubt he's returning anytime soon." He snatches his bottle of water and chugs down several gulps. "You and Knox have a lot in common." He caps it and places it down on the floor.

"You mean, the fact he was in the Royal Marines before he was injured?" You'd have thought that would give us more common ground, but it's only served to rub Knox the wrong way. He refuses to acknowledge my past, and we certainly haven't had any chummy conversations about our service stints. I suppose, being reminded of your injuries in the line of duty every time you see your face in the mirror isn't easy. Perhaps he wants to forget about his past and move on. I can't blame him for that.

"Knox was close to Quentin. He looked up to his uncle, almost hero-worshipped him when he was younger. It's why he became a marine." Brody rises to his feet, then thrusts out his arm. When I take his hand, he pulls me up.

"You're trying to find common ground between me and your brother?" I frown.

He half smiles. "Not that I'm a fan of Arthur. But the one thing I agree with him about is that I want to see my brothers get along."

Technically, I'm their half-brother, but I don't correct him. It's damned inconvenient that I'm beginning to like this guy. When I set out to get to know the rest of my new family, I did it to keep up appearances. But this warmth that fills my chest, this sense of belonging that embraces me like a second skin, takes me by surprise. After my mother died, I became accustomed to being alone, to watching families from the outside as they celebrated holidays. I saw Ben's attachment to his sister and his protectiveness toward his mother, their joint wavelength as a family unit when they were together, and realized I would never have that.

Even when my mother was alive, she was so consumed with her need to make the Davenports pay, it impacted her mental health. There were days when she'd forget to pick me up from school or not be able to get out of bed and go to work. Days when I had to be the adult in our relationship. In a way, it was almost a relief when she passed away. I only had to take care of myself after that. I hated myself for thinking that way, but I couldn't stop it.

The few times I went home to visit Ben's family with him, they welcomed me into their fold. It's the closest I've come to having a sense of connection with anyone since losing my mom. They accepted me for who I was, and the feeling of kinship I experienced with Ben is what kept me grounded.

I'll always be grateful to him for that. I owe him for giving me a reason to not lose myself completely in the missions I ran. It would have been easy to lose perspective with the death and destruction I saw and was often responsible for in the call of duty. But Ben was good and kind, and I owe it to him that some part of me stays human and wasn't lost completely to the emotionless mask I had to do my duty. It's why I'll do my best to watch out for her. To ensure her every need is taken care of. It's how I'll deliver on the promise I made to Ben to take care of his sister.

7

Skylar

"I'm coming!" There's a banging on the door.

I was lucky to find this apartment above the bakery. I rented the bakery space, and the apartment came with it. It has its own separate entrance, so it provides a certain amount of privacy from the traffic to the bakery. It also means, I cut down on commute time and cost. Considering I work into the night, either experimenting on new recipes or trying to balance my books, I can stumble up to my bed and fall asleep, gaining precious extra minutes of rest.

Monday mornings are the slowest and that's the only time I allow myself to sleep in—if you call sleeping until 7 a.m. sleeping in. I don't open until 11 a.m. today but plan to try out some new recipes this morning in the bakery before opening shop. I glance at my phone screen and realize it's already 7:30 a.m.. Ugh, I overslept.

I jump out of bed, pulling a robe on over my sleep shorts and camisole. Whoever's at the door bangs on it again. "Oh, for the love of *Game of Thrones*, I'm coming," I yell again, then reach the door, throw it open, and freeze.

His shoulders fill the doorway, and he's so tall, the top of his head grazes the door frame. It's not that the entrance is narrow, either. He's just a big man.

He grips the door jamb on either side and glowers at me. "The lock on the main door leading to your apartment from the street is broken."

"Good morning to you, too," I drawl at the very irate looking Nathan.

"Did you hear what I said?" His eyebrows draw down further. His eyes flash with anger—what a surprise—and something more. Fear? On my behalf?

"I'm safe, aren't I?" I point out.

"You were sleeping here all night with the downstairs door open?" His jaw tightens. His gaze, as usual, is fixed on my lips. Awareness crawls up my spine. My nipples bead. If I look down, will I find them outlined against my bathrobe? Not that I'm going to risk a peek.

"To be fair, I did lock *this* door." I slap at the door to my apartment to illustrate my point.

"One strong push and its lock could have been broken." He glowers at me.

"Surely, you exaggerate. Also, there's nothing of value here anyway."

He raises his gaze to mine and there's a funny look in his eyes. "You're here."

I blink. Oh. *Oh! Does he mean? Nope, surely not.*

"Can I come in?" Without waiting for my answer, he brushes past me and walks into my living room. And the space immediately shrinks. It's always been enough for me, but with him there, everything seems to be dollhouse-sized in comparison. He glances around the space. I see it through his eyes and wonder what he makes of the kitchenette on one end and my bed and closet on the other. In between, there's a door to my bathroom. It's a tiny place, looking down on a fairly busy main street— which is good for traffic to my bakery. Or so I'd thought. It's one thing to be facing a thoroughfare; another for people passing by to walk in. At least, the window over the bed faces the tiny garden behind the building. In the early hours, things are quiet enough, I can hear the birds.

I shut the door behind me but don't follow him. I don't think there's enough space for both of us in my tiny apartment; not when he seems to take up most of the space.

He does a slow turn, then comes to a stop with his gaze on my features. "You need to come with me."

"Excuse me?" I gape at him.

"You did say you were going to marry me, didn't you?"

That was four days ago, and I haven't heard a peep out of him since then. I almost hoped he'd forgotten about it. But then my landlord emailed me to say if I don't pay for the last three month's rent by the end of the month, he's sending around the debt collector. That's when I realized things were about to get very real, very fast. And that I have no other way out but to marry him, because I need the money.

A part of me wondered if I should message Ben and let him know about the possibility of this happening, but the last thing I want to do is bother him when he needs to focus.

So, I hunkered down and immersed myself in making desserts. I also posted on social media, trying to drum up interest. But without another viral post there was no additional traffic to the bakery. I also didn't have the time to keep up with the posting schedule. I can only focus on one thing, and that one thing is baking. I need someone else who can post to social media. It'll probably take them a fraction of the time it takes me, and it will provide a higher ROI. That's one of the first things I'll need to delegate once I have money.

"Well?" He widens his stance. "You haven't changed your mind, I assume?"

"Did you expect me to?"

"I came here, ready to change your mind back, if you did."

I tighten the knot of my bathrobe, and his gaze drops there. I flush because… My midsection is not where I want anyone's eyes to fall, and definitely not this sexy man I've had a crush on for as long as I can remember.

"You this desperate to marry me?" I tease.

"Yes."

My breath catches in my throat. Goosebumps scatter over my skin. I open my mouth to say something but lose my train of thought. *What does he mean by that? Does he want to marry me, because—all of a sudden, he woke up and realized the feelings I have for him are not one-sided? Likely not.*

His next words confirm that, for he says, "I need Arthur to confirm me as CEO of the Davenport Group. The fastest way to do that is by getting married."

"I still don't understand why you decided it had to be me. You could have asked anyone else."

"There's no one else I could find who'd do it in such a short period of time." He shrugs.

"Don't sound too excited about it." I walk past him, and of course, his ocean breeze scent teases me as I head toward the kitchenette. I switch on the kettle, and spoon coffee grounds into the cafetière, then turn and gasp because he's standing right behind me.

"Oh, I didn't hear you walk over." I half laugh, then tuck a strand of hair behind my ear. "Are you sure you want to go through with this thing?" I swallow.

"If you mean the marriage, yes. Of course I do." He pulls back the sleeve of his jacket and looks at his watch. It's a Rolex. I've seen enough ads of that brand to make out the distinctive pattern of the dial face. Another change. The Nathan I met with Ben was never this stylishly dressed, nor did he wear such expensive brand-names. He was rugged—he's still rugged—but now, there's a sheen of sophistication which sits easily on him. Like he was born into money... And from what he's telling me, it's his right to have been brought up in such luxury.

The kettle switches off. I turn back and pour the water into the cafetière, then reach up on tiptoe to take down the mugs on the top shelf. Before I can touch them, he's there. The heat of his body sears my back. His scent is intense; notes of cinnamon and pepper woven in with that ever-present ocean breeze scent of his teases my nostrils. The lapels of his jacket graze my shoulders, and his fingers brush mine. I freeze; so, does he. We stay there, unmoving—him looming over me, his presence all around me. I sense him move, then he inhales deeply.

What the—! Did he sniff me? I glance at him over my shoulder, but he's already moved away. His features are a cold hard mask, one that does not invite any questions. He steps back and places the mugs on the counter next to me. Then, as if to be certain, he puts more distance between us.

"I assume you take your coffee as dark as your soul?"

He crosses his arms across his chest and glares at me.

"I take that as a yes." I place a teabag in my cup and pour hot water over it. Then I slowly press down on the plunger before tipping the coffee from the cafetière into another cup. I use the espresso machine in the bakery but at home I prefer the simplicity of the French press. I add milk and sugar to my tea—prefer to keep the tea bag in so the brew is strong; blasphemy for a Brit, I know—and mix it. I walk over and hand his cup to him.

He takes a sip of the coffee and doesn't wince; despite the fact it's probably scalding. Of course, he's used to the burning fires of hell where he normally lives, so it doesn't affect him.

He's back to staring at my mouth, and those embers in my lower belly flare to life again. I can't be in his presence without feeling this pull toward him. He must sense some of my thoughts, for he raises his gaze to mine. Once more, the full impact of those uneven eyes overcomes me. The blue is not completely blue. Right now, it's blue-grey, and the amber is almost golden. It's hypnotizing, like the first time I looked into them and lost my breath and my mind emptied of thoughts. It reminded me of looking into the eyes of a storm, filled with rainclouds, heavy with the promise of the first downpour. Like staring into the heart of a forest fire… Dangerous, yet also, alluring, like—*Stop it, right there.*

I pivot and walk over to the couch, where I sit down. For a few seconds, I stare into my cup of tea. Not like I'll find any answers there. His feet appear in my line of sight, but I ignore him. *Maybe he'll leave if I don't talk to him?*

Instead, he lowers his bulk onto the seat next to me. He's not touching me, but he's so huge, he takes up most of the remaining space. The hair on my forearms rise. My body reacts to his nearness with no confusion. *It wants him. I… want him. Oh god, this is going to get so very complicated.* I rub at my temple, where a familiar drumming makes itself known. That's all I need, a migraine. I've had them since I hit puberty at thirteen. Normally, the headaches come at the onset of my period. But since I began taking care of Hugo, combined with scrambling to save my fledging business, the frequency has multiplied.

I hold up a finger. "Hold on, I need to take my medication."

I reach over to where I placed my handbag near the couch, pull out my medicine, shake out a pill, and swallow it down with my tea. I then look up to find him watching me with a frown.

"What's the medication for?"

8

Skylar

"Migraines. Nothing serious."

"Hmm." There's concern in those mismatched eyes. "Have you seen a doctor for it?"

"Of course, I have. How do you think I got the prescription?" I huff.

"And what did he say?"

"That I need to take the medication at the onset of a migraine, so it has the most impact."

His frown deepens. "How often do you get them?"

"Not often."

He continues to stare at me, and it's like he's looking right into my soul. Damn, it's difficult to lie when his mismatched gaze is watching me so closely, I'm sure he can follow my line of thinking. "I get them, maybe... once a month; more often, if I'm stressed out."

"And are you stressed out now?"

"What do you think?"

His lips tighten. He's not happy I answered his question with a question. Well, that's too bad. I'm not a pushover, and it's best he realizes that.

He watches me closely, then nods as if coming to a decision. "I think, you can always back out of this arrangement." He raises his shoulder.

I scoff. "So you keep saying, but you and I both know I need the money."

"There is one more reason I decided it had to be you," he offers.

I stiffen, then incline my head.

"You're Ben's sister. If he were here, he'd want me to help you out."

"He knows I'm a businesswoman. I started this enterprise, knowing the risks."

"But I have the means to rescue your bakery." He takes another sip of his coffee, then, once again, fixes his gaze on me. "We can help each other, Starling."

He whispered that endearment against my lips when he kissed me back on my eighteenth birthday. When I asked him why that nickname, he said I reminded him of one. That I was full of joie-de-vivre, always chattering with enthusiasm like a starling. I've dreamed of his husky voice saying that to me again. I've heard it in my head as I've gone about my life. I've tried to push it away, tried to bury it deep inside, in a place I'd never access. But here he is, in my apartment, sitting next to me, and calling me by that nickname again… Only, it's for the wrong reasons.

"Don't call me that," I burst out.

He frowns. "Why not?"

"It makes me remember the time I embarrassed myself. I'm sure you laughed about it over the years. You must have thought of me as stupid and idiotic and—"

"Beautiful."

"Wh-what?" I stutter.

"I never forgot that kiss, Starling."

"You didn't?"

He leans in, until the heat from his body surrounds me in a cocoon, and his gaze keeps me captive. And when he reaches up to tuck a strand of hair behind my ear, a thousand electric fuses seem to blow out under my skin.

He must be aware of the reaction of my body, for his lips twist. "It's what kept me going through those hard days and long nights when I was on tour. It's what kept me warm when I lay shivering in a ditch in Siberia waiting for enemy soldiers to make an appearance so I could take them out. It's what gave me hope to keep going when I was sure I was never making it back from the last one."

I stiffen. I'd hoped he'd tell me he was as affected as I was by that kiss when I was eighteen. I'd hoped he'd tell me he thought of me over the years.

I'd hoped... He'd confess he, too, wanted me. And now, he's telling me so, and it's overwhelming. My fingers tremble. Following his example, I place my cup on the table and fold my hands in my lap.

I'm not sure how to react to his confession of never having forgotten me, so I settle for not acknowledging at all. "That's the last tour you and Ben were both on?"

He nods slowly. "It was my last mission. I was in charge. The rest of our team were killed." His features grow carefully blank. It's the only sign it's difficult for him to share this. "We made it out by encouraging each other. We'd accomplished what we set out to do, our enemies were dead, but we were both in bad shape. The only reason we survived and made it to the extraction point is because we had each other for company. When he'd lag, I'd tell him he had to survive so he could see you again. And when I slowed, he'd encourage me to keep going by telling me all about you."

That last tour of Ben's is the one he doesn't say much about. The only thing he told me is that he and Nate were both wounded. I put down his lack of communication to the fact he was hurt and needed time to recuperate. Nate must have been more seriously injured because he's the one who came home. "You... You guys spoke about me?"

"You were the one person, not connected to our lives as Marines, that we had in common. He was happy I'd gotten to meet you. Also, talking about you meant we were focusing on the future. On hope. You ignited a sense of possibility in us. As long as we were speaking about you, we weren't in that frozen Siberian landscape, we weren't frostbitten, we weren't soaked through our bones with sweat and blood. As long as we kept focused on you, we knew we'd make it out."

"He never told me." I wring my fingers together. "I wish he'd told me. I wish he'd shared more of what he went through. But he's so stubborn." *Oh, he did the minimum number of sessions with a therapist needed for him to pass the checks and convince his superiors he was fit to return to active duty.* "He simply ignored what had happened and headed right back on the next mission. I wish he'd taken the time to come to terms with everything. Maybe he wouldn't have sounded so preoccupied."

"You spoke to him?" Nathan seems taken aback.

"I spoke to him before he left again. He called me later and told me about his girlfriend."

This time Nathan's gaze widens. "He told you about his girlfriend?"

"Why? Is that supposed to be a secret?"

Nathan slowly shakes his head.

"You know about her?" I ask with interest.

"I haven't met her, if that's what you're asking. But I suspected he was seeing someone."

"He seemed surprised by the speed with which events had moved." I laugh, remembering how dazed he'd sounded on our call. "He also sounded preoccupied, but happy."

Nathan blinks. "He sounded happy?"

He's back to staring at my mouth, and that now-familiar tremor cascades across my nerve-endings. My thighs clench, and I stop myself from squeezing my legs together.

"Yeah, I think he did. He also seemed reluctant to be on a mission, for the first time since he joined the Marines."

Nathan purses his lips. That ever-present wrinkle between his eyebrows deepens. He seems perturbed by my response.

I tip up my chin. "You don't seem pleased. Aren't you happy that my brother seems to have found love?"

He raises his gaze to mine, and whatever he sees in there seems to cause him to relax. He leans back and throws his arm over the couch. His fingertips almost brush my shoulder. I inch away. Not because I don't want him touching me, but the opposite. If he does, there's no telling how I'm going to react. I'll probably like it too much.

He must notice my move, for one side of his lips curl. Then he brings his gaze back to my mouth. "What gives you that idea?"

"The fact that you're still glowering at me? Or wait"—I pretend to think —"I guess that's your resting jerk face."

He chuckles. "Or maybe, that's your imagination?"

"If only it were my imagination that you asked me to marry you," I say in a bitter tone.

"Don't lie." He delivers his words without heat, but that doesn't stop me from flushing.

"What do you mean?"

"Admit it, you were affected by our kiss, too."

I scoff.

"In fact"—his eyes gleam— "I'd wager you spent the last few years dreaming about how it would be when I fucked you."

"Excuse me?" I jut out my chin, ignoring the shiver of need which courses through my veins. "I think you need to leave."

He spreads his legs wider, and that tent between his thighs seems to be bigger than I remember. A tsunami of heat spirals in my belly. My cheeks burn. He snaps his fingers, and I raise my gaze to his face. When I see the curl of his lips, I realize he knows exactly what I've been thinking.

"Do you really want me to leave?" His shoulders swell, and he seems to grow visibly larger, as if he's got an animal inside him that's now filling out his skin and threatening to jump out. His eyes glitter. "Say the word, and I will."

And if he does, I won't get the money. And then, what'll happen to my business? I suppose I should be grateful he isn't reminding me of that. Not that he needs to, considering I can fill in the blanks myself. Isn't that clever of him? Making it seem like I have a choice in the matter, when what he's driving home is, I don't. And without saying it aloud. Aargh! I curl my fingers into fists and glare at him.

His lips curve slightly. "I take that as a no, Starling?"

And how I hate—and love—that nickname. It implies a certain intimacy, which is not real. Except for that kiss. A kiss which he's now admitted also affected him. Something I had not expected to hear from him.

"Well?" He drums his fingers on his chest. "Yes or no?"

9

Nathan

"I… I can't accept that." She looks down at the ring on the tray in front of her, then at me. "I can't."

After she admitted, she wasn't going to tell me to leave, I asked her to change and accompany me. I didn't tell her where we were going. I also overrode her protests that she had to open the bakery. She opens at 11 a.m. on Monday, and I promised to have her back in enough time to prep. She shouldn't need to work on Monday. Given the size of the dark circles under her eyes, she should take the day off and stay in bed. Not that I'm going to mention that to her. If I did, I'm sure she'd extend the operating hours, just to spite me.

But if I'm doing this marriage thing, I'm doing it properly. *And she deserves a ring. Something that proclaims she's mine.* I stiffen. *No, that's not why I'm insisting on having her choose a ring.* It's so my grandfather will believe in the validity of this relationship, which is critical for him to confirm me as the CEO. *Yes, that's all it is. That's the only reason I had the leading jeweler in London open his store early in the morning for a private viewing for us.*

I reach for the ring she's been eyeing since it was placed in front of her. At first, she stared at it with wonder, then with longing, then said she wanted to see other options. But her gaze kept wandering back to this one. Not that she'd ever admit it. She kept looking away from it, until I finally picked it up. Now, she stares at what the jeweler called a bibliophile trilogy ring—one with three interlocking platinum bands to represent our past, present and future together. A whole lot of bull, if you ask me. But I know she's attracted to the emerald in the center, which appears to rise from between the pages of an open book formed from two overlayed 'V' shapes on the ring.

I hold out my palm. She hesitates, then slowly places her hand in mine. I slide the ring onto her finger. For a second, we both stare at it. Her fingers tremble. A drop of moisture falls onto the back of her palm. I glance up to find her eyelashes are spiky with tears.

"What's wrong?"

"It's beautiful." She swallows.

"You're beautiful."

Her chin trembles; she seems overcome by emotion. "You don't have to do this."

"Of course I do."

"It's— Whatever this is you're doing is not real."

"Of course it is."

She raises her gaze to mine, and another teardrop squeezes out from the side of her eyes. Before I can stop myself, I lean in and kiss it away. She freezes. The taste of salt slides over my palate.

I clear my throat. I could tell her I did it because I care for her, that I never stopped thinking about her in all the time I was away from her; but because I'm still cursing myself for telling her I never forgot about that kiss on her eighteenth birthday, when I open my mouth what comes out is, "You're the fiancée of the CEO of the Davenport Group; it's expected."

Her features fall. She pulls her hand from mine. "Of course, it is."

"My grandfather wouldn't believe our relationship otherwise."

"Right." She lowers her chin. Her green eyes are muddied with an emotion that weighs down her eyelids. The hunch of her posture indicates her weariness. Her utter dejection. And damn, if that doesn't piss me off. I did that.

She's the woman I've secretly hankered after all these years. The one who's always appeared smiling and surrounded by a gleaming golden glow in my dreams. The one whose fingers I've dreamed of being wrapped about my cock. Also, her mouth. And being down her throat. And— *Nope, not going there. Not when I'm trying to behave myself. Also, she's Ben's little sister—the reason I've tried to censor my thoughts. And failed.* But I owe it to him to make her dreams come true.

Which also means, keeping her happy, with her lips curved in the opposite direction of the one they are now. "Vanilla or chocolate?"

She rears back as if I've struck her. "Excuse me? What do you mean by that?"

I frown. *I didn't say anything wrong, did I? Unless she thought it to mean... oh. Aha!* I tilt my head. "You didn't think I was asking about your sexual preferences, did you?"

Her features turn an interesting shade of red. "Why don't you scream that louder, so the entire store can hear it?"

"If that's what you want." I raise my voice. "Do you prefer vanilla or—"

She slaps her hand over my mouth. "Shut up, you know I didn't mean what I said."

I flick out my tongue and lick her fingers. The taste of her intensifies, and all the blood in my body seems to drain to my groin. Her breathing grows uneven. Her pupils dilate. She sways closer, and I want to pull her close and close my mouth over hers. I want to wrap my fingers about her neck and hold her in place while I ravage her lips and slide my tongue over hers and drink of her essence... But I'm not going to because... Ben. The only reason I'm marrying her is so I can help her with her business. So I can give her the Davenport family name and set her up for life. A-n-d...

I call bullshit on that. If I wanted, I could throw money at her to pay off her debts so she could revive her business, but I'm selfish that way. I want... these few weeks... Maybe, if I'm lucky, a few months of calling her my wife. Of pretending what's between us is real. Of keeping her close and assuaging that yearning deep inside me. But I'll never sleep with her. I cannot let this pretend marriage turn into the real thing. Where would that leave me with Ben? I cannot fuck his little sister. Not when he's entrusted her welfare to me.

I lower my hand and step back. "You haven't answered the question."

"Wh-what?" She blinks.

"Vanilla or chocolate?"

Her brow knits. She opens her mouth to protest but I raise my hand. "I mean, which ice cream flavor is your preference, of course."

"Oh." The flush in her cheeks bleeds down to her throat and décolletage. I gave her enough time to shrug into a pair of jeans with a pink-pullover that's cut in a V at the neckline. Enough to hint at the shadow between those spectacular tits.

I've managed not to let my gaze slide below her chin but now, I follow her flush to where it spreads into the valley between her breasts. "Not my fault your mind is in the gutter."

She snaps her fingers in my line of sight. I raise my chin and meet her knowing glance. Busted. Also, she mirrored the very same gesture I pulled on her. *Touché, little one.* I allow myself a chuckle, acknowledging she's won this round.

She sniffs, then pushes her hair back from her face with her left hand, which sports my ring. Or maybe, I've won this one, after all? I hold her gaze, and without looking away, nod in the direction of the man standing behind the jewelry counter. "We'll take it."

"I'll take the chocolate, the vanilla and the honey pistachio." She hangs over the display case with the buckets of ice cream showcased behind it. "Topped with peanut butter, sprinkles and strawberry pop-tart."

I wince. "Did you leave anything behind?"

"Hmm"—she presses a finger into her cheek—"now that you mention it, I should add some wasabi peas to it."

I scowl. "Wasabi peas?"

"Also, some potato chips."

My stomach lurches.

"And balsamic glaze."

My gaze widens. "Did you say balsamic—"

She bursts out laughing.

Why, that cheeky monkey! I glower at her. "You know, I'm going to get back at you for this, don't you?"

10

Skylar

Yep, I'm definitely getting back at him for springing this entire ring business on me without warning. He hadn't mentioned anything to me, not until we were striding into the boutique with the name of a world-famous jeweler on it —one so exclusive, there's only one branch in the entire world and it's in this city. And even then, I didn't register what he was about to do. Until the man behind the counter slid a velvet tray with a ring on it toward me. At that point, the penny dropped. And even then, I couldn't chew him out because we were in public. He probably counted on it, well-behaved person that I am.

I went along with the charade, determined to leave without choosing a ring. But when that particular piece was placed in front of me, I knew. And I tried not to show I knew. But he spotted it anyway. He unerringly reached for that ring, and when he placed it on my finger, it felt so right. Both the ring and the man and...

Gah! This is all wrong. I shouldn't be entertaining thoughts of this man, and how it feels to wear his ring on my finger. How it feels like I belong to him. This is all make-believe, a pretense, a fake relationship. I barely know the man, except that he kisses in a way that knocks all thoughts from my mind. He nibbled on my lips in a way I could feel it all the way to the tips of my toes, to the roots of my hair, to the edges of my eyelashes, and... I'll stop now. I swirl my tongue around the heap of ice cream in my cone. He shoots me a sideways glance as he navigates through the traffic.

He refused any ice cream for himself, muttering something about how he hates anything sweet—figures. If he did eat anything with sugar, it'd probably caramelize when it hit his cast-iron stomach where, no doubt, the fires of hell are blazing in full force.

I don't care. More for me to slurp up. And P.S. I'm not holding back my appreciation of my frozen confection, either. Especially not since I realized the effect it's having on him. Each time I lap at my ice treat, he shifts in his seat. Now, when I swallow a particularly big gulp and make an appreciative noise at the back of my throat, he steps on the accelerator. The car leaps forward. There's a chorus of honking from the vehicles next to us.

"Starling, you're playing a dangerous game," he says in a hard voice.

A tremor of excitement squeezes my spine. "Moi?" I turn to him with what I hope is an innocent look on my face. "What did I do?" I widen my gaze, then open my mouth and surround the entire top of the now melting mixture.

His nostrils flare. His gaze, as usual, is on my mouth, and my gesture definitely affects him, for his chest rises and falls. Some of it runs down my chin. He sets his jaw, then swerves to the turn lane. Horns blare, and there's a screech of tires.

"You're crazy," I yell.

"You have no idea." He takes the next turn-off, drives for a few more minutes, then turns again. We're in a residential neighborhood; he eases the car to a stop on the side of the road, then turns to me. "You're driving me insane with your little pink tongue, and your slurping and swallowing, and you know it."

"I—"

He raises his hand. "Don't lie to me."

I glance away, then because the ice cream is melting, and because there's no way I'm going to waste it, I swipe my tongue around the entire outside to catch any drips.

He groans.

I shoot him a glance to see he's facing forward and squeezing the bridge of his nose. He's also muttering something under his breath. I catch the words "fuck" and "bloody" and "buggering hell." *Okay, then.*

I crunch down on the cone, and he widens the space between his legs. I lower my gaze to his crotch and forget to eat. If there were one thing that I'd like to lick and swallow more than an ice cream cone, it would be that thick rod-like appendage outlined between his massive thighs. Some of the ice cream slides down my fingers and plops on my jeans.

"Oh no, no, no." I grab a napkin from my purse and dab at the blot on my thigh, only my hand tips, and the rest of the ice cream oozes down my knuckles, headed for my jeans.

Before it can hit my thigh, he reaches over, circles my forearm with his thick fingers, brings it toward him, and licks his way up the back of my hand. Goosebumps pop on my skin. The hair on the back of my neck stands on end. I draw in a sharp breath as he continues to lave his tongue over my fingers, then closes his mouth around my cone and bites off the rest of the ice cream. Only then, does he look at me. Our eyes meet, and something sizzles in the space between us. The air thickens as he chews, swallows, then slowly straightens.

I lean forward, closing the distance to him until my mouth is in front of his, until our breaths merge, and our eyelashes tangle with each other. Until I can count the individual lines of the wrinkles that fan out from the edges of his eyes. Until I can make out the golden flecks in one eye and the silver sparks in the other. Mesmerizing, haunting, striking. So distinctive. And a tad disturbing.

There are depths to this man, parts of him he's hidden away from everyone else, and I want to reach them. I want to break down the walls he's put up against the world. I want to shatter his defenses. I want to push past his aloof exterior. I want to get a rise out of him. It's why I've been teasing him by licking the ice cream, knowing it was affecting him—which is a surprise. One which I have to leverage because I'll use every advantage I can get with him.

He's taller than me, stronger than me, has seen more of the world, has more experience, and thinks he holds the upper hand in this situation. And maybe he does… For now.

Doesn't mean I'm going to allow him to bend me to his agenda. Doesn't mean I can't have a little fun while trying to worm my way under his skin. I glance down at his mouth, and one side of his lip curls. That sneer of his should not be so attractive. It should not make me want to trace the outline of his lush lower lip and rub his thin upper one. It should not make me want to throw myself at him and crush my mouth to his. It should not—

There's a banging against his window.

I flinch. He pauses, his gaze boring into my face, until he slowly turns.

A uniformed parking warden motions him to lower his window. When Nate does, he looks between us. "Everything okay?" he asks me.

"Yes." I clear my throat.

He glares at Nate. "You're in a no-parking zone, Sir."

Nate jerks his chin. "Sorry about that." He flashes the guy a half-smile.

I blink. It was a *half*-smile, but still, an upturn of his lips, which is more than I've gotten out of him. If you don't count the half-smirks. I swear, I'm going to tease a full-smirk and a full-smile from this man if that's the last thing I do.

The parking warden nods. "Best you moved on now."

"Of course." Nate nods, then rolls up his window and eases the car onto the road. He drives down, then turns at the next crossroad, and back onto a thoroughfare. He follows the flow of traffic until he's back on the main road he veered away from earlier. We drive in silence until he reaches my bakery.

When he comes to a stop, I reach for the handle to open the car door when—

"Starling, you haven't paid your due," he rumbles.

"D-d-d-ue?" I curse myself for stuttering. I'm not afraid of him. Nathan would never hurt me. In fact, I feel safe with him. I always have. From the moment I first saw him, I knew he'd protect me. And it's not only because he's a former Marine. There's something solid about him, something which invites me to trust him, but which also excites me. It's a combination that tells me, if I ever need help, he'll be there for me.

It's no wonder he's my brother's best friend. I'd be so much more comfortable if he were on duty with Ben. He'd make sure to back him up if he needs help. He'd do anything to keep Ben safe. But nothing's going to happen to Ben.

I square my shoulders. He's going to complete his tour and come back and marry the love of his life and have lots of children.

So what if he seemed pensive as he was leaving? That's normal. He was leaving a newly discovered love behind; that's why he seemed upset. So what if I haven't heard from him as often as usual? He's probably been using his downtime to call his girlfriend. He's a seasoned Marine. He'll find his focus. He'll put everything behind him and zero in on the job at hand. He'll fulfill his duties and be back before I know it. Yep, he will.

I turn to Nathan. "You mean, because I distracted you while you were driving?"

He nods slowly.

"That's not my fault," I protest.

"Oh?" He goes preternaturally still. So still, he's like a marauder marking his prey, knowing full-well he's not going to let his quarry escape. A current of electricity squiggles in my belly. The thrill of anticipation sparks at my nerve-endings. I reach for the door, and he doesn't stop me.

"Indeed." I nod. "Not my fault you were taken in by how I licked my ice cream cone. Bet you were imagining something else in its place, huh?"

His gaze widens, and something sparks in the depths of those mismatched eyes, but he banks it. His lips curl. "My creative powers are not as developed as yours. Perhaps, it's you who wishes your visions would materialize."

It's my turn to stare. Now, that's one way of turning the tables on me. I'd do well not to underestimate my brother's best friend.

"And if I said there's an element of truth to what you're saying?"

"Then I'd say, I'll have it out of you yet. Besides, I always collect my dues."

"I don't doubt you, but"—I glance about the car, then back at him—"you'll have to catch me first."

I shove the door open and jump out.

11

Nathan

She races for the steps leading up to her flat. I push my own door open and follow at a leisurely pace. Mainly, because I want to give her a head-start. Also, because she may not realize it, but I'm the one in control here. The vixen may have teased me with the way she licked that frozen dessert, and I admit, I got turned on by it. But she was aroused, too. I could tell by the way she wiggled in her seat, how she squeezed her thighs together, how the pulse at the base of her neck increased in intensity, how her shoulders rose and fell. How she monitored my reaction, and how her own mirrored mine.

We affect each other, and that's the truth. I might have tried to deny it in the years we were apart, but I never forgot her response to my kiss. I've never gotten over how she felt in my arms. There's not a single morning I haven't woken up without thoughts of her crowding my mind. Not a single night has passed when I haven't wished I could taste her again. The chemistry between us blew my mind. It filled me with craving, a hankering which has grown over the years. There's no question that I'm following her in. No question that I'm going to mount the steps, reach her apartment and push open the door—which, by the way, she hasn't locked.

I step inside and let the door shut behind me with a bang that echoes through the space. That should give her enough notice that I'm here, and that I'm going to find her. I raise my head and sniff the air—and maybe it's my imagination, but I can smell her sweet cherry-blossom scent under the smell of freshly-baked bread. I follow it to the door of the bathroom, but when I push it open, she's not there.

I blink, turn, survey the space, then draw in a deep breath, and fill my lungs with Skylar. It has the predictable effect—my thighs harden, my groin stiffens, and my cock stabs against the restraint of my pants.

That yearning inside me swells to a full-blown craving. What I wouldn't give for one taste of her. Just one lick of her lips, one bite of that peach of her behind, one squeeze of her soft tits. *Goddam.* I curl my fingers into fists and shake my head to regain my composure. This time, when I look around the space, I notice the door on the far side of the studio. I must have missed it because it blends into the woodwork. But it's slightly ajar, which is why I notice it now. I stalk toward it, pull it open and step onto a small landing.

I climb the ladder onto the roof and find her sitting on the ledge, with her legs dangling over. Around us, the city spreads out. I walk over and sit down next to her, copying her by pushing my legs over. We sit for a few seconds in silence, then she says, without turning around, "You found me."

"It wasn't difficult."

"I wasn't hiding from you; not exactly." She raises her shoulder.

We sit quietly, and there's no missing the tension radiating from her that I can't ignore. "You don't have to worry; I'm not going to do anything... Nothing that you don't want, at any rate."

She blows out a breath. "That's what I'm afraid of. This... thing between us... It's clear it hasn't ebbed with time."

"It hasn't," I agree.

"It's only gotten stronger."

"It has."

"You going to agree with everything I say?"

"Only for the moment, and only because you're saying things I want to hear."

She throws up her hands. "You're maddening."

"And you still owe me."

"Oh." She seems taken aback. "Wh-what do you want from me?"

I hold out my hand. She hesitates, then slowly places her left palm in mine. I rub my thumb across the ring I placed there less than an hour ago. It looks right. It looks like it belongs to her. And she belongs to me. I promised Ben I'd look out for his sister. And this is the best way I can deliver on it. I bring her palm to my mouth and kiss the ring. "I want you to marry me. I want you to let me take care of you. I want you to... let me give you everything you deserve."

She pulls her hand from mine, and I let her. She places it in her lap and looks out over the rooftops. "I wish he was here." She swallows.

"So do I."

"Do you think he'll be happy when he finds out?"

"I think... He'd be happy if you're happy," I offer.

She half laughs. "Not that I need his permission, but I would like to have his blessing."

"He'd want you to do what you think is right for you and your business," I murmur.

She turns to me. "Why are you being nice to me?"

"Why shouldn't I be?"

"I'm not used to you being this agreeable. Almost pleasant. It's not the kind of man I thought you were."

"But then, you don't know me well, do you?"

Our gazes meet, and that connection which has always been there, flares to life between us.

"We're both to blame for that. I was mortified I threw myself at you. I never told Ben what happened. After that day, I never asked him about you, either. Every time he mentioned you were coming home for a visit; I made sure I wasn't there."

"And I tried my best not to accept his invitations home. But there were times I couldn't say no. I'd dread running into you, then be disappointed when I didn't."

"And now, here we are—engaged." She glances down at her ring.

"And you're going to get the money to save your bakery."

"Right." She swallows.

"The money will be deposited in your account as soon as we're married."

"Which will be—"

"In a week's time."

"So soon?" She jerks her chin up. "I... I thought it might be a little later... In a month, or three, maybe?"

"Can your business survive without the cash for that long?"

She shakes her head.

"So, it's best we go through with it as soon as possible, isn't it?"

12

Skylar

"Next week?" Zoey looks at me in horror. "You're getting married next week?"

"Seems like it." I slide the tray of Splcy Booktoks—a new book-shaped dessert I've been experimenting with—into the oven and straighten.

"And you're standing here, cooking?"

"I'm baking," I point out.

She cuts the air with the palm of her hand. "Let me get this right; you're going to marry that man who asked you to marry him?"

"Umm, that's generally how it works." I half smile.

"Sorry, I'm surprised and confused, is all." She rubs at her temple. "When we last spoke, you weren't sure you were going through with it. What changed your mind about marrying him, and are you sure you're doing the right thing?"

Zoey's the only person who knows about the situation I'm in. Not that I don't trust the others with the circumstances surrounding my upcoming nuptials, but I don't feel ready to spill the gory details to anyone else. Harper works such long hours as a chef, I rarely see her. Grace's TV career is so full-on, she has no time for anyone else, let alone herself. Zoey is the only one whose job allows her to have somewhat of a personal life. Which means, I don't feel bad about bothering her with what's happening in my life.

The others might not like it when they find out I told her first, but I've known her the longest, and I need someone to talk to and share what's happening. I walk over to the small island opposite the oven and grab my glass of water. I take a sip, more to gather my thoughts, then turn to her. "I was hoping you'd tell me that I am," I confess.

She reaches for one of the green-colored cakes in the shape of a worm.

It's another new dessert I've been experimenting with. "It's called Bookworm."

"Oh, that's a good name." She laughs.

"Go on." I nod toward the tray. "Try it and tell me what you think."

She plucks one and takes a bite, then closes her eyes. "Oh, my god, it tastes like—"

"—caramel, peppermint and dark chocolate, topped with pistachio and cream."

She chews, swallows, then opens her eyes and looks at me dreamily. "It makes me want to curl up with a book, in a seat by a window, pull up a blanket around me, and read."

"Right?" I clap my hands. "I'm so happy the flavors took you on a bookish journey."

"But seriously, this cupcake is epic."

"Thanks." I beam at her.

"It's so good, I don't know why there aren't more people beating down the doors to buy them."

"I guess I need to be smarter about my marketing. I need to hire someone to take care of my social media, and also put some money behind advertising to get the word out, which means—"

"You need the budget for it." She taps her finger against her cheek. "Which, I suppose, answers the question I posed earlier."

"It does?"

She nods. "You need the money to tell people about your bakery."

And to take care of Hugo.

"And you need to do it before you go into more debt," she warns me.

"Whoever said you need money to make money knew what they were talking about, eh?" I place my glass on the table.

"Have you tried other ways to raise the money?"

"The banks turned me down. Not surprising, considering my credit rating

is shot. What other way is there? If Nate hadn't come along with the offer...
I'd be looking to declare bankruptcy about now."

"Shit." She pushes her glasses up her nose. "I had no idea things were this
bad."

"Didn't want to bother you guys with my problems."

She walks over to me and squeezes my shoulder. "You're insulting our
friendship by saying that. You do realize that, right?"

I flush. "I didn't mean to."

"Well, you are. What are friends for if you don't share your problems with
them? You're always helping us out, but you never want to talk about
yourself."

"That's not true." I shuffle my feet.

"Yes, it is. When my horrid ex broke up with me, you were the first person
to reach my place. And you baked me a special batch of Macarons. You
remember?"

"The Movin' On Macarons." I smile.

"And boy, did they help me move on. The ingredients you chose spoke to
the hurt in me and healed it."

"It had bittersweet chocolate, symbolic of the complex emotions with
breakups, lemon zest, representing fresh starts, honey to soothe feelings and
bring in sweetness, and chamomile flowers, for calm and relaxation," I say in
recollection.

"And the textures... It cut through the noise in my head and helped me
ground myself."

"Graham cracker crumbs for an unexpected crunch, popped wild rice to
play into a sense of feeling free, crushed pretzel crisps for a salty bite, candied
ginger, to add some spicy zing, and of course, dark chocolate chunks for rich
intensity." I nod.

"Of course"—she laughs—"you think it's obvious, but really, you are a genius
when it comes to choosing the right ingredients and combining them all in a fashion
that's unique to you. The way you baked it and the flavors you packed into it healed
my heart and helped me look beyond the sorry feelings I was burying myself in."

My cheeks warm. "You're being too nice."

"No, I'm not. The texture of the macarons alone was so light and airy, it
lifted my heart and left me with a feeling of optimism, like the best part of my
life was yet to come."

"I'm so pleased they helped you," I murmur.

"I never would have gotten over my breakup so quickly if it weren't for you. Your baking speaks to the soul, to the cells of the body. You know how to appeal to the baser instincts inside —" She touches the lower part of her stomach. "It's why I know you're going to be successful. Once people taste your desserts, they're going to be all over it."

I lower my chin. She's right. A part of me, deep inside, knows I'm good. It's not me being egotistical. It's because all I've ever wanted is to bake. There's something inside of me that comes alive when I'm measuring and mixing and creating a dessert that I know is going to soothe or excite or calm or simply help someone find their center. A cake which speaks to your soul. I know it sounds fanciful, but the mixture of flour and sugar and eggs has always been more than the parts of the whole. Infused with cocoa or herbs or essences, it takes on the powers of a lodestone, or a charm, or a talisman — something endowed with mystical powers that appeal to the emotions inside of you. Like a key to a lock, it opens up a side of you, you didn't know existed. Like I want to do with him.

I want to unravel his control. I want to get under his skin. I want him to lose touch with his logical thinking when he's with me. I want him to go over the edge and admit he can't keep his hands off of me. It's why I indulged in that little skit with the ice cream. It's why I ran out of the car — hoping he'd follow me (which he did.) Hoping he'd throw me over his lap and spank me — which he didn't, and I don't miss it. *How can you miss something you've never had?* Also, I don't want him to spank my bum. Not at all.

That part of me, deep down, which has been so confident of my future as a baker, knows Zoey is onto something.

Once enough people taste my cakes and cookies, they'll want more. They always do. I just need to up my marketing game. Ergo, I need money. Which means —

I hunch my shoulders. "I don't have a choice. I have to go through with the wedding."

She firms her lips. "Whoa, hold on, let's not be hasty."

"I'm not. I've thought this through. There's no other way." That didn't stop me from taking off my engagement ring after Nathan left yesterday. I have another week until the wedding, a week where I can pretend I'm not about to turn my life upside down, doing something that's going to end with my heart being ripped out. I'm going to end up falling for him, and this is going to end badly for me, but I'm going through with it because that's what one does to manifest one's dream. One makes choices and does not shirk hard decisions.

"How about if I ask Summer, on your behalf? Her husband Sinclair is loaded, and —" Zoey begins to say, but I shake my head.

"I'm not going to mix money into the equation with friendship. It's the fastest way to mess up relationships. Everybody knows that."

"But you're mixing money into the most important relationship of your life."

She's right. "Difference is, I'm going into this association as a transactional one. So, the rules of engagement are clear upfront."

"Hmmm, I don't agree, but I can see your mind is made up." She purses her lips. "Besides, people have married for less. History is littered with arranged marriages between kings and princesses, not to mention all of the romances I've edited. Marriages of convenience have blossomed into love affairs, which have stood the test of time and re-written the future. So—" She raises a shoulder.

"There is one complication—" I shuffle my feet.

"Only one?" Her tone is amused.

I scoff. "Okay, more than one. But the biggest of them all is that he's my brother's best friend."

Her jaw drops. "You knew him before he came to you with this proposition?"

"It's *why* he came to me with this proposition."

Her brow clears. "O-k-a-y, some of it is beginning to make sense now. I wondered how this man found you. And why he walked in off the street and asked you to marry him."

"He also stands to gain from this. His grandfather wants him to get married. Once he ties the knot, he'll be confirmed as the CEO of his company."

"Aha. So both of you benefit from the match."

"You can say that."

"And you've met before, so it's not like you two are complete strangers."

"He may as well be." I look away, then back at her.

"Skylar?" She slaps her palms on her hips. "What are you not telling me?"

"Nothing," I lie. No way can I tell her just how much his kiss affected me on my eighteenth birthday, how I convinced myself I was building it up in my head, but meeting him again, I realized I hadn't. How his very proximity seems to turn my brain cells to mush and my bones to jelly. How being in his presence makes me want to forget every single rational thought and throw myself at him. My hormones begin to twerk like they're contestants on *So You Think You Can Dance* when he's around. I'm worried that once I marry him and spend more time with him, I'll be helpless to his charms and ready to do whatever he wants. Which may not be so bad. *Argh, don't think that.*

She continues to peer into my face, then sniffs. "So, you have a thing for your brother's best friend?"

"I don't have a *thing* for him."

She stares at me.

I redden, then look away and busy myself by beginning to measure out the flour for my next experimental dessert.

"Then why are you blushing?"

I roll my eyes. "Okay, I have 'something' for him. And not only because he happens to be very good-looking, but also because I've heard my brother speak so highly of him. He came home a couple of times when I was a kid, and I developed a huge crush on him. Not that he knew. Then, I met him when I was eighteen and—" I firm my lips.

"—and?"

"Nothing." I school all emotion from my features. "I didn't see him again until he prowled into my shop with this proposition."

"Why don't we talk with Grace and Harper? Perhaps they'll have more ideas to offer."

"I don't want to bother them, honestly."

She looks like she's about to protest, then shakes her head. "You *are* going to tell them you're getting married, right?"

"Of course I am. I'm going to message them by the end of the day, and—"

The doorbell tinkles. "Oh, I'd better get that." Truth be told, I'm happy for the interruption. I love Zoey, but she's too perceptive. She knows me well enough that if I keep talking to her, she's going to see through my thin sheen of fake confidence to the doubts lurking below the surface. And right now, I don't want to confront them. For someone who's normally confident about what I want to do, this entire marrying-Nathan-business is bringing so much insecurity to the surface, that it's making me a little dizzy. I dart past Zoey and to the front of the shop, where a woman is standing on the other side of the counter.

She sees me and her features light up. "You must be Skylar. I'm Rachel, and I'm a wedding planner."

"O-k-a-y?"

Even before she says the next few words, I have an idea of what's coming. " Nathan sent me."

"He did?" Zoey comes up from behind me. "I'm Zoey, Skylar's friend."

"Wonderful, you're in time to help Skylar choose her wedding dress."

"My what?" My jaw drops.

"I know this is all a little quick, but considering you're getting married in a week, Nathan wanted me to start the process of putting together the wedding right away."

"He did?" I scowl.

She nods. "He wants you to have only the best. He was very specific about that." Her gaze grows soft. "That man clearly cares about you a lot."

"He does?" I blink, then cup my palm over my mouth and tell Zoey in an aside, "It's all an act. Nathan's good at convincing people about the veracity of the situation. He has to, so he can convince his family the marriage is genuine."

Zoey shoots me a glance but doesn't say anything.

Rachel looks between us, a confused expression on her face. "Is everything okay?"

"Yes, of course," Zoey says brightly. "You said something about a wedding dress?"

"Which I am not interested in," I declare.

Both women turn to look at me. There's a distressed look on Rachel's face. "But the wedding is around the corner—"

"And I'm too busy to leave the bakery." I brandish my hand in the air. "I think it's best you go."

"Oh, Nathan told me you'd say that. He instructed me to bring the wedding dresses to you."

"What do you mean?"

She turns to Zoey. "If your friend can man the counter for a short time—"

"I can—" Zoey nods.

I glower at her, and she raises her hands. "Sorry, but if you've made up your mind to go through with it, then you have to look the part, right?"

Rachel gestures toward the back of the shop. "We have a trailer parked in the alley. And all the dresses are ready for you to try on. You simply have to step in there and make a choice."

When I hesitate, she pleads, "It won't take more than an hour of your time. We have fitting specialists on hand to mark out the alterations."

I draw in a breath. "I'm still not—"

Rachel's eyes gleam. "Also, the dresses are Karma West Sovrano originals."

13

Nathan

"No church wedding." I rock back on my heels. "Also, I will not be inviting the family."

"Oh." Arthur looks crestfallen. "I was hoping to have all of my grandchildren under one roof for this occasion."

"You're not invited, either."

"What?" He gapes. "You don't mean that."

"Sure I do. I saw the circus you put Edward through, and I'm not willing to go through that. You're not going to surprise me by pulling forward my wedding date, old man. I'll do it on my own terms."

"But—"

"You get this wedding, or none at all." I focus my gaze on my grandfather. We're in my office in the headquarters of the Davenport Group. And I'm in the office next to the corner office allocated to the CEO. Not the office for the CEO, but the one adjoining it, with a glass wall in between the two. Because that's how my grandfather operates. G-Pa, as we call him, is a canny old operator who'll get his way without regard for the consequences.

He coughs, then rubs his chest. "You'd deprive this old man of one of his last wishes?"

I resist the urge to roll my eyes. What is it about him that makes me regress back to being seven? Oh, wait. When I was seven, I was busy consoling my mother, who couldn't get out of bed because her depression was particularly bad, and her meds weren't helping, either.

He coughs again and shoots me an injured look.

I glare back. I'm a lot like him. Doesn't mean I'm going to let him get away with his machinations. "I know what you're up to."

"You do?" He looks at me with wide-eyed surprise. Add consummate actor to his list of talents.

"You may claim you didn't know that she and I knew each other before you sent me off to 'evaluate'"— I make air-quotes with my fingers —"the potential of investing in her bakery, but even you have to admit, it's too much of a coincidence for me to believe that."

"I'm not going to keep pressing my innocence to you. Besides, what does it matter how you met her? Important thing is, you found the woman of your dreams."

Knew it. If that isn't a declaration of his culpability, I don't know what is.

"The important thing is, as soon as I get married, you're going to confirm me as CEO and give me that office." I stab my thumb in the direction of the glass wall that separates my space from the one next door.

"The important thing is, you consummate your wedding."

"The fuck?" I stare. "If you think I'm going to let you verify that, you can forget about it."

Tiny raises his head from next to G-Pa and looks at me. His mouth turns down. His ears stand to attention. He's not happy at my voicing my displeasure. I scowl at him, and he blinks back, looking as innocent as the man next to him.

"It's okay, boy." Arthur pats his big head. "Nate, here, needs to get things off his chest. Let's cut him some slack. He's been under some pressure, what with deciding to get married and realizing he can't get away with just going through the motions. It needs to be a real marriage." Arthur tips his chin up at me. "A fake relationship won't cut it. And don't think I won't be able to tell the difference. Ahh, don't look at me like that. I don't need 'proof.'" This time, he makes air-quotes. "The truth of your relationship will be evident to anyone with eyes."

Well, damn. The man might be getting along in his years, but he's still sharp as a tack. The tips of my ears burn, but I manage to school my features into an expression of disdain. "Are you suggesting my relationship with Skylar is fake?"

"Of course not"—he leans back in his chair—"but in case you were thinking of going into a marriage of convenience, you're going to have to turn it into the real deal, real fast."

"And why would I think of creating a pretend relationship?"

"I'm sure you're not." His eyes gleam. "Why would you, when you've carried feelings for this girl for a while, and now that you've met her again... Well, I'm sure you're not stupid enough to let her go."

"Of course I'm not." I roll my shoulders and glance around the office. *Is it hot in here?* I pick up my phone and dial my assistant. "Please get maintenance to lower the temperature of the heating system." I disconnect the call.

"So, it's settled." My grandfather smirks. He looks altogether too pleased with himself. Too late, I realize I've managed to give him what he wants. I thought I had the upper hand in this conversation, but clearly, not.

"What's settled?" I ask slowly.

"You'll be married in six days in a non-denominational ceremony."

"A non-denominational ceremony?" A wrinkle mars her forehead.

"Is that a problem? Would you prefer a church wedding?" I purse my lips. *Should I have consulted with her before I made the decision about the format of the blasted event? Probably. But it's too late to change things. Besides, it's not like it's real anyway. Yet.*

Nevertheless, when she shakes her head, the tension lessens in my shoulders.

"Gosh, no, it's not like I grew up going to church."

"What's the problem, then?" I survey her features, which fill the screen of my phone. I immersed myself in work after Arthur left. Only to surface two hours later to the realization I should call my fiancée—my *fiancée?*—and update her on the status of the wedding.

She looks away, then back at me. There's hesitation on her features.

"Tell me," I order.

She draws in a breath; then brings the spatula she's been using to mix the dessert she's been working on to her mouth. She uses her finger to wipe some batter from the spatula, then licks the mixture, and every part of me tightens. I can't take my gaze off how she moves it around with her tongue, then swallows. My cock extends. My balls harden. I shift around in my chair, looking for a more comfortable position. When she still doesn't answer, I glare at her. "What is it? I don't have all day to guess what you're thinking."

She huffs, then looks away.

"You going to tell me, or do I have to come there and kiss it out of you?"

"Excuse me?" She jerks her chin in my direction. "Did you say—"

"Kiss it out of you? Yes."

She gapes. "B-but this is not a real relationship."

"To the outside world, it is."

She wrinkles her nose. "It's only the two of us right now."

"I'm practicing." *Tell that to my dick, which insists this is the real deal.*

"Hmm…" she scowls. "So, the last time you kissed me—"

"I wanted to learn the shape of your mouth, so when I kiss you on our wedding day, I won't be surprised." *That the best you can come up with? You're a loser, make no mistake.*

She flushes, and her lips part. Her pupils dilate, and I know she's turned on. She looks away, then back at me. "I… uh… I…" She shakes her head. "What was I saying?" She sounds dazed.

Satisfaction warms my chest. It's my words causing her to lose her train of thought. I manage to keep the smile off of my face. "You were going to tell me why you're not happy at the thought of a small wedding ceremony with just the two of us in attendance?"

I must distract her enough that this time she says without hesitation, "I was hoping to have my friends there and—" Someone speaks in the background, she turns to the side, and a smile lights up her features. "Hey, Knox."

Knox? I stiffen. *What is my half-brother doing there?* We're supposed to meet right about now, and— My phone pings with an incoming message.

Knox: I'm stopping by to say hello to your lovely fiancée.

Knox: Not that I'm asking for your permission.

Knox: I might buy a bunch of pastries while I'm here. Aren't her Sweet Bits delicious?

What. The. Fuck?

"You won't be without friends on your wedding day," Knox's voice grows louder. The next moment, he appears on the screen behind my fiancée. "I'll be there."

14

Skylar

"That's a nice thing to say." I glance sideways at Knox.

Traffic to the shop was unusually low today, so when Knox wandered in, I used it as an excuse to close early. I asked him to switch the sign to closed and turn off the lights in the front. I also invited him to help himself to some pastries, then join me in the bakery kitchen so I could talk to him as I experimented on another recipe.

This batter has aphrodisiacs in it. And no, it's not for my wedding cake. *Okay, so it is for my wedding cake.* Doesn't mean I'm stressing about my upcoming nuptials. *Okay, I definitely am, but I don't want to admit it.*

When my phone rang and I saw Nate's name on the FaceTime call, I jumped to answer it. I wanted to hear his voice and see his face. Thankfully, Knox had been distracted by the array of deserts in the front, so he was too far away to hear me talk about my marriage arrangement with Nate. Speaking of —

I glance down at my phone to find he's disconnected. "How rude." And he didn't say goodbye.

"I assume you're talking about my brother?" Knox smirks.

"Who else?" I place the spatula aside and, with the help of a rubber scraper, pour the cake mixture into a cake pan. I slide it into the oven, set a timer, and turn to him.

I haven't been formally introduced to Nathan's family, but Knox came by the day after Nathan's first visit and introduced himself. He told me Nathan had no idea he was coming, but he was curious about the woman his older brother was going to marry and wanted to welcome me to the family. I thought that was a sweet gesture. Especially since Nathan himself shows no signs of inviting me over to meet them.

"What are you doing here?"

"Oh, I was in the neighborhood and thought I'd drop by and see how the wedding preparations are coming along." His lips curl. It's not exactly a smile; more like a smirk. An expression which emphasizes the scar he wears across his face. The 'deformity' only adds to the general air of danger this man wears about him. It shouldn't amp up his sexiness, but it does. In fact, I'm sure some women find him irresistible. Not me, though. I worship at the altar of another alphahole. Since I met Nathan, I've never found another man to match up to him when it comes to sex-appeal. Knox comes close, but he doesn't have the charisma that Nathan does. That allure, that something about him which draws me. The chemistry between Nathan and me is a living, breathing thing which stretches and throbs and thrums, and given a chance, would pull me in and swallow me whole.

"No, that's not true." He tilts his head. "What I told you earlier isn't the complete truth.'

"It's not?" I turn to face him.

He shakes his head. "I'm here because I wanted to get a rise out of my brother."

"You did?" I blink slowly.

"I don't know if he mentioned it to you, but Nathan has only recently come into the family fold."

"No, he hasn't actually." He hasn't told me anything about himself. Though, I gathered a fair bit about his childhood from Ben. Nate's association with the Davenports, though, is still something of a mystery. Except for the part his grandfather plays in his wanting to get married, of course.

"I'll be honest, I don't exactly trust the guy," Knox drawls.

"O-k-a-y?" *Why is he telling me all this?*

He must see the confusion on my features, for he gestures toward the tables. "Shall we sit down, and I can tell you more."

I hesitate, then nod. "Would you like a coffee?"

"A coffee would be wonderful." He steps back and gestures. "After you."

I head for the front of the shop and set about readying the espresso machine. "How do you take your coffee?"

"Black, no sugar."

I prepare it, pour it for him, along with my cup of tea, then walk over to take a seat at the table he's occupied. I slide his coffee over.

He takes a sip of his, and an expression of delight flits over his features. "That's excellent."

"Thank you." I sip my tea, then gesture with my chin. "You were telling me about Nathan?"

He takes another mouthful of his coffee, then sets down his cup. "As I was saying earlier, I don't know him very well. He's a virtual stranger, and while he may be blood, our grandfather deciding to make him the CEO of the company was, understandably, a blow for me."

I lower my chin. "Because you were being groomed to take over as the CEO?"

He nods. "As a result, I keep close tabs on my half-brother. And when he produced a fiancée out of the blue—no doubt, spurred on by my grandfather's condition that he marry before his position is assured—you have to understand, I was suspicious."

"Of course you were," I say lightly.

"What became clear, though, is that he's very possessive about you."

I choke on my next sip of tea, then reach for my handkerchief and pat my lips. "Nathan, possessive?"

He looks at me with surprise. "Surely, you're aware of the feelings he has for you?"

"Umm, we *are* getting married. Of course, he has feelings for me." I can't say otherwise. Not when he's told his family we're getting married. I can't tell Knox the marriage is a farce. If Nathan wants his grandfather to believe our wedding is the real thing, I need to play along with his brothers, as well. In fact, Knox being here might well be a test to find out if our relationship is genuine.

"There are feelings and then there are 'feelings.'" He makes air-quotes with his fingers. "My half-brother takes on the persona of a caveman when he talks about you. And then, there's the speed with which he proposed to you—with a little bit of prompting from our grandfather, of course."

"Hmm." I take another sip of my tea. It's hot enough to burn the roof of my mouth. Just how I like it. Knox is here to find out more about my relationship with Nathan, that much is clear. I bet it's because he wants to use it against Nathan in some way. Nathan hasn't mentioned anything about Knox, but I can sense Knox would love nothing more than to put Nathan at a disadvantage. It's more than sibling rivalry. This feels a bit more serious.

"My fiancé is a very intense man." I incline my head. "He has strong sentiments when it comes to anything that belongs to him. He—" The buzzing of what sounds like a helicopter approaching drowns out my voice. The sound grows even louder. In fact, it sounds like it's just outside my front door. The windows and tables rattle. I grab my cup of tea to stop it from spilling. Knox steadies his cup.

"You were saying—"

"Uh, that Nathan can be a bit over-zealous when it comes to what he owns, like his company and—" I peer through the glass windows of the cafe to find a helicopter landing on the road out front. My jaw drops. "Holy *Schitt's Creek*... Is that...?"

"A helicopter? I believe so." Knox leans back in his seat and there's a smug look on his face. "You think he's over-zealous enough to fly over from his office to declare his ownership of his woman?"

The door flies open, and Nathan stalks inside. Without breaking stride, he reaches Knox, who's smirking in his chair. "The fuck are you doing here?" he snaps.

"I'm having a coffee with your fiancée. The fuck you doing here, bro?"

Nate curls his fingers into fists. "Why are you here?"

"You're getting married in less than a week; thought I should meet your intended and get to know her better." His expression turns innocent. "Especially since you seem to be hiding her from the rest of us."

"My prerogative," he growls.

"And it's mine to come by, meet her, and admire this bakery she's worked so hard to set up. As for the desserts"—he gestures to the cakes on display—"I think I'd love to taste one."

"Of course, coming right up."

I jump up—right now, every sale counts—when—

"Sit down," my fiancé says through gritted teeth.

"Oh, but—"

"Knox was just leaving." Nathan's jaw tics.

Knox's grin widens. "Oh, but I haven't tasted her—"

"—don't fucking say it," Nathan snaps.

"—C!i—"

Nathan grabs Knox by his collar, hauls him to his feet, pulls back his fist, and let's it fly, and—

"Nathan, stop," I cry out.

—pauses within an inch of his half-brother's features.

Knox's smile widens. "Don't stop, big bro."

"Don't do it." I lock my fingers together. "Please, Nate."

He releases Knox so suddenly, he stumbles back, then rights himself. He straightens his collar, then clicks his tongue. "Temper, temper. The CEO of the Davenport Group almost beating up his younger brother? Now, that would have made a fine headline in the media. And where would that have left your bid to confirm your position, eh? You know how much Arthur hates any kind of scandal. He loves to run a tight ship, that man."

The vein at Nathan's temple pulses with such force, I'm sure it's going to snap through his skin. "Out." He stabs his thumb in the direction of the door. "Get the fuck out."

Knox laughs. "Whatever you say, big bro." He turns to me and half-bows. "A pleasure, m'lady. Maybe I'll get to taste your Vaja—"

Nathan makes a growling noise and Knox smirks.

"—your desserts, next time."

He brushes past Nathan and heads out the door. The tinkling of the bell fills the space, then fades away. In the silence that falls over the shop, his anger screams louder than words ever could. He's wound so tightly; the tension vibrates off of his big body and slams into my chest. His displeasure is so thick in the space between us, I could cut the air with a knife. I bend to gather my mug and Knox's when Nate growls, "Leave it."

I ignore him, carry the mugs over to the counter, then turn and gasp. Nathan's standing right behind me. So close, the heat from his body is an all-encompassing shield which wraps around me as effectively as a lasso. He's so tall, I have to tip my head back, and further back, to meet his gaze. His blue eye blazes with cold fire, while his amber eye flashes with golden sparks. The combination of those mismatched eyes boring into me is like being pinned in place by a high-powered laser. His chest heaves, and his shoulders seem to swell. The tendons on his throat stand out in such relief, it's clear he's under great duress.

"Nathan," I whisper, "what's wrong."

When he doesn't answer, the silence stretches. The rage that crackles in the air is so heavy, so thick, so hot, it licks over my skin and makes my nerve-endings pop.

"Nate, please." I take a step forward, and my breasts brush against him. An electric current runs up my spine. The hair on the back of my neck stands on end. He must feel it, too, for every muscle in his body turns to stone.

"Talk to me. Why are you so angry?" I say softly.

"Angry?" His voice is like flint being rubbed together; I can almost feel the sting of the sparks. "That's not the word I'd use right now to describe how I'm feeling."

"Oh?" I manage to keep my tone from trembling. "Then how would you describe it?"

"I'm livid, Starling."

"Why?" I frown. "What did I do wrong?"

He moves so quickly, I flinch. The next moment, he curls his fingers around my wrist. Despite how tightly wound he is, his touch is gentle. He holds up my left palm, and without taking his gaze from mine, growls, "Why aren't you wearing your ring?"

15

Nathan

"I, uh, took it off earlier because I didn't want it to get in the way of the baking."

Her explanation is perfectly plausible. And the ring is big enough to warrant getting in the way of her work. So there's no reason for me to be so upset. No reason to justify the anger that filled me when I heard Knox's voice, the rage that overcame me when I saw Knox step into the frame of the camera behind her, the desperation that squeezed my guts when I realized he was there with her. Fact is, I was so overcome with jealousy on seeing Knox with her, I stalked into my grandfather's office and demanded access to the private helicopter that's always parked on the top floor of the office building. I also had my security team radio the traffic police and pull enough strings so they'd cut off the traffic to the road and gave me special permission to land—now, and in the future.

I used the Davenport name to get my way, and no, I don't feel an ounce of remorse about it. If it means I could get to her in record time, that's all that matters. And then I felt that burn of possessiveness when I saw the empty ring-finger. A coalescence of feelings stabs at my chest. *Why am I so upset she's not wearing my ring? Why is it so important that the world know she's mine? Mine. Mine. Mine.*

Some of my feelings must show on my features, for she swallows. "Nathan," she whispers.

The shape of her lips forming my name is the most erotic thing I've ever seen. My balls harden. My cock thickens. I bend my knees and peer into her eyes. "I shouldn't be this upset about you not wearing the mark of my possession, but it bloody hurts that you aren't."

"I'm sorry." She raises her palm and presses it to my cheek. "I didn't realize it meant so much to you."

"I didn't know, either. And when I saw my asshole half-brother talking to you, it felt like my entire world had fallen apart."

"Oh…" Her features soften. "How… How can I make it better?"

I place my hand over hers, then turn my face into her palm. When I kiss the soft skin at the base of her thumb, she shivers. And when I wrap my other hand below her hips, straighten and throw her over my shoulder, she yelps, "Nathan, what are you doing?"

"I could say I'm punishing you for making me envious, but I'm not going to hide behind that excuse."

"You… you're not?" Her voice is breathless.

I shake my head. "I simply want an excuse to do this." I bring my palm down on her behind with a thwack. The sound echoes around the bakery.

She gasps. "Oh, my god," her voice catches.

"You like that, hmm?"

"Of course not."

I slap her butt again, and this time, a whine bleeds from her lips. The flesh of her arse jiggles, and fuck, if that doesn't turn me on further. I want to leave my mark on that creamy flesh. I want to squeeze her behind and bury my face in the cleavage between her arse cheeks. I want to bury myself in her forbidden hole and make her come so hard, she'll remember the feeling every time she sits down for the next week. The blood thuds at my temples. The crotch of my pants is so tight, I have to widen my stance to accommodate my arousal. As if she senses my thoughts, she squirms in my grasp, and when I grab handfuls of her ample arse, she shudders.

"Still going to tell me you don't like it?"

She draws in a sharp breath, then murmurs something under her breath.

"What was that?"

"I do like it," she says in a low voice, then yelps when I slap her left-butt cheek; then the right, then the left again.

"What was that you said?" I growl.

"I said I like it, you bastard," she yells.

I laugh. And that makes her squirm even more. And when I trail my fingers down the fabric of her skirt, which covers the demarcation between her arse-cheeks, she digs her fingers into my hips. "What are you doing?"

In reply, I march behind the counter and into the kitchen. I pull out the only seat—a bar stool at the island in the center—with my boot clad toe and sit down, then lower her to my lap.

She yelps again, then grabs at my legs to right herself. "I... I don't think the barstool can take both our weights."

"What are you talking about?" I cup the curve of one butt-cheek, and when she bucks, I know her skin must be smarting from my spanking and that my touch must send flickers of pleasure-pain sparking over her nerve-endings.

"Don't act like you don't know," she scoffs.

"I have no idea what you're talking about, especially not when your ripe-as-a-peach backside is all I can see."

"Don't you mean, my watermelon-shaped, fat arse, which is the reason they invented double doors?"

I pause, and this time, when I bring my hand down on her backside, she yells, "What in the ever-lovin' *Succession*!"

"That was for insulting my fiancée's gorgeous rear, and this"—my palm connects with her butt with enough force that her entire body jolts—"is because you put yourself down."

"That hurt," she yelps.

"Good," I murmur.

"What the—!" She turns her head and scowls up at me from between the strands of her hair that hang down over her face. "I can't believe you said that."

"Better believe it. I'm not letting anyone disparage my future wife."

"Future *fake* wife..."

"There's nothing fake about our wedding ceremony."

She shoves her hair back from her face. "But this entire relationship is a farce."

Is it?

When I don't reply, her forehead wrinkles. "It is, isn't it?"

"You tell me."

"You're confusing me, Nate."

"Nothing to be confused about. As far as the world is concerned, we're madly in love and getting married."

"Exactly, but the two of us know it's not real."

"But we have to pretend it is, so it comes across as real to the others."

She opens and shuts her mouth, then shoves at me. "Can you let me go, please, so I can stand up and—" I grip her waist, then haul her to sitting position, so she's straddling me. There's a ripping sound, and she glances down at her now torn skirt. "Oh no, that was my favorite."

"I'll buy you ten more."

She scowls up at me. "I like this one."

"I'll get it mended for you."

"You'd do that?" Her features soften.

I'd do that and so much more, if you gave me a chance. I flatten my palms over the flare of her hips and fit her over my crotch.

"Oh!" Her eyes round in an expression of surprise. Which also means her mouth is open in an 'O', which makes me wonder how it would feel to have her lips wrapped around my cock, which causes the blood to drain to my groin, and my cock to extend, and the tent over my crotch to grow larger and wider and fit snugly in the space between her thighs. And she must feel it for... "Oh, my—" She blinks. "I... Is that... I think that's—"

"My dick stabbing into your pussy?" I pause for effect. "It is."

Her cheeks redden. "No need to be so explicit."

"But you blush so prettily when I am."

"I'm not a prude." She tosses her hair over her shoulder.

"Is that right?"

She raises her fingers, then grips my shoulder. "It is." Using me for leverage, she grinds down on my already swollen cock, which instantly fights to escape the confines of my slacks.

"Fuck." I grit my teeth. A bead of sweat slides down my temple.

Her lips curve in a small smile of victory, then she begins to rub herself against the column in my pants.

16

Skylar

Don't do this. Don't do this.

"You don't want to do this," he growls.

Which, of course, makes me want to prove to him I can. I squeeze down on his throat—the tendons of which are so tense, they feel like taut guitar strings. Then I begin to stroke my pussy up and down the column in his pants, and again. His hold on my hips tightens. The pain slithers down to meet the friction in my core, the combination of which turns my entire center into a forest fire of sensation.

"Oh, my god." I throw my head back and close my eyes, focusing on that part where I'm abrading my pussy into the thick pillar between his legs.

He releases his hold on my hip, only to circle my nape with his thick fingers. And when he drags his stubbled chin over the sensitive skin of my throat, goosebumps pepper my flesh. Pinpricks radiate out from the point of contact to circle my nipples, then zip down to my clit. It's like every erogenous part of my body is on high-alert, and the parts I didn't think could be turned on have developed a beating heart at their center. My entire body has turned into a mass of tactile awareness. The blood thuds at my temples, and my pulse booms in my ears, at my wrists, even in my clit. My nipples throb, and my breasts are so heavy, it feels like there are weights attached to them.

He whispers his nose up my jawline and sniffs deeply. And the act is so erotic, so carnal, like he's breathing me in, like he wants to trap my scent in his lungs and carry it around with him, like he wants to imprint how I smell into every cell in his body, which makes it so very intimate that I feel the pulsing sensation in my clit expand out to my thighs, my belly, then speed up my spine. My entire body has turned into a tsunami of feelings, where every inch of my skin can sense more intensely than I ever have before.

His hold on my neck tightens. It's reassuring, and also… Strangely, arousing… And oh, so possessive. I draw in a breath and come up empty. The burn in my chest seems to ignite every cell in my body. My head spins. In response, I squeeze down on his throat and feel the pulse at the base of his kick up in speed. It mirrors the *thud-thud-thud* of my heart, the whoosh of blood in my veins. My toes curl, my back curves, and when he places his mouth next to my ear, loosens his grasp on my neck so the oxygen rushes into my lungs, and commands, "Come," I shatter.

The orgasm crashes into me with the impact of a freight train and pushes me over the edge. I float in space, weightless, filled with a euphoria I've never experienced before. The happy hormones course through my bloodstream, and when they fade away, I slip against his chest. He tucks my head under his chin, cradles it at the nape of my neck, and holds me in place. The funny thing? It doesn't feel constricting. If anything, it wraps a sense of security about me. Any remnants of tension from my shoulders bleed out, and I yawn. He drags his hand down the length of my hair, and it's soothing but also turns me on.

He must sense it, too, for he chuckles. "Still horny, hmm?"

I try to speak, but it comes out as another yawn. He rises to his feet and suddenly, I'm in his arms. "What are you doing?"

"Taking you to bed."

"What?" I begin to struggle, but when his arms tighten, I subside. "I need to clean up and lock down for the night. I have a cake in the oven."

"Did you set a timer?"

"Yes." I point to the minute timer on the counter next to the oven.

"Do you have a cake tester?"

I point to the timer; the tester sits on the counter next to it.

"I'll do it."

"You don't know where to put things." My voice comes out slightly slurred. I try to rouse myself but end up yawning again.

"I'll figure it out," he murmurs.

"Nate, I really need to do this myself."

"You really don't."

I pout. "How do you know so much about baking, anyway?"

He hesitates. "If you mean, how do I know that you need to use a timer and a cake tester to ensure the cake is ready before you put it away for the night, I thought that was common knowledge."

"No, it's not." I yawn again.

"Hmm... I may have to read up more on baking."

I blink. "Y-y-you, read up on baking?"

"Sure." He shrugs. "I'm investing in your bakery; the least I'd do is read up on the baking process."

He's lying. That's not the only reason he read up on baking. I bet he did it because he has feelings for me, and I love baking. But if I confront him, he'll only deny it, so with the remnants of what clarity of thought I have left, I manage to slur, "There's a spare key to my apartment in the bottom drawer of my desk in my office."

He stiffens.

"You're giving me a key to your apartment?"

"Hmm…" I brush my cheek against the smooth material of his jacket, then turn my face into it and breathe deeply. Cinnamon, pepper, that ocean-breeze scent that is so very Nathan fills my lungs.

"You sure you want me to have the key?"

"After that orgasm? You bet. Also, if we want this charade to work, then shouldn't you have access to my place?" I yawn deeply.

The last thing I remember is being tucked into bed. When I wake up, the only light comes from the moon that streams in. I reach for my phone—which is where I normally keep it on the nightstand. The clock on the screen says 3 a.m.. I put it back, turn on my side, and come face-to-face with Nathan.

He's stretched out on top of the covers. He's removed his jacket, tie, and shoes, but otherwise, he's fully dressed. His white shirt has the top two buttons undone. In the dim light, I can make out what seems to be the outline of a tattoo peeking out from under his lapels. There's also a silver chain with what seems like dog-tags which has fallen over his collar. I reach out to touch it and gasp when he grabs my wrist. I look up to find him glaring at me out of those mismatched eyes. The shadows beneath his cheekbones are pronounced, the stubble on his chin thicker than what it was a few hours ago. With his narrowed gaze and his flared nostrils, he could be the anti-hero in a romance novel or the villain in an action flick.

He brings my hand to his mouth, then wraps his finger around my ring finger, which now sports my ring. *His ring. My ring.* He slides my finger across his tongue until my digit disappears inside his mouth. He covers my ring with his lips and sucks.

I feel the tug in my most intimate parts, deep inside me. I'm instantly wet, the moisture sliding down the inside of my thigh. He draws in a sharp breath, and I swear, he can smell my arousal. And how horny I am right now. I inch forward until we're touching from thigh to chest, and when he releases my finger with a pop and brings it to my mouth, I suck on the wetness, and it feels like I'm tasting his need.

He releases his hold on my wrist, only to dig his fingers into the hair at the nape of my neck. When he tugs, I'm forced to tip my chin up, baring my throat to him. It's a sign of submission, a clear invitation to him to own me, to mark me, to run his nose up my throat and sniff me again. I close my eyes and lean toward him, and when I feel his breath on my lips, a whine spills from me. I don't care that I sound so needy, so greedy, so ravenous in my craving for him. I wait for him to kiss me, and he does. He bypasses my lips and presses his own to my forehead. Then he releases me. I snap my eyes open in time to watch him swing his legs over the side of the bed, slip into his shoes, and straighten.

"I'm sorry, I didn't mean for that to happen last evening." Turning, he grabs his jacket from the back of the chair, where he must have placed it earlier, and strides across the floor of my studio apartment.

What the—! I sit up and call out to him, "Don't you dare leave, Nathan."

He doesn't stop.

"Oh, I almost forgot; you've had so much practice running. It's what you do best, isn't it? When things get real, you cut and run."

He pauses at the door, then grips the doorframe before he turns to look at me over his shoulder. "That's right. And you'd do best to remember it."

17

Nathan

"Where in the bloody buggerin' hell are the P&L reports? They were supposed to be in my inbox five minutes ago." The man on the other end of the phone begins to make an excuse, but I cut him off, "If they don't reach me in the next three minutes, you're fired. You know what? You're fired anyway." I slam the phone receiver into its cradle, then look up as my assistant walks in.

She takes one look at my face, then turns and marches out. Good call. The next unlucky sod who walks into my office is going to be relieved of their duties so fast, they won't know what hit them.

The door opens, and Sinclair walks in.

Doesn't he know how to knock? Well, hell. The one man I cannot fire, nor hold responsible for the shit-show that is my life. Also, he's not directly involved in the Davenport Group of companies, so I can't chew him out over a business shortcoming.

"The fuck you doing here?" I scowl.

"The fuck you looking like you haven't had sex in years?"

The anger building behind my eyes pulses against my temples. "It's best you leave, Sterling."

He smirks. "Best you push up the wedding, before you screw things up."

"Too fucking late for that," I mutter. I lean back in my chair and tap my fingertips together. "What brings you here?"

"Can't I visit an ol' friend?"

I lower my chin to my chest. "We're not friends."

"Tell that to your grandfather, who seems to consider me something of a good luck mascot, considering I have an open invitation to visit any of his offices at any time."

"Must have to do with the fact you're not family, so you haven't been subjected to his machinations. Ergo, you're on good terms with him," I scoff.

"Or it might have to do with the fact that I didn't refuse when he asked to move the weekly poker game to his place." He grins.

I glower back. It was one thing to attend the game at Sinclair's place, but now that it's under Arthur's roof, it means I have to put up with seeing him there. Which is what the canny old bastard, no doubt, intended. My grandfather is not above manufacturing creative excuses to spend time with as many of his grandsons as possible, especially at the same time.

Sinclair prowls forward and throws himself into the chair opposite mine.

"I don't recall asking you to stay."

"I don't recall you asking me to leave." He leans back, rests one ankle on top of his other knee, and circles it with his fingers. He's the very picture of confidence and smug satisfaction. Man has everything—a wife he loves, a child he adores, friends who are all well-settled and who check in with each other on a daily basis—that's how close they are. Not to mention, a business that's so well set up, it practically runs itself. No wonder he spends a lot of time at various Davenport events. Still doesn't explain why he's here, though. I scowl.

He smiles back. "I was told you could do with a bit of friendly advice in this time preceding your wedding."

"An event I don't intend to invite you or any of my half-brothers to, nor my grandfather," I warn.

"As long as you do the deed, I don't think it matters. Of course, it's what your fiancée wants, too, right?"

I hesitate.

He tilts his head. "So, she doesn't want a proper wedding with a white dress and friends in attendance?"

I rub at my temple. "You're giving me a fucking headache with your ceaseless prattle."

"It might have to do with the fact it's nine p.m. and you're still here and keeping your staff away from their loved ones."

"You here to run interference?"

"I told your staff to go home. You're welcome."

My pulse rate picks up. "You had no right to do that. I have a shit ton of stuff to get through, deadlines to meet—"

"Promises to keep, miles to go before you sleep, yada, yada. Spare me your tale of woe and accept the fact that I have something to help your condition."

"My condition?" I say carefully.

"I mean your heartburn... Not the heartache you're carrying around behind that asshole exterior of yours. That's something you're going to have to figure out how to fix on your own. As for the former..." He pulls a small bottle of chewable antacids from his pocket and places it on the table. "I have the solution to that."

Fuck him. I eye the antacids with longing. Fact is, I forgot to eat breakfast and skipped lunch, and poured enough coffee down my throat to cause heartburn. That's all it is—heartburn, a result of too much acidity from the caffeine. That's the reason my stomach is lurching at this moment.

The pressure behind my eyes swell. I grimace, then snatch up the bottle, shake out a pill onto my palm and chew on it. When I look back at Sinclair, he has a considering expression on his face.

"What?" I snap.

"I understand what you're going through is scary."

"You have no idea," I say bitterly.

"On the contrary, I do. I've been there." He holds up his forefinger. "It starts as a marriage of convenience, as a fake relationship, one you're getting into for what you think are the right reasons but are actually the wrong reasons. And then, they turn out to be the right reasons; only, you still think they're wrong and keep denying it to yourself. Then, when you wake up and acknowledge your feelings, it's too late."

"First"—I hold up my own forefinger—"not a marriage of convenience."

"If you say so." He shrugs.

"And what do you mean by 'too late'?" I frown.

"You might have lost the love of your life by then." He lowers his forefinger, only to raise his middle finger. "Unless, of course, that's the point of this entire exercise?" He swipes his middle finger under his lower lip.

"You're making no sense. Also, what are you? Ten?"

He continues, as if he hasn't heard me, "What's not making sense is... Your fiancée is on her way to meet a man, while—"

I jump up to my feet. "What the fuck do you mean?"

"I mean, she's in the lobby of The Dorchester, waiting for a man she connected with on an online app—"

"She's on a fucking date?" I bellow. The sound is loud and harsh and echoes around the office with enough force, my headache turns up a notch.

"I believe that's the technical term, yes."

"What the fuck?" I push back my chair, which tumbles to the floor, then race around the desk and past him toward the door, before coming to a standstill. I pivot and stab my finger in his direction. "How do you know where she is?"

"She mentioned it to her friend Zoey, who mentioned it to my wife Summer, who asked me to mention it to you. Her friends are worried about her. They figured if you knew, you'd intervene. Speaking of"—he stabs his middle finger at the door—"you going there, or you going to stand here holding your dick in your hand while, right now, your fiancée might be in bed with—"

"Don't fucking say it." The churning in my gut intensifies. I wince, then shake out another antacid and chew on it. I pocket the bottle, then glare at him. "If I find out you're wrong—"

"I'm not."

"—I'm going to smash my fist in your face."

18

Skylar

"You sure about this?" Zoey's worried face looks up at me from my phone screen. She's the only one who knows about my plan. I mentioned it to her yesterday, and only because she called me after I'd arranged the date with a man I'd matched with on a dating app.

Last night, she didn't react in a way that made me think she was concerned. But clearly, she was, since she called me back to check in on me. I love my friends, but this is why I don't want to share too much of what's going on in my life. Sure, it makes me come across as being closed off, but it also means I don't have to explain myself to others. It's not that I'm not grateful for my friends being concerned about me. But honestly, at the moment, I just want to get on with the program before I lose my nerve. That said, I knew it was prudent to let Zoey know where I was going to be, as a safety precaution. After all, I'm going to meet a stranger.

"Skylar? Did you hear what I said?" Zoey frowns

"I'm sure." *I'm not.* But I'm not going to tell her that.

When I went on the dating app, I made it clear I was looking for a no-strings-attached, one-night-only encounter to lose my virginity. Of course, losing my V-card attracted a host of responses. When 'Larry,' if that's his real name, recommended we meet at The Dorchester, one of the finest hotels in the city, I knew he had money. It also meant my first time would be in the lap of luxury.

After Nate walked out on me—again—and after he made it clear everything that happened between us was a mistake, I was pissed. Sure, he closed up shop for me, then carried me up to my apartment and put me to bed, which shows he cares for me. And he slept on top of the sheets fully clothed, and on his side of the bed so there was no accidental touching. Not until I reached out to touch him, that is. But then, he withdrew and made it clear what happened the night before was a mistake.

He may be attracted to me, but not enough to sleep with me. He may have feelings for me, but not enough for him to make love to me.

He'll marry me, consolidate his position as CEO with his grandfather, then likely, divorce me. He'll find someone who's a svelte, five-foot ten-inch, icy blonde with long legs and a figure so flat, you can see the light pass through her. Everything he's told me so far about how much he loves my figure is a lie. If he actually liked how I look, he'd have slept with me last night.

I saved my virginity for him, but maybe he doesn't want it. Maybe he doesn't find me alluring enough. I am a plus-size, after all. Maybe he's put off by the thought of having sex with someone as big as me? I hunch my shoulders.

The marriage between us isn't real. *The chemistry between the two of you is real, though. It has been from the first moment you met. So is the connection you've felt with him.* Too bad he doesn't want to acknowledge it.

Worse, when he gives in to the temptation, he regrets it.

Once we get married, I'm sure he'll want me to move in with him, and then I'll never be able to resist the urge to sleep with him. I'd probably throw myself down on the bed and beg him to take my virginity... And chances are, he'll refuse. Ugh!

And if, for some reason, he wants me enough to consummate the marriage? Then, along with having feelings for him, he'll also be the first man I sleep with. That's something I'll never recover from.

I'll never be able to put him behind me and move on. I'll be forever stuck in a limbo where my emotions are connected with him. He'll become my sun, moon and stars, and I... will be nothing but dust to him. *No, I can't let that happen.* I have enough pride to not give up everything I am to him. I will hold onto something for myself. Something I will not let him have access to. Something I choose to give to someone other than him—my virginity. It's what gave me the courage to come here today, and—

"Skylar, have you thought this through? What if you regret it later?" Zoey's voice interrupts me.

"I won't. I have thought this through. This is what I want to do." I set my jaw.

She scans my features, and her own soften. "I know how independent you are. And I can't claim to understand why you want to go through with this, but I want to make sure you don't hurt yourself in the process."

He already hurt me; not that she's aware of it, of course. But then, I also haven't told my friends about Hugo. Another secret I've kept from them. I realize, it's unusual to support someone who's not even blood family when I can barely support myself. But it's my choice, and I don't want to have to explain it to anyone else.

The only person who knows about him is Ben. And my brother supports me. He even wanted to share in the cost for Hugo's treatment, but I refused to let him. It was my choice to help Hugo, which doesn't mean Ben has to pay for his treatment, too. I could do with Ben's emotional support right about now, though.

My phone buzzes with an incoming call; the caller ID says 'unknown,' which normally means it's Ben calling me from whichever location he's been posted to.

"Uh, Zoey, I have to go."

She stiffens. "If I don't hear from you in an hour, I'm coming over there."

"You're a good friend, Z." I blow her a kiss.

"I'm not joking, Sky."

"I don't doubt you. Gotta go." I disconnect her call and answer Ben's. "Hey big bro, how're you doing?"

"Little sis, you sound like you're up to something you shouldn't be doing." Ben's voice is so clear, he might as well be in the same room as me. Which is a change from the static that normally crackles across the telephone lines when he speaks to me from whichever corner of the world he's in. You'd think the Marines would provide clear lines of communication for their men who are putting their lives on the line for our safety but apparently not.

"I'm exactly where I should be," I manage to say around the ball of emotion in my throat. And no, it's not because I'm lying to him, either. I miss my brother, is all. I miss having someone to talk to, someone I can go to for advice, though probably not in this instance. I don't think he'll be very happy when he finds out I'm married to his best friend, and without telling him. But it's for the best. I don't want to distract him during his mission. The last thing he needs is to find out about matters of my heart. Compared to the challenges he's facing, what I'm going through is nothing. "How are you doing, wherever it is you are?"

"I'm doing well, honey. I'm just a little tired from being out here and away from all of you."

"You're missing her," my instincts prompt me to say.

There's silence, then he sighs. "I am. I didn't think I would. I thought when I left, I'd be able to get back into the groove of things. That I'd pick up where I left off, when it came to leading my team on a mission—"

"But it's not the same anymore."

"It's not," he agrees.

"And it wouldn't be. After all, you're in love."

He laughs. "When did you get so wise. Wait—" He hesitates. "Is it because you're in love? Is that why you sound so mature?"

"Hey, I've always sounded older than my years."

He chuckles. "You were born an old soul. It's why I've often felt like I'm talking to one of my peers when I speak with you. No matter, you're so tiny."

"I'm not tiny," I protest.

"Five-feet four-inches is tiny; counts as tiny." He snickers.

"Okay, fine, but physical attributes are not as important as emotional maturity, which I lead on."

"That you do." His voice is sober. "You're the best of both of us, the best of our parents. Every time things go to shite out here, I draw strength from the fact you're safe. That everything I do will ensure you live a long and happy life."

"And I'm so grateful for that." I swallow down the worry that clogs my throat. "I miss you, big brother."

"And I miss you, too. I wish we had more time together. I wish I hadn't had to leave when I did—"

"Don't talk like that. You'll be back soon, Ben. You're going to deliver on this mission; you're going to surpass all expectations."

"Of course I am. After all, I am the best at what I do." His voice is cocky, then he coughs.

"You okay?" I frown.

"Yea. Picked up a chill. The nights here can get real cold, real quick." There's a beeping sound on the line, and he sighs. "I gotta go. There's only one phone line in this place, and the rest of the men need to call home, too. I love you, little sis. Just remember, you're worth a lot more than you give yourself credit for and you deserve a lot more than you realize. Don't just give yourself away to any—" The call cuts out.

I lower my phone to my lap and stare at it. How like Ben to be cut off in the middle of another of his pithy sayings.

It's almost as if he was in my head and knows what I'm planning to do, but that's not possible. Did he sound more tired than usual? Is he unwell? Under the weather? He definitely wasn't his usual self-confident and optimistic self. Every other time he's called me, he's always been itching to get back in the game. This time... It felt like he couldn't wait to come back home. And he will. And then he'll find out I'm married to his best friend and, no doubt, both Nate and I are going to get an earful. But he'll be happy for us—less so, when we divorce... But when he finds out the reasons behind why I did it, he'll understand. He'll know I did it because I wanted to save my business and take care of Hugo... And do it on my own. He'll be proud of me, I'm sure of that.

And if what I'm going to do right now makes me a little less proud of myself, that's okay. At least I'm choosing to do this. Unlike this marriage, which I've been coerced into. Sure, I'm benefiting from it, but if I had another way of getting the money, I wouldn't marry Nate. *A-n-d I'm trying too hard to convince myself. I cannot let thoughts of Nate sway me. I can't. I—*

"Taylor?" A man's voice interrupts my thoughts.

I look up to find a slim man with thinning hair and a pleasant face smiling down at me.

"Larry?" I rise to my feet and hold out my hand. "I'm Taylor Smith." So, I used my girl crush's first name and couldn't come up with a more exotic surname. It works though, doesn't it?

"Larry Jones," he says with a knowing smile. He's probably also using a pseudonym. I glance down at his left hand and, thankfully, there's no mark where a wedding band might be. Good. One less thing to feel bad about.

"Would you like a drink?" He aims an awkward smile in my direction.

I wince. "Um, actually I'd prefer to get this over with."

He seems taken aback, then nods. "That's a good idea. Why beat about the bush when we can head straight for the sack, eh?"

I wince.

So does he. "Sorry, that came out sounding a little creepy. I promise I'm not." He holds up his hands. "Creepy, that is. You sure you don't want that drink?

19

Nathan

"Where the fuck is the goddamn elevator?" I stab my finger into the button that's supposed to summon the elevator, but which has shown no sign of doing so for the last thirty seconds.

On my way over, I used the Davenport name to talk to the manager of the hotel, who confirmed to me that my fiancée was in the hotel. He also obtained the room number she'd gone into and messaged it to me. Apparently, the Davenport clout is good for something.

The elevator doors open, I stalk inside, turn, then bare my teeth at the couple who were about to enter. They freeze, then skitter back. I punch in the floor number where the room she went into is located, then drag my fingers through my hair as the elevator climbs the floors. It comes to a stop, and when the doors slide back, I rush out. Down the corridor, toward the room where she's supposed to be.

I use the keycard I took from the manager to let myself in. I rush inside, then come to a stop. She's standing at the far end by a big bay window. Her back is to me, her thick blonde hair flowing down her back. Her hips are outlined in the dress she's wearing, which comes to just above her knees. On her feet, she's wearing stilettos, with chain-like straps that go around her ankles. Something about the erotic effect of how it clings to her skin twists my stomach. *She wore this for another man?*

She turns to look over her shoulder. There's a smile on her face, which disappears when she spots me. Her gaze widens, and her color fades. "You," she whispers, "what are you doing here?"

"I should be asking you that question, dear fiancée. Speaking of"—I glance down at the empty ring finger on her left hand—"where is your ring?"

She turns around to face me, then shoves her hand behind her back. "That's no business of yours."

"On the contrary." I take a step forward; she moves back. "It's all my business. *You* are my business. In fact,"—I look her up and down—"your business is my business."

She looks at me suspiciously. "Wh-what's that supposed to mean?"

"Have you checked your bank account lately?"

She shakes her head.

"The money you need to pay off your debts has been deposited."

Her jaw drops. "So soon? But I just signed the paperwork an hour ago."

My lawyers informed me they'd received her e-signature, and I ordered my banker to deposit the money in her account.

"I fulfilled my part of the bargain." I take a step forward, and she stiffens. "You have no choice but to go through with your end now."

She firms her lips. "So, this is you making sure I can't back out?"

"Do you want to back out?"

Before she can reply, the door to the ensuite bathroom opens, and a man steps into the room. He spots me, and his features harden. "You're in the wrong room, buddy."

"No, *you're* in a hotel room with my fiancée, *buddy*; that's what's wrong."

His gaze widens. He turns to her. "You're engaged?"

"Hey, don't talk to her; talk to me." I plant myself between them, cutting her off from his line of sight.

He has no choice but to address me. "I didn't know." He raises his hands.

"Now, you do."

"But she's here, so maybe she doesn't want to be—" he argues.

"Don't fucking say it." I take a step in his direction, and he shuffles back.

"Whoa, whoa, I didn't come here to be caught in any marital discord." He continues to sidle in the direction of the door, which is the only reason I don't grab him and shove him out. "But I have to point out, if she's here, despite being engaged to you, then it stands to reason, you're not satisfying—"

I stalk toward him. He turns and races out the door. I slam it shut, lock it for good measure, then turn and place my shoulders against it. "Answer the question."

"Wh-which one?"

"Do you want to back out of the deal?"

She hesitates.

My heart slams into my ribcage. I cannot... *Will not* let her back out. "Why don't you check the money in your bank account? That might help you."

She looks like she's about to refuse, then nods. She heads toward where she's placed her handbag on the nightstand on the right side of the bed. That's the side she prefers to sleep on.

So, she came here with the intention of staying the night. I curl my fingers into fists at my sides. My fiancée came to this hotel room with the intention of sleeping with another man days before our wedding. My shoulders bunch, and the blood roars at my temples. This is my fault. I walked out on her after telling her what happened between us was a mistake. I made her come but I didn't fuck her. I didn't satisfy my woman. And she decided to turn to another man. I watch as she reaches the nightstand, pulls her phone from her handbag, and swipes her fingers across the screen.

Her eyes widen, and she turns on me. "That's much more than the figure stated in the contract."

"It's three times the sum," I snap.

"Why? Why would you do that?"

"To make sure you never need money again. You can invest it in your business. Or use it for anything else you want."

A strange look comes into her eyes—one mixed with relief, and a hint of suspicion. So, she does have use for the additional money. Why didn't she ask me for it in the first place? Haven't I made it clear to her that her needs are my priority? Probably not. Not with the way I've behaved with her. Kissing her, making her come, then walking out on her. I need to make it up to her. But how?

"You needn't have done that." She firms her lips. "I don't need your handouts."

"Oh, I didn't do it for you."

She blinks. "What do you mean?"

"I did it to make sure my future wife wants for nothing. You're mine. And I take care of what belongs to me."

"I'm not a possession." She scowls.

"Oh, you're more than that." I prowl toward her.

She stiffens, but when I come to a stop in front of her, she doesn't move away. I bend my knees and peer into her eyes. "You're my best friend's sister." *And the only woman I want in my bed.* "Which is why, you realize, I can't fuck you, right?"

20

Skylar

"What? Why not?" I hear the words coming out of my mouth, and it sounds like I'm desperate. But I don't care. Until this moment, I wasn't aware how much I want him to make love to me. He left me in my bed and walked away, but in some corner of my mind, I was sure it was only a matter of time before he did. In fact, the romantic part of me wondered if he was saving making love for the first time on our wedding night. So what if this is a marriage of convenience? The chemistry between us is off the charts, and Nate's a virile man. He's not going to deny himself. Not when it's clear being together is going to be good for both of us... Unless he doesn't want me?

"You don't want me," I say flatly.

He frowns. "What do you mean?"

"Is it because I'm not the kind of woman you normally go for?"

"You're not making any sense."

"Oh, you want me to spell it out; fine. I'm a big woman. I have curves. My size dresses are difficult to find. I have large tits and huge hips."

"O-k-a-y?" He looks genuinely confused.

I squeeze my fingers around my phone. Men. How dumb can they be? Do you have to spell out every single detail to them and slap them over the head with it, and even then, they don't get it?

"Argh!" I shake my head. Then, with my free hand, gesture to my figure. "I'm a plus-size girl."

"So?"

"So, I'm fat. And you, clearly, are not the kind of man who wants to bed someone of my dimensions."

His forehead clears. "You think because you're curvaceous—"

"That's a diplomatic way of putting it."

"—I don't find you attractive?"

"Clearly, you don't. You put me to bed but didn't undress me. You slept on top of the covers. Then, told me what happened between us was a mistake, and then you left."

He squeezes the bridge of his nose, his massive chest rises and falls, then he lowers his hand. "Let me get this right. You think I find you unappealing—"

"You do."

"—because I didn't take off your clothes when you were sleeping, and didn't fuck you while I was at it, and then left in the morning."

"And you told me it was a mistake."

"I did not—"

I tighten my lips. "Are you denying—"

"I said, what happened between us shouldn't have; I didn't say it was a mistake."

"Oh." I bite the inside of my cheek. "But I thought—" I shake my head, trying to recall his exact words. "Doesn't matter what you said. It was a rejection."

"I'm sorry it came across like that. I wanted to leave before I did something I would regret."

"Like sleeping with me?"

He nods.

"But why? Why can't you, uh—"

"Fuck you?"

"Why not, Nathan?"

"You're Ben's sister. You're my best friend's little sister."

"I'm aware. And he's going to find out about us at some point."

The wrinkle between his forehead deepens. "Doesn't make me feel any better about desiring you. If I had a choice, I'd—"

"Prefer not to be attracted to me?"

"Yes," he says without hesitation.

A knot of hurt tightens in my chest. My throat closes. "So, I *was* right. You don't want me."

"Didn't you hear what I said? I am so attracted to you, I can't think straight when you're around."

"You have a funny way of showing it; you—" I gasp, for he's grabbed my free hand and placed it on the tent between his legs. The unmistakable bulge which fills my palm seems to grow bigger under my touch. The heat of his arousal soaks through his pants and sinks into my skin. The pulse between my legs throbs in response. I try to pull my hand away, but he holds it captive. He swipes my palm up the column between his thighs, and a groan rumbles up his chest.

"Fuck." He grits his teeth. "Now do you see how much I want you?"

I manage to nod, my gaze fixed on the flush which stains his cheekbones, the beat of his pulse at his temple, the tic at his jaw, the way his heterochromatic eyes blaze with a blue-gold fire that tells me he's this close to losing control. And oh, I so want him to. He's always been the unapproachable one. The confident one. The one who rejected me first, and again. The one who's been able to walk away from me.

To see the naked desire on his features, the need in his eyes, the evidence of his arousal, hot and throbbing under my palm, the way the tendons of his throat stand out in relief, like the mountains jutting out from the earth you see on a flight path... All of it tells me, he has a hankering for me. So then, why doesn't he do something about it? That's right, my brother. I hold up my phone. "Call him."

"What?"

"Call my brother. Leave him a message and tell him we're together. Tell him you want to marry me. He has to find out at some point. Why not now? Let's put this issue to bed, once and for all, so you can take me to bed."

That strange look I've seen a couple times earlier flits across his features. It's a mixture of confusion and sadness and resolve. He reaches for my phone and tosses it over his shoulder, so it hits the bed.

"Why did you—"

He shakes his head. "We don't want to disturb him when he's on a mission and weaken his concentration."

"But—" I begin, but he cuts me off again.

"Trust me. I've been there. When you're away from home and missing everything and everyone—even though you convince yourself you aren't. When you focus on the directives you've been given and try to carry them out, even though you may not agree with all of it. When you convince yourself the high you get from putting your life on the line is something you enjoy, even though the reality is that you're shitting bricks..."

I can't stop the giggle that spills from my lips. It's a nervous sound, but it draws a quirk of his lips, and OMG, that smirk on his lips is so hot. Also, his cock jumps under my hand. My pussy clenches in response. My belly trembles. The smile fades from my lips. Our gazes hold, and the sparks that fly between us could light a cigar. This time, when I tug my hand, he releases it.

"So, you see, I do want you. Very much." He tucks a strand of hair behind my ear.

I shiver. "But you don't want to make love to me?"

He shakes his head. "Oh, I want to, but I can't. You're Ben's little sister. I can't betray him."

I roll my eyes. "I am also my own person. And once we're married—"

"It's not a real marriage."

"It's a real marriage when it suits you, not otherwise. Typical," I burst out.

"Starling, I—" he begins, but I hold up a hand.

"You won't make love to me, even when we're married?"

"Not even then," he says softly.

I tilt my head. "But it's okay if *I* make you come?"

His gaze narrows. I can sense the thoughts whirring behind his eyes, which widen when I sink to my knees.

21

Nathan

What the—? One moment, she's accusing me of not wanting her; the next, she's on her knees. And before I can protest, she reaches for my belt and undoes it. For someone who relied on his wits to save his life, I seem to have lost my edge. Before I can react, she lowers my zipper. My cock springs free. Her eyes go so round, it's clear she must have been expecting me to wear boxers— which I've stopped doing, since I've needed easy access to my dick to jerk off during the day in my attempt to get some relief from the aching hard-on which has refused to go down since I saw her across the counter at her bakery. Not that I'm going to tell her that.

She stares at my length, and I feel myself extend. Feel the blood drain to my groin. Feel my thighs grow rock hard and have to widen my stance to accommodate my arousal. She gulps. My cock twitches and grows even longer.

"Oh, my god, you... You're so big."

Her half-fearful, half-lusty tone serves to make me even harder, if that's possible. I feel the veins in my shaft throb. Pre-cum oozes from the crown, and she flicks out her tongue and touches her lower lip. A-n-d, that's it. All my good intentions go out the window. I've wanted her for so long, and she's here on her knees and staring at my dick like she's both terrified of it but also wants to lock her lips around it. "What are you waiting for?"

"Wh-what?" she manages to choke out.

"You going to look at it, or are you going to do something about it?"

"I... Uh, I'm not sure," she confesses. The vulnerability in her voice, combined with the uncertainty on her features brings out the protectiveness in me.

I scan her wide-eyed gaze, her parted lips, the blush on her cheeks, which extends to her neck, and what I can see on her décolletage and— *No, it can't be.* I try to temper my tone, so I won't scare her away. "Are you a virgin?"

"What?" She jerks her chin up. "What gives you that idea?"

The fact that she asked me a question in response to mine? *Fuck.* "Oh. No... This is not happening."

I take a step back, begin to tuck myself back in, but she leans forward, brushes my fingers aside, and wrapping her fingers around the girth of my cock, closes her lips around the head. Wetness, heat, and the suction of her too small mouth around my shaft send a jolt of awareness screaming up my spine. My legs tremble, and my vision blurs. Once more, my reflexes abandon me. All I can do is groan as she begins to lick around the rim of the crown. I take in her fingers that don't meet around the girth of my dick, the way she licks down the length, only to retrace her steps back to the crown, and when my cock disappears inside her mouth again, my entire body trembles. "Jesus Christ, woman, you're killing me."

She looks up at me, and her eyes gleam. All hesitation is gone from her features. The uncertainty is replaced by a stubbornness I noticed the first time I met her. She brings her other hand up to cup my balls, and a growl rumbles up my chest.

"You don't know what you're doing," I bite out.

In response, she tilts her head and manages to take my dick down her throat. She promptly chokes. Drool slides down her chin. The sucking sensation zips down to my toes and ricochets up to my brain, which communicates to me this is a very good idea.

With my last remnants of sanity, I dig my fingers into her hair and tug her head back, so I have an unrestricted view of her eyes. "This changes nothing," I warn.

In response, she rolls her eyes, but it's so quick, I can't be sure. Then, she massages my balls and *f-u-c-k*, all thoughts drain from my head. All my attention is focused on her hands, her mouth, where we're connected, where she holds my life in her hands. Maybe I looked down the barrel of the gun of the last enemy soldier and managed to shoot him first. Maybe I was fighting for survival then, but it didn't feel as intense, as real, as on the knife's edge of something momentous, as the way it does to look into her eyes and see the resolve, the need, and the desire to please. It's the last that pushes me over the edge.

"If we're doing this, then it's my way, you understand?"

She nods, indicating she hears me, but it's not enough.

"Tap my thigh anytime you want me to stop."

She dips her chin.

"Take a breath," I order.

When she does, I pull her head forward gently, fighting every instinct to yank her into place. My cock slides down her throat again. She swallows, and goddamn, but I almost come right then. I urge her back, until my cock is poised at the rim of her lips. This time, when I feed her my dick, it goes down smoothly. More spit drips from her mouth, teardrops squeeze out from the corners of her eyes. Her mascara runs down her cheeks, and she looks destroyed, and erotic, and every wet dream come true. My balls tighten, my thighs harden, and I'm so fucking close, I know I'm not going to last long.

This is what happens when you haven't had sex, except with your hand, in years. This is how your control threatens to shatter because you haven't been able to fuck another woman because every time you're with one, you see *her* face, and it reminds you, it's not the one woman you want. And now, the object of my dreams is here—with my cock down her throat, and the feel of her gaze on mine, her touch on my balls, the warmth of her mouth around the crown of my shaft, and it's too intense. Too deep. Too much. I ease her back; my dick slides out with a plop. And without fanfare, I come over her face, her mouth, the part of her chest uncovered by her neckline. She looks at me with dazed eyes, and I pull her to her feet and fix my mouth on hers.

22

Skylar

His kiss is soft and slow, and I feel it all the way to my feet. My scalp tingles. My fingers quiver. I hold onto his shoulders and shiver from the intimacy of how he holds me. How he cups my face with his massive hands. How he begins to massage his cum into my cheeks. How he stares into my eyes as he continues to kiss me. It's more erotic than having him come on my face. More personal than anything I've ever experienced. More moving. More everything. He's marking his claim on me, and it feels so right. Tears slide down my cheeks. He wipes them off with his thumb, then slides his hand down to curve his fingers around my throat. His lips touch mine, and we share breath. He swipes his other palm down to the space above the neckline of my blouse. He proceeds to rub in his cum, and I can't stop the shiver that grips me.

"You're mine, baby. You've been mine since the first time I kissed you."

"I'm yours," I whisper against his lips.

"I tried not to want you. Tried to keep away from you. Tried to tell myself it was wrong to need you. To take you in my dreams with such intensity, it felt like I didn't know where my skin ended and yours began. I tried to keep away." He leans his forehead against mine. "God knows, I tried."

"I'm glad you stopped."

He chuckles. "Not sure I agree."

What? I begin to pull away, but he wraps his massive arm about my waist and holds me. "Sorry, that came out wrong. I mean,"—he searches my features—"I'm not sorry I stopped resisting the pull between us. Only, it doesn't negate the fact that I feel like I'm being disloyal to Ben."

"Or maybe, he'll be happy? Maybe, he'll be overjoyed that his sister and his best friend, the two most important people in his life, are together."

"Maybe." For a second, hope lights up his features. His heterochromatic eyes blaze with unbridled joy... Which fades away, leaving a tortured look in its place. "Maybe not." He scans my features with a hunger that sends little tingling sensations zipping under my skin. He looks at me like he can't resist me, and almost hates me for that. And I hate that he can't accept what I knew was inevitable from the first time we kissed. That we're meant to be together. Once again, I try to pull away; once again, he doesn't let me go. "No, don't be angry. I know I'm being an asshole at the moment for not throwing you down and fucking you right now —"

"You can say that again," I huff.

"But you have to understand, after years of dreaming of you, to have you in my arms is something I'm still trying to get my head around." His expression turns almost reverent. He presses his thumb into the hollow of my throat where my pulse drums. "It feels almost too real, too enormous, too everything. I'm holding you, my fiancée, close to me, and it's everything I ever wanted. I wish—" He hesitates, and it's so uncharacteristic of him. As are his words of the last few seconds, the tenderness he's displaying, the way he's looking at me with an almost fearful look in his eyes...

It's all so *not* very Nate that my heart stutters. A shiver of apprehension squeezes my spine. I stare into his gorgeous mismatched eyes and see the fear there. *For him, me? For Ben?*

Yes, that must be it. Ben hasn't been himself, and Nate must have sensed it, like I did. Of course, he's worried about my brother. "Ben's going to be okay. I know he's going to come back to us. He has to come back to us."

Nate's gaze widens. There's a flash of what looks like panic in them, then that shutter drops over his eyes. The one he uses to hide his feelings from the world... From me.

"Don't do that," I snap.

"Do what?" His forehead furrows.

"You know what," I hiss.

"No, I don't."

I pull away, and this time, he releases me. "Don't lock yourself away behind that impenetrable shield you like to throw over your emotions so nothing and no one can get through to you."

He seems taken aback, then a softness penetrates his gaze. "It's because I'm vulnerable to you, because I can never say no to you, because I worry you can read what I'm thinking too easily, that I hide from you."

I shake my head. "I want to believe you—"

"Believe me." He steps forward, taking my hand in his. "Believe me, Starling. You can see through me. Only you have the power to read me. It's why I must guard my true self from you."

"What? Why? I don't understand. If you know there's a connection between us, that you're compelled to share yourself with me, why stop yourself?"

"Because—" He swallows "Because it's for the best."

I laugh. "You're joking, right?"

He drags his fingers through his hair. "I wish I were."

I stare at him in frustration. "This is not helping at all. In fact, this is pissing me off."

"Me too, more than you can imagine, but can you trust me on this?"

I bite the inside of my cheek. *Should I?* What he's saying makes no sense... And yet... He seems so sincere. There's no mistaking the plea in his voice, the coaxing expression in his eyes. There's almost a hint of desperation in how he draws circles with his thumb over the pulse at my wrist. A gentleness in how he cradles my palm between his giant ones. And when he brings the back of my palm to his mouth and kisses the skin there without taking his gaze off mine, my bones melt in surrender.

"Okay," I whisper, already hating myself for giving in. Knowing I'm going to regret this later. But also knowing, I don't have a choice. "Okay." I nod.

"Okay." He exhales, and his lips curve.

I tip up my chin. "On one condition."

23

Skylar

"That's one way of ensuring you have a fucktastic consummation on your wedding night." Zoey snickers at me from the phone screen.

I cough, then grab a glass of water from the counter next to my baking tray and take a sip. "That's one way of putting it."

My condition was that we consummate our relationship on our wedding night. He was surprised when I told him. I was sure he wasn't going to agree, but he finally nodded. Maybe that's not the done thing, asking your husband-to-be for sex, but when Nate revealed that fucking me seemed like the ultimate betrayal of Ben, I knew he intended not to sleep with me. And I haven't come this far to have the man of my dreams decide not to make love to me. Although, given the chemistry between us, perhaps I needn't worry? Either way, I saw the opportunity and took it.

"But you haven't told him you're a virgin?" Zoey pauses midway in applying her lipstick and turns away from her vanity to look at me. It's eight p.m., and I closed the shop—the traffic today was slightly better than yesterday, so that's a positive. I was unable to go up to the apartment and relax, so instead, I decided to work on another new recipe.

"I think he guessed it." I add a pinch of cinnamon and the seeds from a vanilla pod into the cake batter. "He asked me if I was, and I managed not to reply."

"Why not? Isn't it best you're upfront with him?"

Like he needs another excuse for not wanting to sleep with me. I keep silent as I shake in the cocoa powder, then the almond extract, followed by a cup of espresso.

It's part of the recipe I'm trying out for my wedding cake. I wasn't aware that's what I was doing until I was a ways along. But as I mixed the ingredients and imagined the finished product in my head, I realized, this one was going to be special. Sure, people normally get their wedding cake catered, but I want to come up with a mix of ingredients that mean something to me—and perhaps, to him—and evoke memories for everyone else who eats the cake at the wedding. Of course, there's no guarantee I'll have the kind of ceremony I can invite people to, but that hasn't stopped me from playing around with the components, either.

"Skylar, you need to be upfront with him. It's one thing to marry him so you can stop your business from going under. It's another thing to not share things that are going to impact your relationship. Assuming you do want to have a relationship with him?" She peers into the camera.

I shuffle my feet. "You're right; he needs to know."

"So, you'll tell him?"

I nod.

"And while you're at it, you're going to find out more details about your wedding?"

"I guess you must think I'm a pushover for not knowing more about my own wedding?"

She looks at me with censure in her eyes. "I'll never judge you, Skye. And the situation is unusual, to say the least. Do I wish you'd confide in me more? Yes, but that doesn't mean you have anything less than my absolute support in anything you decide to do."

Tears fill my eyes. "You're a good friend." I sniffle.

Zoey looks alarmed. "Girl, please. Don't go all sentimental on me now. Also, your tears are running into whatever it is you're making there."

"Oh, shoot." I snatch a tissue to mop at my cheeks, then roll it into a ball and toss it into the bin. The doorbell to the delivery entrance rings. I lowered the shutters in the front earlier and wasn't expecting any deliveries. "I need to go. There's someone at the door." I reach for the tap to wash my hands, but the doorbell rings again. "Someone who's in a hurry." I frown.

"Okay, I'll call you tomorrow." Zoey blows me a kiss. "And remember, you hold the power in this relationship."

"Do I?" I can't keep the skepticism off my features.

"He needs you as much as you need his money; maybe even more. Surely, there's more at stake for him, considering he needs to get married to confirm his position in the company."

I nod slowly. "We're equal partners in this."

"As it should be in a marriage." She nods.

"There's no reason for me to think I'm the helpless one here."

"You and helpless?" She rolls her eyes.

I manage to laugh. Of course, she hasn't seen how I melt into a puddle when I'm in his presence. Nor am I going to tell her that. Having her think I'm able to resist the powerhouse that is Nathan Davenport gives me the courage to think I really can hold my own in this relationship. There's a banging on the door.

"I'm coming," I yell, then wave at Zoey. "Talk soon, babe!" I disconnect the call, toss my phone aside, then head for the service entrance.

I throw the door open and am faced with Nate's very angry countenance.

He has his fist up like I've caught him mid-action rapping at the door—a fist he now lowers. "You opened the door without checking who it was."

"I thought it was a service delivery."

"Were you expecting a delivery at night?"

"Well…"

"And I'm standing in an alley," he says through gritted teeth.

I look past him into the darkened space. "So? That's why I thought it was a delivery."

"I could have been someone who wanted to harm you."

You've already harmed my heart; beat that! is what I want to say aloud. Instead, I brush at the strand of hair that's fallen over my face and sigh loudly. "Are you going to stand there yelling at me? Or do you want to come in?"

He raises his gaze from my mouth to my face, and a peculiar look overcomes his features.

"What?" I frown.

"You have something—" His voice is both harsh and soft, at the same time. He swallows, then raises his arm and touches my cheek. He shows me his hand, and I spot the dough on his fingers.

"Oh, *Star Trek.*" I scratch my head, and some more dough comes off on my hand. I shake it off.

"You used *Star Trek* as a swear word." He sounds dazed.

"Old habits." I shake the hair strands again, and this time, my fingers come away empty.

"It's gone," he murmurs. His gaze caresses my features. His mismatched eyes are alight with an expression I can't quite place. He pulls out a handkerchief (silk) from his pocket and hands it over.

I hesitate. "I'll dirty it."

His brows draw down. "That's the general idea."

When I hesitate, he takes my hand in his, then gently runs the cloth over my fingers. Goosebumps trail up my arm. And when he drags the cloth between them, a line of fire zips down to my clit. My pussy throbs. My thighs quiver.

I pull my hand from him, turn on my heels and walk inside. I'm aware of him following me, of the door closing with a snick, and it feels so final. I walk back to my place behind the cake batter. I reach for the buttermilk and pour that in. Then place the bowl on a wet cloth and hold it in place. I grab the mixer, dip it into the ingredients, and turn it on. If I were making a batch for the bakery, I'd use the stand mixer, but because this is an experiment and I much prefer having complete control over how I mix the ingredients, I prefer the hand mixer.

The sound of the whirring fills the air. A few minutes later, I stop, raise the whisk and survey the batter for clumps. Satisfied, I set the whisk aside and turn, holding the bowl.

And of course, he's there. He's standing with his legs in a wide stance, his broad chest blocking out the sight of the kitchen behind him. His arms are crossed so his biceps strain at the sleeves of his fitted jacket. His blue eye blazes at me; his brown eye seems to be spitting sparks. His gaze is so intense, I'm forced to lower my own—which means, I catch the bulge between his thighs. "Oh," I gulp.

"Indeed," he says in a dry voice. Then leans over, dips his finger into the batter and brings it to my mouth. "Open."

24

Nathan

She opens her mouth without hesitation, and that's what tips me over the edge. The fact she has her lips in an 'O', and when I touch my batter-soaked finger to her tongue, she closes them around my digit and sucks on it, and I can feel that suction all the way to the crown of my cock. I'm so hard, my pants feel like they're about to split at the crotch. She swipes her tongue up my fingernail, and all the blood drains to my groin. She releases my finger with a plop, then licks her lower lip, and my vision tunnels. All of my senses home in on her. I reach around her, take handfuls of her ample butt, and she gasps.

"Nate," she breathes, then yelps when I haul her up. She locks her ankles around my waist, her pupils, so blown, I can see myself on the black surface.

"I'm heavy," she protests.

"How many times do I have to tell you, you're fucking perfect."

The color of her cheeks deepens, and her lips tremble, and I can tell it's because she's trying to stifle a smile. She's pleased by my words. And if I could, I'd spend every single second of my life making her smile. I'll have to settle for showing her how good it's going to be when I fuck her.

With the bowl of that delicious-smelling mixture—what's in it, anyway? — between us, I take a few steps forward and place her on the countertop. Then,

I take the bowl from her, place it to the side, and step between her thighs. She's forced to push her legs apart, and her dress rides up. She begins to pull at it, in a bid to cover herself. That is, until I glare at her.

She stops shuffling and locks her fingers together. "What are you doing?" she asks in a breathless tone.

"Looking at what's mine." I take her left hand in mine, rub my finger across the ring—my ring—that she's wearing. I bring her hand to my mouth, kiss the ring, then in a quick move, twist her hand behind her back.

"Oh." Her cheeks grow even pinker, the blush extending down her neck to the tops of her breasts.

"If I were a better man, I'd apologize in advance."

"For what?" She frowns.

"For this." I hook a finger in the 'V' of her neckline and tug with enough force the cloth tears down the center.

"Oh, *Breaking Bad*!" she yells.

I laugh. I can't help it. "Only you would use a show about a meth cooking professor as an expletive."

"It does the job, doesn't it? Also, I happen to love this dress."

"I love what's inside it more." I stare at her breasts spilling out of her bra, and I swear, I almost come in my pants. I reach for the nipple that is outlined against a bra-cup, and when she tries to stop me, I twist her other arm behind her and shackle both wrists together. The result: she's forced to thrust out her chest. All the more for me to play with. I pull down her bra-cups. As I stare at first, one berry-colored nipple, then the other, they tighten into little buds of tasty morsels. I scoop up some of the batter from the bowl, dab it on both nipples, then lean down and bite on one.

"Oh, *Sopranos*," she groans.

"I must not be doing my job very well, if you're still talking." I lave on the nipple, then kiss my way to her other breast and suck the other nipple, while weighing the first with my free hand. And when I pinch her nipple, her entire body jolts. She throws her head back and cries out, but I don't let up. I twist her nipple, while nibbling on the other one, then push my palm into the center of her chest.

I straighten, stare into her eyes and apply gentle pressure. I release her arms, ease her back, then grab the pair of scissors nearby. I bring it down to her hem and cut up the length of her skirt. The fabric falls to each side of her thighs with a soft swish. I look down at the dark curls shadowed through the crotch of her panties. Her very wet panties. Seems my touching her has turned her on. Good.

I allow myself a small smile. Then, because I can't stop myself, I slide the scissors under the waistband of her panties and cut through it on either side of her crotch. When I'm done, I place the scissors aside, then flick back the cloth. Her pussy lips gleam back at me. "Fuck," I growl, then lower myself to my knees. I throw a leg of hers over each of my shoulders, then pull open her pussy lips with my fingers.

"Nate," she exclaims, then cries out when I lick her from back hole to clit. The taste of her is like honey and cardamom and everything that warms my soul. I circle her clit with my tongue, and she squeezes her thighs around my face. I can barely breathe, but that's okay. If I were to die right now, I'd be fine, as long as my breath was stolen by the pressure of her flesh against mine. I stab my tongue inside her slit, and a whine slips from her lips. And when I flick my tongue in and out of her, in a parody of how I want to fuck her with my cock, she digs her fingers into my hair and tugs with such force, I can feel it all the way to my toes.

My cock weeps, my balls groan, and I can't stop the rumble of satisfaction that vibrates up my chest as I continue to fuck her with my tongue as she pushes her hips forward and rides my face, as I slide a finger between the cleavage of her butt cheeks to touch her forbidden hole. She freezes. When I play with her rosette, a trembling grips her. Incoherent sounds come from her mouth, and when I stuff my tongue inside her wet channel, and grind my palm against her clit, while inching my finger inside her forbidden hole, she climaxes. Her entire body jolts. A keening cry emerges from her lips, her thighs tremble about my ears and moisture hits the inside of my mouth. I swallow greedily. *What the—did she just—?*

25

Skylar

"Did you squirt me?"

I hear his voice as if from far away, try to open my mouth to answer, but all that comes out is a purr. Heat flushes my cheeks. I try to understand the question but lose the battle against the contentment that pervades every part of my body. I float down from the climax that thundered against me with the force of a deluge. Aftershocks undulate my body like the wake of a ferry. I'm aware of wetness between my legs. Sweat beads my forehead, my neck, and pools under my armpits. I sense him straighten, then heat envelops my front. When I open my eyes, I'm not surprised to find his face is above mine.

"You squirted me." It's not a question this time. "Who'd have thought, hmm?"

I blush to the roots of my hair. When I begin to look away, he shakes his head. "Don't hide. That was a compliment."

"It… It was?" I clear my throat.

He nods. "Nothing like a squirt to confirm you enjoyed everything I did to you." One side of his mouth curls. His hair sticks to his forehead, his blue eye is so dark it's almost brown, and his brown one has lightened until it could be almost blue. So that's what it takes for his heterochromatic eyes to match—

desire. That's the key to get to this man. Offer yourself up to him. Let him use your body as he wishes. An instrument of his pleasure.

"Use me," I murmur.

"What?"

I slide my fingers through his hair and tug, and when his face almost touches mine, I lick the wetness off his mouth. "My body. Use it to satisfy your needs."

His gaze widens. "You don't know what you're saying."

"I know there's a part of you that you want to keep hidden. A part you dare not bring to the fore. A part you don't want to let loose because—"

He tilts his head, a look of polite curiosity in his eyes. And damn him, but I hate that. I want to shock that distance from his gaze forever.

"—because I know you're into BDSM." *Umm, actually I don't, but why not?* He seems like a man who'd love that entire kinky side of sex. And I bet I'd enjoy it, too, as long as he's the one administering that kinkiness.

"BDSM?" he says slowly.

"Uh, yeah." I wriggle around, trying to find a more comfortable position. Considering I'm lying back in a pile of flour and droplets of various essences and food stuff I used in the cake batter, that's no mean feat. "You know, bondage and discipline and sadomasochism."

"You forgot dominance and submission." In what seems to be an absent-minded gesture, he cups my breast. Pinpricks of heat radiate out from his touch.

"S-submission?" I wish my voice didn't shake. I wish my entire body didn't feel so heavy. I wish I didn't feel this lethargic.

"Do you want to submit to me, baby? Do you want me to show you how it can be when you give yourself up to me? Do you want to experience how it feels to have me direct you, to understand how it feels to please me. To allow me to find out what you like, what turns you on, to wring pleasure from your body such that you've never experienced before?"

"If it's more like the orgasms you give me, then bring it on."

He barks out a laugh. "You surprise me, baby."

"And you… make me want more. You make me want to not be scared anymore. You make me want to live expansively. To reach for everything I thought was once out of reach."

Once more, his gaze is on my mouth. It's almost as if he's reading my lips. As if he likes to see my lips form the words as I speak. Then, he raises his gaze to mine, and once again, his mismatched eyes no longer resemble each other.

Combined with his mussed-up hair, it gives him a crazed look, which I much prefer over that cold, stern mask he normally wears.

Then, he bends and rubs his nose up my cheek, and I whimper.

"The sounds you make drive me crazy," he whispers against my mouth. Something stabs me between my legs, and I become aware of how aroused he is. I begin to slide my hand between us, but he circles his fingers around my wrist. "Touch me now, and we're never moving from here."

"I don't mind that, though I confess, I've been more comfortable."

In response, he straightens, then pulls me to sitting position. He tucks my hair behind my ear and his touch is so tender, a lump of emotion forms in my throat. He tucks my boobs inside my bra, then tugs the edges of my dress over my chest.

"You didn't come," I remind him.

"It's more important you did."

I blink rapidly. "I'm not used to you being this nice."

He half smiles. "Don't get used to it."

"A-n-d, you had to spoil everything by saying that, didn't you?"

He raises his shoulder. "Wouldn't be me if I didn't show my true colors, hmm?"

"Which I'm beginning to think is not the growly, grumpy, I-hate-the-world mask you show everyone."

His features sober. "I'm not a nice man."

"But you are a good man."

"Definitely not. I've killed men."

"To defend our country, so people like me are safe."

"I've also… lied," he says this in a tone that seems exploratory. If he thinks that's going to shock me, he's sooo mistaken.

"I'm sure you had good reason."

"I did… I do."

I blink. "Are you lying to me? Is that what you're trying to say?"

He nods. "Remember how I said we were getting married in a week?"

I nod slowly.

"I lied. We're getting married tomorrow."

26

Nathan

"I suppose I should be grateful you invited me to the wedding," Arthur growls. I lead him to a seat in the front row. It's a good thing the relationship between the wives and girlfriends is strong enough that my fiancée's wish to be married on a beach found its way back to me, the same way I found out about her trip to that hotel room.

She almost went to bed with another man, and all because I felt guilty about fucking her. A mistake I'm not going to commit again. Not after how I almost took her in the bakery yesterday. I managed to stop myself, but only because her queries about my BDSM proclivities took me by surprise. She's well-read enough to have recognized what I want. Whether she can withstand the rigors of the lifestyle is something I'm looking forward to finding out.

At some point, when I was on my knees with my face pushed into her sweet pussy, when I licked at her slit and found myself craving to be inside of her hot, throbbing, channel, when I wanted to ravage her every hole, I realized I was fighting a losing battle.

From the moment I saw her all grown up on her eighteenth birthday, I fell for her. Every step in my life since has brought me closer to her. I might have tried to run away from her, but really, I was always finding my way back to her.

And Ben asked me to look after her, after all. And this is me, keeping my promise to him. I'm ensuring she'll land on her feet and be looked after for the rest of her life. He'd want that.

As for my marrying her and bedding her… I don't think it's something he'll accept that easily, but hopefully, he'll come around. Hopefully, he'll find it in him to forgive me for taking advantage of his sister. I'm using her situation against her. Of course, she's helping me, too… We're helping each other. I cross my fingers. I can only pray that Ben will see it that way. *I'm sorry, Ben, you couldn't be here, but I hope when we finally meet again, you'll find it in your heart to understand why I did what I did.*

"You okay, grandson?"

I tug at the collar of my shirt. "Of course I am." I'm only getting married. It's a walk in the park, compared to tracking down enemies of the country via drones, and deciding to take the hit, only to find a group of children walking into the frame and having to make a split-second decision whether to go ahead with the mission or not.

It doesn't explain why I've been sweating like a whore in church all morning, considering we're not even in a church. A gust of wind raises the hair from my forehead, and I turn my face toward it. I managed to secure the only natural beach in this area, which happens to be a few miles from London. It's not normally available to be rented, but thanks to my contacts, I managed. As I keep discovering, it pays to be CEO of the Davenport Group sometimes. There was never a question of whether to make it happen, considering my fiancée secretly wanted a beach wedding.

"You're nervous," Arthur says with something like satisfaction.

You would be, too, if you knew what I have in store for you and your 'legitimate' grandsons.

When I don't reply, Arthur tips up his chin in my direction. "It's a good sign."

I grunt.

"I'd have been worried if you weren't."

What-fucking-ever. I resist the urge to scratch my chin, knowing that's my tell. I am *not* nervous. *I am not.*

Arthur tugs at my sleeve, and when I look down, he beams at me. "I'm glad you decided to invite your family to the ceremony. I'm guessing it's what your fiancée wanted, and a happy wife is a happy life. You couldn't have found a better way to start your marriage."

"That's not the reason I opted for this ceremony," I say through gritted teeth.

"Of course it was." He waves a hand in the air. The sound of bottles being clanked as the caterers set the buckets of Champagne down on the long table at the side of the massive tent I asked to be erected reaches us.

Next to him, Tiny, who's been sprawled on the ground, sits up and cocks his head. "Now, you need to behave, boy. The Champagne is not good for you." Arthur wiggles a finger under Tiny's nose.

The Great Dane makes a rumbling sound at the back of his throat.

"This mutt not only understands me, but he also answers back." Arthur pats his head. "Remember our discussion. The only reason I brought you along is because you sulked when I said I wouldn't. And you promised you'd stay away from the bubbles." Tiny looks up at Arthur and blinks. There's a very innocent look in the Great Dane's eyes. One I do not trust.

"What are the odds he's going to be downing the Champagne before the night is out?" Sinclair says from next to me.

It's true. Tiny has a hankering for Champagne. Not wine. Not even sparkling wine. It has to be Champagne. And the more expensive, the better. If I hadn't seen it with my own eyes, I wouldn't have believed it. I watch the Great Dane yawn, then slide his big head between his paws. His ears flop but his eyes... They're trained on the catering staff pouring the bubbles into the vintage, sixties-style Champagne glasses I instructed the wedding planner to arrange for—because I found out my wife-to-be loves the look of them.

"Ready to tie the noose... Sorry, I mean knot, ol' chap?" Knox, who walked up behind Sinclair, slaps me on the back.

"Fuck off, ol' chap," I say in a casual tone.

Knox laughs. "Considering you decided not to have any groomsmen at your wedding, I don't know if I should be insulted or grateful."

I turn to find he's dressed in jeans and a T-shirt, his only concession is a jacket, though this one has seen better days. "I'm not insulted you decided not to wear a black tie."

"I fucking hate black suits and ties, and anything that needs me to loop a piece of cloth around my neck," he says with vehemence.

"Clothes don't make the man," I shrug.

He seems taken aback, then nods slowly. "Maybe I'll find a reason to not abhor you, yet."

"Not holding my breath on that."

He cracks a half-smile at that. And I thought I held the patent on being the scary, unapproachable mofo. But Knox, with his scarred face, and his I-don't-give-a-fuck appearance, has me beat.

"Now, that wasn't so difficult, was it?" Arthur looks between us.

"The fuck you mean?" I scowl.

"The two of you are on your way to becoming friends." He nods.

"I wouldn't say that." Knox coughs.

"Nonsense, I can see the beginnings of a beautiful relationship between the two of you."

Sinclair laughs. "I'd like to be a fly on the wall when that happens."

Knox gives me a can-you-believe-this-bullshit look.

For once, I agree with him.

"I think I'd better go in search of the hard liquor, the kind I can actually get drunk on." He turns and stalks off in the opposite direction of the Champagne, where I've arranged for a bar to be set up with the kind of alcohol my half-brothers seem to favor. And only because I'm not petty like that. They're my guests. The least I can do is cater to their tastes. I wish I could get drunk, too... But sadly, I'll have to contend with water to see me through.

"How're you holding up?" Sinclair surveys my features.

"I'm good," I say with a confidence I don't feel. I wish I could fast-forward to the end of the ceremony. This thing is supposed to be fake, but it feels too bloody real. Like I've reached a turning point in my life and now, there's no looking back.

"It's okay to be nervous," he begins, but I cut him off.

"Why does everyone keep telling me that? I'm not bloody nervous. Also, what happened to the damn breeze?" I pull out my handkerchief and mop my brow.

He exchanges a look with Arthur, something seems to pass between them, then Sinclair nods. "Right, I'll see you on the other side."

He walks over to join Summer, who's chatting with a group of women. As he joins the group, he says something witty, and they all laugh. They must be Starling's friends. I told the wedding planner to ensure she invited all of them. It's what she wanted, after all, and I want to make sure I give her the wedding of her dreams.

The muted hum of voices fills the air. My half-brothers seem to be everywhere. Connor, who's taken on the role of bartender, pours Knox a drink. Ryot is standing at a distance, his hand shoved in his pocket, a glower on his face. Tyler is talking to a redhead, and Edward has his arm around his new wife Mira. The two of them are engaged in conversation with Dr. Weston Kincaid, and a woman who I assume is his wife.

The roar of a bike cuts through the muted hum of voices.

"As I was saying, there's nothing like family to have in your corner when things get tough, and—" Arthur looks past me in the direction of the noise, and his gaze widens. "Who's that?" Arthur's voice is filled with awe and something like... Admiration? It's enough to cause me to turn to where a figure parks a bike and disembarks. She takes off her helmet and runs her fingers through her shoulder-length hair. The sunlight glints off the silver strands threaded through the brown and blue-colored ones. She's wearing a dress which comes to mid-thigh, combined with tights and motorcycle boots that come to over her knee. She clips her helmet on the side of the Harley, then proceeds to walk toward us.

"Granny Imelda, you made it!" The redheaded woman walks past us and embraces the older, Harley-riding woman.

"As I was saying—" Arthur seems to lose his train of thought before swallowing in an audible gulp. "Uh, do you think you can introduce me to her?"

27

Skylar

"It's time." Imelda holds out her arm. I asked her to walk me down the aisle at the last minute. Mostly because she's such a confident woman, I hoped some of it would rub off on me.

I opted against having bridesmaids — not least of all, because my darling fiancé announced yesterday that the wedding was today. He'd already taken care of the paperwork, including having the registrar arrive at the venue to officiate at the wedding, so we'd simply have to sign the forms on the spot. The man thinks of everything, although I'll admit, arriving at the venue and realizing it was at a beach surprised me. Zoey saw my shocked expression and confessed to me that she might have mentioned my preference to Summer, who mi-i-ight have mentioned it to Sinclair with the explicit instruction to pass on that information to my fiancé. What he did with it was up to him...

She confessed she didn't think he'd actually track down the only natural beach within miles of London and rent it for the day. The cost of it — Oh, my, *Stranger Things* — I don't want to hazard a guess. Rachel, the wedding planner, mentioned to me that he'd been very specific about how he wanted the big gazebo where we're standing to be put up.

It'll shield us against the wind, and there's a plush carpet underfoot and heaters every few feet. So, despite the fact it's a blustery January afternoon outside, it'll be warm there. He also had a separate tent put up, which I'm using as a dressing room.

Grace peeked in earlier, as did Summer and Zoey. Apparently, he invited my friends, after I mentioned that I'd love to have them at my wedding. This, despite the fact his preference was to turn up at the courthouse, sign the papers, then go back home and consummate the marriage. My nipples tighten. C-o-n-s-u-m-m-a-t-e. Meaning, soon I'll be his wife and he'll expect to penetrate my vagina with his huge cock. And it is huge. It barely fit down my throat, and he'll stuff it inside my aching channel, which is already a mass of wetness in anticipation.

"You, ah… You're all flushed." Imelda glances around the space. "Funny, I hadn't thought the heaters in here were that intense."

"They're not."

She turns to stare at me.

"I mean… I'm, ah… Having a hot flash, is all."

"Hot flash?" Her eyebrows knit, then her forehead smooths out. "Oh, *that* kind of hot flash." Her eyes twinkle.

I feel my flush deepen.

"Looking forward to being in the arms of your beloved. Aren't you cute?" She sighs.

"It's not—" I begin, but she waves away my explanation.

"It's quite all right, my dear. I remember how it was to see the face of my husband for the first time in front of the priest. He lifted my veil, and I looked into his blue eyes and thought he was the most handsome man on the planet."

"That's when you saw him for the first time?"

"It was an arranged marriage. My family expected me to comply, of course. Not that I'd have dreamed of going against them. I thought I was the luckiest woman in the entire world, especially since I'd known friends who'd had a rude surprise when they found out their husbands were nowhere near as good-looking as they'd hoped they'd be. Mine was handsome. Unfortunately, he also liked to drink and beat me many nights."

"Oh, Imelda," I gasp.

She shrugs. "Once the kids were born, he lost interest in me, thank fuck. He had mistresses on the side. But I was just happy he left me alone. As he got older, he seemed to want to spend more time with me and the children. And once the kids were older and left home, we finally seemed to find a balance. Our last years together were our happiest. But then he died, and I found I still had a lot of the world to discover."

"Thank you for sharing." I lock my arm with hers. "I hope I'll have half as much courage as you when it comes to making decisions related to my married life." *Especially when it's time to walk away.* Once I'm sure Hugo is taken care of and that the bakery is self-sufficient.

I used some of the money he deposited in my bank account to pay off my debts and to cover the pending bills at Hugo's care home. A portion of the rest went toward hiring the woman who interned with me earlier this year. I wasn't able to keep her on because I had no money to pay her, but now I do. And she was looking for a job. She was able to fill the position right away and took on duties at the shop today, which is why I was able to leave to come here. This whole wedding thing happened so quickly, but it's a blessing. Instead of having the rest of the week hanging over me, this is like pulling off a Band-Aid. Get the deed done, so we could both move on with our lives.

"I'm sure your experience will be very different." Imelda pats my hand. "After all, you know who you're marrying."

Do I? I know the parts he's shown to me. And I know of him from what Ben told me. I know he's much more tender than he likes to let on. And that he has tattoos, which I haven't yet seen. And that he has a raging sex-drive, which I'm not complaining about. Also, there's a darkness to him, which should put me off but doesn't. Maybe there's a darkness inside of me which responds to the depravity within him.

In the last few days, I've come to know Nate better, but that doesn't mean I know him well at all. If anything, it's made me realize how much of himself he's kept away from me. How much I want to find out everything about him. Especially his proclivity to BDSM. My toes curl. That slow pulse between my legs speeds up.

Then we walk out of the tent, and Rachel ushers us toward the main gazebo. We enter, and a hush falls over the small group.

Zoey's face bursts into a big smile. She nudges Grace, who's staring at her phone. She looks up, then over her shoulder, and her features soften. "You got this," she mouths to me.

I smile, feeling tears form behind my eyes. I sniff, and Imelda squeezes my arm. We pass by the row with Summer and Sinclair, who has his arm about her. Next to them, is a couple I don't recognize. I don't know the couple seated in front of them, either. They must be Nathan's friends.

On the opposite side of the aisle are his half-brothers. Knox nods in my direction, before looking forward. One of his brothers, who wears specs, flashes me a smile. His other two brothers, however, wear bored expressions. One of them yawns as I pass. The other glowers at something in the distance.

Apparently, he's angry about the world, in general. Jeez, these men take tall, dark and grumpy to another level. It's clear they'd rather be anywhere else but here.

A slight breeze blows in from the open flap that frames the beach. Nate's other half-brother, Edward—who used to be a priest, and who agreed to officiate the wedding, *and* who I met today when he came to introduce himself in the other tent—beams at me. Facing him, with his back toward me, is my future husband. I take a step forward and he stiffens. Then, as if sensing my perusal, he turns to look at me.

28

Nathan

"You may kiss the bride."

My muscles relax, and I frame her face with my palms. She looks up at me with a dazed expression that mirrors how I feel inside.

Throughout the ceremony, a sense of being disassociated from my body, of looking down at the proceedings from afar, engulfed me. Luckily, it's a small crowd, the noise from them minimal, yet enough that when they fell silent, I knew she'd entered the tent. It might also have to do with the ripple of awareness that swept up my spine.

I turned to face her and had my first sight of my wife-to-be. She was clad in a form-fitting, cream-colored gown that hinted at her cleavage, nipped in at her waist, and outlined her lush thighs, before sweeping down to her feet. As she approached me, I took in her thick blonde hair flowing around her shoulders, her glowing skin, her pink cheeks, and when she came to a halt in front of me, I couldn't look away from her sparkling eyes.

She is stunning.

My heart skips a beat, and I know. I've been fooling myself. I'm in love with her. Possibly have been since I kissed her the day she turned eighteen. I knew she was going to be my wife from the second I laid eyes on her. *My wife.*

This elaborate setup of offering to rescue her bakery in return for her marrying me, is because I'm a coward. I couldn't risk her turning me down, not after how I walked away from her the first time. So instead, I used her circumstances to ensure she couldn't say no to marrying me.

"My wife," I whisper against her lips. Her green eyes lighten. Her chest rises and falls. There's so much emotion in them, so much feeling… So much I haven't shared with her. What complicated situations we weave in the name of love. It's because I love her that I did all of this. It's because I'm never letting go of her that I found a way to bind her to me forever.

I may have fooled myself by saying this arrangement was temporary. That I was marrying her to please my grandfather and consolidate my position in the company. That, once I was confirmed as the CEO, I'd destroy Arthur's legacy and the future of my half-brothers and walk away from her. The former, I'm close to delivering on. The latter? It's just an elaborate lie I told myself.

She's my past. My present. My future. She's everything. She's mine.

"Mine."

I close my mouth over hers and kiss her. And she melts into me. She parts her lips and lets me take from her. She opens herself up and lets me taste her sweetness, her willingness, her complete acceptance. Her body bends to mine. I wrap my arm about her waist; with the other, I hold her chin in place as I plunder her mouth. And she lets me.

She moans in her throat, and that little sound turns my need into a raging inferno. My thighs are hard, my cock so turgid, it's a wonder I haven't stabbed through the crotch of my pants. It's the agony in my loins which forces me to raise my head. I stare into her flushed features, her closed eyelids, the way her eyelashes fan against her cheekbones. "Open your eyes and look at me, wife," I growl.

She flutters open her eyelids, and her dilated pupils tell me she's as aroused as I am. I want to scoop her up in my arms, tell everyone here to fuck off, take her home and make love to her. I want to show her I'm the man for her. I want to imprint myself so deeply into her body, her mind, her soul, to absorb her emotions and turn them into my own, to wring enough orgasms from her that she'll never forget how it feels to have my cock inside her, my fingers marking her skin, my teeth, my mouth biting down on that curve of where her throat meets her shoulder, so everyone knows she belongs to me.

I want to… Bend her over and fuck her, take all of her virgin holes. I want to… Make sweet love to her and paint my name across her skin with my cum. I want to fuck her so thoroughly, she'll never want to be with another man.

That's right, be selfish again. Think only of yourself. Your needs, your wants, how you cannot hold yourself back anymore. How you're going to break her heart. How she'll never forgive you when she finds out the truth.

I release her and step back. When she sways, I right her with a hold on her shoulder. And when I know she can stand on her own, I grab her hand and turn to face my family and our friends. I ignore the bewilderment on her face and nod at my grandfather, who's the first to reach us.

"Congratulations." He takes her hands in his and kisses her knuckles. Anger flushes my chest. Possessiveness is a demon that holds me in thrall. My guts twist. I can't stop myself from putting my arm about her waist and drawing her close.

"Well done." He turns to me. "This might be the first sensible thing you've done in your life."

No kidding.

"What an amazing ceremony!" The redheaded woman throws her arms about my wife—*my wife*—and kisses her on both cheeks. My wife hugs her back. "Oh, my god, you look so beautiful." The redhead sniffs.

"Couldn't have done it without you, Zoey." My wife smiles, then turns to me. "This is my husband, Nathan Davenport."

"Zoey Malfoy"—she holds out her hand—"no connection to Draco."

I look from her to my wife. "Isn't that the surname of Harry Potter's arch enemy?"

My wife gasps. Zoey stares at me with big eyes, then she clutches my wife's arm. "D-does he know who Draco is?"

"Evidently." My wife narrows her gaze on me. "You know who Draco Malfoy is?"

"Considering I'm now married to a Potterhead, the least I could do was brush up on the Potterverse." I smirk.

"Ohmigod, ohmigod!" Zoey slaps her palms over her mouth. "He knows about the Potterverse?"

"I take it, you're also a fellow Swiftie?" I drawl.

"Jesus!" Zoey sways, and my wife grips her arm to right her. "Are you for real?" She looks at me as if seeing me for the first time. "Can I touch you?"

"Excuse me?" I frown.

"To make sure you're real? You know about the Potterverse and about us Swifties. I want to make sure you exist, and I did not dream you up."

I chuckle. "Sure." I hold out my arm. "You can touch me."

"No, you can't." My wife closes the distance and grabs my arm, before waving her free hand in her friend's direction. "Go get your own. This one's mine."

Mine.

A hot sensation stabs at my chest. A warmth invades my veins. I do belong to her. I always have. Now, I only hope she'll feel the same when it comes to forgiving my mistakes.

Zoey looks between us, and a genuine smile splits her face. "I'm so happy for you Skye."

She swallows. "Me too," she says almost shyly.

More of her friends head our way. They start talking altogether. The sound builds on itself, and a warning buzz infiltrates my ears. My muscles stiffen, my head spins, and she must feel my discomfort because she looks up at me with a curious expression. "Everything okay, husband?"

29

Skylar

"Here you go." My husband pours Champagne into a flute and places it in front of me.

After the wedding ceremony, he asked me if I wanted to stay for the reception organized by the wedding planner. Of course I wanted to, and not only because the setting in the third tent looked so pretty. Once more, he seemed to have read my mind, with the long table set up in the center of the tent so our friends could sit around the table and relax while a team of staff served us. We sat at one end of the table, Sinclair and Summer at the opposite end. Zoey sat next to me, and to her credit, she hadn't even looked in Nate's direction. There had been a toast from Sinclair, who seemed to have taken on the unofficial duties of a best man. Then Zoey raised her glass and said how happy she was about our union. She also managed to weave in a warning aimed at my husband that he'd better treat me right, to which he graciously nodded his head. He didn't say a word throughout the dinner. He also didn't eat. As the Champagne was downed and the noise level at the table increased, his jaw had grown increasingly tense. His color began to fade, and his hold on his glass of water grew tighter. His gaze was focused on some faraway place where I couldn't reach him, and he didn't answer any of the good-natured ribbing coming his way.

I sensed Dr. Weston—who my husband had introduced me to earlier—shoot him a couple of strange glances, but my husband didn't notice. He seemed to grow more and more distant as the minutes wore on. When I finally told him I was ready to leave, he didn't respond. Not until I touched his shoulder, when he visibly flinched. And when he raised his gaze to mine, I spied shadows in them. He rubbed his temple, and I was sure he was suffering from a headache. I gestured to him that I wanted to leave, and he didn't waste a second. He jumped up, and without bidding anyone goodbye, he hustled me out of there.

To be frank, by then, everyone was in high spirits. Sinclair and Summer were kissing, Dr. Weston had pulled his wife onto his lap. G-Pa was trying to engage Imelda in conversation—though she was having none of it. And Edward was seated near them, looking deeply into his wife Mira's eyes. As for my friends? Grace was on her phone, while Zoey had taken on the role of keeping Tiny away from the Champagne. Nate's other half-brothers were busy glowering at each other. Connor is the only one who, seeing us leave, raised his glass.

All in all, none of them would miss us. My husband hustled me to the waiting car and instructed the driver to take us to his place on Primrose Hill.

He was engrossed in swiping his phone screen, and I was left with a sense of letdown. I stared at my wedding band—a simple platinum affair, which I thoroughly approve of—and tried to talk to him, but he didn't reply.

I shot a sideways glance at the slimmer version of the band he sported on his left hand. Apparently, he's traditional enough to wear one, and OMG, I couldn't stop that warmth of possessiveness from squeezing my chest when I looked at it. I'd tried to broach the issue of our wedding bands with him, but then he accelerated the timing of the ceremony, and everything had happened so fast. Rachel told me not to worry about it, that Nate would be taking care of it, and that was that. I raised my gaze to my husband's face, but his brow was furrowed as he stared at his phone.

He seemed to have retreated to some part of himself with a do-not-disturb sign hung on it. Or maybe, he just needed a little time to decompress? It's not every day one gets married, after all. And that ceremony... It felt real. Genuine. Honest. When he kissed me, it felt like a pact. The start of something new. I wanted to ask him if he felt the same, but it didn't seem like the right time to broach the issue. And to be honest, I'd have been devastated if he'd said no.

I turned to share my feelings with my husband, but the frown on his face was so uninviting, I held off.

By the time we reached his place, he was more relaxed. He told the driver to take the rest of the day off, then unlocked the door to his beautiful Victorian home and guided me inside. He escorted me to a small table laid for two, with a bucket of Champagne on it and two chairs facing each other on the deck outside the living room.

Now, he pours Champagne for me and sparkling water for himself. Huh? Come to think of it, I've never seen him drinking alcohol.

"You're a teetotaler?" I frown.

"I was never a big drinker. And once I joined the Marines, I found I was more focused, and my faculties were sharper when I abstained from alcohol. I chose to steer clear of the booze in my downtime after I returned to civilian life. It… it felt right to stay that way." He hesitates. "Probably has to do with seeing my mother hitting the bottle in the latter half of her life. It was her crutch for forgetting how she'd been turned away by my father's family."

"I'm sorry," I whisper.

He shakes his head. "It's in the past."

There's so much I don't know about him. So much I want to know about him.

"Thank you for sharing…" I swallow.

He looks at me strangely. "You're my wife. Of course, I'd want to share that with you."

My wife. A thrill dances up my spine. There's a fizzing sensation in my chest that bubbles out to my extremities. *Why do I feel like I'm in over my head? Why do I already feel so much for my husband?* I glance away and pretend to be absorbed in the view of Primrose Hill, which stretches out before us. There are a few people jogging up the slope, but otherwise, it's quiet.

Beyond that, the city stretches out, and in the distance, I can make out the dome of St. Paul's Cathedral, the soaring glass and steel facade of The Shard, the bullet-like shape of The Gherkin, and the huge wheel of the London Eye.

He turns to me and raises his glass. "To us."

I clink my glass with his and meet his mismatched gaze. "To never hiding anything from each other."

His features shutter at once, and I curse myself. My sub-conscious must have been working overtime for me to say those words. And I'm one to talk, considering I haven't told him about Hugo yet.

His gaze narrows. "Something you want to tell me, wife?"

I swallow. It's now or never. And I haven't done anything wrong, after all.

I place my flute of Champagne on the table between us, then fold my fingers together. "There was another reason I accepted your proposal of marriage in return for the money you offered."

"You wanted to rescue your business." He nods.

"Not just that." I hunch my shoulders.

The skin around his eyes tightens; otherwise, there's no other reaction on his features. He raises his glass of water to his mouth and takes a sip.

The silence stretches, and I curse myself. *Why did I have to bring this up now? And on our wedding day? Maybe I don't like having this secret between us? Maybe I want to start our life together on a clean slate?*

"After completing my baking course from the Master Baker Program—"

"Ben was so proud when you won the scholarship to study there. He did mention you had to take out a loan to finance your living costs though."

"Wow, he really kept you abreast of the details." I scowl.

"Only because he was upset he wasn't able to help you more with the costs." He holds up his palm. "I was his best friend, and I knew you; it was natural for him to share."

I lock my fingers together. "I'm still paying off the loan, though the money you paid into my account should help with that, too." I hunch my shoulders. "Anyway, I moved to London, and apprenticed at a well-known pastry-shop, which is where I met Hugo. He was eighteen and had transitioned out of the care system. He was a brilliant baker but hadn't been able to study it professionally, so he was stuck doing odd jobs. He was the little brother I never had. And with Ben being away so much, I was alone. I pretty much adopted him.

"When I told him about my plans for *The Fearless Kitten*, he was excited. He decided to join me." I swallow. "A week after we opened, we were both working long hours. He'd been at the bakery until 2 a.m. the previous day and I told him he needn't come in early the next day to help me open the shop, but he insisted. He was exhausted and in such a hurry, he didn't strap on his helmet. As he reached the bakery, I ran onto the road in front of him. I still don't know what possessed me to do that. He swerved to avoid me and ended up losing control of the bike. His helmet fell off and he hit his head on the sidewalk. I was hurt in the accident, but my injuries weren't serious. Hugo, on the other hand…" I rub at my temple. "It changed his life forever. He changed the trajectory of his bike so he wouldn't hit me and ended up changing the trajectory of his life instead."

I hunch my shoulders.

"That smiling, laughing boy who'd been destined for big things, turned into someone who has the disposition of a five-year-old. He needs around-the-clock care. Thanks to the state, I was able to find a place that could accommodate him, but I had to cover some of the costs. Between spending time with him and trying to keep the bakery afloat, the workload became too much for me. I wanted to shut down the pastry shop, but in his moments of coherence, Hugo would tell me to hang in there. He'd tell me I had to give it a shot, for both of us."

"So, you kept it going."

I nod. "Only, it began to bleed money, almost from day one. This venture has been the most intense learning experience of my life." I glance down at my hands. "It's also been the most frightening. Every day, I've hoped the business would turn around. Every day, I've been disappointed. You know the scariest part?"

He tilts his head.

"If I could do it all over again, I wouldn't change a thing. Except, I'd stop Hugo from riding his motorcycle over to the bakery that day. I can't remember why I was standing on the road that day, but it's my fault he crashed trying to avoid me."

Nate's jaw tics. A muscle works below his cheekbone, but he doesn't say anything.

"You know what's worse?" I shift my weight from foot to foot. "Looking at Hugo now, taking in the dimmed light in his eyes. The way he often doesn't know where he is and who I am. How he sometimes thinks I'm his mother, and sometimes his sister. How he's still able to cook up the best burger I've ever tasted when you put him in a kitchen, which can only be when he's supervised. His muscle memory still works. Can you believe that? It's only his recollections of all the other incidents in his life which are deteriorating. The doctors think his condition could worsen, and if that happens, it won't be long before he's catatonic."

I look away then back at him. "I sometimes think, he'd have been better off if he'd died." I squeeze my eyes shut. *There, I've said it aloud.* "I feel responsible for Hugo but also, sometimes, I resent the fact I decided to take it on. If I could have relinquished his care to the state completely, I'd have been better off... Or so I think. And then in the next breath, I know I would never do that. And then, I resent myself for being so selfish."

There's a touch on my shoulder. I snap my eyes open to find he's squeezing it.

"It wasn't your fault he was in an accident."

"But it was. If it weren't for me, he wouldn't have veered off course and lost control of his bike and collided with the sidewalk. Besides, he's like my brother. If something happened to Ben..." I draw in a breath. "If it had been Ben who was hurt on a mission, wouldn't I take care of him? I can't think of Hugo as my brother in one breath, and in the other, abandon him when he needs me most."

30

Nathan

"You're a good friend." I release her shoulder, only to cup her cheek. My words sound so inconsequential. My heart hurts; my chest squeezes in on itself. The buzz in my head, which has faded away since we left the crowd of people behind at the wedding venue, picks up again. "I am so sorry for what happened to Hugo."

"Thank you," she murmurs.

"It must be very difficult seeing him in this state."

"It is." She sniffles. "He was a brilliant chef. He had a brilliant future. He had... Has a natural knack for cooking any dish, be it an entrée or sweet dish. He could have gone all the way to the top. And now... He can barely remember his name most days." Tears pour down her cheeks.

My guts churn. I can't bear to see her cry. Can't tolerate seeing the distress she is in. I lean over the small coffee table and press my lips to hers. It's meant to be comforting, a way for me to distract her from the sadness that grips her. I merely want to console her, but the touch of her mouth, the warmth of her breath, the taste of her goes straight to my head. I draw her sweet cherry-blossom scent into my lungs, and every cell in my body seems to burst into flames. I tilt my head, slide my tongue over hers, and she makes that little moan at the back of her throat, the one that drives me crazy. I lean in further, tipping my glass of water, which falls to the floor with a crash.

The sound cuts through my brain, and the pain in my eardrums escalates. The sound of gunfire. Of screams. The thud of footsteps racing toward me. The images overwhelm me. I flinch, pull away and squeeze my eyes shut. Take a breath, another. Try to rid the wave of static that overwhelms my hearing. When it abates to a bearable level, I open my eyes.

She's looking at me with worry on her features. "Are you okay?"

I shake my head. "I will be." I reach for the bottle of water and take a sip.

"Was it the noise of the glass crashing to the floor that set you off?" she asks in a soft voice.

I retrieve my glass and place it on the table. "Loud noises hurt my ears."

"You're suffering from PTSD?"

I nod. "That last mission I was part of went south. The other two men on our team were killed by enemy fire. Ben and I took the rest of them out. Carrying our dead team-mates, we were making our way back to the extraction point when a bomb went off next to me. Ben shoved me away, got the brunt of it instead. I owe him my life."

"He never told me," she whispers.

He shrugs. "Modest bastard. Never liked taking credit for his bravery."

She nods, her cheeks glisten with her tears, and she wipes them off. "He's always been that way. Every time I thought taking care of Hugo and running the business was too much, I thought of him on the front lines. I thought of you on the front lines, too. And how brave both of you were, and it gave me the courage to keep going."

"I'm not brave." I twist my lips. "If I were, I wouldn't have coerced you to marry me in this fashion."

Her gaze widens. "Are you admitting that what you did was wrong?"

I rub the back of my neck. "I wouldn't go that far."

She rolls her eyes. "I should have known, getting an apology from you is too far out to imagine."

"I should have told you upfront that I never stopped thinking about you. That we made a good match. That we could help each other. I could have used a softer approach, I suppose."

She blinks slowly. "Wow, should I be grateful that the great Nathan Davenport has extended me a half-apology?"

I quirk my lips. "That was half-assed, as far as apologies go. You and I both know that. So no, I wasn't apologizing. I'm not sorry for finding a way to make you mine."

Remember me thinking that our marriage would end and that I'd have to walk away from her? Also, that I'd be okay with that? Bugger that. I have her here with me, in my house, under my roof, and I know now, I'll never be able to live without her. She's my wife. And I intend to do everything to convince her to stay mine.

I intend to own her heart, and her thoughts, and her body. I intend to pleasure her, so she never forgets who she belongs to. So her skin only ever wants my touch. So her soul knows who's her mate. So she has eyes for me, and no one else. I intend to win her over and monopolize her heart, such that when the time comes to forgive me, she won't think twice. And if it means I use underhanded means to win her sympathy, then so be it.

She tilts her head, "When the bomb went off next to you, were you hurt?"

"I was, but not seriously." I shift my stance. "I got to keep all of my limbs. But my hearing was impaired."

"Oh." Her eyes grow huge. "Is that why you often stare at my mouth? You're trying to make up for your loss in hearing by lip reading?"

"That's part of it. The other part is, I can't stop thinking of our first kiss."

She draws in a sharp breath.

"Couldn't forget the shape of your mouth, the softness of your lips, the little whines you made at the back of your throat, the sweetness of your breath, the beat of your heart as it picked up speed, the thrum of your pulse at the base of your throat. The sensation of finding something so precious, so unique, so once-in-a-lifetime was so overwhelming—"

"—you turned and left me."

I wince. "You were too young."

"I was eighteen."

"You were my best-friend's sister."

She scoffs. "He'd have come around, like he's going to do now, when he finds out we're together."

That familiar flutter of unease slithers through my veins, and I push it away. Now's not the time to tell her everything. *Then when?* When I know for sure, she's so in love with me, it'll override all other emotions. When I know she won't want to leave me. When I'm sure she'll understand why I did what I did. When... I know it's the right time to tell her the truth, knowing she has the strength to bear it. When she trusts me enough to allow me to support her as she deals with the aftermath of it.

"You were a virgin."

She tips up her chin. "I still am."

"Not for much longer."

She blinks rapidly, then color flushes her cheeks. "If that's your way of saying you are going to—"

"Run." I jerk my chin in the direction of the doors leading to the house.

"Excuse me?" She gapes.

"Unless you don't want to? Unless you want to give in to me without a fight, which I admit, would be a disappointment."

She stares between my eyes, then reaches for the bottle of Champagne and slowly takes a sip. "Is this one of your kinky-fuckery games?"

I bark out a laugh, then take the bottle from her and place it down on the table with a soft thunk. "Does saying those words turn you on?"

"Of course not." She pouts.

"Hmm…" I drag my thumb under my bottom lip. She follows my movements, her breathing growing rapid. I lift the bottle of water to my lips, then pause, "Open your mouth, wife."

She seems like she's going to refuse, and when she finally complies, I'm sure I'm going to come in my pants. That's how little control I have around this woman. I take a sip of my water, then beckon her forward. When she leans in, I close the distance to her and spit it into her mouth. She swallows, and her cheeks flush crimson. Then, she licks her lips. I lift my bottle to my mouth again and drain it. When I place it back on the table, she's watching me with a hint of fear and excitement woven through her gaze.

"This is your last chance."

"For what?"

31

Skylar

"Run. I'll give you a head start, and when I catch you—and you know I will—you'll no longer be a virgin, and—"

Before he can complete his sentence, I jump up to my feet, and race for the doorway leading to the house. He hasn't shown me around yet, and now, I curse myself for not having insisted he did. *Which way do I go?* I race across the living room, into the large entry with the high ceilings and a staircase. The staircase. I dart up it… Then realize, too late, I should have gone out the front door. That might have given me a fighting chance. Now, I'm going to be trapped inside the house. *Maybe I wanted to be trapped inside so he'd find me?*

When he declared I'd no longer be a virgin, I won't deny, a thrill rushed through me. It seems like I've been waiting so long to be in his arms, to have him make love to me… And for it to be on our wedding night…

My steps slow. Fact is, he's right. I want him, so why am I running from him? I stop halfway up the stairs, then turn to find him standing at the bottom of the staircase. He's looking at me with a quizzical expression, one foot on the step above him. He's still in his tux, not a hair out of place, while I feel disheveled and sweaty. His gaze meets mine, and it's like a traction ray drawing me to him. He doesn't need to chase me, when I already want to be his.

And damn... but that feels like I'm giving up my power when I'm not. I'm owning this... connection between us. I'm reveling in it, when he's always tried to run from it. I take one step down, then another, until I stop halfway down to him. I throw off my heels and look up to find him watching me closely.

I bend, pull up my dress and slide off my garter. I hold it up, and his blue eye flashes silver, while his brown lightens with golden stars. I certainly have his attention. I throw it at him, and he catches it, then watches me with a speculative look.

"I see you've decided to give into the inevitable without a fight?"

"On the contrary—" Without taking my gaze off of his, partly so he can read my lips, I slip off my panties. When I straighten, a flush blotches his cheeks.

I was right; he wants me, very much. He can't hold himself back. He was trying to swing the balance of power in his direction with that primal play. Yes, I know what that was, having read enough spicy books. Even if I didn't know the technical term for that, my instincts tell me he was trying to take control of the situation. And while I'm more than happy to let him have that, I plan to, at least, hold my own against him, even if it's only for a short period of time.

I toss my panties at him. Of course, he catches them. He brings them to his face and sniffs, and that action is so erotic, so filthy... My knees buckle. I grab at the banister to hold my balance.

He slides my panties inside his pocket, then reaches up and loosens his bowtie. It should not be titillating, but the way his biceps stretch the sleeves of his tux turns my brain cells to mush. He undoes the top button of his shirt, and the next. When he undoes the third, strands of his chest hair are visible. My mouth goes dry.

He unhooks the button holding his jacket lapels together, and when they fall apart, showing the stretch of his shirt across that lean waist, my pussy clenches. Moisture bathes my core, and I have to clamp down on my inner walls to stop the cum from sliding out.

His nostrils flare. His gaze darts down to my pussy, which is only covered by my gown, then back to my face. He shrugs off his jacket, which slithers to the floor. My gaze is drawn to his chest, to the shadows of his nipples visible through the white of his shirt, to the cleavage of his pecs.

As if in a dream, I reach forward to undo the next button, but he grabs my wrist and twists my arm behind my back. The action forces me up on my toes.

He drags his gaze down to my breasts, and his throat moves as he swallows. "Your tits are going to be the death of me." He lowers his head to the valley between my breasts, then licks my cleavage. The action is so primal, so lust-filled, a moan spills from my lips. It seems to snap him into action, for he straightens, then bends his knees and throws me over his shoulder. He *throws* my size sixteen frame over his shoulder. He is the first man to want me enough to touch me, and make me feel beautiful, and carry me, and run up the stairs like I weigh nothing. I'm too shocked to move, too surprised to say anything. Then, he enters a room — his bedroom, I assume, for the next moment he's throwing me down on the bed.

I bounce once, then shove the hair out of my face. I begin to sit up, but he grabs my ankle and pulls me over to the edge of the bed, my dress riding up my body in the process. I yelp and try to back away, purely on instinct. In response, he grips my other ankle and holds me down. I look into his face to find his gaze locked on mine. There's an intense look on his features; his jaw is set. He shoves my legs apart, and when I yelp, one side of his lips twist.

"Fight me," he growls.

I'm not sure what makes me follow his direction, but my hindbrain kicks into gear. All of my senses narrow in on him. There's something in his eyes. Something that tells me he's serious. And when my gaze drops to the tent between his legs, I realize, he's turned on. I begin to struggle. "Let me go."

He doesn't reply. But his breathing grows rougher, so I know I'm doing the right thing. I try to tug my legs from his hold. The next moment, he's pushed my legs up, so my knees are next to my ears.

"Nate." I swallow.

He doesn't reply. He's busy staring at my bare pussy. The way he devours me with his gaze, I'm sure his next move is going to be—I cry out, for he's bent his head and licked me from back hole to clit. "Oh, *Twilight Zone!*"

He glances up from between my thighs. "Your swearing is a fucking turn on."

"It... It is?"

"Makes me wonder what you'll do when I—"

I yell, for he's slapped my pussy.

"What in the *Peaky Blinders* are you doing?" I try to pull away from him, and he laughs. It's a dark, evil sound, filled with promises of all the dirty things he can do to me. And I want them. And I want to please him even more.

Okay, so I'm a slut. We've established that. Can we just... cut me some slack? I'm just a woman parting her legs for the man who's the love of her life, the only one I've ever wanted to be with.

And then, he slaps my pussy again. This time, my entire body jolts. I growl at him, and he smirks at me. Then he lowers his head and bites my clit.

"Bloody *Bridgerton*!" I try to pull away from him.

He looks up and smacks his lips. "You taste so fucking delightful."

"And when you release me, I'm going to smack your balls. We'll see, then, how much you like it—" I huff, for he releases his hold on my one leg, only to stick that finger inside my pussy. I gasp. It's only a finger—his one thick finger—but it already feels like he's stretching me. He scoops up my cum, then proceeds to smear it around my forbidden hole and—nope, not ready for that yet.

I press the foot he's released against his shoulder and push. And somehow, that unbalances him—bet he does it on purpose—so I can get free. But I don't care. If he wants to shove his monster cock up the wrong hole, then I'm taking him up on his offer to run and to fight him. I scramble back, then manage to jump to my feet.

He slowly straightens. Even standing on the bed, I barely reach to eye level with him. He's so tall. And the way he rolls his neck, the tendons of his shoulders pop. I feint to the left, and when he follows me, I race to the right of the bed, jump down and around the foot, and toward the doorway. I burst out of the room, and a fierce ball of emotion fires in my chest. At least I'm making it difficult for him to catch me.

I wail in protest, for he's caught me around the waist. "You animal! Release me!" This time, I yell with real anger. But he stalks back to the bed and throws me down with enough force that I lay there, stunned. Before I can jump up, he's pulled off his belt, walked around to the head of the bed and pulled one of my arms up, then the other, and tied my wrists to the headboard.

"What are you doing?" I gasp breathlessly.

In reply, he walks back around to the foot of the bed. He shoves off his shirt, toes off his shoes and socks, then grabs a condom from his pants before he steps out of them. My jaw drops, and not only because some part of me is disappointed by the condom, but because his chest is a work of art.

He has a picture of the goddess Justitia, blindfolded and holding the scales of justice in one hand and a sword in another, tattooed across his chest. The line *Per Mare Per Terram* is scrawled under it. The robes of the goddess are colored in jeweled hues which... I peer closer—yep, it covers the scars which mar his chest. The robes billow around her ankles, drawing attention to her feet, which, in turn, point in the direction of... that... That thing between his legs.

I was wrong. It's not a monster... It's the freakin' mother-of-all-dragons-in-size cock. I've already had it in my mouth, but the thought of him cramming that inside my pussy is still alarming.

As if my gaze turns him on more, his shaft expands in size.

"You—" I swallow. "You're not going to put that thing in me, are you?"

In response, he sheaths himself with the condom, then pumps his cock once. He digs one knee, then the other, onto the bed between my legs, forcing them further apart. The entire time, that freakin' jumbotron of a dick stands up straight against his stomach. The vein that runs up the underside of his shaft throbs in tandem with the beat of my heart.

I shake my head. "Oh no you don't."

He moves forward until he's positioned between my legs, then pushes up my wedding dress so it's bunched over my breasts. I bend my knee and kick out a leg, but he catches it and positions it over his shoulder. And when I try to strike out with my other leg, he grips my foot and hooks my ankle over his other shoulder.

"Nate—" I swallow.

In response, he positions his cock against my opening. I'm so turned on, the nudge of the swollen head against my throbbing slit makes me cry out. He stops then and looks deeply into my eyes. His pupils are dilated with lust, his jaw is set, and a pulse throbs at his temple. He's so turned on; it takes my breath away. My lungs burn. Every bit of oxygen seems to have been sucked out of the room. The very air itself is electric with need, and a desire so intense, my scalp tightens. My nipples turn into little rubber bullets of desire.

"Yes? Or no?" he snaps.

I swallow.

"Starling?" His tone is hard and there's a warning note to it. "Tell me you want this, or else, I'm not doing it." His lips thin, and his biceps bulge.

There's a tension radiating out of him that pushes down on my chest and pins me in place. There's so much emotion packed into that space between us, I wonder how I ever thought this man was unexpressive. He merely packed away all of his feelings in a space inside of him, which he's revealing to me today.

Is it the fact that I finally resisted him that drew that darkness inside of him to the fore? Did it take my saying 'no' for him to come fully into his desire? Did it—

He begins to draw away, and all thoughts drain from my head.

"Yes," I cry out, "yes, I want you to fuck me, right now and—" The breath is forced out of me in a keening cry, for he's propelled his hips forward and breached me.

32

Nathan

With my cock half inside her, I freeze. "Baby"—I push my palms into the bed —"I'm so fucking sorry I hurt you."

She shakes her head, opens her mouth, but nothing comes out. Instead, a tear rolls down from the corner of her eye.

I bend and lick it up. That makes her breath hitch. I lower my face over hers, look into her features. "I should have gone slower, but I got carried away. And you're so fucking hot and tight and moist, and—" I freeze, for she's tilted up her hips, enough that my cock slides in further. The muscles of my shoulders bunch. My groin tightens. Tendrils of need radiate out from where we're joined. I want so badly to ram all the way inside of her, but I'm not going to risk causing her more pain. I reach down between us and rub at her clit. She cries out, then locks her ankles around my neck.

"It aches," she groans.

I freeze, every muscle in my body locking up. "I knew it. I knew I should have held back." I begin to withdraw, but she digs her heels into my back.

"Don't you dare stop now."

"You need time to adjust to my size. I should have prepared you more for my intrusion."

"Well, you're in now, aren't you?"

I wince. "Not exactly."

"What do you mean?"

"I'm only halfway in."

"Wh-a-a-t?" Her mouth falls open. "You're joking."

In response, my cock twitches inside of her.

"You…" She swallows. "You seriously aren't all the way in?"

I lower my head and brush my mouth over hers. "I'm a big man."

"You don't say?" she scoffs.

"Did you roll your eyes at me?"

She assumes a look of innocence. "I wouldn't dare."

"And still sassy. Maybe you need your pussy slapped again, hmm?"

Her flush depends. "No!"

"Or maybe you need your arse spanked."

"Maybe," she says coyly.

"Why, Mrs. Davenport, I do believe you might enjoy that too much."

"It, uh, has its merits." She tips up her chin.

"And I'm sorry I took you in such a hurry."

"I don't know"—she flutters her eyelashes—"it's flattering that you couldn't wait. I'd like to think I was the cause of you losing control."

"More than you'll ever know." I circle her clit, then touch the place where I'm joined with her. A shiver grips her. And when I trace the outline of her pussy lips, moisture bathes my cock. I slide my hand behind her to the valley between her arse cheeks, and when I play with her forbidden entrance, her entire body shudders. Her inner walls spasm, and I slip further inside her. And when I lower my head and lave at her nipple, she arches her back. I bite down, and her pussy clamps down around my dick.

"Ffffuck!" I push my forehead into her shoulder to calm myself down. I will not lose control. I need to make this really good for her. I press little kisses up her neck to her mouth, and when I lick her lips, she relaxes again.

"Let me in, baby," I whisper.

She shudders and pants and writhes against me. And then she pushes up and into me. I slip in all the way to the hilt. I stay there, with my balls knocking into her cunt, and when I play with the rosette of her back-entrance, she groans, "Not today."

"Not today," I agree, "but you'll offer me your virgin arse very soon."

"That depends." She cracks open her heavy eyelids.

"On what?"

"On how good you make it for me—" She gasps as I pull back and stay poised against the rim of her entrance.

"You were saying—"

She blinks slowly. "Was I?"

"Hmm…" I tease her back hole. "Something about how good I make it for you?"

"Awfully cocky, aren't you?"

I dig my knees into the mattress, and with a lunge of my hips, I sink inside her to the hilt. Hot and tight, and so fucking wet. My brain cells seem to short-circuit from the pleasure. I manage to get a hold of my thoughts and focus my gaze on her features, "Does that feel good, darling?"

She swallows, opens her mouth, but no words come out.

I cup her cheek. "Not continuing until you reply, Starling."

She blinks, then nods. "I swear, I can feel you in my throat."

I half smile. "That's flattering baby, but my question was, does it feel good for you?"

"It feels like"—she looks between my eyes—"I'm yours."

My heart feels like it's going to burst through my ribcage. A sensation of floating on thin air fills me, and I haven't even orgasmed. This… This is how I knew it would be with her. This is why I stayed away from her. This is why, now that I've had a taste of her, I'll never be able to give her up. "I'm going to make love to you."

I pull back again, and still holding her gaze, I kick my hips forward and slide into her, all the way, until I can't fit further. I brush up against the wall of her cervix, and a low groan emerges from her.

"You like that?"

She nods, her green eyes filled with lust. It makes me feel so fucking good that I'm pleasuring her. I reach up and loosen the belt on her wrists. When her hands are free, she wraps them about my neck and pulls me close. I gaze deeply into her eyes, our breaths mingling, and begin to fuck her in earnest. The next time I thrust into her, her entire body jolts. The bed squeaks, and the headboard crashes into the wall. I push into her again, angling my hips so I sink even deeper. At the same time, I curve my finger inside her back channel.

"Nate," she cries out, and her body jolts again. Her pupils are so dilated, I can see myself reflected in the sheet of black.

I plunge into her one last time, and when she arches her back and digs her fingernails into my shoulders, I growl, "Come with me."

33

Skylar

I'm still looking into his eyes when I shatter. The orgasm sweeps through me, carries me to a place far away, and my entire body seems to catch fire. The vibrations seize me, and moisture bathes my core. My thighs tremble, and I clutch at the only thing solid in this world—him. He continues to fuck me, putting his entire self behind it.

Nathan fucks like he lives his life. With one-hundred percent intensity. He gives all of himself, and it's as if he's consuming me. As if he's infusing his very soul into me, and with a groan, he empties himself inside of me. He holds my gaze for a few seconds more. Long enough for me to see the pain-pleasure of his climax in his eyes. Then he presses his head into the side of my neck, and for a few seconds, rests the weight of his body on mine. His heart thunders against mine.

The heat from him envelops me in a cauldron of future dreams. A life together. Getting up with him by my side. Opening my heart to him. Falling asleep to him throbbing inside me. Hearing his words, seeing him smile, taking in that freakin' sexy smirk of his, trailing my fingers over the veins on his arm, seeing the tendons on his neck pop when he's angry, his smooth gait which reminds me of a predator, his heart, which is as squishy as that of a teddy bear

—I want all of this and more.

I want a future with him. I didn't realize how much until this moment, when every inch of my body is covered with his. Looking into his eyes while making love is the most intimate experience of my life. Nothing can top this. Nothing can make me feel this treasured, this wanted, this sexy, this desirable. *This everything.* The rush of emotions brings tears to my eyes. I swallow them away, but that slight movement makes him lift his face and search my features.

"You okay?"

I shake my head.

He frowns. "Did I—"

"Hurt me? Yes, but in a good way."

He frowns, then pulls out of me. I wince. His frown deepens. He sits back on his heels, and when he glances down, I follow his gaze to where blood streaks the condom.

"Oh." I blink. I didn't think I would bleed. It didn't hurt that much.

I glance up to find his jaw tic. His face is set in a harsh line. He shoves off the bed and puts distance between us.

I frown. "Nate, are you okay?"

He runs his fingers through his hair, a tortured expression on his face. "I'm sorry I wasn't gentler with you, Starling." He stares at my pussy, and I should be embarrassed, but really, I'm too preoccupied by the emotions flitting across his face. I've never seen him this disturbed. This... Slightly horrified. I once thought the man was unfeeling, but watching his reaction, I could laugh at how wrong I was.

"I thought I could contain myself. When I've already waited so long to be inside of you, I should have been able to wait another few minutes, but the feel of your melting pussy milking my cock was more than I could bear. Suddenly, all I could think of was fucking you—"

"I wanted you to fuck me."

His jaw hardens. "—and taking my pleasure from your body."

"I got a lot of pleasure from it, too," I counter. "I came... hard, and only you could wring that kind of reaction from my body."

He goes on as if he doesn't hear me. "I wanted to be gentler with you. Instead, I couldn't stop from putting my needs first. This is what happens when—" he firms his lips.

"When?" I scowl. *Why is he so upset?* It was good—better than good. That was a move-the-earth-kind of orgasm he gave me. I mean, I'm the virgin here. Or rather, was a virgin. If anything, I should be emotionally upset about what happened, but I feel good. Better than good. I feel like I belong here in his bed, with his big, fat cock bringing me to climax over and over again. Instead, he's the one who's so pissed off with himself. If I didn't know him better, I'd say... *Naaaah*... I freeze. *It's not possible. Is it?*

"Nathan?" I rise up to my feet, my skirt still bunched around my waist. That's what happens when you wear something slim fitting, with hips and thighs that form a natural resting place for the fabric. You have to tug on the fabric to smooth it down, but before I can do that, a drop of something — Blood? His cum? Mine? A mix of all three runs down my inner thigh. His gaze latches onto that and, when I come to a stop in front of him, he reaches out, scoops up the moisture, brings it to his mouth and sucks on it.

It should gross me out, but instead, a thousand little fireflies seem to light up in my blood stream. "Nate, look at me," I whisper.

Something in my voice — or maybe it's the emotions vibrating off of me, which communicate themselves to him — makes his chin jerk up. His gaze locks with mine, and it's like a physical blow to my chest. I'll never not be impacted by this man's gaze. "Nate" — I swallow — "when... when was the last time you had sex?"

He glares at me. The hair on my forearms rises, and that giddy feeling in my belly is back, but I manage to ignore it. I rise up on tiptoes and cup his cheek. He flinches but doesn't move away.

"Tell me, baby, when was the last time you fucked —"

" —a few days before your eighteenth birthday," he bites out.

I blink.

"A... A few days before my eighteenth birthday?" I can't have heard that right. "So, you haven't had sex for more than five years?"

"Not that I haven't wanted to." He laughs in a self-deprecating manner. "Trust me, I tried. But I couldn't even bring a woman home, not when the only one I wanted in my bed was you. I tried fucking them at their place, but it felt all wrong. I couldn't bring myself to touch them, let alone, have sex with them. I tried beating off to porn; didn't work. Not until I imagined it was your pussy I was inside, that it was you I was bending over and taking from behind, that it was your arse I was taking, your nipples I was squeezing, your breasts I was weighing in my hands. And then... I finally find a way to get you in my bed, and what do I do?"

"You make love to me."

"I shagged you —"

"You showed me how good it could be. I couldn't have chosen a better man to lose my virginity to. I couldn't have asked for a more amazing experience on my wedding night."

He flinches again.

"And for the record, I found it even more pleasurable when you asked me to run and chased me. It heightened the entire experience—"

His gaze grows stark.

"—uh… thought I should let you know."

A vein pops at his temple.

"Just in case you were wondering…" My voice peters out.

The muscle working at his jaw tells me that was not the right thing to say. *Huh?* Before I can ask, he pivots and stalks off in the direction of the ensuite.

"Nate? Nathan?" I call out, but he doesn't stop. *Or maybe, he didn't hear me? Is his hearing problem exacerbated only when there's noise? Or does he always need to compensate for his hearing loss with lip reading?* There are so many questions I have for him. So much I don't know about my new husband.

The one thing I have learned about him is that he wants me to fight him when it comes to sex. He wants me to protest that I don't want him. When I struggle, it excites him. When I run, and he gets to chase me before he fucks me, it turns him on even more.

I hear the sound of water running, then he returns from the bathroom with a wet cloth. And he's wearing a pair of grey sweats. His cock is outlined through the fabric at the crotch, and my mouth waters. It's not fair the man fills out a pair of sweatpants even better than he looks in a pair of tailor-made formal pants. His hair is mussed-up, and with his bare chest, and the makings of a five o'clock shadow, he looks deliciously rumpled.

"It's called Primal Play." He leans in and presses the cloth to the flesh between my legs.

It's my turn to flinch… Not because it hurts, but because it's cold. The slight burning sensation subsides. He looks at the cloth and his features harden more, if that's possible.

"So that's your kink?" I survey his scowling face.

He takes a few steps toward the bathroom and tosses the cloth into the sink. "To me, it's as natural as doing it in the missionary position is for other people. I'm turned on when my woman struggles against my hold and uses the tools she's born with: nails, hair, teeth, and skin—

"You want me to fight you?"

He lowers his chin to his chest. "I want you to act on instinct. I want you to get in touch with your base self and express yourself freely."

"You're a primal Dom," I try out the word in my mouth, and a buzzing sensation shivers up my spine. There's something powerful about that word. *Dom.* Dominant. *Husband.*

"And you're my prey." He holds out his hand.

My pussy squeezes in on itself. My toes curl. I should not find that arousing. He's saying he's going to hunt me and... My scalp prickles, pins and needles dot the soles of my feet, and when he holds out his hand, given the glower he's sporting, I decide not to ask any more questions. Not when I know I'll love the answers he gives me, and then hate myself for loving them. I've discovered enough of that darker side inside of me for today. I place my palm in his.

He turns me around and proceeds to unzip me. He slides the gown down my arms, and then my hips. When it pools around my ankles, I step out of it. Thanks to the built-in bra, and since I took off my panties earlier, I'm naked. In front of my husband. For the first time. He applies light pressure on my shoulder, and I pivot to face him. He rakes his gaze down my face, my breast, my stomach. I begin to wrap my arms about myself, but he stops me with a touch on my arm. "Don't hide that beautiful body of yours."

I swallow. My cheeks burn. He's been inside me. He's touched parts of me, inside and out that no one else has. But standing without clothes in front of the gorgeousness that is Nate makes me feel so inadequate. "You're so handsome, and I"—I look away and mumble—"I'm fat and ugly and—"

"Hey, stop insulting my wife," he growls.

"You don't have to be polite."

I try to cover myself with my arms again, and he wraps his fingers around my wrists to stop me.

I'm still not comfortable with him seeing me like this, so I try to explain. "I've been teased enough times in school, and then at university. Even my fellow bakers in the Master Baker Program couldn't resist, pointing out that I was a big girl. Obviously, I like my desserts."

"They were stupid idiots who should be waterboarded, tied up in the dark, and not allowed to sleep for a week," he snaps.

I crack a smile. "That seems a little over-the-top."

"They deserve worse. You're gorgeous. Your figure is the kind the master artists drew on canvas and sculptors rhapsodized about in stone. You're natural, and curvy—"

"You mean, I'm fat."

"Lush and full-bodied and curvy."

"Gosh, who knew you had so many different ways of saying fat in a diplomatic way," I say lightly, darting my gaze around the room.

He makes a growling noise at the back of his throat, and my nipples perk up. *Ugh*. Also, my pussy clenches. *Stupid pussy*. My body hasn't gotten the memo that I'm not supposed to react with such intensity to him. Although, what else can you expect me to do when he's standing in front of me dripping sex from every pore and revealing his perfect V-cut abs? And then, there are those grey sweats, which ride low enough to show off that happy trail pointing to the promised land, a.k.a. his rather substantial prick. And what a surprise to find he's not as much of a prick as he'd like to make himself out to be.

He notches his knuckles under my chin, so I have no choice but to meet his searing mismatched gaze. "You will not put yourself down. You will not say things which you and I both know are untrue. You are a gorgeous, intelligent, courageous, independent entrepreneur with more brains in your little finger than most people have in their heads."

"An entrepreneur who needed to barter herself for money to keep her business going," I scoff.

Muscles work at his jaw. Those tendons of his throat I love so much pop out in such relief, I'm sure they're going to snap. "Did you not want to marry me? Is that what this is about?"

I shake my head, then begin to brush past him. "I don't want to talk about this."

But does he let me go? Of course not.

He circles my wrist with his fingers and pulls so I fall into him. He locks me in the circle of his arms, and glares into my face. "You doing a runner?"

"Just copying you, is all."

A nerve pops at his temple. His shoulders grow in size, and I'm sure he's going to burst out of his skin, but then he laughs. I stare in surprise as his entire face lights up and makes him look so much younger.

Is this what he looked like before he joined the Marines? When he was a young man with dreams in his eyes and hopes of making the world a better place? Why is it that, from the time we're born, we begin inching our way toward the cynical beings that life turns us into? Only on him, the grumpiness looks attractive. In fact, the more standoffish he is, the more I want to find a way to get close to him. And then, the fact that he didn't have sex with anyone else after he saw me on my eighteenth birthday... Yes, he did let those women touch him... But he didn't fuck them. A fierce hope pulses through my veins.

He walked away that day. I thought he hated me, but it turns out... He, too, harbored powerful feelings for me all this time. Everything I felt wasn't one sided. My head spins. My scalp tingles. I place my palms on his chest, and his muscles twitch. It's like touching a powerhouse of raw, steel cable, covered in flesh. My toes curl, and that pulse between my thighs spikes. I draw my fingers over the raised scars colored in by the jeweled robes of Goddess Justitia, up to her blindfolded eyes. "Is this tattoo to declare you believe justice is blind?"

"That's a wrong preconception most people have. The blindfold represents that justice is impartial. I got the tattoo to remind myself death comes for all of us. Some, sooner than later. But Death is the ultimate equalizer."

"How long have you had it?"

"About a year," he says.

I look up to find him watching me with curiosity.

I shrug. "If you think I'm disturbed by your rather macabre explanation, I'm not."

"I didn't expect you to be. Not after the gumption you've shown thus far."

"Gumption, and me?" I slide my fingers up his shoulders. His sinews writhe under my touch, and when I wrap my arms about his neck, the pulse at the base of his throat speeds up. His features, though, don't change expression. Tough customer, this one. "If I had more courage, I'd have held out and not accepted your proposal to bail me out."

"And risked losing the business?" He shakes his head. "You were smart enough to know when you needed help. And I'm not saying it because it brought you back into my life. No, being a smart entrepreneur means knowing when to seek help."

"Wow, more praise from you? Is it sunny in London today?" I pretend to look toward the window.

"What about your tattoo?" He runs his thumb across the tiny cat-shaped outline I have etched into the inside of my left wrist.

"That's in memory of Cocoa, my first and only kitten. She kept me company when Ben left to join the Marines. She ran away one day and never returned. I missed her so much, especially because she was my constant companion... My best friend, given I didn't have that many friends in school."

"I'm sorry." He brushes his lips across my mouth, and I sigh.

"It was a long time ago."

"Is your bakery —"

"Named after her?" I smile. "It is. She was a fierce little thing. I swear she thought she was more dog than cat, given the number of fights she got into with any dog she came across."

He nibbles his way up my jawline, then tugs on my earlobe. My thighs tremble, and my pussy clenches. My breasts seem to swell, and I squirm against him. "Nate, please," I whine.

"You ready to take my cock up your arse?"

I blink, then pull back. When I jerk my chin up, it's to find he's smirking.

"Very smooth change of subject. Not!" I slap at his chest. "Don't get your hopes high on that, buster."

"Aww, wife…" His lips turn down. "You're not going to deny me, are you?"

My heart does that little dance in my chest that it does every time he calls me 'wife.' Ugh, all he has to growl is 'my wife,' and I'll probably let him fuck me there, too.

He must see the capitulation on my face, because his own brightens. "I take it, that's a yes?"

"It's not a no." I toss my head. "What is it with guys and anal?"

"It's the forbidden, baby. Not to mention, it's that tight chokehold on our cocks that makes it the best possible sex ever."

"For you, maybe."

"That's where you're wrong…"

"Well, it's not very intimate." I purse my lips.

"How would you know?"

34

Nathan

"Um, because—" She opens and shuts her mouth. "You're right, I don't. But I'm going based on what I've read about it."

"In your romance novels?"

"There, too, but not only. There's this thing called the internet; you know?"

He snickers. "That sassy mouth of yours is going to get you into so much trouble."

"The kind I'm going to enjoy, I hope." She raises one brow.

I look between her eyes. "Did you enjoy what we did earlier?"

"You mean, when you fucked me?"

"That, too… And it was more than fucking. You know that."

I hear the chiding tone in my voice and berate myself. I don't want to sound like I'm admonishing her. Sure enough, she flushes and tries to pull away, but I hold her in place. "We made love, baby. Unadulterated, passionate, intensely heated, feverish, vehement, fiery, and searing-me-to-my-bones kind of love."

Her gaze widens. "I didn't think you knew how to put your emotions into words."

"I'm learning from the best. You've been chipping away at that wall around my heart since we met. One kiss, and I could feel myself retreating into that primal part of me I prefer to let out to play on very specific occasions."

"So earlier, when you said you enjoy consensual non-consent—"

"Apparently, I feel comfortable enough with you to show my proclivities. It's something I've generally preferred to indulge in, in controlled circumstances."

She frowns. "You mean, with someone who you pay for sex?"

"No sex." I click my tongue. "While I have paid for role play, it's always ended with me jerking myself off."

She sets her jaw. "So those women... Did they—"

"Blow me off? No."

She nods slowly. "But did you let them—"

"Touch my dick? The answer is yes, a couple of times." *Only I didn't like it at all and put an end to it. The only woman whose hands I wanted on my cock was you.*

Her green eyes blaze.

So fucking cute.

"You jealous?" I murmur.

"What do you think?" She tips up her chin.

"I think"—I turn my head and nuzzle her arm, then twine my fingers with hers and bring our joined hands to my mouth. I kiss the rings that I put there— "these look good on you."

She scoffs.

Her forehead is furrowed. There's a downward tilt to her lips which I want to kiss away. I look into her eyes. "I didn't fuck them, baby. They were paid to role-play, and that's all I did," I say gently.

"But you had sex with other women, those who you didn't role play with?"

I merely smile.

When she opens her mouth to ask the inevitable question, I click my tongue. "I don't keep count. I also don't go around talking about who I slept with. That would be ungentlemanly."

She snorts. "You're not a gentleman."

"Not with you, I'm not. With you"—I press her palm to my cheek—"with you, I can't seem to hold back the truth. With you, I want to share my filthiest, dirtiest secrets. I want to play out my most secret erotic fantasies with you."

She takes a few seconds to digest that. "I think that's good. I'm your wife. You should be able to tell me what you want."

"I never intended for our relationship to take such a turn." I roll my shoulders. "I certainly didn't want our wedding night to turn into an initiation into the pleasures of kink for you."

"And what if I liked it?" She juts out her chin. "You know I did."

I nod slowly. "And that surprised me."

"Did you expect me to run from the room screaming?"

"Maybe?" I whisper my knuckles up her jawline. "I certainly didn't expect you to play along without missing a beat. I didn't expect you to turn me on to the extent that I couldn't stop myself from taking you so quickly. I didn't expect you to give me your virginity wholeheartedly."

"I've wanted you to have it since our first kiss."

I blow out a breath. "You shouldn't be so honest with me, baby. You shouldn't wear your heart on your sleeve."

"Why not?"

"Because I'm a bad man. Because I'll take advantage of you. Because I'll use everything you share with me to mold you into the kind of woman who'll relish the kind of sex I like."

"I see no problem with that." She smiles slyly.

"I'll corrupt you, Starling. I'll debauch you. I'll pervert you and turn you into someone you won't recognize when you look in the mirror."

"You'll turn me into someone who's not afraid. Someone who's courageous enough to own her sexuality. Someone who isn't going to hide her need for the kinky-fuckery stuff I've only read about so far."

I groan. "Fuck, when you talk dirty, it's such a turn on."

"I can tell." She pushes her pelvis into the tent that's been steadily forming at my crotch. "I'm a whore for your brand of depravity. A slut for your kind of corruption. It thrills me and makes me so horny that I get to explore everything I only read about with you, my husband."

Fire sweeps under my skin and zips down to my groin. I'm instantly hard. She called me her husband and now, I'll turn the world upside down to ensure she always has a smile on her face. The possessiveness I felt when I placed that ring on her finger multiplies. She's my wife. My soulmate. Mine.

She must sense my thoughts, for her pupils dilate. Her lips part. Her breathing grows ragged, and she leans in toward me. The air between us crackles with lust and need and something so honest, something that's so intense, it turns my chest into a seething mass of need.

"The emotions I'm feeling"—she swallows—"are too much."

I release her, only to scoop her up in my arms bridal-style. "I know the remedy."

35

Skylar

"Taylor Swift? You're playing Taylor Swift?" The familiar words of "All Too Well" play over the speakers in the background. After placing a robe around my shoulders—one which looks like the one I own, and which he confirms is mine, because he enlisted a team to pack up most of my possessions from my apartment while I was getting dressed for the wedding—he cinches it firmly at my waist and walks me over to the island in the kitchen.

I should feel upset that he packed up my stuff without asking me, but there's something to be said about having him take charge. Besides, he did mention to me that I'd have to move in with him so the relationship would look genuine. I wasn't happy about that, but it wasn't something I could refuse. It's important his grandfather buys into the veracity of this marriage. Also, I'm keeping my apartment, since it's so conveniently located over my bakery, and that means, I can go up whenever I feel the need for space.

"Does it not bother you?" I ask.

"What do you mean?" He frowns.

"Having music in the background." I point in the direction of the speakers. "Does it not hurt your, uh, hearing?"

"If the sound increases over a certain decibel, or if there's too much heavy bass, then yes. But at this decibel, it doesn't bother me... much."

"So, it *does* bother you?" I chew the inside of my cheek.

"It's worth it." He half smiles.

Something softens in my heart. "How did you know that song was my favorite?"

"I happened to catch the video of the song during my research, and I admit, it pulled me in."

"You researched her and listened to her songs?" That melting sensation in my heart spreads to my belly and, lower still, to between my legs. Is there anything more freakin' romantic than your husband spending time to find out more about your tastes?

"It wasn't exactly a hardship, especially when her lyrics do seem to come from a place of genuineness."

"Oh, they do. She writes based on her real heartbreaks. The lyrics of 'All Too Well,' for example, are inspired by her affair with Jake Gyllenhaal," *who I have a secret crush on, and who my husband resembles. Gah!* I'm married to a Jake Gyllenhaal lookalike, and not just his face. That gorgeous body of his is every bit as sculpted and molded into a piece of art as any very fit Hollywood movie star.

I take in the way the planes of Nate's back flex as he reaches up to take down a couple of glasses from the shelf. His very distracting, very chiseled back has a tattoo of a trident with the words *"I am the captain of my soul and the master of my fate"* scrawled in a semi-circle under it. Below that, what appear to be the names of people? The elaborate style of the script renders the names themselves illegible at this distance.

He must sense my perusal, for he rumbles, "They're the names of the men from my regiment who've given their lives in the course of duty."

The last of the names disappears under the waistband of his sweatpants. The first letter of that name looks like B—

He turns before I can decipher it. "I forgot to pull on a T-shirt."

Before I can protest and tell him that's not needed, he marches out of the kitchen and returns a few minutes later, wearing a T-shirt. Not that it helps, for the thin, much-washed fabric clings to his biceps and stretches across his chest, lovingly outlining every sinew of his shoulders.

There's a look of intense concentration on his features. His brow is furrowed. "You know I'll never hurt you, right?" He scans my features. "You know I'll do everything possible to take care of you, whether we're married or not?"

I blink slowly. "Are you thinking of a time in the future when we're not married?"

He hesitates.

That's not very reassuring, is it?

He fills the glasses with water from the tap, then walks over to slide one in front of me. "Drink" he orders.

I roll my eyes at the command but reach for the glass because I'm parched. When I set down the water, he rounds the island to stand next to me. "The one thing I've learned is that life is not to be taken for granted. Everything and everyone we love has an expiry date on it. And the more we love them, the more it hurts when they're gone."

There's a thread of seriousness running through his words, something earnest, something almost pleading. Something that causes the hackles on my neck to stand up. "Nate, what are you trying to tell me?" I whisper.

The furrow between his eyebrows deepens. He turns me around to face him and plants his hands on the island, bracketing me in. "That all good times in life are temporary. That we need to remember the memories as we create them, for they'll soon be gone. That the moments in life when everything seems right are fleeting."

"That's a bleak outlook." I stare into those mismatched eyes of his, and the shadows of pain and regret in his look back at me. "What is it? What is it that you've seen that makes you this cynical, this weary, this... disillusioned?"

"What have I not seen?" He laughs, and the sound is bitter. "A mother losing her son; a child being killed through no fault of his own; a fellow soldier surviving war, only to take his own life, leaving his family shattered." The skin around his eyes tightens, and his lips thin. "Life is cruel."

"Life rewards you when you least expect it," I counter.

"Life teaches you never to trust, for the people you think you can count on are the ones who disappear." He snaps his fingers, and I flinch. "*Poof*, and they're gone, just like that."

The sorrow that vibrates off of him is so dark, so filled with agony and regret and grief... So much, I know, he's talking about someone in particular.

"Who did you lose?" I cup his cheek. "Tell me, Nate. Who are you talking about?"

That's when the doorbell rings. He blinks, and the emotions from his face vanish, like he's turned off a tap. Once more, he's wearing that mask of slight boredom, the one that helps him put a wall between himself and the world.

"That must be the food." He straightens and begins to walk toward the door of the kitchen.

"You ordered food?"

He waggles his eyebrows. "It's our wedding night. I knew we'd need to replenish our energy." When I begin to respond, he adds, "I scheduled this about a week ago; something special to celebrate a special night." Then, he winks.

I'm speechless. This man is so thoughtful. I begin to follow him out, but he glances over his shoulder and stabs a finger at me. "Stay here."

I should have known when he said he arranged this about a week ago. Of course he didn't order food from a delivery app because that would be too normal. No, a team of caterers bustle in, led by a man wearing a suit.

They head over to the round dining table under the large window in the kitchen, which looks out over the garden below. There's a flurry of activity as they spread a tablecloth, set the table for two, even plant a vase with flowers on the table, before placing a variety of dishes on the surface. When the team is done, they line up along the side—I kid you not, they line up like this is an army drill—and the man in the suit turns to us. "Sir, Ma'am,"—he looks between us—"if I may, I'd like to tell you what's on the menu."

"This is Otis, my grandfather's butler." Nate gestures to the man. "He was there at the wedding, but you might have been too pre-occupied to notice."

Otis dips his chin at me. "My congratulations to the both of you."

"Thank you," I murmur.

Nate waves his hand. "Go on then, Otis, tell us what James has sent us."

Otis clears his throat. "The Champagne is a Louis Roederer Cristal Brut."

I raise my eyebrows. *O-k-a-y. That must cost, at least, one-thousand dollars per bottle.*

"For the starters, we have Burrata cheese with heirloom tomatoes, basil pesto and balsamic reduction, seared scallops with cauliflower puree, and a basket of warm bread." For each item described, he uses his hands to point out their location.

Yum! My mouth begins to water.

"For the salad, there's mixed baby greens with shaved fennel, crispy prosciutto, and lemon vinaigrette. This is followed by a salmon en croute stuffed with spinach and ricotta in beurre blanc sauce for the lady."

How did he know I prefer fish? I shoot Nate a glance, and he tilts his head. *Hmm, so he found a way to obtain more information about my tastes.*

"And for you, Sir, there's chicken saltimbocca with sage, prosciutto, and a madeira wine sauce over risotto."

"Much appreciated." Nate offers a polite smile.

"The sides include sautéed wild mushrooms, and roasted Brussel sprouts with pancetta and parmesan risotto."

I do love both mushrooms and Brussel sprouts—weird, I know.

"And for dessert—" He pauses and looks at me.

I straighten my spine.

"There are chocolate molten lava cakes, and fresh berries with sweet ricotta and honey."

"Those are my favorites!" I clap my hands. "Thank you so much. All of it looks delicious."

"I'll pass that onto the chef." Otis' lips twitch.

"Thank you." Nate walks over and claps the man on his shoulder. "Tell James I owe him."

Otis dips his chin. "You know he's only too happy to make the time for you. As am I." He turns and claps his hand once, and the team turns and marches out. Otis follows them.

When they're gone, Nate turns to me. "Shall we?" He walks over to pull out a chair for me.

The scent of food teases my nostrils, and my stomach grumbles. I slip off the stool and head toward the table. Even though the team laid it out in front of me, I can't stop marveling at how pretty everything looks. Each of the dishes is beautifully presented, the cutlery sparkles, and the bottle of Champagne in the ice bucket looks crisp and refreshing. "I assume James is the chef?"

He nods. "James Hamilton is a chef I happen to know well, and who agreed to—"

"Not the Michelin-starred James Hamilton?" I glance up in time to see him nod.

"The same. He's a former Royal Marine and served with me."

"I had no idea."

"I don't think he talks about it much. He's one of us who managed to carve out a whole new career after leaving the Marines.

"Like you did?"

His face closes further. "When my grandfather called me, I couldn't say no. This was my chance to find out more about where I came from. Besides, he needed me, and it was my duty to help him out." His words sound smooth. *Too smooth. Too rehearsed, perhaps?*

My stomach does a nervous flip. *Why do I get the feeling he's hiding something from me again?* I open my mouth to ask, when he pushes my chair in, then walks around to take his seat.

He raises the Champagne bottle and pops the cork. He pours the sparkling liquid into my flute and places it back in the bucket before pouring sparking water for himself. He raises his glass, and when I mirror his action, he clinks his glass with mine. "To you, my wife."

36

Nate

Her breath hitches, and a blush coats her cheeks. She likes it when I call her my wife, and fuck, if I don't love the sound of it from my lips. She raises her glass and takes a sip, then makes a sound of approval in her throat. My cock twitches, and my thigh muscles bunch. Those little noises she makes are going to snap my restraint. I knock back the rest of my water like its tequila, and wish it burned its way down my throat. Unfortunately, the sparkling water is much softer. Yet, as I watch her tuck into the salad, as she licks the vinaigrette from her lips, the sight of her pink tongue unbalances me enough that I lose my hold on my glass. I manage to catch it before it crashes into the table, then place it down with exaggerated care. I take a few mouthfuls of my own appetizer. Not because the food isn't delicious, but because my mind is racing ahead with thoughts of the many different ways, I'm going to fuck her tonight, I give up all pretense of eating and watch her.

She wipes up the dressing on her plate with a piece of bread, then flicks a look in my direction. Whatever she sees on my face has her cheeks turning pink. "What?" she grumbles.

"You have something, here—" I reach out and scoop up a drop of the vinaigrette from her lower lip, bringing it to my mouth to suck on my finger.

Her eyelids grow heavy. Our gazes catch, hold. The air between us grows electric. She swallows, reaches for her glass of Champagne and takes a sip. When she places it down, I top her up, and refill my glass of water. I rise, walk around, and swap out her now empty appetizer plate with the entrée.

She seems amused by my gesture. "You playing at being my waiter?"

"I'd be happy to wait on you hand and foot for the rest of my life."

Her lips part, and her expression softens. "You're a closet romantic." Her tone is almost accusing.

"Because I like to take care of you?"

"Exactly." Her eyebrows knit. "When I think of how much I hated you all these years... Maybe I still do, because you're so effortlessly charming, it's unfair."

"Can't help it if I'm naturally charismatic." I smirk.

"A-n-d there he is." She waves an arm in the air. "And just as I was starting to think you're more likable than you let on."

"Don't make that mistake. I'm not the kind of man you want to develop feelings for."

I wince. I want her in my life. I want to bind her to me so she never leaves, yet every time I sense her getting close, I say something to push her away. Something inside me is resistant to the idea. Perhaps it's my time on missions where I've had to be hyper vigilant about everyone and everything around me that's ingrained this deep sense of mistrust. The only person I let myself rely on was Ben, and I failed him. I can't fail his sister. Already, I feel too much for her. Already, fucking her has made me feel closer to her than anyone else. Already, I'm losing my perspective when it comes to her. And if I lose my edge, it's not long before I fail her in some way.

She firms her lips. "Well then, you shouldn't fuck me like it means something."

I tilt my head. "It does mean something. It means *everything* when we fuck." *And that is the problem.* When I'm around her, I can't think straight. I lose all sense of time and place. I lose the ability to ensure nothing ever happens to her.

I round the table and slide back into my chair, then reach for my own entrée. It was kind of James to make the chicken just how I like it, but right now, I might as well be eating mud, for all the taste I have in my mouth. Nevertheless, it is my wedding dinner, so I manage to scoop a few forkfuls into my mouth. When I look up next, it's to find an intense expression on her features.

"Why do you say that?"

I set down my fork, then pat at the corners of my mouth with a napkin before dropping it at the side of my plate. "Because it's true. Because in all these years, I've never fucked a woman while I looked into her eyes."

"Oh." She seems taken aback, then reaches for her Champagne and takes a sip. "I think you're telling the truth."

I'm about to say I don't lie, then realize, that's not true. Not anymore. So, I settle for tossing back the rest of my sparkling water, before topping myself up again.

"I guess the advantage of your not drinking any alcohol is that, uh... that... You know—"

"My performance won't be hampered in any way?" I look at her from under my eyelashes.

"Exactly." She tips up her chin, as if to counter the blush on her cheeks.

How did I get so lucky, to end up with a woman who has that core of innocence at heart? And this, despite her being an entrepreneur and taking care of a man she's as close to as her own brother.

How can I think of living without her? Is there any way she won't leave me when the truth comes out? Maybe. If I own up and tell her everything now... If I stop with the lies and tell her why I did it. If I don't delay the inevitable and let her decide for herself that what I did was for her own good. But it's too early to do that. We've only just gotten married. If I had a month or, at least, a couple of weeks to consolidate our relationship... And then, once I've made sure she's been added to the Davenport's list of successors in G-Pa's estate... Once her future is taken care of... I can tell her everything. Then, no matter what she decides about us, I'll be able to rest easy.

"When it comes to you, it's the opposite, that's the problem."

"Eh?"

"There's not a moment when I haven't thought of you in these past years. There hasn't been a single night when I haven't wished you were next to me. There's not a single morning I haven't woken wishing I was buried inside of you. I've fucked you exactly three-thousand six-hundred fifty times in my head since the day I kissed you."

She gapes. "But... How could you... I mean, how did you—"

"Keep count?"

She nods.

"It's easy when you've yearned for someone, and cursed yourself for it, and tried to stop yourself from thinking of them, only to have your dreams betray you, for they're filled with images of the one person who's off limits."

"Yet, here we are," she says softly.

And it's how I've let down Ben. Losing any appetite I had left, I place my fork on my plate and push it aside. She rises to her feet, begins to walk around, then winces. I frown, but before I can ask if she's okay, she places the dessert in front of me, then climbs into my lap.

"What are you doing?" I arch an eyebrow.

"Trying to cheer you up."

"Do I look like I needed cheering up?" I smirk.

"You looked like you were thinking of things that make you unhappy."

"They don't." I brush a strand of hair behind her ear. "They give me food for thought, is all. A reality check. But also, a realization."

"A realization?" She scoops up some of the sweet ricotta cheese with a fingertip and holds it out to me. I curl my fingers around her wrist, then close my mouth around her digit and lick it off.

Goosebumps snake up her skin. Her fingers tremble. The fact that I affect her so much shoots a burst of satisfaction down my spine. My cock thickens, and when her eyes widen, I know she feels it against her ample beautiful butt.

"That you mean the world to me. That when we part ways, my life will never be the same."

37

Skylar

"Why do you have to say that? Why are you convinced we'll separate?"

"Because this is but a marriage of convenience. We went into it, each of us, to get something specific. And once we get that, there's no need for us to be together, is there?" He peers into my face like he expects me to deny it. Like he wants me to say this is more than just an arrangement. Like he wants me to come out and tell him how I feel. It almost feels like a test, in some ways. Except for that insistent thrust of his cock into the valley between my butt cheeks, and the sparks in his eyes, and the way his biceps bulge and stretch his T-shirt, which tells me he's far from unaffected by our proximity. Then there's the way he cups my cheek and scowls. "Is there?"

I shake my head. "You're right. We went into this with our eyes open. Once my business is stable and Hugo is taken care of, and you've consolidated your role as CEO, there's no need for us to be together."

His features tighten. A pulse throbs at his jawline. He lowers his arm, only to lock it around my waist. "But I get the time until that happens. I'm your husband, you're my wife, and you'll satisfy my needs, isn't that right?"

I frown. *Where is this conversation going?* "If you mean, your kinky-fuckery stuff—"

"Which you happen to like."

"I do." I blush as I say it because, apparently, I'll never be able to discuss our sexual proclivities without feeling bashful. This man's been inside of me, and I can feel how aroused he is by me, and yet, I'm unable to come to terms with how much he wants me and how he wants to do all these erotic things to my body.

"And you'll tell me if you don't?" His gaze grows intense. "At any time, if you feel I'm going too far, you'll speak up?"

I nod slowly. "Am I not supposed to have a safe word for it?"

He considers my question for a few seconds. "By now you know, I have a primal fetish." He pauses... *Clocking my response?* "But I sometimes lean toward sadism."

I draw in a sharp breath. I skirted around that word in my head, mainly because thinking of it made my situation too real. But hearing it from his mouth sends a pulse of desire thrumming through my veins. I've wanted to know about this world. Wanted to know how it would be to be dominated. I resorted to books, mainly because I didn't have the time or the energy for hookups.

In school, I was the geeky nerd, the one who salivated at the jocks from afar, but never had the courage to approach them; and they definitely never noticed me. The couple of boyfriends I had were more interested in taking my virginity than anything else. Besides, their fumbling didn't exactly give me the confidence they knew what they were doing. And then, I turned eighteen and kissed him. I immediately knew he was the one I'd give my virginity to. All of the other men I met paled in comparison.

A year later my mother passed away. And when I moved to London and met Hugo he became the younger brother I never had. When he met with his accident, my life became all about staying afloat. Staying ahead of the responsibilities that came with caring for him, the sorrow I felt from losing my mother, and then Ben leaving on his tours, the frustration I felt at not being able to make my business a success...

When Nate walked into my life again, I was drowning. But seeing him fired up my desire to survive, to win, to reach for the goals I thought were no longer within reach. Sure, he frustrated me and made me angry, but that's what gave me the impetus to get ahead of my self-doubts. He kickstarted that desire in me to wake up each morning and want to do better than the previous day, and isn't that what the definition of living is? To look forward to each moment, to want to do more, to enjoy each second you're alive. That's what Nate has given me. He's changed my world; shown me a future I didn't know was possible. *Only… Is he going to be in it? I don't know.* But it's not going to stop me from enjoying the time I have with him. "The thought had crossed my mind, yes," I murmur.

"I love inflicting pain, but I adore it when it's on someone I care about. Feeling the flinch, hearing the gasp, seeing the marks on your flesh, inflicting pain on you, my wife, arouses me like nothing has before."

"Oh—" I swallow. "Is that good?"

"For me, yes. For you? Definitely. Because you're the recipient of my ministrations. You're the one who benefits from my teasing and taunting, and my chasing you—"

"Chasing? Because you love primal play?"

He nods. "It's the thrill of the chase. Apparently, being on a mission is what gets me going. And when the mission is to catch my woman and spank her and tie her up and take her to the edge a dozen times before I finally fuck her, it satisfies something in me."

"Especially when I resist?" Something in my subconscious pushes me to ask.

I know I'm on the right track when he strokes his chin and rumbles, "Especially when you give me a chance to overpower you and hold you down and touch you and learn every dip and hollow of your body and bring you to the edge again and again and deny you an orgasm so that when I finally allow it, it'll be the single most superlative experience in your life."

"Wow," I breathe. A thousand butterflies flutter in my belly. If he keeps up this dirty talk, I'm going to be a sodden mess.

"I may like inflicting pain, but I also remain human. I can often see when it's too much. But *often* isn't *always*. And I want you to feel free to speak to me. To tell me if you don't like something, or if we go too far. I want you to continuously communicate with me. I will keep checking in with you to make sure you're okay. And when you tell me to stop, I will."

"Just like that?"

"Just like that." He wraps his fingers about my nape of my neck and tilts my head, so I have no choice but to hold his gaze. "What do you say?"

38

Nate

"Yes," she says without hesitation, and it's enough to make me bend her over this table and take her from behind. But I won't. Because today is our wedding night, and she deserves it to be the most special one of her life.

"And you'll do as I ask of you?"

She nods again.

"And you'll let me fuck you in any hole I want."

This time, she purses her lips. "You mean, the one that shall not be named?"

"That, too." I smirk.

"You wouldn't be smirking if you were facing the prospect of having something stuck up your backside." She sniffs.

This time, I bark out a laugh. "You can say no."

"Hmm." She looks torn. "I would, except—"

"Except?"

"I have a sneaky feeling I might be missing out."

"You would." I slide my palm down to grab a handful of her wide backside. "When I bear down on your A-spot, while stimulating your G-spot—"

"Hold on, there's an A spot?" There's skepticism in her voice.

"Indeed, there is. And no, I'm not making it up. And when I stimulate both at the same time—"

"It's a double orgasm?"

"Or an O to the power of—" I let the sentence hang in the air.

She narrows her gaze on me. "You're not saying this just to—"

"Get in your backside? Nope, you can search for it online, if you want."

"Hmph." She flattens her palm over my chest, and I can feel the *bam-bam-bam* of my heart against it.

"Again, you have every right to say no, and—"

"That's so not fair."

"What's not fair?"

"You give me the choice, and that puts the onus on me, and it makes it very difficult for me to refuse, thanks to the FOMO I have around this."

"You're saying I shouldn't give you the choice?"

She blinks slowly. "I'm not sure."

"There's no shame in that. If you'd prefer for me to decide what's best for you and make decisions for you—"

"Wouldn't that be handing over all the power to you?"

"On the contrary, you hold the power. I'll do all the hard work. I'll interpret your needs and do everything in my power to satisfy you and make you feel good, and anytime you feel it's not working out, you just have to say stop."

"So you say."

"I mean it." I release my hold on her neck to hold up my hand. "Promise."

She looks between my eyes, and whatever she sees there must convince her, for she slowly nods. "Okay."

"Good girl." I press my lips to hers. She opens her mouth, and I sweep in my tongue, tasting the fruity notes of the Champagne and the tang of the vinaigrette, combined with the saltiness of the salmon she's eaten. And past that is that honeyed essence of her, which goes straight to my head. My breath catches in my chest, my pulse knocks at my temples, and when my balls tighten, I have to slide my thighs apart to accommodate the rush of blood to my nether regions. She presses her ample tits against me, and her erect nipples dig into my chest, which in turn, sets off a wave of need that washes over my cock.

"Jesus,"—I manage to tear my mouth away and press my forehead against hers—"one touch, and I can't stop until I've consumed you completely."

A moan bleeds from her lips, and it's so needy, so carnal, the lust in my blood skyrockets. I grip her hips and set her back on her feet to put some space between us.

"But I wanna kiss you." She sways toward me, but I grip her hips and stop her.

"Not yet, baby, and not tonight."

"What?" She stares.

"You're still sore. I took your virginity. I'm not selfish enough to want to fuck you again when you need time to recover."

She looks like she's about to protest, then glances away. "Of course, there's the hole whose name shall not be spoken."

"Not if it's going to add to your discomfort."

"How do you know I'm in discomfort?"

"Every time you walk, you wince. And not that it doesn't add to my ego, knowing it's the imprint of my cock inside you that you feel when you do, but I don't want you to be in so much pain that you don't enjoy it when I fuck you again."

Once more, there's that soft look in her eyes. "You're really a teddy bear, you know that?"

I lean back in my chair. "Not how I've been described before."

"You are. Also,"—she grabs a spoon and scoops up some of the chocolate from the lava cake—"I think you should taste this." She holds it to my mouth, and I lick the spoon clean. Her breath catches; her own lips part.

I take the spoon from her, set it aside, then use my finger to retrieve a dollop of the cake. I hold it out to her. "Open."

When she does, I slide it over her tongue, and when she sucks on my fingertip, lust grips my entire body. "I need to be inside you, baby. If you're not serious about what you said earlier—"

"I am." Her voice is breathless. Then, she unties the sash at her waist, and the robe slithers to the floor. Her hourglass figure is on display. Those tits, that waist, the flare of her hips, which only add to her appeal, those fleshy thighs, and between them, her glistening, swollen pussy lips.

As I stare at the flesh, a fat drop of cum slides down her inner thigh. I reach over, catch it with my fingertip, and bring it to my mouth. When I suck on it, her flavors mix with the chocolate, and my cock extends. I slide my hand inside the waistband of my sweats and pull it out. I pump it, and pre-cum squeezes out from the crown. She watches me jerk myself off, and I watch the gathering desire on her face. I run my thumb across the slit of my shaft and when I hold it out, she leans in and licks it off. Then closes her eyes as she swallows.

"It's salty and rich and umami." She opens her eyelids. "Who'd have thought you would have such a complex taste." Only a master baker like her could identify those individual flavors.

I make a circling motion with my forefinger. She slowly turns, and when she has her back to me, I can't stop myself from slapping her arse.

The sound echoes around the space, and she jumps. "Ouch!" She stares at me over her shoulder. "Why did you do that?"

"Because"—I rise to my feet—"this time, I will not be denied the pursuit."

"Pursuit?" She swallows.

"The hunt, the stalking, the tracking,"—I crack my neck—"the way I'm going to come after you now."

She takes a step forward, and another, and then she takes off.

39

Skylar

My heart bangs into my ribcage, and my blood pressure spikes. Once more, I'm naked and I'm being chased through my husband's house—I suppose I should start calling it my house—by my husband. Only this time, I know a little more about the reason behind it, and the fact that I enjoy it. That's why I'm not going to be caught out by him... Not quickly, at any rate.

I race into the hallway and toward the living room, then through to the conservatory and push open the doors. The sun has set, and lights dot the pathway that runs across the garden. I step out, shiver a bit, and hesitate. *Am I stupid stepping out when people on the hill can see me? Not to mention when the temperature is about to drop further and I don't have a stitch of clothing on? Bet he wouldn't expect me to do so, which is why I should do it. Right?*

There's a sound behind me. It prompts me to shut the door and step onto the patio, then down onto the garden path. I move forward and shiver. This was a stupid idea. I race forward, toward the hedges at the bottom of the garden, which are so tall, they block the sight of whatever is behind them. That's when I realize I'm in a maze. I glance over my shoulder once, hear footsteps approaching, and move forward. I jog down one path, then turn to the left, then the right, and again.

Footsteps speed up behind me. Then his voice rumbles, "I can hear you."

He's so close, I cry out, turn and look around, but can't see him. He's not behind me, but he must be nearby, on the other side of this green wall created by the hedge.

I face forward and keep going. His footsteps seem to fade, and then I burst into a clearing. There's a fountain in the center, and in the middle is the statue of a bird in flight. *A bird? Is that a... starling? Did he have it put up to remind him of me? Nah, not possible. Is it?*

I head toward it and stop when I'm in front of it. It's carved out of white marble, the wings spread out on either side of its body, its head lifted to the skies. Water pours out of the beak and falls back into the water. Each feather is so carefully carved, it seems to quiver in the breeze.

The blood is pumping through my veins, my pulse rate so high, the cold I felt earlier has been chased away. Heat rolls under my skin. A bead of sweat slides down the valley between my breasts. There's something so breathtaking about this statue, I can't stop looking at it.

I hear footsteps behind me and turn to face him. He walks toward me, his gait unhurried. He's naked, and his heavy cock sticks up from his crotch. I swallow, and my mouth fills with moisture. He's so hot, so freakin' sexy, the epitome of manliness, the height of masculinity. Pheromones swirl around him and seem to reach out to me.

My body temperature seems to turn up another notch, and despite standing outside without a stitch of clothing, it feels like I'm close to a furnace. He closes the distance to me, and I skitter back. I hit the wall of the fountain and freeze. He slows to a stop, jerks his chin to the side, and I don't give myself time to think. I burst into a run, around the fountain, into the hedge on the other side. I'm sure I can hear his footsteps echo through the maze. *No, no, no, I'm not going to let him catch me, not that quickly.*

I increase my speed, the dirt of the path digging into the soles of my feet, but I don't let up. I dart down one path, then another, and into a part of the maze which seems to be denser than the rest. The hedges on either side meet above me, and the sound of my footsteps is blanketed by the leaves lying on the ground. It would be completely dark, but for the faint moonlight that glows at the end of the green tunnel.

I rush out of it and cry out when he steps in my path. The momentum of my body carries me forward, and I crash into him. Skin against skin, hard muscles, ridged planes, and so much heat, I feel I've been scalded. I try to push away, but he throws me over his shoulder.

"Let me go." I begin to struggle in earnest, then yell when he slaps my butt.

"Got you." He stomps around and into what I see is a smaller clearing. There's a bench in the center and a small pond in front of it, teeming with koi and lit by lights at the bottom. He reaches the bench, sits down and throws me across his lap. "You did well, Starling."

I try to jump up but—*thwack-thwack-thwack*—the continuous spanking to my alternating butt cheeks arrows lust straight to my core. *No, no, no, I'm not giving in yet.* I manage to maneuver myself so I can sink my teeth into his thigh.

He doesn't even flinch. He merely places his heavy arm across my shoulders, so I'm rendered immobile. Then, he trails his fingers down my spine to the cleavage between my butt cheeks. A shiver grips me, and when he slides his fingers down to my slit, a whine bleeds from my lips.

"You're soaked, baby," his voice is hushed. He scoops up my cum and smears it around my forbidden hole. Those butterflies, which had taken flight in my belly earlier, soar to my extremities. My breasts hurt. Every part of me feels heavy and slow, like I'm swimming through honey.

"Nate, please," I whine.

"Tell me what you want, wife."

"Fuck me, husband, please."

I add the 'husband' because I've seen the effect it has on him, and I must succeed, for he stills. Then he removes his arm, and that's when I roll off of him. I hit the ground with a thud—*ow!*—but jump up and race off.

I must take him by surprise, for he doesn't lunge forward and grab me as I thought he would. But then, I hear his footsteps racing after me, and I know he did it merely to give me a head start. He really does like the chase. He wasn't kidding about that. I hear his footsteps draw closer and speed up.

"Run," he growls from somewhere so near, I yelp. I speed up even more, manage to round a corner, and keep running. His footsteps seem to fade. I look behind me to find he's not there. Huh? I slow down to a walk, my heartbeat ringing in my ears, my breath coming in pants. Sweat clings to my shoulders and trickles down my back. *Where is he?*

I reach the next turn, and the hair on the back of my neck rises. I stop, retrace my steps. *Nope, can't be.* My instincts blare, and the hair on my forearms rises in alarm, even as my pussy squeezes down on itself. *No, it's not possible.* I cry out, for he suddenly emerges from a narrow gap in the hedge I hadn't seen. "That's cheating!" I protest.

"When it comes to having you, I'll break all the rules. I'll set the world on fire if it means I can spend a few more minutes with you."

I throw up my hands. "You can't sweet talk me."

"Not trying to, not when I mean every word I say."

"You're trying to get in my good graces."

"Guilty as charged."

"You still haven't caught me." I continue to walk backward.

"Now I have." He lunges forward.

I cry out, turn and run.

40

Nate

Her butt twitches and jiggles as she begins to run, and for a few seconds, that heart-shaped behind of hers distracts me. But that iron focus, which has been my hallmark throughout my military career, kicks in. I race forward, closing the distance to her. She looks at me over her shoulder, yelps, then lowers her head and speeds up. I'm almost upon her, when she turns and charges me. I'll admit that takes me by surprise.

My Starling is putting up a fight, and that only makes her even more desirable. She feints to the right, I mirror her move, and that's when she darts to the left and past me. And I let her. I let her race forward for a few seconds, enough to make her think she's gotten away. Then I put on a burst of speed and reach her. Grabbing her around her waist, I twist her body up and over my shoulder.

"What the—" She tries to break free, but I increase the pressure around her thighs, then slap her gorgeous butt for good measure. "Let me the hell go," she snarls.

"Not happening."

She tries to dig her knees into my chest, and succeeds, enough to surprise a breath out of me. But then I squeeze her butt, hard enough for her to cry out, and when I massage the curved flesh, a full body quake runs through her. She continues to protest, though; manages to bury her fists a couple of times into my back, too.

I reach the marble bench facing the fountain with the starling and lower her onto it, on her front. When she resists, I slap her arse. She cries out, and I take advantage of her surprise to push her legs apart so she's straddling the bench. Then I follow her down, so my front is plastered to her back. She shivers, pants, grunts, and tries to break free. That's when I lower my head and dig my teeth into the curve where her shoulder meets her neck.

"Oh, my god." She throws her head back and into the crook of my shoulder. I reach around, cover her breasts, and squeeze.

She jolts, then throws her arm back and around my neck. She arches her tits into my palms.

"So fucking beautiful." I massage her breasts, then pinch down on both nipples. She groans, trying half-heartedly to pull away. That's when I release her, then slide back and flatten my palm into the small of her back. I apply enough pressure that she's forced to bend over.

She pushes her cheek into the bench, then turns and scowls at me. "What are you doing?"

"Preparing you for my penetration, of course."

Her eyes grow wide. "B-b-b... Don't you need lube?"

"I have lube." I scoop up the cum from the crown of my cock and smear it around her forbidden entrance. She gasps, then tries to wriggle away, but there's no escape. I keep my hand on her back and hold her steady, then use the moisture dripping from her cunt to ease my finger into her back hole.

"Oh god." She closes her eyes and pants. "That feels..."

"Good?"

"Different."

"Just wait until you have my cock there, baby."

She opens her eyelids and glares at me. "You're trying to scare me."

"Am I succeeding?"

"It's going to h-hurt?" she stutters.

"I hope so." I smirk.

She scowls. "You're an asshole."

"I'm going to be inside your arsehole, actually."

"Fuck you," she spits out, and I laugh.

She's so fucking delightful when she fights back. It's this version of Starling that I fell for. I walked away after kissing her, and she flew at me, and raged, and I fell head-over-heels in love with her. Go figure.

So, when I saw her at the bakery and found her on the defensive and sad and desperate, I hated it. I wasn't happy when she accepted the marriage arrangement without demurring. Apparently, she needed this little mock fight to find her mettle, and fuck, if I'm not going to be the beneficiary of it.

I slide closer, fit the head of my cock to her opening, and she stills. Her muscles seize up. I massage her shoulders, her neck, and when she relaxes, I slip inside and past the ring of muscle that resisted me.

"You feel so big," she whines.

"Shh." I grit my teeth to stay where I am. Sweat drips from my forehead, down my temple and onto her back. She shivers. I shudder. "Let me in, baby. I promise, it's going to be so good for you."

She groans, then begins to hump the bench.

"That's it, get yourself off. Push your little clit into the stone and let it arouse you further."

She whimpers, then sighs.

I slide my finger under her breast and pinch her nipple. She clamps down on my cock, and it's such a strong chokehold, I almost come. I grip the base of my cock and stop myself, then bend and kiss the nape of her neck, her shoulders, slide my fingers into her hair, and massage her scalp. She relaxes again, and I slide in further. "That's it, just a few more inches."

She half laughs, half cries. "I fucking hate you."

"I love you." I close my mouth over hers and absorb her cries, even as I hold her in place and pull out, then tilt my hips and breach her again. This time, I sink in all the way to my hilt. I growl, and her cry joins mine. I pant as I stay still, allowing her to adjust. She gasps, then mewls. I push her hair to the side. "You okay, darling?"

She swallows, then slowly nods.

"A few seconds, then I promise, it'll get better." I kiss her nose, her cheek, her eyelid over the eye I can see. Then back to her lips, where I lick her mouth.

Her lips curve. "You're messy."

"And you make me so fucking horny."

I pull out again, and this time, when I propel my hips forward, she pushes back to meet me.

41

Skylar

He thrusts into me, and this time, hits a spot inside of me that sends vibrations up my spine. My arms tremble, and I have to hold onto the edge of the bench to stop myself from overbalancing. Not that he'd let me, for he has his fingers around my throat in a possessive clasp. The stone is smooth under me and cold to my overheated skin.

Then he pulls out, rises to his feet, and once again, maneuvers his body so my one leg is bent with the foot placed on the bench, the other is flat on the ground. In this position, he has my legs spread and can reach my pussy, which he does right away when he stuffs two fingers into my slit. I groan and squeeze my eyes shut, then gasp when I feel his cock once again at my back entrance. He pushes aside my hair with his chin and presses a kiss to my neck, up to my ear, and when he nibbles on my earlobe, everything inside me melts. That's when he impales me again.

I'm lubricated enough for him to slip all the way in, and when he hits my A-spot, then adds a third finger inside my pussy and works them in and out of me and hits my G spot, I see stars. The orgasm crashes over me with no build up. My limbs shake, my toes curl, and even the ends of my hair seem to feel the sparks of heat and lust and sensations that sweep through me. I'm faintly aware of him groaning as he empties himself inside me. And then my knees give way as I allow the darkness to swallow me up.

I sense him pulling out, then he planks over me. The heat from his body pours over me, and beads of sweat pop on my forehead. He straightens, only to lift me up, and carry me. Then the softness of the sheets cover me. I snuggle into the pillowy softness, but before I can let sleep overcome me, I mumble, "The statue of the Starling... Did you—"

"Have it installed because it'd remind me of you? Yes." There's a touch on my forehead, and I know he kissed me. I smile and drift off. When I open my eyes next, it's still dark. He sits next to me on the bed.

"Skye, baby, wake up."

"Hmm?" I yawn. "What is it?"

"How are you feeling?" He reaches over and switches on the lamp.

I wince as my eyes adjust. "I'm good." I yawn, then wince again when every muscle in my body protests. "Maybe a little sore." I sit up, then take the glass of water he hands me. I chug down most of it, then return it to him. He places it on the bedside table, then holds out my phone. "It vibrated while you were sleeping, and kept vibrating over and over again, so I took the call."

"Oh?" I look at the screen and notice the missed calls and the voice mails. I raise the phone to my ear and listen to the first one, then the next, and the third. The blood drains from my features. "Hugo, I need to go to him."

"I'll take you."

"Apparently, he became violent, threw things around, attacked an orderly, then collapsed." The doctor's gaze flicks to the man standing silently next to me, then back to my face. "He's stable now."

The scent of antiseptic stings my nose. The fluorescent lights from above bounce off the walls and hurt my eyes. A headache begins to drum at my temples, and I rub at them. Nathan drove to the hospital in record time. I'm sure he broke a few speed limits, but we weren't stopped by the police. Evidently, even the law bends to this guy. Or luck was on our side. Not that I'm feeling very lucky standing in this hospital corridor.

"I don't understand. Hugo has never been violent before. In fact, I've never seen him display any form of aggression, and he was doing so well."

The doctor's gaze grows sympathetic. "There are lots of things we don't understand about a traumatic brain injury. The brain has enough neural pathways that, sometimes, they fire in a way that causes this kind of behavior that doesn't follow a pattern."

I try to follow along with what he's saying, and my headache increases in intensity. "And you're saying he collapsed?" I move my hand to the back of my neck, trying to ease the tension.

"We're not sure exactly what caused it. We may never know, given how the brain works." He raises a shoulder. "All we can do is eliminate possibilities. There's nothing we can pinpoint as a cause for what happens. We have, however, changed his medication to better manage his symptoms, and hopefully, prevent such an outburst from happening again."

I glance past him into the room where I can make out the prone figure on the bed. At least he's not surrounded by tubes or machines. But for the fact we're in a hospital, he could simply be asleep.

"So he's going to be okay?"

"There's no change in his current condition," the doctor replies.

So that's not a no, but that's also not a yes. A shiver runs up my spine, and when Nathan wraps his arm around my shoulders, I move into the warmth of his chest. It's the first time I've had someone to lean on in such a situation. All this time taking care of Hugo, I didn't realize how lonely I felt, how overwhelming the situation really is. Just having someone here with me while I'm talking to the doctor gives me that reassurance I didn't realize I needed.

The doctor looks between us again. "There's a waiting room down the corridor. We'll let you know as soon as he regains consciousness."

"I'd prefer to stay with him in his room, if that's possible, so he sees me as soon as he wakes up." I lock my hands together.

The doctor nods, then turns and leaves.

Hugo was violent. Does that mean the care home wouldn't want him back? I hope not. "I… I need to call the care home."

"Probably best you call them in the morning. Also, why don't we move to the waiting room? You'll be more comfortable there?"

"No," I say with more force than necessary. "I want to make sure I'm here for him." *I can't be there for my brother through whatever hell he's going through on his tour. Surely, I can do this much for Hugo?*

So maybe I'm assuaging my guilt for leading my life as normal while my brother puts his at stake so I can be safe, but right now, I'm going to do what feels right. Which is staying with Hugo. I march inside the room, Nathan on my heels.

I take in the pale features of the young man on the bed. He's thinner than when I last saw him. There are hollows under his cheekbones. He's tall enough to fit the entire length of the bed. The result: he looks like he's made of all gangly arms and legs. And he looks so young. The headache begins to knock at the backs of my eyes. I rub my forehead and allow Nate to guide me to a chair next to Hugo's bed.

"Oh, Hugo,"—I place my hand on his—"I'm so sorry."

A tear squeezes out from the corner of my eye, and I swat at it. I'm not going to cry for him. Hugo's going to be fine. He has to be. "With a little bit of help, he could be back to baking daily. It's the one thing he's still good at. His talent is being wasted."

"Perhaps it's time to move him to a facility with those amenities, where he'll get a better quality of care."

"I looked into it, but all of the good ones in the city have waiting lists of up to a year." I rub the back of my neck.

"I'm sure I could make a few calls and find him space in the best one among them."

I look at him over my shoulder. A gooey feeling unfurls in my belly.

"Also... Weston happens to know the top brain surgeon in the country."

"He does?" Hope bubbles in my chest.

Nate nods. "I'm sure he'd agree to examine Hugo and come up with the best route to speed up his progress."

My heart contracts in my chest. That gooey feeling in my stomach combines with that euphoric feeling in my chest and spreads to the rest of my body. "You'd do that for Hugo?" I swallow.

His gaze is intense, and when he looks into my eyes, I'm sure he's touched my soul. "Of course. I'd do it for you; I know how much it would mean to you. And there should be some benefit to being a Davenport, right?" He quirks his lips. "Being part of this family opens doors, and if it can help Hugo—"

I release Hugo's hand, only to jump up to my feet, turn, and throw my arms around Nate's shoulders. I stand up on tiptoe and tip up my head, which still means I can only reach his chin, which I manage to kiss. "Thank you. You didn't need to offer to do that, but I'm glad you did."

I must take him by surprise, for he stiffens, then places his hands on my hips. He pulls me in, so my breasts are crushed to his chest, then lowers his head so our lips meet. Then, he proceeds to devour my mouth. I'm aware that we're in a hospital and Hugo's sleeping on the bed, but I seem unable to stop my body from responding. My nipples harden, my thighs quiver, and I'm so drenched, I'm sure my panties are soaking wet. When he finally releases me, I sway. He steadies me. "I'll arrange a time for us to take Hugo to see the specialist right away."

"But your job—"

"Is not more important than you. Nothing is more important than you and anything you hold dear."

A pressure builds behind my eyes. "Don't be so nice to me, please."

A strange look comes into his eyes. "You deserve this, Starling. You deserve every good thing to happen to you. You deserve this, and so much more."

I sniffle. "You're being too generous."

"You should know, I did not deposit the money in your account as a favor to you."

"No, you did it because we had an arrangement."

"And if you'd refused to marry me, I still would've transferred the money."

"What?" I stiffen. "Why would you do that?"

He cups my face. "It's what your business is worth. I see a lot of potential in your bakery. There's no reason why you couldn't expand to a chain across the country, and beyond. Soon."

I laugh. "Hold on. One step at a time. And first, I need to make sure Hugo's taken care of."

That strange look is back on his features.

"What?" I scowl.

He shakes his head, "You're so fucking generous. You always think of others first. You should learn to take care of yourself first."

"Isn't that what you're here for?"

His lips quirk. "That's the only job I want in my life. Speaking of..." He pulls out a strip of pills from his pocket and hands it over.

"Is that my migraine medication?" I take in the familiar packaging.

He nods. "I could tell you sensed one coming on."

"You could tell I was getting a migraine?" I manage to choke out the words.

"You were rubbing your forehead, baby—a clear sign you had a headache coming on. I make sure to carry your medication on-the-go, in case you need it."

My head spins, and this time, it's not the migraine. It's the fact that this man noticed something only my doctor knows about me. The fact that my 'marriage of convenience' husband made it his business to carry around my medication, should I need it.

"I know it's best taken while the migraine is in its early stages. That way, it fades faster." He heads out into the corridor and returns a few minutes later with a juice box.

"What else are you carrying in those pockets?" I joke.

"Only my love for you." He punches the straw into the hole and hands it to me, and my heart... It melts. Literally. He urges me to take the medicine, and once I've swallowed the pill, he sits down in the chair, then pulls me into his lap. I curl into his chest, and he strokes my hair.

"I'd have never guessed you were so tender, so thoughtful, so caring, so everything." I rub my cheek against his jacket. It's more erotic than the orgasms he pulls from my body. It denotes a level of intimacy I never thought I'd have in my life. He kisses the top of my head, and I close my eyes.

The next thing I know, I hear Hugo's soft, "Sky Pie?"

42

Nathan

"You want to bequeath all your money and assets to your wife?" Arthur frowns at me from under his bushy eyebrows. We're in his den at his place.

It's been two days since Hugo woke up in the hospital. He seemed to be absolutely fine and delighted to see Skylar. He was remorseful and told her he was sorry for the temper tantrum he'd thrown. Apparently, he remembered his meltdown.

He said it'd felt like he was having an out-of-body experience, like he was outside his body and watching himself have that blow up. He knew it was wrong but was unable to stop himself. He wanted to apologize to those he'd hurt. He proceeded to apologize to Skylar again, profusely. Then, he admitted he'd been pretending to swallow his medication for the last few days, instead, spitting them out, which might explain why he lost control.

Then, just like that, he transformed in front of our eyes. His voice shifted, becoming younger, his features softened, and he asked Skylar why she was there. It was like he'd switched off that aware part of his brain and lapsed into someone younger.

Skylar stiffened, but she didn't show her sadness on her face. She switched gears and spoke to Hugo like he was a child. Hugo referred to her as his older sister, and she played along. He slowly became aware he was in the hospital and wondered what had happened. By the time she finished explaining, he'd fallen asleep.

I got breakfast, both for her and Hugo, and while they were eating, I left the room to make some calls. By the time I rejoined them, I'd made the arrangements to move Hugo to an enhanced facility. While money alone wouldn't have been enough for such a quick turnaround, it's amazing what the Davenport name can get you in this city.

My wife called up his existing care home and explained to them that Hugo wouldn't be returning, and from what she told me, they were relieved. Not the least because there was a waiting list for people to take his place in the state-run place.

I arranged for a team to help with the transition, and as soon as they arrived, we set off toward the new establishment. There, I left my wife to help Hugo get settled in. I told her not to worry about the bakery, that along with the girl she'd hired, I'd arranged for a team to help her with interviewing more people, so she could get additional help behind the counter. When my wife seemed like she was on the verge of tears, I kissed her hard, thus distracting her, then told her I needed to get to the office. Enroute, I'd stopped at Arthur's place.

"You're sure about this?" He scrutinizes my features, as if trying to understand my intentions.

"She's my wife—"

"Of a few days."

"I've known her for almost ten years," I point out.

"True." He absent-mindedly pats Tiny's head. The big dog had walked into the den, and after sniffing me and making sure I scratched him behind his ear, he padded around to sit his butt next to Arthur's chair and watch our conversation, looking between the two of us like he could understand every word. "But you haven't been married for very long."

"You don't have to be married for years to know when something is right. I knew she was the one when I set eyes on her, and the feeling has only grown since she became my wife."

Arthur looks at me with something like shock. "Why, my boy, who'd have guessed there's a romantic underneath that bluster?" His eyes sparkle.

"Don't say I told you so—"

"I told you so," he says with satisfaction in his eyes.

Tiny adds a woof. I scowl at the big dog, who pants at me.

"Fine, I concede this. Maybe there's some method to your madness; or maybe, it's luck that your machinations paid off."

"Does it matter? You found your soul mate."

And it won't be long before she hates me, which is why it's important I get this contract drawn up and signed by Arthur. "There's one more thing."

"Oh?" As if he senses what's coming, and wants to prepare for it, he reaches into the humidor on his desk and pulls out a cigar. He offers it to me, and when I refuse, takes his time cutting off the tip, then places it between his lips and lights up. I shift in my seat as he blows out a puff of smoke, then leans back. "Let me guess. You want me to make sure I add her name to the list of Davenports who are eligible for the monthly allowance from the company? This would cement her status as one of the family, and should something happen to you, or god forbid, you decide to sever ties from us, she continues to benefit from the growth of the business."

I nod. "And if the business fails, for some reason, or is sold off—not that that's going to happen—"

"Of course not." He puffs out another cloud of smoke.

"—but on the outside possibility that it does, I want your word that she gets the proceeds of whatever settlement is reached."

He lowers his cigar and narrows his gaze. "Why, dear grandson, if I didn't trust you as much as I do, I'd say you're not above divesting the company." He smiles, a shrewd look about his eyes. "Not that you'd do that."

Fuck, I never planned on letting my intentions be this transparent. I must be losing my touch at the negotiating table. All that experience from bartering with the enemy and persuading them to release hostages has come to naught. Caught up in the emotion of the situation, with my heart not my own anymore, I wasn't thinking clearly. That's the only explanation for why I've given away my intentions to my grandfather. But no matter. I can salvage the situation and get what I want. Just as long as she's taken care of.

"What can I say, except that I like to think ahead? Strategy has always been my strong point. It's why you hired me to run the company."

"My choice was to have you and Edward run it together—"

"But he didn't want to have anything to do with the leadership role. So, I guess you're stuck with me."

He strokes his chin. "You want to ensure the love of your life is taken care of, no matter what happens to the business."

"Exactly."

"In fact, you probably had this in mind when you decided to marry her?"

"She is my wife and the sole beneficiary of my will. That should demonstrate how much I care for her. How much I believe in this marriage—"

"Despite your protests to the contrary—"

"—how much I have faith in us surviving the ups and downs of a marital relationship."

"Or perhaps... You're sure you won't stick around long enough to see these mythical ups and downs."

I lower my chin. "Why, Arthur, you've all but called me a traitor. Someone who's going to sell out the company, as well as leave his new wife."

"Aren't you?"

I laugh. "Why would I? I love my wife. The Davenports are my family. Why would I do anything to hurt either of them?"

"But what if you didn't have a choice?" He smiles sadly.

I frown, taking in the droop of his shoulders. Nope, he has no idea what I've done to get this far. And he definitely has no inkling of what I have in mind for the future. I open my mouth to reassure him, when his phone vibrates.

He looks at it and frowns. "Sorry, I need to take this."

He answers the call. There's a voice on the other side. I can't make out the words, but whatever that person says leads to the blood draining from his face.

Tiny must sense the change in his mood, for he barks, then jumps up, every muscle in his body rigid.

Arthur lowers his phone, then looks at me with dazed eyes. "He's coming home."

43

Skylar

"When do you finish work?"

My husband's features soften on my phone screen. "Soon, baby. How are the interviews going?"

It's been two weeks since we moved Hugo to a top-of-the-line facility—one with expansive grounds and separate, serviced apartments allocated to the residents, instead of rooms. And round-the-clock help with a patient to staff ratio of five to one. That means there's always someone looking in on them, including one person to check in with them as they sleep. That's what money can buy.

I should be grateful for it, and I am; Hugo is well looked after. Especially when my husband made sure to fix up the kitchen in his apartment, so he can practice his dishes, making sure there's someone watching over him when he does it, so he's safe. All of this was accomplished over the course of a week.

I've insisted on checking in on Hugo every day, spending time with him until I'm sure he's happy. And each night, I return home to the arms of my waiting husband. He started working from his home office, so he's always there when I return. And he takes care of me, too.

The first time I returned, he signed off of his video call mid-conversation, then bent me over his desk and fucked me. The second time, he pushed me to my knees and insisted I blow him while he was talking. It was both demeaning and hot, especially when he came down my throat, then kissed me and carried me to our room, and proceeded to fuck me while looking into my eyes in the way only he can.

Every night, he's shown me how innovative he can be when it comes to bringing me to climax... Or rather, edging me until he brings me to climax.

One night, he took me to the verge of orgasm over and over again.

Just thinking about it sends a wildfire of electricity humming across my nerve-endings. I manage to keep the blush off my features and lean back in the chair in my tiny office in the bakery. "The interviews are going well." I clear my throat. "I identified one team member from the ten candidates I met."

He whistles. "You've been busy."

"Not as much as you. When did you get the time to put in calls to the employment agency, so they'd not only put forward the CV's of eligible employees, but also talk to me first to ascertain my requirements, then prioritize me over their other clients?"

"I can be persuasive." He schools his face into an innocent expression.

"You mean, you didn't give them a choice?" I scoff.

A one-shouldered, casual shrug, and there's something in the way he's looking at me with just the right amount of casual boredom that tells me —"Hold on, you own that employment agency, so they had to prioritize your call?"

"You might be right," he concedes.

I laugh. "Why am I not surprised? In fact, I should have expected that." I should be grateful that he thought of the demands of my business and anticipated my needs again, just like he did with the migraine medication. But there's a part of me that can't help but feel resentful.

He must notice the dueling sentiments on my face, for he frowns. "What is it?"

I shake my head. "Nothing."

"Tell me," he murmurs.

When I hesitate, his gaze narrows. "Tell me, Starling." He lowers the tone of his voice, and the hushed dominance inherent in it causes a flurry of goosebumps to scatter across my skin. That cascade of electricity across my nerve-endings intensifies, and yet again, I manage to school my features into one of seriousness.

Apparently, I've learned a lot from my husband in the few weeks we've been living together. Namely, how to hide my emotions.

"I don't want to come across as ungrateful, but I also can't stop myself from thinking about how easy it is for you to make things happen. You wave a hand, and a company drops their current projects and prioritizes yours. You raise an eyebrow, and I have a line of people waiting outside my door to be interviewed. Do they even want the job, or were they promised money to pretend to be interested and—" I break off because he's flared his nostrils, and anger clings to the contours of his beautiful cheekbones.

"Are you implying I had to bribe people to come to you for an interview?"

I shift around in my seat. *Shit. Guess I shouldn't have said that? But it's the truth. And why should I be afraid of saying what's on my mind with him?* "I'm saying, because of who you are and how clever you are with your negotiations, people likely don't have a choice when you ask something of them." *Like I didn't when you asked me to marry you.*

I don't say that last line aloud, but he must hear the implication in my words, for the furrow between his eyebrows grows deeper. "I'm not going to apologize for who I am and how I get what I want."

You wanted me, and you got me.

"I did." He nods, doing that mind-reading thing again. Ugh! How does he always know what I'm thinking?

"And I want your talent to be seen and recognized by the world," he growls.

My treacherous heart flips at his praise. Those little bubbles of electricity cascade to my extremities.

"And you're selling yourself short again, if you think people don't want to work with you." He sets his jaw.

"Why would they want to work with me? I'm a little, one-woman, almost-bankrupt business—"

"—who makes the most delicious desserts in this city, probably in this country, and has the most innovative names, which are bound to be a hit with your audience, provided"—he holds up a finger—"they know about it. Which is why you need the team, so you can up your game—"

"Fine, got it. I know all the reasons. It still feels wrong that it should all come so easily, now that—"

"You're my wife?"

That cascade of desire under my skin, turns into an inferno. Jesus, he only has to say *my wife*, and I'll do anything he asks of me. My breathing grows shallow, and sweat beads my forehead. I can no longer keep my reaction off of my features, and he notices, for a sly look comes into his eyes. "Are you wet, wife?"

"What?" I squeak.

"Is your pussy moist and needy and yearning to be wrapped around your husband's big, hard, thick cock?"

Husband. He called himself *my* husband. Heat bursts through the pores of my skin like lava through a volcano, like steam gushing out from a geyser. And if I touch myself between my legs, no doubt, I'll find a pool of moisture dripping down my thighs.

"Touch yourself," he growls.

"What?" I glance around the little office. "Here?"

"There. Where anyone can walk in and find the boss writhing around her fingers and moaning my name."

"Ohmygod." The picture he paints is so hot, so erotic, so pornographic in its detail, that the heat spreads to my extremities. My toes curl, my scalp tingles, my fingertips tremble, and before I can stop myself, I've slid my fingers up my skirt and pushed aside the gusset of my panties. When I brush my clit, little jolts of electricity arch out to my nipples, which in turn, tighten into points of desire.

"Hmm…" He drags his thumb under his lip. "Now, slide four fingers inside yourself."

"Four?" I swallow.

"We both know, I'm at least twice that in girth, but it'll have to do. For now."

"For now?"

"Until I get there, I mean." He rises to his feet and exits his office.

"You're coming here?" I gape at him.

"My wife's horny and wants to get off. Of course, I'm coming to you."

That melting sensation in my chest becomes bigger and bigger and spreads to other parts of my body. I'm one hot, gooey mess, and every particle has little hearts drawn on them. That's how sweet and arousing this entire conversation is.

"I might be done by the time you get here," I murmur.

"I doubt it." He walks down the corridor. "Also, did I tell you to stop, wife?"

I shake my head.

"Keep going." His tone brooks no argument. The dominance in his words sparks a thrill of anticipation across my nerve-endings. I thrust four fingers inside myself, then gasp when I'm stretched around my digits. Of course, it's not the same as having his cock inside me, but when I begin to fuck myself with my fingers, tendrils of sensations course through my veins. I pant and grip the edge of my desk, allowing myself time to adjust when he urges me on again. "Don't stop." His harsh command sinks into my blood and arrows directly to my core. Something frantic begins to build inside of me. Something like a ticking time bomb, which begins to speed up, faster and faster.

On screen, he makes a noise like a groan and a growl and everything in between. "That's it. Keep that cunt hot and wet and lubricated for my cock."

"Oh, my god, you're so filthy," I gasp out.

His lips twist. "But you knew that when you threw yourself at me on your eighteenth birthday."

"Did not," I manage to choke out.

"What a little liar you are, Starling. Your big eyes practically ate me up as I walked toward you that day. You were wearing a frilly white dress that ended above your knees, with pink over-the-knees socks, black Mary Janes, and a pin holding up one side of your hair. A pin with Hello Kitty on it."

"You remember that?" I ask, surprised.

"I remember everything about that encounter. Especially how young you seemed, how innocent, and how everything about you was soft and pliable and waiting to be marked by someone. And knowing I was going to hell for hoping that man was going to be me."

"And now you are." I swallow.

He walks out of the elevator, climbs a few more stairs, and steps onto a terrace of sorts. And then, the *whump-whump-whump* of a chopper can be heard in the background. He slides in wireless earplugs, and the noise recedes.

"And every part of me is thankful for the moment I bartered a deal with you. I'm your first, and I'll forever be humbled you gave me that privilege."

"Virginity is notional," I scoff.

"Only a woman would say that." He smirks.

"Why is it so important to a man, anyway?"

"It's not the concept of purity, if that's what you're asking." He steps inside the chopper, then nods his chin at the pilot. The screen tilts as the helicopter takes off. "It's the fact that I am the only one who's been inside you. The only one who knows how your pussy feels around my shaft, the only one who knows how you taste. Call it primitive, or elementary, or base, or all of it, but knowing you've only been with me so far, that you're my wife, and only I can make you come, fills me with a sense of pride and possession, and a fuck-load of satisfaction, like nothing else can. Also, did I give you permission to stop?"

I shake my head, trying to wrap my mind around what he's telling me—the fact it means so much to him, the fact he's so grateful that I waited for him. And I did it because I wanted to. Because no one else would do, but him.

Because I've always known he's the one for me. Because really, there was no other possible reality in my life. Because I still can't believe this man, who's flying toward me across the city in a helicopter, because it would have taken too long if he'd taken a car, like everyone else—is mine. Because I'm his, only his. The thought sends a spurt of need lancing through me. "Nate, I need you."

"I'm almost there," he says in a grim voice.

"Me too."

"Don't you dare come without me," he snaps.

I circle my clit with my finger, and my body convulses, "Ohgod, ohgod, oh—"

"—Nate. Say it."

"Oh"—I curl my fingers inside myself, and the climax swells up my hips, up my spine—"Nate."

That's when the walls seem to shake. The *whump-whump-whump* of the helicopter definitely sounds closer.

"Don't you dare come," he growls at me as he shoves open the door of the helicopter, then races down the steps. A part of me registers that he's landed in the middle of the road, and that he's headed across the sidewalk and is now pushing open the door. I hear the familiar tinkle of the doorbell over the entrance, then the voice of my employee asking him to stop, before the sound of footsteps approach, the door to my office is shoved open with such force it almost flies off the hinges, and then he's there.

44

Nathan

"Sir, you can't be here." Her sales assistant hovers behind me.

"That's my wife," I growl without moving.

I walked into the bakery, barged past the surprised sales assistant, and headed to her office, threw open the door and paused.

She's seated behind her desk. Her features are flushed, her back is straight, but the tell-tale movement of her arm gives away the fact she's engaged in something else.

"Skylar," the salesperson behind me yells, "are you okay?"

"Yes." Starling clears her throat, then in a strong voice says, "He's telling the truth. He's my husband."

"Oh, okay."

I sense the woman behind me backing away. That's when I step in, shut the door behind me and lock it.

"You came." Her voice is breathless.

"You didn't." I prowl toward her, rounding the table as her movements get more frantic. She throws her head back, showing off the creamy length of her throat. Her tits stretch the blouse she's wearing. The neckline dips enough to show off her gorgeous cleavage.

"I'm going to —"

"You will not come until I give you permission," I say, almost gently—confident her body will obey me, knowing she's trying her best to reach the edge of this climax, which holds her in thrall—absolutely fucking adoring every inch of her curvy, plus-size body, and her beautiful hair, and the dip of her waist, and the flare of her hips, and most of all, her big heart. Her generosity of spirit, which insists she put everyone else before herself. It's this quality that wouldn't allow her to stop Ben from pursuing his dream. And now, she's trying to fill that gap in her life by taking care of Hugo. The least I can do is give her enough orgasms and make her happy.

"But, Nate, I wanna." She looks at me from under her heavy eyelids, and continues to fuck herself, only it's clear her orgasm isn't progressing. Her expression turns fierce, and she shoves her fingers in and out of her cunt. A squelching sound fills the air; that's how wet she is. Also, her scent—the complex perfume of wet pussy tinged with the sweet yearning of her arousal permeates the air. It sinks into my blood and tightens my groin, until I'm sure my cock is going to burst out of my pants. And still, she doesn't come. Not even when I walk over to her, push down her panties, then circle my fingers around her wrist and hold her hand in place. I twist her wrist, knowing it will cause her fingers to curve against her pussy walls. I'm rewarded by a mewl.

"Your body knows who its master is, baby." I begin to fuck her with her own fingers, moving them in and out of her. The trembling begins anew in her body, and when she whimpers, I'm there with my mouth over hers to absorb the sound. I slide my tongue over hers, drink from her, and hold her gaze with mine, seeing the need inside her to come. Then, I plant my bulk between her legs. I sink down to my knees, and pulling her fingers from her cunt, bring them to my mouth and suck on them.

Her pupils dilate, and she parts her lips, but seems incapable of speaking. And when I lick my lips, she draws in a sharp breath. I ease her panties down her legs and pocket the scrap of cloth. Then I hook my arm under her knee and push her leg up and over the arm of her chair. When I look down, her plump pussy lips glisten at me. And when I bend and lick her from back hole to clit, she sinks back in her chair. I begin to eat her out in earnest, flicking my tongue in and out of her sopping wet slit, and when I suck on the nub of her clit, she cries out, "Nate!"

My name from her mouth drives me over the edge. I grip her around the waist, rise to my feet, lifting her with me, then plant her on her table. I carefully push her laptop to the side, and shove at everything else. Papers flutter to the floor, a notepad crashes, some pens, her phone. I kick her chair aside, and it overbalances with a crash.

She blinks, but otherwise, doesn't react. Only when I notch myself at her opening, does she wrap her legs around my waist. "Nate," she whispers.

"I'm going to fuck you now."

Before she can react, I'm buried inside her in one smooth move.

She cries out.

I wait there, throbbing, pulsing inside her. Each breach is echoed by the loving clasp of her pussy around my cock. Each thump of my beating heart is mirrored by the pulse at the base of her neck. I push my nose into the curve of her shoulder, take a long sniff, then bite down through the fabric of her dress.

She wails, and the sound causes my dick to jump inside her.

I push her back to lie on the desk, then twist one of her arms up and over her head. I pin it to the surface, then the other, before locking them in place with my hand. With the other, I cup her breast, then give into temptation and lock my mouth around her nipple. I bite down again, and this time, she whimpers. I pull down on her dress, so her tit is bared, then suck on her reddened nipple. She shudders, tries to pull her hands from my grip, but I don't release her. I place my face over hers, looking her deeply in the eyes. Then I pull out and ram into her with enough force that the entire desk screeches and moves forward.

"My... My employee will know what's going on."

"I'll pay her off."

"Money can't buy everything." She holds my gaze. "Definitely not love."

"Maybe not forever, but right now, it's you and me, and there's nothing between us."

A shadow crosses her features, but she seems to shake it off. "Only us."

I begin to fuck her more intensely. Each time I bury myself in her, her entire body jolts. Each time I pull out, my body misses her. All of my blood is in my balls. There's nothing left of me to give to her. Nothing except my cum. I pull out, and this time, when I thrust into her, I hit that spot deep inside her. She begins to shiver and tightens her hold around my waist, as I continue to stuff myself into her channel, continue to brush up against that sweet secret spot of hers, over and over, until tears squeeze out from the corners of her eyes.

"Please, please, please," she chants.

And I can't hold back. I lower my face until our noses bump, and our breaths mingle, and my lips brush hers. "Come with me."

She shatters, and I absorb her cries and fuck her through her aftershocks, until I follow her over the edge. My orgasm goes on and on, and when I'm finally spent, I bury my face in the curve of her shoulder. Only then do I realize, I didn't use a condom.

45

Skylar

"Fuck, fuck, fuck." He pulls out of me. "I shouldn't have come inside you without protection." He looks down to where his cum, and mine, I'm sure, drips down my thighs. His features tighten, his lips curl, then as if he can't help himself, he pushes the moisture back inside me. "But now that I have, there's no going back."

"There isn't any going back for me, either."

He glances up at me, and a resolute look settles on his features. "Promise me, you'll always trust me."

"Of course, I trust you."

He scoops up some of the mixture from my pussy, then paints it on my lips. "Even when it seems you can't, especially when you're sure you can't... It's then, I want you to remember this conversation. Remember the taste of us on your tongue."

I lick my lips and the salty-sweet, tangy taste fills my senses. "I'll never forget it."

"The weight of my body on yours." He pushes his hips into mine, so his cock settles into the space between my thighs. "Remember that."

"It's imprinted into me." I tug on my arms, and he releases me.

I cup his cheek. "What are you not telling me, Nate?"

He opens his mouth, then shuts it. "I want to tell you everything, but I can't." There's something tortured in his eyes, something that raises the hairs on the back of my neck. "It's not time yet."

"I'm so confused." I look between those beloved mismatched eyes of his. "I'm not sure what you're trying to tell me."

He looks away and seems to compose himself. When he looks back at me, his gaze is clear again. "You'll know everything when the time is right, I promise."

I told him I trust him, but for the first time, tendrils of doubt slither across my mind. *What is happening? What is going on with him? Does he really love me? Is that what this is about?* "Is there something about Hugo's condition that you're not telling me?"

"Hugo?" He frowns. "No, of course not. You consulted with the doctors; you know everything there is to know."

I relax slightly. "Okay."

"Okay." He straightens, then pulls my panties back into place, before tugging my dress down to cover my thighs. "You'll let me know if there are any... consequences?"

He pulls me up to sitting and I tilt my head. "You mean, if I get pregnant?"

His jaw stiffens, then he jerks his chin.

"Are you worried I might be pregnant?"

"If you are... We'll deal with it."

"Hold on." I push at him, but of course, he refuses to step away. "What do you mean, deal with it?"

"I mean, we'll figure out what to do about it."

"It... You mean your child and mine?"

"It's hypothetical at this moment, but that's what I mean, yes." He rubs the back of his neck. "I don't want to make a big deal out of it. There's probably nothing here to discuss, but if you are —"

"Then I'd be so very happy. Wouldn't you?"

He looks away again, then takes a step back. And the cold air seems to rush in between us.

"Nate?" I slide off the desk, then draw in a sharp breath when the cum slides down between my legs. He turns to me at once. His sharp, heterochromatic gaze must follow mine to where I'm staring at the moisture that glistens below the hem of my dress.

"Jesus," he breaths, then once more, sinks down to his knees. "Fuck." He wraps his thick fingers round each of my calves, his digits long enough to meet around the other side, and it's not like my legs are on the slimmer side, either. But the way he slides his fingers up, until he's able to scoop up the trail of liquid, makes me feel fragile and ethereal. But I've always felt delicate with him. The way he handles my body with care, but also with a confidence that says he's comfortable with my size, does wonders for my self-confidence. It's only with him, I feel myself. It's only around him, I can act like I'm normal size and not fat. Oh, I'm good at putting on an act in front of everyone, but there are still times when I look at the mirror and wish I was an M, if not a S.

He brings his finger to his mouth and sucks on it, and I can almost taste our joined-up cum.

"I'm sorry." He looks up at me from his position at my knees. "I'm a selfish bastard. I should be worried about how you feel that I was bareback inside you. Instead, all I can focus on is my hang ups."

"For the record, I'm happy you didn't use a condom."

"For the record, I'm fucking turned on that you're going to be walking around all evening with my cum dripping out of your cunt."

And just like that, sparks unfurl again in my belly.

"So, you'll be fine if I'm pregnant?"

His gaze widens, before those damn shutters come down over his eyes. "We'll cross that bridge when we come to it." He smooths my skirt down, then stands, so once again, he's towering over me. "Arthur's expecting us at the 7A Club."

"The 7A Club?"

"For some reason, it's not his place today, and he wants the family together." He raises his shoulders.

"I can't leave my employee to close the shop again."

"She's doing well, so far, isn't she?"

"She is," I acknowledge.

"And you have the money to pay her overtime."

"I...do," I say slowly.

"Bet she'll be happy for the extra cash."

"Do you always have to be so annoyingly right?"

"Not always." He takes my hand in his, and bringing it to his mouth, kisses my knuckles. "Though, I wish I were."

And there it is again—cryptic words, that hidden expression in his eyes. I open my mouth to ask him about it, but he shakes his head. "Not this evening. I promise, I'll tell you when the time is right."

I don't want to let it go; I don't. But it's not like belaboring the point is going to help me, either. If anything, it's making him pull away from me further. So I nod. "Not this evening."

"Good." He hooks my arm through his. "Ready to leave?"

No, we didn't take the whirly-bird, which had, apparently, taken off at some point when he was inside me. And it's a good thing, too, else it would've resulted in a traffic jam. Instead, his car and the driver, who I now recognize, were waiting for us at the curb.

And yes, my employee was only too happy to close up. She was thrilled at the prospect of overtime pay, and she didn't show any reaction to the sounds she must have heard from my office. No doubt, she's going to gossip about it to her friends, but whatever. What I don't know won't hurt me, right?

On the ride over, he busied himself on his phone. Looking at his hard profile, it was difficult to reconcile this emotionless, distant man with the one who took a helicopter across town, just so he could get his wife off.

Is the prospect of having a child that worrying for him? And yet, he was turned on by the sight of his cum leaking out of my pussy. So why is he being so aloof now?

I reach for my phone, mostly to stop myself from saying anything to him. There are a series of messages from the girls in our shared chat group.

> Zoey: I know you're in post-marital bliss but you're not allowed to forget your friends *crying face emoji*
>
> Grace: Girl that was the most beautiful ceremony ever and I can't get over how your husband couldn't wait to get you out of there to consummate the wedding! *eggplant emoji, cat emoji, sweat emoji* Enjoy!!!! But I want to know all the details.
>
> Harper: I'm so sorry I missed it. I am so pissed at my boss right now! I can't believe he refused to give me the day off!!! *angry face emoji*
>
> Me: Haven't forgotten you guys... Okay so maybe I did forget everyone and everything for a few minutes there but... You know how it is. *winking emoji* And no I'm absolutely not sharing those details. Harper I missed you too. Look on the positive side. Your boss couldn't do without you for even a day which means he needs you which is always a good thing. Oh and Grace? It's more like *snake emoji, peach emoji, hand emoji*

· · ·

The three dots at the bottom of the group begin to jump around at once. I'll bet that's Zoey or Grace; those two are never far from their phones. Unlike Harper, who, like me, doesn't look at her phone when she's in the kitchen.

"What's so funny?" I glance up to find my husband watching me.

I put my phone away at once. Not that I have anything to feel guilty about, but considering I was describing the fully-loaded, XXL-sized banana split he sports between his thighs, I can't stop myself from reddening.

"Nothing's funny." I cough into my hand. "What gave you that idea?"

"You were chuckling to yourself."

"Was I?" I school my features into a look of what I hope looks like innocence. "I have a bad habit of talking to myself."

"Hmm." His lips twist, and something tells me I am not fooling him.

"How are you friends, by the way?" he drawls.

I blush all the way to the roots of my hair. "M-my friends?"

"You're talking to them, aren't you?"

I nod dumbly. Surely, he doesn't know what we were discussing?

"Give them my regards."

"I will," I squeak.

Thankfully, he goes back to whatever it was he was doing on his phone and doesn't ask me any more questions. Some of the tension drains from my shoulders.

"Do you meet Arthur and your brothers—"

"—half-brothers," he corrects me.

"Half-brothers. Do you meet them often?"

"Arthur wants us to have lunch as a family on the weekends."

Of course, being in the service industry, every day is a working day. In fact, Sundays are when I make a lot of sales from families who are out and about. It's another thing I didn't fully understand when I started this business. It's like having a real-life baby. You can never leave home, unless there's someone tending the baby—I mean, bakery—for the day. Most days, I don't mind, but sometimes, I want to sleep late on a weekend and just be lazy.

And now, with the team I've hired, I can do that, from time to time. Honestly, the morning prep is so essential, I don't like to miss it. But most days, I don't even have to close, the staff takes care of that. And it's thanks to him giving me the money to hire them, and then he went a step further by arranging for me to interview the prospective candidates. It facilitated the process and helped me onboard the team in a much shorter time than I thought possible.

He's so thoughtful, and that's so unexpected. Given his gruff, sometimes distant persona, I never did expect him to be this caring. And he shows me he is at every turn. *So, why can't he share whatever it is that's weighing on his mind? Is it something that's going to upset me? Could it be an ex-girlfriend or an ex-wife, even?* I never asked him if he was married before.

"Were you married before?"

"What?" He blinks.

"Do you have an ex-wife? Or someone you fell in love with before? Is that what you want to tell me?"

He finishes whatever he's typing into his phone, then puts it away before turning to me. "You are the only woman I've ever loved. The only one I ever *will* love. You're it for me. Why can't you accept that?"

46

Nathan

"I..." She swallows. "I... guess, I'm still having trouble accepting that you want me. I know you find me attractive, I know you like my curves, or so you've told me, but—"

"You don't believe me."

She wriggles around in her seat. "I do believe you, but—"

"But you're not entirely convinced."

"Some part of me thinks you asked me to marry you out of some misplaced notion of responsibility to my brother. I'm sure he made you promise to take care of me before he went off on his mission."

Something in my features must give me away for she nods. "That's what I thought."

"He did ask me to take care of you, but that's not the only reason I asked you to marry me."

"So, you did it because you needed a wife, and I was available."

"That, too, but it's not only these logical reasons you're trying to fix on my intentions."

"You're a logical man."

"I am," I agree.

"And you wanted to consolidate your position in the company by getting married."

"And I loved you. I wanted to make sure I kept you near, and this seemed like the best way to tick all these boxes."

The skin between her eyebrows wrinkles. "So, I'm a box to tick?"

I blow out a breath. Heaven help me from a woman's reasoning and need to know everything all at once. I take her left palm in mine and run my thumb across her wedding ring. "You know you're more than that. I haven't hidden what you mean to me."

"And I'm trying to understand why you turned up in my life now, when my bakery was floundering, and I was looking for help. The timing was auspicious, you have to agree."

"I suspect Arthur knew of our prior connection and wanted to set things up so the two of us would get together."

"Arthur would do that?" Her frown deepens.

"He says he wasn't aware we knew each other, but given his machinations with Edward, and how much he wants us to settle down, I wouldn't put it past him."

"So, you had no idea you were going to meet me that day?"

"I did. I had been determined to keep my distance from you, but when I saw you face-to-face, I knew I couldn't let you go... Not without finding a way to help you."

"And now?" She searches my features. "Do you feel the same way?"

"I'll never feel differently about you." *Not even when you come to hate me for what I did and decide to leave.*

The car pulls up in front of the 7A Club.

I release her hand, get out of the car, then walk around to open the door for her. I help her out, then kiss her forehead. "I love you. Don't ever forget that."

"Anyone know why the old man asked us to meet here?" Knox drawls from his position by the window. Of course he'd be by the window. My half-brother isn't the kind to want to be anywhere near the rest of his family if he can possibly keep away. He's positioned himself so his features are in shadow while the evening sunlight slants in and over his body. Those scars of his are probably enough to give him a complex. Probably enough to make him want to hide his face from strangers. Even the people at the office don't look directly at him when they speak to him. Except for the Davenports, who, to give them credit, never let on that they notice his disfigurement.

"Has he ever asked to meet us at the club instead of his home?" Ryot stands by the other window in the room. These Davenports, always on alert, always making sure they have their exits mapped. And I'm one of them now. Only in name. To ensure I bring them down and take revenge for how they abandoned my mother. Only, I didn't count on meeting a woman who'd deflect me from my focus.

Meeting Starling, marrying her, thinking of a future with her; it's changed me. The need for revenge is not as strong or as important as it once was. I haven't forgiven Arthur for turning his back on my mother... But my future lies with Starling. My wife. And for the first time, the fact that the Davenport fortune could benefit her is making me reconsider my purpose.

Tyler, Connor and Brody stand in another corner. The three of them seem to have a bond which Knox and Ryot don't share. For that matter, Knox and Ryot don't seem like they have a bond with each other, either. Loners that they are, Ryot being the most unsocial of them.

The one thing they do share is their mistrust of me—the usurper, the one who came in from the outside to take over the role as CEO. Not that Arthur has confirmed my position yet. I should be getting impatient, but for the fact I've been too focused on my wife. On enjoying her cunt, her lips, the touch of her fingers on my skin, the feel of her fluttering round my cock as I come inside her. *Without a condom. Jesus, what was I thinking?* Or not thinking, as the case may be. Since seeing her at the bakery and realizing I could help her, I've lost sight of the goal that has driven me this far.

I take a step away from the settee, where she's seated with Mira, Edward's wife. They returned from their honeymoon yesterday, and as I watch, Ed reaches down to touch her shoulder, as if reassuring himself that she's real. Mira looks up and beams at him. Ed lowers his head and kisses her. A kiss which seems to go on and on, until Connor clears his throat.

"Maybe you two came back from your honeymoon too soon? Weren't you supposed to be gone a few more days?" he quips.

"Damn right, but Arthur called. And while I did, at first, tell him to fuck off—"

Connor coughs. "You told him to fuck off?"

"Or words to that extent, but he insisted we return."

"Hmm." Knox rubs his chin. "Anyone else get the feeling we're being set up for a big reveal?"

Tyler grunts in assent.

Brody nods.

Ryot's glower deepens.

Connor looks between us. "Let's cut the old man a break, shall we?"

I snort. "He's far from a helpless old man."

"Granted. Arthur's the most Machiavellian person I've ever met. But his intentions are good."

I exchange glances with Edward.

"If it weren't for Arthur, I'd never have met my wife, so I can't completely disagree with that statement. But I'm not sure his manipulating our lives is something I condone, either." Edward sits down on the edge of the settee and wraps his arm about Mira's shoulder.

"No fucking way is he arranging my marriage," Brody growls.

Ryot raises his middle finger, making his opinion of the topic at hand clear.

Connor holds up a hand. "All I'm saying is —"

He breaks off as a man walks into the room. A stranger, who's tall and broad enough to indicate that he either works out a lot or has the kind of job that involves being on the move and carrying out a certain level of physical activity daily. The jeans he wears are worn at the knees, and the sleeves of his beaten leather jacket stretch across his biceps. His scuffed military-issue boots give away his profession, as does his erect bearing. There are hints of grey at his temples, and while his hair is still short, it's not shorn as close to the scalp as it would be if he'd come off active duty. The shadows in his eyes hint at the action he must have seen, while the lines on his face indicate he's older than the rest of us in this room.

He pauses at the edge of the informal circle we're scattered around in. There's no hesitation, as much as wariness in his stance as he surveys the group. Silence descends, but from the ripple of awareness that runs through the room, I realize the others know who he is.

The man's gaze runs over the faces of those gathered, until it alights on Ryot. A look of regret comes over his features. "I'm sorry, I —"

Before he can complete the sentence, Ryot crosses the room and swings his fist.

47

Skylar

"Oh my god." I clap my hands over my mouth.

On the other side of the room, the new arrival takes Ryot's hit on the chin and doesn't flinch, which is saying something. Because Ryot is built like a tank. He's as tall as the stranger, but his muscles are thicker. He pulls his fist back again, and my husband plants his body in front of me, no doubt, to protect me. It also means I can't see what's happening.

I jump up and try to look around him, in time to see the new man take another hit, this time, to his side. Ryot swings a third time, but this time, the other man—who, while older than Ryot, is every bit as fit as him—steps aside, then trips Ryot, who crashes down on his front. The other man moves so quickly, he blurs. The next moment, he has his knee pressed into the small of Ryot's back. He also has Ryot's arms pinned behind him. Ryot growls and tries to shake off the other man, but doesn't succeed.

"You gotta listen to me, mate; it wasn't my fault. I'm sorry for what happened, but it was a mistake."

"One that resulted in the mission being compromised. You called the airstrike on the wrong coordinates. You killed her." Ryot's eyes blaze.

I don't think I've heard him speak before, so it's a shock to hear his voice.

"It was a mistake," the other man bites out through gritted teeth.

"There are no mistakes. There is only death and no return. Not a single day goes by when I don't wish it was me you killed and not her." He bangs his forehead into the wooden floor, and the sound echoes through the room.

"I'm sorry, man. If I could, I'd take back my actions. I had no way of knowing the intelligence was wrong. Not a day goes by when I don't blame myself for what happened."

Ryot looks at the other man with so much venom, I flinch.

The stranger's jaw flexes. He must loosen his grip, for Ryot shakes him off and rises to his feet. He turns and points his finger at the new arrival. "I hope you go through what I did. I hope you lose the one you love, and then you'll realize how it feels to live, knowing you'll never see her again. Never hold her again. Never hear her laugh or hold her in your arms again. While day after day, you have to go through this farce of a life and pretend to live, when what you are is a dead man walking. And there's no way you're going to kill yourself because she'd be disappointed in you. So, you keep living, when actually"—he swallows—"all you want is to die, so you can see her again."

There's silence in the room. Strike what I said earlier. Ryot doesn't hate the man. He abhors him, which is obvious since he decided to speak what's on his mind.

He pivots and walks out of the room, leaving the other man on the floor, still on one knee.

His shoulders rise and fall. For a second, he lowers his chin to his chest, head bowed as if in penance. Then, he slowly rises to his feet and turns to face the room. "Anyone else? Might as well get it all out now, boys."

The rest of the Davenport brothers stay silent. The seconds tick past as the other brother's glower at him. He's family, that much is clear from the resemblance between him and the others, but he's not welcome. Not when the animosity in the room is so strong the hair on the back of my neck stands on end.

Edward and Nate exchange glances.

Then, my husband closes the distance to the new arrival and holds out his hand. "Nate Davenport."

The other man does a chin jerk. "M Squadron?"

Nate nods slowly. "You're X Squadron."

Something passes between the two men, an understanding of sorts.

"Quentin Davenport." The other man tilts his head. "You're my nephew."

"And you're a fucking coward." This, from Knox.

"You have the gall to show your face again?" Tyler's jaw works.

"You fucking hurt him. You turned Ryot's life upside down and now, you expect him to forgive you?" Brody moves forward.

It's as if there's a signal, for suddenly, the four remaining brothers surround Quentin.

That's when Edward steps in and stretches out his arm to block Brody. "Hold on, chaps, we don't want to come to blows here in the Club."

"Oh, we do. And it's going to be more than blows, considering what he did to Ryot," Knox says in a low voice. Anger vibrates off of him. The feeling of menace permeating the air is so thick, it pins me in place.

"It was an error." Quentin raises his hands, palms facing outward. "A slip-up in intelligence. There was a mole on my team, and I didn't know. If I had known, I never would've given the orders."

"It was poor planning and communication on your part. You were the leader. It was your responsibility," Brody snaps.

Quentin lowers his chin. "I take responsibility for what happened. It was my fault. It's why I left the Marines."

"Not enough. You get to leave with honors, while Ryot goes ballistic and is stripped of his colors and told to leave the career he loves?" Knox shakes his head. "You need to pay."

"He does; that's why I called him here," Arthur says from the doorway. He shuts the door behind him, then unhooks the lead from Tiny. The dog pads over to Quentin, sniffs him, looks around at the other guys with one ear quirked, then he butts Quentin's hip. Quentin scratches the mutt's big head, and Tiny makes a purring noise in his throat. The interaction seems to break up the tension a little. Arthur walks past Quentin and takes a seat in an armchair by the fireplace. It's a position from which he can survey the room. Somehow, he's already maneuvered things, making it clear, he's the one in charge.

"Step back, everyone," Arthur commands.

Knox takes a step forward, and Arthur booms, "Back off. That's an order."

Knox hesitates, then to my surprise, he slowly moves back. "This isn't over." He bares his teeth in Quentin's direction, then pivots and heads back to his position by the window. Connor, Brody and Tyler stay in place for a few seconds, then retreat.

Nate's features relax. He and Edward walk back to stand next to me and Mira. Nate squeezes my shoulder, and I turn my face into his hand. Seeing this showdown brought home the level of testosterone in this family. It's quite a sight to see these men gathered under one roof again, and then to see them almost come to blows.

A secret part of me knows I'd have enjoyed it, too. It's that bloodthirsty part of me, the darker part of me that my husband has loosened. The honest part of me, I suppose. The part that can no longer stay hidden. The part he's brought to the fore, with the way he's possessed my body and taught me to love my figure, to trust my instincts, to believe in myself.

Of course, I had a measure of self-confidence to begin with. And no, I did not hate how I looked, but I haven't been as comfortable in my skin as I am now. And it's thanks to him. Some of my emotions must communicate themselves to him, for he rubs his thumb across my cheek. I look up to find his eyes shining with that emotion I now know he reserves for me.

He told me he loved me, but right here, surrounded by his family, and having seen how he intervened to keep the peace, it sinks in. He's my husband and he loves me. And I love him. I need to tell him. I open my mouth, but for some reason, the words stick in my throat. An instinct, or perhaps, it's the fact that he's holding back something from me. If I overlooked that, everything would be perfect, but I can't. A part of me insists, I need to know. That when I do, everything might change. A shiver runs down my back.

"Cold?" His lips curl in that half-smile that I can feel all the way to my toes. Then, he shrugs off his jacket and places it around my shoulders. "Better?"

Before I can answer, Arthur's voice booms through the room. "Quentin, I wasn't sure you'd come."

Quentin's jaw firms. "Me neither. But"—his throat moves as he swallows —"I needed to make amends."

Arthur nods. "I'm glad you've realized that. As your nephews pointed out, it's time for you to pay."

"Oh?" Quentin's features grow wary. "What do you want, Arthur?"

Not father, or Dad, just Arthur. Jeez, this entire family hates this old man. He must have been a terror in his younger days. Correction he's still a terror. A vein tics at Arthur's temple. He's pissed off by Quentin calling him by his name, but when he speaks, his voice is even. "Why do you think I want something from you?"

Quentin snorts. "Because you're a mean ol' bastard, is why. And because everything is a negotiation and a means to an end, especially the lives of your family."

Arthur clicks his tongue. "You don't have a very good opinion of me, do you?"

"To say the least."

"So, it's not going to make it any worse when I say I want you to join the family business and take over the info-communication arm of Davenport Industries."

"What the fuck?! You're carving up the company again?" Knox bursts out.

"Just making sure everyone's strengths are used in the best way. It's the only way this family is going to survive the challenges we face in almost every sector." Arthur tilts his head. "There's more than enough companies for all of you to become CEOs of your own portfolios."

"You groomed me to be your heir. You said I would be group CEO," his left eyelid twitches.

"A title Nathan has the experience to take on more than anyone else in this room." Arthur's voice is firm.

Knox's nostrils flare. He narrows his gaze on Arthur. "I will get back at you for this."

Arthur smiles, and his expression is so similar to the way Knox bared his teeth at Quentin earlier. This family... They'd happily tear out each other's throats when it comes to delivering on their own ambitions.

At the same time, when there's a challenge to one of them, everyone steps up, as I saw earlier when the brothers came to Ryot's defense. Of course, it helps that all of them are united against Quentin. It always helps to have a central figure to rally against.

Hold on a second, is that why Arthur asked Quentin to return? Another way to bring the brothers together? No matter that it might be at the cost of Quentin losing whatever relationship he has with them? Or is it a chance for Quentin to redeem himself with them?

"Nathan, you should find the confirmation letter of your position as Group CEO on your desk."

My husband inclines his head. This is something he's been working toward for a while, but there's no change in expression on his face. How strange. I'd have expected him to be happy, even excited, but his forehead is furrowed. It's as if he's not quite sure how to react to the news. He also doesn't seem surprised to see Quentin here. Apparently, he knew his uncle was coming today.

"As for you, Quentin"—Arthur looks him up and down—"I assume you accept my proposition?"

Quentin nods slowly. "Do I have a choice?"

"You always have a choice." Arthur's smile is sly.

"More like a non-choice." Quentin rubs the back of his neck.

"You in or out, son?"

"Don't fucking call me *son*."

Arthur sighs. "Can we leave the emotions out of this discussion? You are my son. It's a fact of life; deal with it."

"And I'm in, only because it's a way to make amends with my nephews; deal with it," Quentin snaps back.

Arthur nods. "I do have a condition."

48

Nathan

"So, you agreed to get married." I top off the whiskey in Quentin's tumbler and pour sparkling water for myself. We're seated on chairs, which have been set to one side of the room, with our drinks on the coffee table between us. The condition Arthur imposed on him... To marry within the next six months, and to a woman the old man approves of. What a shocker, eh?

When Quentin didn't protest, Arthur seemed to relax. I thanked him for confirming me as group CEO, but he waved it off. He told me I deserved it, that I should make sure to collaborate closely with Quentin, then he took his leave.

None of my half-brothers protested seeing him leave early. If anything, the tension in the room reduced with his departure. Edward saw him out before leaving with Mira.

Starling wanted to check in on her bakery to make sure her employee had closed up properly, and Edward and Mira offered to drop her off. I didn't want her to leave, but it's important she focuses on building up her business, especially with the funding flowing in and a new team to onboard. So, I kissed her hard and told her I'd pick her up in a few hours.

Which left Quentin and me, and the rest of my half-brother clan. Knox broke out the liquor, and everyone accepted a glass like it was the answer to all of their problems. Which I know from experience, it isn't.

I pour some of the sparkling water into a glass and take a sip.

"You don't drink?" Quentin asks.

I look at him in surprise. Only my wife noticed I abstain from alcohol. None of the other Davenports have noticed, or if they have, they haven't mentioned it to me. But nothing escapes Quentin's gaze.

"You sure you don't want to vie for the role of Group CEO?" I joke.

"Not a chance." He swirls the amber liquid in his glass. "That's not what I returned for."

"No, you came back to make peace with your nephews." I gesture toward the other end of the room, where Knox, Connor, Tyler and Brody are gathered around the bar and talking in low voices. You know what I said earlier about Knox being a loner? Strike that; it took a threat to one of the brothers for them to close ranks. Which is a positive thing. It's going to stand the Davenports in good stead when I break down their companies and sell them off, except the info-communication division, since Quentin's leading that now.

"I suppose I should make a start by going over and talking to them." He shoots a sideways glance toward his nephews. "But then I think, I'm not a masochist, and there's going to be enough time to take them on in the future. Besides, to begin, I'd rather face them one at a time."

"Good strategy." I drain my glass of water and pour myself more.

He clinks his glass with mine, before taking a sip. "Why did you get out?" he asks me.

"It's the same ol' story." I rotate my neck. "Mission gone wrong. We were ambushed. I made it out alive."

He swallows another mouthful before he asks, "Was that a good thing?"

I bark out a laugh, the sound nowhere as joyful as it's supposed to be. He knows, sometimes making it out of a war is to be cursed spending the rest of your life fighting the demons that never leave you. "For me; not so much for the others."

He waits. The silence stretches, inviting me to fill it with my confessions. Edward's the former priest, the man to whom I've been tempted to confess in the past. It's the first time someone else has invited the same confidence from me.

"Two of my team were killed in front of my eyes."

He whistles. "Tough on you."

"Tougher on their families."

He searches my features, a shrewd look in his eyes. "You understand, they knew what they were signing up for?"

"They expected to fight. They gave up their youth, their laughter, their hopes and dreams for the country. In return, they expect the country to help them when they and their families need it."

"You think the system failed them?"

"Ask their families, who were handed a flag and compensation that's barely enough to take care of their living costs. Then, there are those who succeed at their given mission but, like me, suffer from PTSD. So many are given an honorable discharge, and then what?"

He tips up his chin. "There are career transition programs, housing assistance, grants, and benefits in place to help vets adapt back to daily life.'

"Bullshit." I slap my palm on the table. "What's on paper and what happens in real life are two very different realities."

"Nevertheless, there is help for them, provided they're willing to be helped."

"You mean, they come back irreparably broken, unable to help themselves, and the inevitable happens. A higher percentage of veterans take their lives than any other demographic."

"Not you," he murmurs.

"Not you, either," I point out.

"I had a reason to live. A family— As dysfunctional as the Davenports are, I had blood to come back to."

"So did many of these men. But it didn't seem to help."

"No, it depends on the person. If they can find the resources within themselves to crawl out of the hole."

"The hole we put them in." I stare into my empty glass.

"If by we, you mean—"

"The country. The system. Call it what you want, but this endless cycle of serving up our youth as fodder to serve the bidding of politicians is something I have always questioned."

"Yet, you joined the military."

"I was young and foolish. I thought I could change the system from inside." I rub the back of my neck. "Why are we talking about this, anyway?"

"Because you feel for the lives that were lost. And you want to do something about it."

"Perhaps." I roll my shoulders, glance around the room, then back at him. "You, on the other hand—"

"—still believe in the power of the armed forces, yes. If that last mission hadn't gone wrong in the way it did, if that one particular life hadn't been lost, I'd never have left."

"Who was she?" I tilt my head. "I assume it's someone Ryot had feelings for? Did the two of you serve together?"

"We served at the same time, yes. As for the rest, it's his prerogative to talk about it; not mine."

"Understood." Both of us lapse into silence for a few minutes. He tosses back the rest of his whiskey, then tugs at his sleeves. "I'll see you around." He rises to his feet.

The movement catches the attention of the rest of the men. Knox pushes away from the bar and walks over to stand in his path.

"Where do you think you're going, old man?" he growls.

Brody and Tyler join him, flanking him on either side. Connor watches with a frown on his face. Clearly, he's not happy with his brothers' actions. He's not stopping them, though.

"I don't want any fighting." Quentin holds up his hands. "Also, not sure our eighteen-year age difference warrants your referring to me as old, but if it makes you feel better..." He shrugs.

A vein throbs at Knox's temple. The tips of his ears grow white. Never a good sign.

I rise to my feet. "Guys, this is something Ryot and Quentin need to sort out between themselves. I understand it's a good thing you're all doing by backing up Ryot, but not sure if fisticuffs are the way to solve this."

"Whose side are you on?" Tyler growls.

"I'm on no one's side."

"That's because you got the Group CEO role," Knox growls.

"Is that what you want? The role? Say the word, and I'll be happy to hand it over to you."

I sense the others staring at me in surprise. Knox frowns. He seems to consider my suggestion, then shakes his head. "Nah, it doesn't work that way. The old man promised it to me, and he broke his promise. You deciding you don't want the role and handing it over doesn't cut it."

"Ah"—I stroke my chin—"it's Arthur's approval you seek?"

He grunts. "You a pop psychologist?"

"Nope, just seen enough of the world. No matter how much we grow up, or"—I shoot a glance at Quentin—"or how far we run, we're always looking for our parents to accept us."

"Is that what you want from Arthur? Is that why you returned to the family fold?" Quentin murmurs.

"In some ways, I suppose I was. My mother didn't let a day go by without talking about my father. Arthur's wife may have paid her off, but she always saw herself as a Davenport. Maybe that's why, when Arthur called, I came." *And also because it gave me the opportunity to take revenge.*

Silence follows my announcement. Guess the men weren't expecting me to be this honest? Hell, I wasn't expecting to be this honest. Apparently, along with falling in love, I've also forgotten how to keep my secrets. Or perhaps, my subconscious has decided it's time to be vulnerable? Share a little of myself with my half-brothers. Make them feel more comfortable around me, so when I break up the company and sell it off, it's going to hurt so much more. Nothing like one of your own betraying you to wreak the worst devastation. And that's what I want, after all. I want them to suffer the way my mother did. I want them to feel the anger, the pain, the rage, the helplessness I felt every single day of my growing years. All because my father and his family thought she wasn't good enough for them.

I'll never allow that to happen to my wife. Which is why it's important Arthur acknowledges her as a Davenport, and ensures she gets all the advantages that go with it. She'll never face the loneliness and the isolation my mother did. She'll never feel she's been abandoned. Of course, it's not just the money that matters, but the fact that my mother did not have to worry about that, is the only reason I'm still alive. Yes, my grandmother took care of us in that way, but the lack of emotional acceptance is what ate away at my mother.

My wife will never face that. She was chosen by my grandfather, after all. I used to think it was a coincidence that it turned out I already knew her... But was it?

I'm convinced Arthur had it all planned out. He knew that we knew each other, that her brother Ben was my best friend, and that I never forgot her. I bet he found out that I was keeping an eye on her bakery. But he must have noticed that I didn't approach her. He must have thought I needed a nudge — anything to get me to come face to face with her, so as to trigger a reaction in me — which he was right about. I saw her that day in her bakery and knew I could no longer stay away from her. I'm more convinced than ever that he planned everything so we'd meet, knowing a possible outcome was that I'd marry her. All Arthur cares is that everyone of marriageable age is settled before he pops it.

The worst thing? In this particular case, I can't fault him. Gramps has his merits, after all. Just not enough for me to spare his life's work.

And it's not like any of them are going to end up the streets after this. The Davenports have enough money stashed away in accounts and real-estate around the world to lead a very good life. Enough to inject capital into the formation of a new company, if they choose. Enough to buy back the shares of the existing companies, if they choose. All I'm doing is providing them a reality check. Enough to not take their money for granted anymore. Hell, they should be grateful I'm giving them a life lesson.

And what does it say about you? I squeeze the bridge of my nose. Falling for my wife is making me vulnerable in all areas of my life. It's fucking confusing, feeling this way. It was a lot easier when my goal was clear. Take revenge for how they treated my mother. That's what's guided me to this point. And now...? Now, all I know is she's the most important thing in my life. Spending time with her is what matters most. Taking care of her, protecting her... Coming clean to her? That, too. I can't keep putting that off. I look around and notice that all eyes in the room are on me.

"What?" I scowl at the men.

"Something on your mind, bro?" Knox prowls over to stand over me. "You look disturbed."

"You'd be, too, if you were pussy whipped," Brody snickers.

I lean back in my seat. "Sounds like you're jealous."

"Sounds like you can't stand an hour's absence from her, " he scoffs.

"Never denied that." I hold up my hands. "I'll be the first to admit, I'm in love with my wife. I'd rather spend an evening with her than any more time with you jokers."

I rise to my feet. "I wish I could say I don't envy you—"

"But you do."

He chuckles. "In this respect, I'm wiser than my nephews. I saw the way you two looked at each other. What you have... It's not an easy thing to come by."

I take in the shadows in his eyes and realize this man has as many secrets as me, perhaps more. But that's none of my concern. He's come this far; he's survived running strategy for dangerous missions. Question is, will he survive the Davenports? Only one way to find out.

"Right, I'm out. Give you uncle and nephews a chance to get to know each other."

49

Skylar

"What?" Grace stares.

"What?" Zoey squeaks.

"I agreed to it. I was fine with it, guys. Not that I'm into voyeurism or anything—"

"Jesus, he sees you getting off when you're on your own in your office?"

"And in the bakery," I say in a low voice. "I keep it hygienic. Not when I'm baking. Okay, maybe once, but I stepped away from the counter"—*to where he could have a clear view of the proceedings*—"and washed my hands before and after."

Zoey begins to laugh. "I'd say that was stalking but clearly, you like him watching you."

"I do," I admit in a small voice. "Also, uh, it began because he realized I was… Uh… Turned on, and he, uh… Took a chopper over, so he could, ah, you know—"

"Make you come?" Grace drawls.

My cheeks, my chest, even my arms and legs feel hot. My skin feels too tight for my body. Ohmygod, I'm going to burst into flames from mortification. I'm not used to sharing so much, not even with my best friends, and definitely not about this specific kink my husband and I seem to have developed.

Zoey laughs harder. "I mean, whatever floats your boat. And if you're a consensual partner in it, then why not. Although, even if you weren't—" She bites down on her lower lip. "I mean, even if you weren't and he was watching you, he's your husband, so I'd still find it hot."

"You've been reading too many romance novels." Grace frowns.

"No shit, that's my job." Zoey smiles widely. "Why do you think I love what I do so much? Imagine editing spicy novels for a living. I looooove it."

"It's all very well in romance novels, but in real life, um, I'm not sure." Grace's lips settle in a stern line.

"That's because you've never met a powerful, confident man who'll sweep you off your feet," Zoey scoffs.

"If he hadn't had her consent in it, I would be worried. I'd even call his behavior controlling." Grace tosses her head.

"He is all of that, and I do like it when we're together. But he's also tender and caring and does things like carry my migraine medication around so he has it on hand, if I forget it."

"He did that?" Grace seems taken aback.

"Also, he helped me move Hugo to a better facility after he had a meltdown in his current one." I lower my chin.

"Hugo?" Zoey inclines her head. "Isn't that your ex-colleague from the bakery you worked at?"

"Yeah. I never told you guys before, but he'd decided to join me at *The Fearless Kitten.* He was on his way to help me open the shop when I happened to run out onto the road in front of him. He tried to avoid me, ended up losing his helmet and hitting his head on the sidewalk. It's my fault he was injured. My fault his entire life changed. The strange thing is I still don't remember why I was on the road in the first place."

"You don't?" Zoey frowns.

"I spent a few days in hospital after the accident. While I made a full recovery, my memories about what happened prior to being hit by the bike are fuzzy. Either way, I was back on my feet very quickly. Except for follow up check-ups, I was able to go on with my life. As for Hugo--" My chin trembles. "Poor Hugo ended up suffering from a traumatic brain injury. No way could I leave him helpless and at the mercy of the state. I decided to take care of him and have been paying his additional needs bills for the last year."

"Oh, honey, I'm so sorry." Zoey wraps her arm about me. "If I'd been around—"

I sniffle, then shake my head. "This was before I met you guys. I was at my lowest when you walked into my shop, Z. I am so grateful that you did. It's thanks to you I met everyone else, and I found a circle of friends in this city."

"And you know we're here for you. You should have asked us for help." Grace purses her lips. "All this time, you've been trying to manage on your own. I wish you'd told us."

"I'm sorry, Gracie, really. I wanted to share, but I didn't want to be judged for doing this. I didn't want to be told it wasn't my responsibility. I wanted to do it. I couldn't abandon him, you know?"

"You have such a big heart," she murmurs.

"Oh, Skye." Zoey's eyes glimmer with tears. "You must have found it so difficult to cope on your own. It's why you always seemed so tense. I thought it was the issues you were having with the fledgling business, but it was so much more."

"I'm really sorry I didn't tell you guys. I thought I'd be imposing on you. But now I realize, I was being selfish. I didn't give any of you a chance to be good friends. I wasn't generous enough to let you into my life. I'm sorry, truly."

"Hey, it's okay. You do what works for you. Don't feel compelled to do what you think is right according to the world. Do what is right for you, first." Grace smiles. "And if that means you want to indulge in exhibitionism, more power to you."

Zoey's eyes round. "And how do you know about that particular kink?"

"I might have read a spicy book or two." Grace smirks.

"Why you secret filth slut," Zoey gasps.

I laugh. "So, you guys don't mind if I admit that my husband watching me getting myself off keeps me in a state of hyper arousal and makes me want to do even more dirty things to myself to turn him on?"

Grace rolls her eyes. "Now you're showing off."

"So, is he watching you right now?" Zoey asks in a breathless voice.

"Probably, but I don't care. I have nothing to hide." *Unlike him.*

The timer on my oven dings. "Gotta go, guys, and get the next batch of Cream Horns in."

Zoey barks out a laugh. "Cream Horns?"

"Get your mind out of the butter, babe."

She snorts. Grace snickers.

"And that's what they're called, by the way, so I didn't even have come up with a spicy booktok name." I pretend to blow on my nails and rub them on my collar. "Not my fault if my customers decide these innocent conical choux pastry filled with whipped cream remind them of certain parts of the male anatomy."

"Of course not." Grace nods.

"I might have exaggerated the conical shape, so it resembled said parts, of course."

Both burst out laughing.

I blow them a kiss. "See you two very soon." I disconnect, then pull out the tray of desserts and set it aside to cool, before popping the other into the oven. By the time I'm done with the next tray, Nate still hasn't arrived. I check my phone and notice I missed a message from him.

> Husband: Heavy traffic due to an accident on the freeway. Be there soon. Love you, wife.

Warmth suffuses my chest. I begin to type, 'love you, too,' then delete it. I settle for liking his message with a heart, then glance around the space. It's dark outside, and when I check the time on my phone, I realize it's almost nine-thirty p.m. I ended up tasting some of the Cream Horns—you know, the ones that came out of the oven not looking perfect, and which I wouldn't have been able to serve anyway; *keep telling yourself that, girl*—and they were soooo good. But now, I'm not hungry.

I stretch, yawn, and start cleaning up the kitchen. When the oven dings, I pull out the cakes and slide them onto a sheet tray on the counter before covering them with a cake dome with vents to let air through. I'll leave them to cool overnight and frost them tomorrow. I decide to go up to my flat and wait for him. I've been thinking of turning it into an office, now that I don't use it as a living space anymore. Maybe, at some point in the future?

I take off my apron and yawn again, grab my phone and my handbag, and locking up the shop, make my way upstairs. I'm so sleepy, I could probably grab a nap before he arrives. In fact, I might as well make myself comfortable. I bought a few essentials and keep them in the apartment just for times like this, including the pair of sleep shorts and camisole that I change into.

By the time I hit my bed, my body feels so heavy. Guess it's from all those nights of not having much sleep—thanks to those lovely orgasms my husband has drawn from me, and which I'm not complaining about, at all. I'm so tired. I close my eyes and drift off.

A tapping on the door wakes me up. I sit up, shove my legs over the side of the bed and stand up.

"Coming!" I shove my hair on top of my head into a messy bun, then head to the door and throw it open. And blink.

Nate's standing there. But... He's in uniform, and he's holding his cap in his hand. There's a woman standing next to him. She's also in uniform, but she's wearing a collar that marks her out as a chaplain. A chaplain? Why is she here with Nate?

A strong sense of déjà vu grips me.

I'm dreaming. I must be. But it all feels so real. Is it a memory? Did this already happen? Why is my heart racing? Why is my pulse racing? Why is my stomach knotted?

I push down my rising panic, already suspecting there'll be no waking from this. I know what's coming, but I can't stop any of it. Because in the back of my mind, there's a little voice telling me it's time to face reality. *I don't want to!* But time has run out. And there's no running from what happened. Images flood my brain, and I can't stop them. I struggle to breathe.

I watch, as if from a distance. It's like it's not me. More like, I don't want it to be me. And I don't want to feel what I'm seeing, but I do. I feel every bit of it.

I frown at Nate. "What are you doing here?"

He looks me directly in the eyes. "Can I come in?"

"Nathan?" My heart turns into a heavy anchor, slowly beginning to slide down my body. Pulling me down with it. My chest feels like there's an entire building collapsed on it. I draw in a breath, and my lungs feel like they're on fire. "Nate?" I manage to speak around the boiling oil clogging my throat. "What is it?"

"Skylar... Skye." The skin around his eyes tightens. "Please, can we come in?"

I step back, and he moves forward, cupping his hand around my elbow and guiding me to the sofa. The next moment, I'm sitting down, and he's on his knee in front of me. "Skye, I have to tell you something."

I see it in his eyes then. That mixture of regret and anger and sympathy... And failure. It's the failure that signals to me that something's very wrong. That, and the fact that Nate fucking Davenport is taking my hand between his, and he's on bended knee.

Something I've wanted, but not like this.

Not. Like. This.

I tug my hand from his, and he releases me.

I lock my fingers together and shake my head. "No. No. No. No. No."

"Skye, please, let me."

My palm connects with his cheek with such force, his head snaps back. A ripple of pain shoots up my arm. The outline of my fingers stands out on his face. I should feel regretful, but I don't. Should feel shocked, and I do, but not because I slapped him.

"Skye, please." He takes my hand in his again, and this time, I clasp it tightly.

A tear squeezed out from the corner of my eye. "No—" I swallow. "No, please," I whisper.

"Skye—" His voice cracks. His throat moves as he swallows. His mismatched eyes are dull, lifeless. The color has leached from his face, except for my fingerprints, which stand out in vivid red mockery. "I'm so sorry, Skye."

I shake my head, and the tears flow freely down my cheeks. "It can't be true, it can't."

"Ben, he—"

"No!" I throw off his hand and jump to my feet, then dart around him. "I won't hear it." I race toward the doorway. The chaplain steps into my path, but I push past her, out the door, down the flight of stairs, and onto the sidewalk. I don't stop.

It's not possible. Nothing has happened to Ben. Nothing. My heart is a shark that bites its way out of my chest, chewing through my ribcage, my flesh, my sinews. Spilling my blood, so it flows down my front.

I'm spinning. My entire world has turned upside down. I can't be alive without Ben. I can't. I won't. I notice the motorbike a second before it hit me. There's a screech of brakes. I'm screaming, flying through the air. Then blackness.

"Starling, are you okay?"

I jolt and see my husband staring at me with a worried expression. And I know it's true. It really happened. I remember now. I remember how my brother's best friend came to break the news to me. How he tried to tell me, and I wouldn't listen.

I clear my throat and meet his mismatched gaze. "You came here… To tell me about Ben."

"What?" The color drains from his face. "What did you say?"

50

Nathan

"Ben," she says in a low voice. "You came here, to my apartment, to tell me about him."

My heart stops, then starts again. The blood, which threatened to drain out of me, begins to pump through my veins, and tears fill my eyes. *I'm here, alive. And so is she. But Ben. Oh god, Ben.* I place my hand on her shoulder, but she shakes it off. "Don't touch me."

My chest collapses in on itself. My stomach threatens to turn into a tornado, which twists up through my throat, before I push back the bile that threatens to spill out.

She must see the anguish on my face, for her features soften. "I meant, if you touch me, I'll lose my train of thought, and right now, I need to be clear-headed... So I understand what happened."

I nod, then stick my arms behind my back and lock the fingers of one hand around the other wrist to stop myself from reaching out to her, holding her, and soothing her. Right now, she doesn't want that. So, I'll do as she says. *For now.*

She turns and walks into the apartment, I follow her. I can't keep my gaze off her bare legs, those creamy thighs, the curve of her hips. As she opened the door, I noticed she was wearing pink cotton sleep shorts and a camisole that stretched across her breasts. Her nipples were outlined against the fabric, and I'd be lying if I said my fingers hadn't twitched to reach out and tweak those buds.

How can I be thinking of her body, of how much I want to bury myself inside her sweet pussy, when she's finally remembering the events following her brother's death?

She glances over her shoulder, and when she sees my gaze, a pink color smears her cheeks. She looks away, then veers toward her sleeping area. She grabs her bathrobe from the foot of her bed and shoves her arms into it. She ties the belt around her waist, before walking to the window to look out. I take a step forward, then stop. I want to go to her and take her in my arms. I want to console her. But she asked for a little space. I owe that much to her, no matter, every cell in my body insists I stay close to her.

She wraps her arms about her waist, the gesture, one of defensiveness. Doesn't she know she doesn't have to protect herself from me? That I'll never hurt her? That everything I've done is for her. That I'd kill myself if I could shield her from pain. That I'd do anything for Ben to be standing here instead of me, so she wouldn't have to face the grief of what's coming.

"He's dead, isn't he?" she whispers.

I flinch.

I never had to get those words out because she understood it by looking at my face. That day, I witnessed how the understanding dawned in her eyes when she saw the chaplain. I'd told my superior in the Marines that it was better to take a grief counsellor or welfare officer, or someone whose very presence wouldn't scream that there'd been a death, but I'd been over-ruled. Another reason I'd known my days in the Marines were over. If you couldn't bend the rules when it was in the best interest of the person concerned, then what use were they? And I'd never had thoughts like this before. Rules were what governed my life.

After my chaotic childhood, and moving around so much with my mother, it was a relief to find a home amidst the discipline and the black and white of the Marines. Until I wasn't able to save Ben. Until I stood there facing his sister and had to convey the news to her. I was only authorized to be the one to do so because I'd threatened the chain of command with outing them about the corruption I'd seen. They'd agreed at once. But insisted the chaplain go with me. Something about being able to justify my presence, as I was Ben's senior and had run missions with him, but that they couldn't bend protocol further. Well, fuck them. I'd said so before leaving, knowing I was leaving active service after that final trip to see her.

Only, she ran out of the apartment building. I wasn't able to stop her. I raced after her, but I was too late.

She turns to face me. "You came to break the news to me, and I didn't want to listen." She swallows. "I ran away from you. I stepped onto the street, and in the path of a motorbike. A bike which was driven by Hugo—" Her features pale further. "I remembered being hit by his bike, but I couldn't understand why I was running across the road."

I flinch again. I found her sprawled on her back, with blood pooling under her. And she was still, so still. My breath caught, and my entire body felt as if I'd been plunged into the depths of a cold lake. I have no recollection of sinking down next to her, but I placed my fingers against her neck, and when I caught the pulse—faint, but it was there— Only then, did I come back into my body, the noise of the crowd, and the distant wail of a siren slowly filtering into my sub-conscious. I didn't dare move her, managing to find the presence of mind to take off my jacket and place it around her to keep her warm. I followed her into the ambulance and rode with her to the hospital.

"I stayed with you until you regained consciousness."

"I never saw you."

"I couldn't face you. I saw the devastation on your face when you realized what had happened."

"You mean, when I realized Ben was dead?"

I nod, unable to bring myself to say the words. I've never said it aloud. Not to my superiors. Not to those who were there at his funeral. Not to myself. On the surface, it might seem like I'm coping better, but that's because I've had her in my life.

Her voice is soft and hard at the same time, her eyes dry. Her entire being is one straight line. Stiff. Unyielding. Those beautiful curves stamped with defiance and suffering and anger. So much anger.

I deserve it, though. I deserve her hate, her bitterness. Everything she throws at me. *Why doesn't she yell at me? Or tell me to leave. Why doesn't she slap me again?* Anything is preferable to this cold, unfeeling woman who faces me.

"Your loss of hearing"—she narrows her gaze on me—"you said a bomb went off next to you?"

I nod, knowing what's coming next, but staying silent. My wife is so fucking smart. Of course she'd piece it all together.

"Was Ben injured on this mission, as well?" Her chin trembles, but she doesn't cry.

"He was. A mission gone wrong. It's always a mission gone wrong." I rub the back of my neck. "We ran a dozen successful ones. We knew our luck was going to run out. I told him…" I pause. "I told him I didn't have a good feeling about this one, but he waved it off. You know Ben." I laugh, the sound hollow.

"I know Ben, the eternal optimist." A small smile graces those gorgeous lips. "He preferred to see the positive side of things. It was almost as if he could change the future to be what he wanted it to be."

"And he succeeded, always," I say softly.

"Until he didn't…" Her voice is low, her features anguished. My heart stutters. All I want to do is gather her up in my arms and console her. But will she let me? I take a step in her direction; she doesn't protest.

"You—" She swallows. "You brought him back home?"

I nod.

"And came to tell me."

"I managed to persuade the powers that be it was the right thing to do. That I was the person to tell you about what had happened to him. I wanted to be there for you."

Her lips droop. "But you weren't there when I woke up."

"I couldn't be there with you." I take another step in her direction, "Not when I could have stopped the mission from going forward. It was more than a feeling; I had information the mission could be compromised—"

"You had information?" she asks slowly.

I widen my stance, shoulders squared, spine straight. *You can do this, soldier. You owe it to her to do this. You owe her the truth.* "It wasn't confirmed, but there were indications." *Why is this so hard? I faced down an enquiry for this and was cleared and yet, the guilt has never left me. Is that why I want to come clean to her? To assuage my conscience? No, it's more than that. I want her to know everything about what happened to Ben. I want to do the right thing by her.*

"There were indications?" Her forehead wrinkles.

I nod. "I'd heard from unconfirmed sources that the mission could be compromised. That the enemy soldiers knew about our move. That our team could be ambushed. I told Ben it was best to cancel, but he knew how important it was to move. He knew, if we didn't take that opportunity, it would lead to other, much bigger losses on our side."

"You let him sacrifice himself?" Her voice is cold.

"No, not at all." I walk over to her and sink down on my knees in front of her, but when I try to take her hands in mine, she pulls away. I'm left looking up at her with an imploring expression on my face. "That's not what happened at all. He was a soldier; he had a right to decide if he wanted to move forward. He, and everyone else in our battalion."

"You were their leader—"

"And their strategist. I had no family. I had nothing to lose. I decided to move forward. I *wanted* to do it on my own, but —"

"Ben wouldn't let you go alone."

"I told him not to come." I shake my head. That scene is fresh in my mind. "I told him he needed to stay back. He could coordinate the mission from base instead. That's as important as being on the front lines. But he laughed at me. He asked if I wanted to keep all the fun for myself. He asked why I was being that selfish. I told him to think of you."

"And?" She swallows. "What did he say?"

51

Nathan

"That you were a soldier's sister. You knew how important it was for him to give his best for our country. He was insistent. He was filled with a sense of purpose, a sense that this is where he was needed."

"So, you both went on that last mission, and Ben saved your life."

A ball of emotion clogs my throat, and I nod. She remembers that. She remembers who I am. I was worried that when her memory of what happened to Ben returned, she might forget who I was, but she hasn't. *Thank fuck.* I nod slowly.

"The bomb that hurt my hearing on that mission, the one Ben saved me from"—I swallow—"it also injured him. He was bleeding profusely from a chest wound. I patched him up. I wanted to carry him to the extraction point, but he insisted on making it on his own steam, so we could carry our dead comrades with us. Once we got on the chopper, he collapsed. I held his hand on the journey back."

The scent of copper, of burned flesh, of death on the fringes of the space washes over me again. My stomach lurches. Acid burns the back of my mouth, but I choke it down.

"I told him he had to live. I asked him to think of you, and you know what he said?"

She shakes her head, her eyes wide in her pale face.

"He said as long as I was there, he knew you'd be fine."

Her lips tremble.

"He asked me to look out for you. He made me promise I'd always be there for you."

"Oh, Ben." She takes a step back and comes up against the ledge of the window.

Emotion squeezes my chest. I shift my weight from knee to knee. "He made it back to base, made what seemed to be a full recovery but —" I roll my shoulders. "But he wasn't ready to return to civilian life. He knew he'd lost his edge and could never be sent on a mission again. It was as if he'd lost his purpose."

"He survived the mission?" She chews on her lower lip. I keep my gaze off the glistening flesh. Now's not the time to think of how my cock twitches every time she worries her lip with her teeth.

"He did. But he didn't want you to know. It was as if he knew his days were numbered."

"What... What happened?"

"They found him on his bed, dressed in his uniform. He'd put a bullet through his head."

"Oh, my god!" She slaps her palms over her mouth.

"It was my fault. I never should have left him alone. I'd stayed by his side throughout everything. I thought he was getting better. That was the first day I stepped away for a walk. Turns out, he'd bribed one of the cleaning staff in the hospital to procure a gun. I should have realized how desperate he was. He was no longer the cheerful soldier I knew. He'd become withdrawn, depressed. I should have realized he'd gone into a dark place inside. I should have helped him. Should have insisted he was watched around the clock. I failed."

That weight in my stomach sinks to my feet. I lower my chin to my chest. "I'm so sorry, Starling. It's my fault he's not here. If I could exchange my life for his, I'd do it. If there were anything I could do to take his place, I would."

"Don't say that."

There's a touch on my head, and when I look up, she runs her fingers through my hair.

"I'm not sure I would've survived your dying," she whispers.

"I live with the guilt of having survived every single day."

She lowers her hand, and this time, when I catch it, she doesn't pull away. "I love you, Starling."

She shakes her head. "Yet, you played me. All along, you knew the truth and you never told me."

I set my jaw. "You were fragile. The doctors said your memories could come back at any time, but I had to allow it to happen naturally, on your timetable. I had to protect you from the truth until you were strong enough to face it."

"You mean, you were waiting until you could use the situation to your advantage by asking me to marry you in return for your helping to save my business."

I square my shoulders. "No, it wasn't until I saw you again that I realized I couldn't continue living without you. And maybe, it was a bit heavy-handed to push you into a marriage you didn't want, and I'll admit, I was being selfish. But as far as reminding you of the truth, I was warned, if I revealed anything before you were ready, it could make your condition worse. No matter how much it would have relieved my conscience, I couldn't burden you. You were my priority. I had to do everything in my power to ensure you were shielded—"

She purses her lips. "You mean lied to, don't you?"

I flinch. "I mean, sheltered"—I swallow— "from anything that could upset your already fragile state. Meanwhile, you had to live life as usual. It was tough for me to watch you from a distance, but I forced myself to comply. I knew it was better for you to let things be. I forced myself to bide my time and not approach you. Until my grandfather insisted I go to your bakery that day."

"You knew you were going to see me when you came into the bakery that day?"

I nod.

"But you seemed so angry. So unapproachable. You seemed to resent the fact that you were seeing me again. I was convinced you hated me because I'd thrown myself at you and kissed you the last time we'd met."

"Not you, me. I hated how much I wanted you when I came face-to-face with you at the bakery. I'd been watching you from afar, but being so close to you"—I draw in a breath— "I realized how much I wanted you in my life. I knew I was going to use the situation to my advantage. I knew I was going to ask you to marry me in return for saving your business. Seeing you forced all of my feelings to the surface. I didn't want to wait any longer. What if someone else found you, and I never had another chance? I couldn't let that happen. I knew I'd regret it forever. I thought about coming clean then, on everything—"

"But you didn't."

"I couldn't." I square my shoulders. "The memories had to come back to you in an organic fashion. I couldn't risk saying or doing anything that might trigger you."

Her throat moves as she swallows. Her chin quivers. I see the rejection in her eyes, and my heart seems to shatter.

"Don't hate me, Starling, please."

"I... I don't hate you, Nate. I can't. Ben wouldn't have wanted that."

"And he probably wouldn't agree with everything I've done so far, but I swear, I only had your best interests at heart."

A tear runs down her cheek.

"Don't cry, baby, please." I wipe away the moisture, then cup her cheek. "I'm so sorry I hurt you. I didn't mean to. I was sure I'd be able to handle the meeting with you, but seeing you, talking to you, brought back all the guilt I associated with you, and it all snowballed from that. First, the kiss on your eighteenth birthday—"

"I kissed you," she reminds me.

"And I kissed you back." I tip up my chin. "You were a kid—"

"I was eighteen. An adult."

I firm my lips. "You were my best friend's little sister. And I took advantage of you."

"Oh, please, you didn't do anything I didn't want you to then. Or now."

I shake my head. "I thought I'd be able to resist you this time around. My idea was to meet you and tell you I had the money to help your business."

She scoffs. "I never would've accepted it. Not after the way you walked away from me on my eighteenth birthday. You never spoke to me again, until—"

"Until the day I came to your place to tell you about your brother. A day that caused you so much agony, you wanted to block it out of your memory."

She swallows. Anguish clings to her features. Every part of me insists I take her in my arms and hold her close to console her. I lean toward her, then stop. If I do that, I won't be able to stop myself from carrying her back home and keeping her there until we've sorted things out, and... That would be unfair to her. After everything I've said and done, which has complicated both of our lives further, I owe it to her to come clean on all of the facts.

She tugs on her hand, and I release it.

"And the proposal to marry me? What was that about?"

"I saw the opportunity, I took it. I thought we could help each other. I thought I could use the money I had toward some good, while keeping you close. I did not...did not...mean to..."

"Fuck me?"

"To fall for you all over again. I realized living under the same roof as you, there was no way I could keep my distance. Not when everything in me wanted our arrangement to be real. Not when I realized I'd known you were the woman for me from the moment I kissed you."

She rubs at her temple. "Did... Did Ben know how rich you are?"

"He knew I was independently wealthy, thanks to the investments I made. I was lucky in that. I didn't need the Davenports' money. But when Arthur asked me to return after I left the Marines, I figured, why not? It was a way of getting to know my half-brothers. I figured that this was my way to—" I look away, unable to complete my sentence.

When I look back at her, she searches my features. "What are you not telling me? Are you going to hide something else from me, after everything that's happened?"

I shake my head. "No more lies. No more omissions. I'm going to use my position within the Davenport organization to implode the company. This is my revenge for what they did to my mother."

"So, the reason you're here is because you wanted to get vengeance for what happened to you and your mother?"

I peer into her face. "The reason I'm here is because of you. Everything else is secondary."

"And yet, you never told me about my brother."

"I tried," I protest. "Then, I had to wait until the right time. I had to wait so it wouldn't hurt you further. When you woke up at the hospital, the doctors realized you didn't remember what had happened before the accident. But you hadn't suffered a hit to the head. When they spoke to me, they concluded it was because of the emotional trauma you'd suffered. That, combined with the physical shock of the accident, had resulted in you temporarily blocking out the news of your brother's death. They told me your memories would come back to you, but I had to let it happen on its own."

"So why didn't you meet me in the hospital? Why weren't you there for me?"

"I... I felt responsible for what had happened. For not being able to save your brother. For being the one to tell you the news. I figured, if you saw me, I'd serve as a reminder of what had happened. The memory was so new, even if you had repressed it. You were so fragile then. I discussed it with the doctors, and they agreed that if you saw me, everything related to your brother would rush to the fore. It was too soon. They advised me to give you a little time to recover. And to be honest, it was a relief... Because I knew that every time I looked at you, I'd feed the guilt I felt over what had happened — and I wouldn't even be able to tell you."

"You didn't have those concerns when you walked into the bakery and asked me to marry you?"

"A year had passed since the death of your brother. I figured you were in a stronger place. Also, I checked in with your doctor."

"The one I've had regular check-ups with since the accident?"

I rub the back of my neck. "It wasn't easy getting him to... agree to talk to me, but I was persistent."

She stares. "You threatened him?"

"Nothing as crude as that. I paid enough money to build a new wing for the hospital, and I named it after him."

"Of course you did," she scoffs.

"All that money I had access to was of some use. I didn't take what I did lightly. I knew I was making him infringe on doctor patient confidentiality. And I might have played the card of my being a veteran, as well, but needs must. When I explained the situation... That, combined with the generous donation, helped him come around."

"I... I don't know what to say." She looks at me with anger and frustration. "I am so angry with you right now."

"And you have every right to be. But I was desperate. When I saw you that day, I knew I wouldn't be able to leave you again. I knew I needed a reason to keep you close. I knew I couldn't live without you. I needed a legitimate reason for being in your life, Starling."

She rubs at her forehead. "If you came in that day, knowing you were going to invest in my business, then why did you say you were leaving before you'd even tasted any of my cakes."

I half smile. "That was a tactic to get you worked up. If you thought you were going to lose the investment, you'd want it even more."

"I forget how good you are at negotiating," her voice is bitter.

"No, baby, please don't get upset. I... I was in the same boat. Being so close to you had brought back all of the memories. All of the reasons why I needed to find a way to have you in my life."

"I don't know what to say." She shakes her head. "I knew there were gaps in my memory, but I never would've guessed there was something so significant."

"All that time, I kept my distance, but I never stopped looking out for you. I made sure you were safe. And then, when you found out Hugo had been injured in that same accident... That he hadn't gotten away unhurt... That he was in bad shape —"

"I blamed myself for the accident. If I hadn't asked him to come in that day and open the store with me. If I hadn't run out in front of his bike, he wouldn't have lost control." She looks away. "I knew I couldn't leave him at the mercy of the state. I knew I had to take care of him."

"In a way, I knew you were replacing the gap in your memory and everything that had happened to Ben by creating a different story and taking care of Hugo."

"He's my friend. I had a responsibility."

"And you didn't shy away. It's why I knew —"

"—that you had to help me. And since you were watching me, you knew I was in financial trouble with the bakery." Her lips thin.

I hold out my palm. She looks at it for a second, then slowly places her hand in mine again. *Thank fuck!* I thread my fingers through hers. "I did. I admit that. But I didn't interfere in that, and I haven't asked you to change the location of the bakery, either."

"What's wrong with this location?" She frowns.

"You know it's not the safest part of town."

"It's an up-and-coming, gentrifying area, and the most sought after by hipsters," she points out.

"It's also rough around the edges. It's why I —" I break off. Didn't mean for that to come out.

But my wife spots my hesitation, and her lips set in a firm line. "You're hiding something again."

"It's not important."

"Oh?" She tries to pull her hand away, but I hold on. "It really isn't."

"Tell me."

I look away, then back at her. "I watched you from a distance to make sure you were okay."

"You watched me?"

"Most nights, I parked outside. It's not like I was getting much sleep. I figured I might as well ensure you were safe."

"And I'm supposed to be grateful that you stalked me?"

"I didn't stalk. I never interfered in your life. I simply made sure I did what Ben asked of me. I made sure you were watched over. I couldn't let anything happen to you."

"We're in London; what could happen to me?" she scoffs.

"I know it seems crazy to you. But I'd just come back from war. I'd lost my best friend, my teammates. I couldn't just go back to being a civilian and discard the alertness that had kept me alive. I'm a soldier. That never goes away. I simply directed all of that vigilance into making sure you were okay."

For a few seconds, there's silence. She stares at me, and I hold her gaze.

Yes, I've done many things wrong. Maybe I've gone about this entire situation the wrong way. Maybe I should have come right out and told her everything when I walked into her bakery. But I didn't. I couldn't. I couldn't take the risk that she'd hate me for not being there for her brother. I couldn't lose her. I couldn't let her walk away from me.

And now? I know I could still lose her. I know she might never forgive me, but I know I have to come clean. Now, she remembers everything. Now, she's in a stronger place than she was before. Now I know Arthur's acknowledged her as part of the Davenport family, and that she'll get the monthly allowance all Davenports are eligible for. Now I know she'll be looked after, no matter what happens between us, or to the Davenport Group of companies. Now, she knows that... "I love you"—I kiss her hand, then look up into her face—"and I always will, even if you never do."

A tear rolls down her cheek, and plops onto mine. "Oh, Nate, why does everything have to be so complicated?"

52

Skylar

"And then you asked him to leave?" Zoey slides a cup of hot chocolate across the table. She called me, saw my face, and told me she was coming over to the apartment. I didn't protest. Not when I felt so lonely.

"I told him I need a little time to figure things out. I just need to get my head around everything he revealed."

I'm strangely dry-eyed. You'd think I'd be in tears, maybe hysterical, because I found out my brother is dead.

All those conversations I had with him on the phone, the messages I exchanged with him, the fact I saw him like he was real… Clearly, it was my imagination working overtime. It felt so real. Which, if I'm being honest, scares the crap out of me. How could my mind play tricks on me like that?

And yet, when I think about it, maybe a part of me knew I was talking to someone who wasn't alive anymore. Maybe I knew my brain was trying to fill in the blanks in my life with images of Ben. That I was holding conversations with him as if he were alive, as a way of coping. And now, I can't. And I don't want to admit it, even to myself, but I'm embarrassed. How can I trust anything I see anymore without wondering if my brain is trying to shield me from some kind of trauma?

I glance at the phone I placed next to me on the table. It's been silent since he left. Not that I've been expecting him to call me. Okay, maybe I am. But why should he when I'm the one who told him to leave? I told him I needed some space to consider everything. I need a little time.

His features had closed, but not before I saw the anguish in his eyes. Then he nodded. He told me he wasn't going to rush me into anything, that I have to decide what's best for me. He understood I'd need to digest everything. He also told me he'll always be there for me, but that almost makes it worse. How can he be so patient, so calm, when it feels like everything around me is collapsing? Like one part of my life is over, and I'm on the precipice of something huge.

I take a sip of the chocolate, and the bitter-sweet taste of the cocoa coats my tongue. The fragrance of cinnamon fills my nose. The depth of nutmeg, the pungent tang of cardamom, the aromatic warmth of vanilla and cloves—all of it thaws the ice in my veins. "This is good," I murmur.

"It should be; it's your recipe." She laughs.

"Of course it is." Another of my little inventions. "Chocolate Cinnamon Hero. That's what the mix is called."

"A good name, considering we want all our alphaholes to be cinnamon rolls at heart," she agrees.

"As is Nate." I swirl the spicy chocolate around my tongue. "He's growly on the outside like crisp dough that crackles on your tongue, and tender on the inside like the gooey center of a cinnamon roll."

"So you aren't pissed with him?"

"I think I am. But not because he couldn't protect my brother. I know he feels guilty about what happened to Ben, which is understandable, but Ben knew what he was getting into. It was a mission and"—I bite the inside of my cheek—"if anything had happened to Nate, I'd be a hundred times more heartbroken. I'm a terrible sister for thinking that."

"You're human." Zoey raises her own chocolate drink to her mouth and takes a sip. "And so is he. And love is messy, like the mixture of one of your experimental desserts. You put in all the ingredients, but before you bake it, it's just a lump of spiked dough sitting in a bowl. Until you bake it, you don't know how it's going to taste, or look, or if it will rise the way you want it to."

"Wow, that's a very good analogy." I look at her with admiration.

"I know, right?" She seems taken aback. "I suppose there's a reason I'm an editor. I forget sometimes—I'm good with words." She laughs.

I take another sip of chocolate and lick the mixture from my lips. "I am upset that he didn't tell me about my brother, but I also understand why he didn't. It's not like I made it easy for him. And… I don't think I could have coped with it if he'd come out and told me."

She nods.

"But I'm upset that he didn't just tell me he loved me —"

"He did; you told me so."

"I mean, that he didn't come out and tell me he loved me and he wanted to marry me when he first came back to the bakery."

"And how would you have reacted to that?"

I think about it, and heat steals over my cheeks. "Not well. I'd have thought he was joking. Or he was taking pity on me for having walked out on me after I kissed him. I'd tried my best to forget him all these years."

"So, how do you feel about what he's done now?"

"It still feels like he could have been more open about it. He told me he pressured the doctor until he was willing to discuss my case."

"He did?" She frowns.

"And then, many nights, he parked outside my window and watched over me for the last year."

"That's both persistent, and a little unnerving."

"He's clearly skillful about it, because I never spotted him. But it also means, when he walked into my bakery and asked me to marry him, he knew about my situation with the bakery. And with Hugo."

Her eyes grow big. "Wow, okay. That's a lot."

"Yeah. But you know what's even more messed up?"

"You love him?"

"Damn him, but I do. And he's my husband. I can't think of living my life without him. Is that weird?"

She places her cup on the table, then leans over to place her hand on mine. "It's not weird. Anyone has only to see the two of you in a room to realize there's a connection between both of you. Somehow, you fit."

"If that's meant to make me feel better —"

"It's what I see. Doesn't mean you have to condone what he did. And not even because he thought it was in your best interests to do so."

53

Nathan

"I'll have the same." Quentin slides onto the barstool next to mine. I'm at the 7A Club because I couldn't bear to be home without her. And I didn't want to end up at her doorstep just twenty-four hours after she asked for time to think things through. Also, I'm not going to park my car outside her place and watch her, the way I've done so many nights over the past year.

I promised her I'd let her be. I promised myself I'd let her come to me. And I have to stick to that. No matter, if it's turning my guts inside out and making me feel like my skin is being peeled off of me. So, after my meetings today, I find myself at the 7A Club because, where else does a man go on a night when his wife is not home?

The bartender pours out a glass of sparkling water and slides it over to him. He looks at it with distaste. "On second thought, get me a Macallan." He pushes the glass of fizzy water in my direction. "I forgot you don't drink. Here, knock yourself out."

"I already did." I push aside my empty glass, pick up the one he passed me, and take a sip.

"Do I detect a note of self-pity?"

"And more." I stare into my glass of water. If there were an occasion I could do with a drink, it's now. But there's no way I'm going down that path again. Instead, I take another sip of the water. "She hates me. I made sure she hates me. I'm a self-sabotaging prick and I brought this upon myself."

He whistles, then snatches up the tumbler of whiskey the bartender placed in front of him. He tosses it back, then slaps it back on the wood. "Needed that. Can't listen to confessions without alcohol in my veins." He turns to me. "Now, tell Uncle Quentin everything."

I snort. "You're what, fifteen years older than me?"

"Doesn't change the fact I'm your uncle."

"What-fucking-ever." I throw back the rest of the water, then signal to the guy behind the bar to top me up.

"Don't overdo it, eh?" He smirks.

I half laugh, then... *What the hell? It's not like I have anyone else to talk to.* Ben's gone. And regardless of what my wife says, regardless of the Marines absolving me of all wrongdoing; yes, there was an enquiry into my actions, before they decided to reward me with a medal. Another reason I lost faith in them. How could you deem my actions wrong one day, then, just because a panel of people find you did nothing wrong, decide to praise you for the same? It makes no sense. But then, little in the world does—except her. And I couldn't look her in the eye after she regained consciousness. I watched her from afar, and convinced myself she was better off without me. I couldn't forget the shock and anger in her eyes when she saw me and then, the devastation when she realized what I was about to say. She wasn't able to hear it from me. She didn't want it to be her reality. It's why she ran out of the apartment. And I wasn't able to stop her. I wasn't able to get to her in time.

Once again, I'd failed her. And this, despite promising Ben I'd look after her. Then, I took advantage of her situation and coerced her into marrying me. Nothing makes what I did right. I can't justify it. I'm in the wrong, period. I need to pay for it.

"Hey, where did you go to?" I look up to find Quentin's worried glance on me. "You okay, mate? You don't look so hot."

"I'm afraid I've committed a mistake I'll never recover from."

"Did you try apologizing to her?"

I nod.

"And?"

"It's not enough. What I did to her, no apology can put right."

He rubs his chin. "So what will put it right?"

"I... I'm not sure." For the first time in my life, I'm completely and utterly at a loss. How could I have come to this? The man who's survived on his own since he was eighteen, who made it through some of the highest profile missions the Marines ran, the man who took out enemy soldiers in hand-to-hand combat, laid low by a curvaceous siren who occupies his every thought.

A new voice growls from behind me, "I'll tell you what I'm sure of, you're a mother-fucking traitor." I hear the whistle of the breeze, and I could duck, but I don't. Instead, I let Knox's fist connect with my chin. The force of the blow knocks me off the bar stool. I hit the floor, the back of my head smashing into the hard tiles. Searing pain splits my skull. I see sparks behind my eyes. When it clears, Knox's angry face looms over mine. "You bastard. How long have you been planning this?" He grabs my collar.

I let him haul me to my feet. When he pulls back his fist, I go lax in his grasp. *I need this. I deserve this. I should be beaten up for everything I did to her.*

He lets his fist fly, but Quentin blocks it. A sharp cut to Knox's other arm has him loosening his hold on me. Quentin shoves him away. "Hold on, now."

"Don't fucking interrupt, old man. This is between me and my fucking half-brother." Knox says half-brother in a derisive voice, which I must admit, is a fine touch. What's more, I deserve it.

"What the fuck is wrong with you?" Quentin growls.

"The fuck is wrong with you?" Knox turns on him. "This fucker tried to sell us out, and you're protecting him?"

Quentin frowns. "Sell us out?"

"He made a deal with our competitors, the bloody Whittingtons."

Quentin scoffs, then he sees the look on my face, and all mirth disappears from his features. "The fuck have you done, Nathan?"

"Nothing the lot of you don't deserve. Present company excluded." I move my jaw this way, then that. "Doesn't seem like anything's broken." I smirk at Knox. "Couldn't do one thing right, hmm?"

Knox's nostrils flare. Rage lights up his eyes. With a snarl, he charges, but once more, Quentin slaps his arm against Knox's chest. "Cut it out."

"I am going to kill you." Anger leaps off of Knox, a thick wall of hate, which I welcome.

"Join the queue." I bare my teeth at him.

Quentin looks around. "You lot may not care about the reputation of the Davenports—"

"Like you do?" Knox snorts.

"Only to the extent it hurts my inheritance."

"Thought you didn't care about that?" I narrow my gaze on him.

"Things change. Turns out, I'm more of a family man than I'd like to admit, what with my son getting married—"

"You have a son?" I blink.

"Of marriageable age? You're old," Knox growls.

"Had him at twenty-six, not that it's any of your business. But"—he looks between the two of us—"what happens to the Davenport Group is important to me, now that I run one of the companies." He glances around at the interested eyes watching us. "I think we've attracted enough attention. Shall we take this behind closed doors?"

54

Nathan

"He's got it wrong. I wasn't selling off the company; I was saving it."

Knox tosses his head. "You're going to deny you met with the Whittingtons on their turf yesterday?"

He's right. After leaving her place, I called up Toren Whittington, their CEO, and arranged to meet him. "Doesn't mean my actions are detrimental to the company." I'm seated on one end of the rectangular table in a conference room of the 7A Club. The table has four chairs at the center of each side.

Quentin raised an eyebrow at one of the staff and secured the room for us. Impressive, considering the club is frequented by those who wield the kind of power that can change the fate of nations. He wears authority like he was born into it, which he was. He was a Rear Admiral in the Royal Marines before he took early retirement. He's used to commanding men who, while trained to follow orders, did not always do so with readiness, as I know from experience.

"So why did you meet them?" He scowls at me. He's foregone the chair and is standing at the midpoint of the table between Knox and me. A neutral zone to indicate he's not taking any sides, but he's remained standing in order to show he's the one in charge. Man's canny as fuck.

"I was staving off a hostile takeover."

Knox snorts. "Fucking lies, he —"

Quentin holds up his hand. Knox seems like he's going to defy him, but to my surprise, he lapses. Though his gaze promises all kinds of retribution. I hold his gaze and cross my arms over my chest. I'm not backing down, either.

"If you'd bothered to check the movements of stocks before you came, you'd see that our other rivals, the Madisons, began buying up stock from the five percent owned by our non-family, minority shareholders over the last week. While that, in itself, is not a threat, if they'd succeeded in buying up the entire five percent, it would've given them a seat on the board, which would have made things very difficult for us. It's why I approached the Whittingtons."

"Why would you do that?" Quentin frowns.

"They own five percent of our group."

"Not possible. Arthur hates them." Knox scoffs. "There's a family feud with them."

"— because a Whittington and a Davenport fought over a Madison woman generations ago. They settled it with us selling five percent of the company to the Whittingtons. The Madisons were left out, which is why they're hungry to get a portion of the company. Not that selling a stake in the company to the Whittingtons back then helped," I widen my stance. "The hate between the Davenports and the Whittingtons never died down. All of this is, of course, a well-kept company secret. Until now."

"The fuck?" Knox narrows his gaze on me.

"How do you know this?" There's an almost admiring note in Quentin's voice.

"Research into family history, one of my favorite pastimes."

"You mean, you had an investigator look into it?" He smirks.

When I don't reply, Knox jumps up and slams both of his hands on the table. A glass of water tips over, rolls to the edge, then thumps against the carpeted floor. Not one of the three of us react.

"You didn't think I'd join the company, no matter that you're blood family, without due diligence, did you?" I drawl.

His nostrils flare.

"It's what anyone would do in his position," Quentin murmurs.

"Is that what you did?" Knox rounds on him. "Did you investigate us before you accepted Arthur's offer of becoming the CEO of the info-communication division?"

Quentin smiles slowly. "I didn't need to; I already knew Arthur couldn't be trusted. But did I ask to look at the books of the info-comm companies before I accepted the proposal? You bet I did."

"Motherfucker," he growls.

"Now that we have that out of the way" — Quentin turns to me — "let me get this right. You found out the Madisons were buying up shares in the Davenport Group, so you approached the Whittingtons?"

"I sold them five percent of my shares." When I agreed to take over as interim CEO of the group, Arthur transferred nine percent of his shares to me, bringing down his stake to forty-two percent. It made me the second largest shareholder in the group, after him.

"You what?" Knox explodes.

"As of this morning, the Whittington Group owns ten percent of the Davenport Group, giving us the capital to buy back the Madisons' shares."

"The Madisons sold back the shares?" Knox asks in a disbelieving voice.

"They did when I revealed a family secret they weren't keen on being made public."

Quentin smirks. "You blackmailed them?"

"I prefer to think of it as light coercion," I drawl.

Knox sets his jaw. "And the secret — "

"Is between me and them. Suffice to say this ensures they'll never attempt such a tactic again. Once the transaction is complete, my share will be back at nine percent, and none of your holdings will be impacted."

"Except, we'll be in bed with our worst enemies." Knox drags his hand through his hair. "Fucking hell."

"Should prove interesting, for sure." I smirk.

The sound of clapping reaches us. All three of us turn to the doorway of the room to find Arthur standing there. He walks into the room, Tiny at his heels. The mutt pads over to butt my side, waits for me to pet him, then walks over to Knox.

"Good boy." He tugs at Tiny's ears.

The Great Dane makes a rumbling noise at the back of his throat. He brushes his head against Knox's thigh, then heads to Quentin. He pants up at the man, his tongue lolling. Quentin quirks his lips and scratches him under his chin. Tiny's smile seems to grow wider. He wags his flagstaff-like tail, barks a soft woof, then circles around back to where Arthur has taken up position on the opposite side of Quentin.

Arthur lowers his bulk into the chair and sighs. Man's looking every one of his eighty-two years today. There are shadows under his eyes, and his cheekbones are pronounced. However, when he places his elbows on the table and steeples his fingers together, his hands are steady. He glances at Knox, then Quentin, before turning to me. "You did well."

I blink. "I did?" I ask, caution in my tone.

"What are you saying?" Knox bursts out. "He's ensured we're joined at the hip with those Whittingtons."

Arthur pays him no heed. "You prevented the Madisons from buying up shares in our company, didn't you?" He addresses his question to me.

I nod slowly.

"Then you did the right thing."

"Even though it means that the Whittingtons now have access to all our accounts and our secrets. Have you forgotten how they sabotaged our entry into the Asian market?" Knox argues.

"And blocked us when we tried to launch our new media company; I'm aware," Arthur replies without taking his gaze from my face.

"Don't forget, there's a Whittington in the position of Prime Minister of the country," I prod.

"You're talking about Hunter Whittington?" Knox frowns.

"He's Toren Whittington's cousin. Don't believe the two men see eye-to-eye on much, but they're family. I'm sure it doesn't hurt to have the Whittington surname opening even more doors," Quentin murmurs.

Arthur leans back in his chair. "Not that I'm happy with the Whittingtons acquiring additional stake in my company."

"You still own fifty-one percent of the shares," I point out.

"You mean *you* own fifty-one percent of the shares."

"I do?" I ask, a cautious note in my voice.

"As of this moment, since I confirmed you as group CEO. With it, I am transferring thirty-five percent of my stake to you. You're the majority shareholder now." Arthur's smile is grim.

"You still hold seven percent in the group, second only to the Whittingtons. And you're Chairman; you can veto any decision you don't agree with."

"Not when it's, clearly, in the best interests of the company. I will not be seen as bringing my emotions into play when it comes to making the right decision." He sets his jaw.

I stroke my chin. Interesting. Hadn't expected Arthur to play along with me. I hadn't expected him to take the news of sharing interest with the Whittingtons so calmly.

Quentin looks between us. "Everything okay?" he murmurs.

"Why wouldn't it be?" Knox frowns.

"Because I sense there's something unsaid here?" Quentin narrows his gaze on me. "What is it, Nate? What are you not saying?"

Silence descends. The tension in the room feels like the approach of a thunderstorm. Heavy, silent, but with that growing static that sets my teeth on edge and prickles the hair on my forearms taut with urgency. A heavy weight pushes down on my chest. The tension in the room is so evident, even Knox straightens. "Arthur? Gramps? What's happening?"

"Ask your half-brother," he murmurs.

Half-brother, huh? Arthur's never treated me like anything less than family before. He's never referred to me as half-anything. I place the tips of my fingers together, making myself comfortable in my chair.

"Nate?" Knox's gaze is piercing across the space. "What have you done?"

"You sure you want to know?" I half smile, still holding Arthur's gaze. A bead of sweat slides down my spine, but I ignore it.

"Of-fucking-course, I do. Will you come out and tell us already?"

I turn to Knox. "I'm appointing you as the deputy CEO."

Knox blinks, then barks out a laugh. "Deputy CEO."

"Gives you all the powers of a CEO—you can step in when I'm not around. And you can bet I'll take advantage of that, considering I want to spend more time with my wife."

Knox's frown deepens. He opens and shuts his mouth, then shakes his head. "The fuck? I don't think I trust why you're doing this."

"Does it matter?" I half smile. "It puts you in the driver's seat. Isn't that what you want? Also"—I turn to Quentin—"in addition to taking over as the CEO of the info-comms division, I'd like to appoint you as Group Chief Operating Officer."

He scans my features. "That's a big responsibility."

"It is."

"I've yet to acclimate to my existing role."

"I'm sure you can manage."

He nods slowly. "Can I think about this and give you my answer later?"

"Of course." I look around the table. "If that will be all…" I rise to my feet.

"Sit down," Arthur snaps.

Fucking hell, and I thought I'd pulled it off. I thought I'd made it through this meeting without having to be interrogated by Gramps, but apparently not.

"I need to speak with Nathan"—he sets his jaw—"alone."

Both Quentin and Knox hesitate. Then Quentin spins around on his heels and walks out, followed by Knox. The door snicks shut. Silence descends. Tiny sneezes. It seems to shake Arthur out of his reverie.

He glances away and sighs. "Were you going to tell me at all?" he finally asks.

"That I had the option of selling out my shares to the Madisons, which would have resulted in them increasing their stake in our company? That I could have then coerced your grandsons into parting with their shares for the right amount, setting things up for a takeover?"

Arthur scowls. "They'd have never agreed to that."

"Considering how pissed off they are at you, and for a generous asking price—"

A shadow crosses Arthur's gaze. "But you didn't go through with the plan."

"I didn't."

A vein pops at his temple. "What stopped you? And don't tell me it's because you had an attack of conscience at the last moment."

"And if I said I did?"

Arthur's features grow more pinched. "Then I wouldn't believe you."

I hold his gaze for a second longer, then sigh. "You're right. It wasn't an attack of conscience. I did not sell out because I want to be the kind of man my wife is proud to be married to."

Surprise flits across his features, then a kind of satisfaction, before he masks it. I bet the old man is thinking he was right in making me marry. And I can't fault him.

"You wanted her to be proud of you," he says slowly.

"I did."

He lowers his chin to his chest. "And how does that make you feel?"

"Proud as hell and also, shit," I confess.

"Because you haven't gotten your revenge for how we treated your mother?"

It's my turn to be surprised, but I keep the emotion off of my features. At least, I hope I do. Since I met my wife, it's become increasingly difficult to retreat to that hardened part of me where I can hide behind the barriers I put up against the world. She's brought my emotions to the surface, and now, there's no going back to the unfeeling, dispassionate person whose focus was to avenge the wrongs done to my mother. There's no going back to the dumbass who denied his feelings for his best friend's little sister. There's no going back to staying detached from how I'd be hurting my own flesh and blood if I went through with the plan of selling out to the Madisons, then watched as they broke up the company Arthur built and sold it off for parts.

Pain laces Arthur's expression. The shadows from under his eyes seem to creep into his gaze, so when he looks at me, there's remorse etched into his features. "I don't blame you for wanting vengeance on your father's family. If I were in your shoes, I'd have wanted to do the same thing. Still, you shouldn't blame my wife for buying off your mother. Times were different then. She wanted to protect her family from what she saw as scandal that would have touched every part of our lives."

"So, she sacrificed my mother instead."

"She ensured the two of you would never lack for any creature comforts."

"Just no emotional support from the Davenports. She made it clear she didn't want me to ever know my father. And because she moved away from her family and friends, my mother found herself isolated."

"She was wrong in that." Arthur smiles sadly, the expression tinged with tiredness. "Forgive your grandmother."

"I can't forget what she did, but I'm ready to forgive and move on, thanks to my wife."

Relief floods his features. "And are you ready to forgive yourself?"

55

Skylar

"You sure you're ready to forgive him?" Grace eyes the Clitasaurus with a longing expression.

"You don't have to." Imelda snatches one of the double-chocolate bonbons shaped like a woman's butt—the ones called Spanked—and pops it into her mouth.

"Unless, of course, you want to." Summer flutters her fingers in the air. "Which one do you think? The Spicy Scene, the Red Room, or The Earth Moved?"

She's joined our weekly book club meeting. Every week, it's been a struggle to get the customers out of the shop in time to close up. Eventually, I gave up. I extended the hours, as evidenced by the people at different tables.

Hiring someone to do social media has paid off big time. That, and putting some money into advertising the bakery locally. Foot traffic has increased, mothers have begun coming in for coffee with their girlfriends, and the packed goodies are flying off the shelves. And being able to introduce free-Wi-Fi for all customers is a game-changer.

The best part? I know there are at least two romance authors who've been writing their novels in the seating area of the bakery, and they've featured the desserts in their books. For the first time since starting *The Fearless Kitten*, I'm in the black.

And it's thanks to him. Not just the money he deposited in my account, but the feedback he gave me when I showed him my business plan. The gentle nudge toward hiring staff, which I knew I should do, but couldn't find the courage to do it. He steered me in the right direction, then stepped back. If only he could see the place now.

I glance around the still-crowded shop. We managed to grab one of the bigger tables so the book club could meet. Every Friday night, the girls and I have been catching up here. It's a welcome break, and my one social activity of the week. That, and meeting up with Hugo. Initially, I went every day, but when it was clear he was getting on swimmingly well—partly due to the new medication he's on, that resulted in longer pockets of lucidity where he could communicate with me on the phone—I dropped the frequency of my visits to weekly.

I've visited him four times since Nate left. Four weeks since I last saw him.

Of course, I told him to give me time. I told him I needed space. But I didn't expect him to actually give me space. I've been sneaking glances out of my apartment window and scanning the street below, but there haven't been any cars parked there—at least, no one who looks like my husband stationed outside keeping a look out on the building. Apparently, he's sticking to his word, which is good, right? It's what I wanted, after all.

He had some of my clothes sent over and messaged me to say he'd arranged to have food delivered to me thrice a day, so I wouldn't starve. I told him he needn't have bothered, but he said he knew how hard I'd be working and that it would take me time to get my new team up and running. Meanwhile, he'd rest easy knowing I was being fed.

His words brought tears to my eyes. That's so Nathan. He cares for me so much. And he's not doing any of this as a way to push me into coming around. I mean, obviously, that's what he wants, but he's doing this because he really wants to take care of me. He's the kind of guy who'll stand by the ones he loves. Who'll do anything for his family and friends. It's why he blames himself for what happened to Ben. My phone buzzes.

I look at the message. It's not from Ben. I know I'll never hear from him again, and that's bittersweet. It's still difficult for me to believe he's gone but I'm beginning to accept it. Probably because I've lived with this reality for a year. Somewhere inside of me, I think I knew he wasn't coming back. Subconsciously, I've had time to absorb it. Maybe that's why I didn't fall apart completely again? Or maybe, I'm waiting for the opportunity to do so.

"Who's the message from?" Grace manages to tear her gaze away from the Clitasaurus long enough to ask.

"Hugo." I smile. "He's been experimenting with his new menu."

"New menu?" Zoey's voice is surprised. "He's cooking again?"

"And how." I show her the picture of the dish he texted me.

"That looks delicious." Summer smiles.

"What is it?" Imelda peers at the screen. "Is that an omelet?"

I cough, then take a drink of water before nodding at the screen. "A crab and asparagus omelet, with cherry tomatoes and rocket leaves, drizzled with balsamic glaze on the side."

Imelda whistles. "Fancy-schmancy!"

Another message comes through, and I read it out loud, "I'd love to cook for you and your book club one day soon."

"Oh, that would be great," Grace exclaims.

"He's been wanting to meet the rest of the Spicy booktokers." I laugh. That's the name we've given ourselves.

"I'd love that." Imelda nods.

"Me, too," Summer chimes in.

"Maybe we can meet him next week?" When my friends nod in assent, I text him back.

Hugo: *smile emoji* *smile emoji* I'll plan the menu
right away

"He can't wait." I laugh and set the phone aside.

"So he's doing well?" Grace finally reaches for a Clitasauraus and stares at it with reverence.

"He's improving so much. I hardly recognize him. It's amazing what the right care and medication will do." I take a sip of my tea.

"It was Nate who found the facility for him, right?" Imelda brushes the crumbs off her fingers.

I nod. We should be exchanging opinions on the last book we read, but really, we found that we got along so well, the weekly meetings have become more of an excuse to catch up on each other's lives. The very first Friday after he left, I met all of them, and before I knew it, I'd shared the entire story with them. It was such a relief, too. It felt like a weight had lifted, especially when

Grace, Imelda, and Summer empathized with me. There wasn't any judgement. Which is what I'd worried about. Zoey looked at me with an I-told-you-so expression, to which I rolled my eyes.

It gives me a warm feeling to realize I've found my tribe. Friends who have my back. A bakery that's doing well enough that I'm already thinking of expanding. And Hugo's on the mend. If only I had a chance to share his progress and that of my business with my husband. I do miss him. Don't get me wrong; I love my friends. But it's not the same as having my man by my side. A shiver grips me, and I sneeze.

"Skye?" Imelda touches my shoulder. "You okay?"

"Yes, of course." I reach for a tissue and blow my nose. "I seem to be coming down with a cold, is all. And yes, it was Nate who found the facility for him." And it was Nate who helped me turn around my business. Nate who revealed the truth of what happened to Ben. My husband may not be here in person, but he's infiltrated every part of my life.

"You miss him," Imelda murmurs.

I glance around to find the other women watching me. "I thought I wouldn't. No, that's not correct. I knew I would, but I didn't think it would be to this extent." I sniffle, then blow my nose into the tissue again. Ugh, I really am coming down with a cold. At least, I hope it's a cold and not a flu. I can't afford to get sick — not now, when I still need the new team to settle in. I have a new person behind the counter, and two new people who help fulfill deliveries within a five- mile radius of the bakery. And in addition to a social media manager, I have an advertising manager, as well as an accountant. I've gone from a one-woman operation to a small business unit employing six additional people, in a matter of weeks.

"Oh, honey, your cold seems to be getting worse." Zoey clicks her tongue. "Have you been taking your vitamins?"

Nope. I've been rushing around trying to keep busy, trying not to think of my husband. In the process, I seem to have forgotten to do basic self-care stuff, like take my daily vitamins, or work out, or eat healthy... For that matter, I probably wouldn't be eating at all if it weren't for my sweet, thoughtful husband. Who I miss.

"You've been working too hard." Grace's forehead wrinkles.

"When was the last time you took some time off?" Summer frowns. Her phone buzzes; she looks at it and sighs. "I need to go relieve the baby-sitter."

"So glad you could make it." I blow a kiss in her direction. "I'd kiss you, but I don't want to risk passing you the germs."

She blows a kiss back at me, then at the others. "It was so lovely to meet all of you. I'm going to try to make it next Friday, if all goes well. And you"—she stabs a finger in my direction—"you take care of that cold. And if you need anything—"

"I'll be fine." I laugh. "Some sleep, and I'll be right as rain tomorrow."

Ugh, I am not right as rain. In fact, it feels like a storm has taken up residence in my head. I groan, then turn on my side. The others fussed over me, including helping me to shut down the shop, and seeing me upstairs. Imelda tucked me into bed. Zoey made me a cup of hot tea with lemon and ginger and insisted I take it, along with Tylenol. I swallowed it down without protest, then fell asleep to the sound of my friends talking. When I woke up at midnight, I managed to go to the bathroom, drank some more water, then fell asleep again. I woke up with shivers wracking my body.

I peer at my phone, and realize I didn't charge it. I manage to plug it in and switch it on. It's two a.m., so it must be more than six hours since I took the last dose of Tylenol. I reach for the bottle of pills Zoey must have left behind on my nightstand, then shake out two and swallow them down with the now tepid tea. I slide down under the covers, then curl up on my side, trying to keep my body warmth in. My teeth chatter, the chills seem to intensify, and I can't stop shaking. I stuff my palms under my armpits in an attempt to warm them. I feel terrible. *Terrible.* Tears slide down my cheeks. I will not feel sorry for myself. I will not. I swipe at the moisture. Close my eyes, and sleep fitfully.

Finally, warmth sweeps over me. I sigh, snuggling into it. A heavy hand descends around my waist and pulls me against a hard front. I know it's him. "Nate," I whisper.

56

Nathan

I watch her sleep, thick eyelashes sweeping over her cheekbones. Her breathing is harsh, her cheeks are flushed, and when I push the hair back from her forehead, I feel her burning up. *Damn. I should have come sooner.*

Zoey called my office and told me Starling wasn't feeling well. I wanted to rush to her right away, but I stopped myself. I promised her I'd give her time. I also promised her I'd always be there for her—in sickness and in health. That's my vow to her. It's that vow that finally pushed me to leave the office, by which time, it was past two a.m..

I drove to her place, pulled out the key I have to her apartment, and let myself in. When I reached her bed, I found her shivering with fever. I took off my shoes, crawled into bed, and held her. She melted into me, and her trembling almost instantly subsided. She's still running a fever, but it seems to be slightly weaker in intensity than earlier. I slide out of bed, fill a glass with water, wet a washcloth, and walk back. I slide my arm under her neck, and holding up her head, place the glass to her lips. "Drink, baby."

Her eyelids flicker, then she obediently takes a few sips of water.

"When did you take the Tylenol?"

"Two a.m., I saw the time before I fell back to sleep."

I lay her back against the pillow, then place the washcloth on her forehead. "That feels good," she sighs.

I place my hand on the moist cloth, and she places her much smaller hand on mine. "I'm so glad you're here."

I bend and brush my lips over hers. "Me too, darling."

A tear squeezes out from the corner of my eye. I make no attempt to brush it off. This is how much I've missed being with my wife. How much I've missed holding her. Cuddling her in the mornings. Waking up to her sweet curves against mine. How much I've missed the beat of her heart against mine. How much I've missed the warmth of her body against mine. And yes, I've missed being inside her, too, missed the clench of her pussy around my cock as she orgasms, those breathy little moans and whines she makes when she's close. The curve of her lips, those big eyes of hers when she's surprised. I've missed everything. I've missed sharing my life with my significant other. Missed her even more, now that I know how it can be for us to be together. Missed her much more than those years I spent jerking off to the feel of her mouth against mine when she kissed me on her eighteenth birthday. I'm glad I'm here, for it's a privilege to show her how much I care.

"Maybe I should call a doctor." I begin to move away, but she grabs my wrist.

"No doctor."

"But you're not well, sweetheart."

She looks between my eyes. "You're here now. I'll be fine."

I cup her cheek. "Give me your illness, baby. I can take it."

She scoffs, "Like I want you to get sick."

"I can bear it. But seeing you unwell hurts me so much more. I'd do anything to make you feel better. Anything."

Her lips curve. "I love you." She closes her eyes.

When the cloth begins to lose its coolness, I rise, wet it under the tap in the bathroom, then return and place it on her forehead. I find a basin in her kitchen, fill it with water and place it on her nightstand. I continue to wet the washcloth and place it on her forehead throughout the night. As the silvery light of dawn filters in through the window, her fever breaks. I wipe the sweat from her forehead, then gently run the cloth over her neck, before I toss it back into the basin.

The tension drains from my muscles, and I yawn. I've been in enough fights to realize I'm facing an adrenaline dip. This, nursing her through this fever, is, by far, one of the more serious battles I've fought. And no way am I losing to this illness. But she's better now. I yawn again, then slip into the bed and gather her close. My breathing mirrors hers and I drift off to sleep. When I wake up it's to find her staring at me.

"How are you feeling now?" I tuck strands of her hair behind her ear.

"Like I've run a marathon." She coughs. "But otherwise, much better."

"You need to stay in bed today."

"Will you stay with me?"

I nod, then place the back of my hand on her forehead. "No fever, that's good."

"Did you get any sleep?" She touches my cheek. "You look tired."

"Now that you're feeling better, I'm good."

She smiles. "It's nice to be with you."

"Only nice?"

She laughs. "It's almost decadent that you're taking care of me, to be honest."

I frown. "It's my duty, and my responsibility, and the most important thing in the world."

She flushes. "You say the sweetest things."

"And you're the sweetest thing in my life."

"Sweeter than the desserts I create?"

"Sweeter than even that penis-shaped cake you have in your shop."

"Jealous of a snack, hmm?"

"Hardly. We both know my cock is much bigger and can get much harder than any of those dildo shaped sweet dishes you create."

"Is that right?" She slides her hand between us and squeezes my morning wood.

I groan. "No baby. Not now."

"Why not?" She frowns.

"You're not well."

"I'm feeling much better, thanks to you." She continues to massage my dick from crown to base, and all the blood drains to my groin.

"Fuck," I growl.

"That's what I want from you."

I place my hand on hers and, for a second, hold it there. I'd give anything to have her continue to jerk me off, but at this rate, I'll come in my pants in seconds, and that's not fair to her. Besides, no way, am I letting her do all the work. "And I want to make love to you, but you need to get better first." I manage to pry her hand away from my throbbing shaft and bring it to my mouth. I kiss her fingertips. "I love you."

"I love you, too," she murmurs.

I pause. I heard her earlier, but I was sure she said it because she wasn't fully awake. But here she is, looking at me, and smiling that angelic smile of hers, and telling me the three words I've wanted to hear from her for so long. I trace my thumb around the wedding ring I gave her. "Say that again."

"I love you." She tips up her head and presses her lips to mine. "Only you."

57

Skylar

We did stay in bed all day. More precisely, I did. While he made sure I was hydrated by making first, tea and toast, and then, soup for me. And it didn't come out of a can. He also didn't order in. He used my food processor and insisted on making it from scratch. Is there anything hotter than watching your man cook for you? The bread, he picked up downstairs. But first, he insisted I call my employees and let them know I was taking a day off. Not that I needed much urging.

Not having him for almost a month, I was starved for his company. I couldn't keep my eyes off of him. And god, I want him so much. He took off his jacket, rolled up the sleeves of his shirt to show off those muscled forearms, and I swooned. And when he brought me breakfast in bed, I noticed he'd taken off his socks and shoes. Bare feet on this man were almost as sexy as seeing him naked. Almost.

I was so disappointed when he didn't want to make love to me. So, when he filled the tub with hot water, carried me to the bathroom, then helped me peel off my sweat-dampened pajamas, I was sure he'd follow me in. But nope, that didn't happen. He helped me into the tub, and when I tried to pull him in, he shook his head. He gently ran a washcloth over my shoulders, my chest, my back, without once looking at my boobs, or any other part of me. I was so disappointed. I tried to draw attention to my breasts, but he refused to look at them. He washed and conditioned my hair before rinsing it. He finished washing me, then pulled the plug on the bathtub.

He urged me to my feet, then wrapped a towel around me. He helped me out of the tub, proceeded to dry every inch of my body—yes, even between my legs. He patted my pussy dry, and little sparks of lust fanned to life under my skin. He ran the towel down my inner thigh, and a quiver surged up my back. And when he brushed the skin between my toes, those sparks of lust turned into a full-fledged inferno, which turned my insides to mush. When I swayed, he swept me up in his arms and asked me if I was okay.

I whined and told him I wasn't because he wasn't inside me. To which he laughed and said I needed to get better first. By then, I was feeling a little woozy, so I curled up into his chest. He carried me to bed, seated me in front of him, combed out my hair and blotted it dry. I leaned back into him and closed my eyes.

The next time I open them, it's noon. I feel so much better. I glance across the expanse of the flat to see him cooking. As I pull on a pair of yoga pants and a sweatshirt, he turns and smiles at me. "How are you feeling now?"

"Pretty good."

He surveys my face, then nods. "You look much better." He gestures to the tiny kitchen table. "Have a seat."

"Gotta use the bathroom first." I smile and head into the bathroom where I take care of business before rinsing off my face and quickly brushing my teeth. Exiting moments later, I cheerfully state, "Now, I feel better."

He chuckles as I take my place at the table. He places a bowl of soup in front of me, and toasted bread next to it. "Eat." He slips into the chair next to mine.

"What about you?"

"If you eat, my hunger is assuaged."

"Aww." Warmth coils in my chest.

"It's true." He spoons out some of the soup and holds it up to my mouth. I allow him to feed me a few mouthfuls. "I really think you can eat."

"I want to see you eat first."

"Please?" I curl my fingers around his wrist. "I am feeling much better, and I'll enjoy this meal a lot more if you eat it with me."

He searches my features, then his lips quirk. "As you wish." He places the spoon in the bowl, gets up and serves himself.

"This soup is delicious." I butter some of the bread and pop it into my mouth.

"My mother's recipe. She had her faults, but she was a big believer in the power of chicken soup. I have so many memories of her taking care of me and making me soup when I was unwell. Funny how your memories tend to focus on the good parts and forget the bad ones." He looks into his soup bowl with a contemplative expression in his eyes.

"Life is too short to dwell on what caused us pain. It's so much healthier to forgive and move on."

"Have you forgiven me?" He looks up and into my face. "Can you forgive me, baby, for not telling you about Ben?"

I place my spoon back in my bowl and lean back. "I know you were doing what you thought was best, and you thought you were protecting me, but now that I know the truth, it almost feels like you were lying to me all that time. And that's not a good feeling. I know what you did was to protect me, and I know I didn't make it easy for you when you first came here to tell me... Of course I forgive you. But I'm not that eighteen-year-old girl you met anymore. I've grown up."

"No kidding," he murmurs.

"You know I have. And I've grown even more over the past year, as my subconscious was slowly coming to terms with the reality I didn't want to face. The thing is, I can take care of myself. I admit my bakery business had a patchy start to it, but it's doing well now, thanks to you."

"Don't thank me. You made the decision to accept my proposal. You did what was needed to pull your business out of the red. The success is all yours."

"Thank you," I say softly.

His lips quirk. "You're welcome."

I prop my elbow on the table and cradle my chin in my palm. "And thank you for taking care of me."

"It was my pleasure—not that you fell sick, obviously, but that I could be there for you. That's all I want, Starling—to be with you. I spent my life looking for a purpose and now, I know what it is." He looks at me with so much emotion in his eyes. He's normally such a grumphole, I wouldn't have thought it possible that he could feel so much.

"It's you, baby." He goes down on his knees and takes my hand in his. "Marrying you is the biggest achievement of my life. Being at your side is my privilege. Becoming your husband is everything I have ever wanted. Calling you my wife is my honor, and something I will never take for granted. I love you, Starling. I swore to protect you, cherish you, worship you with my body and soul, and I intend to never break those vows."

"Nate." My heart feels too big for my chest. There are all these emotions racing through me, and I'm not sure if I can contain them. It feels too big for me. "I love you, Nate."

His features soften, and his eyes darken with feeling. "I'll never get enough of hearing those words from you. And I don't deserve your forgiveness, but I'm selfish enough to take it. I intend to spend every day of my life making you happy. I promise to protect your dreams, because they are my dreams, too. I vow to nurture your ambitions, for they hold our future. I will always honor, encourage, support, and cherish you. I promise to always hold your hand, to make you laugh, to encourage you to achieve your goals, and to be your safe space when the world gets tough."

"Oh, Nate." A tear rolls down my cheek.

He wipes it away.

"Every moment with you feels like the greatest gift life could have given me. With every beat of my heart, I hear your name. All that I am and all that I can be, I owe it to you. You are my inspiration, my safe refuge from the storms of life, my happy place, and I want to call you mine, forever."

That lightness in my chest spreads to the rest of my body. A burst of joy, of happiness, of rainbows in the sky and birdsong in the air. A feeling of being given everything, of how lucky I am, fills me.

He kisses my knuckles, then leans in until his breath brushes my cheek. "Let me lift you up when you can't lift yourself. Let me have your back. Give me the chance to love you unconditionally, until my last breath." He holds my gaze. "Will you do that?"

58

Skylar

I whisk together the flour, sugar, baking soda, and salt. My wedding band—the simple, no-frills platinum one that my husband got for me so I could wear it even while I'm baking—glints in the fluorescent lights of the bakery. Business is booming, and footfall to the bakery has tripled in the last few days. So much so, we keep selling out by noon and have to close. It's a problem I'm not complaining about, but we definitely need to make some adjustments, so it doesn't become a habit. Besides, it gives me time to test out recipes in the kitchen, something I love doing.

I beat the egg yolks into the cooled butter-stout mixture I made and set aside earlier. Yep, this one has stout beer, in this case, Guinness, which was Ben's favorite beer.

The first time he took me to our local pub, when I turned twenty-one, was after much cajoling, and only after I threatened to go there on my own if he didn't. I asked for a glass of wine, and Ben allowed me a small one. He insisted I have a spritzer, giving in when I scowled at him. For himself, he ordered a pint of Guinness. When our drinks arrived, we raised our glasses.

"To my gorgeous sister, who's all grown up—but remember, all of your boyfriends need to be approved by me." He smirked.

He had the last laugh. He wasn't around to approve of the men I dated, but he did give his blessing for me and his best friend—now my husband—to be together when he made Nate promise to look after me.

I rolled my eyes, clinked my glass with his mug, took a sip of the wine— and made an oooh noise. Inwardly, I winced because the wine tasted more acidic than I'd expected.

Ben took a sip of the Guinness, and when he looked at me, I laughed. "You have a beer mustache."

"You talking about my yeasty crumb catcher?" He chuckled.

"Whatever."

"Here, give it a try." He offered me his mug of beer.

I took a sip of the Guinness and promptly gagged. "Ugh!"

"Don't like it?" He cackled.

"It tastes bitter, almost metallic." I made a face at him.

"It's the nectar of the gods." He took another long pull of the beer, then licked off the foam. "Remember Skye, life is like a foam 'stache," he intoned.

I fixed him with a disbelieving look. "Oh?"

He nodded. "Here one minute, gone the next. It's what you make of it when you're wearing it that counts."

I shot a dramatic glance upward, as if praying for divine intervention. "Is this another of your kernels of wisdom?"

He thought for a minute, then shook his head. "Nah, just made that up, but it sounded profound, didn't it?" He laughed.

I shook my head. My big, goofy older brother.

This had become our tradition whenever he was home between his tours. We'd head to the pub, where he'd buy me a spritzer. It didn't matter that I drank wine when I was out with my friends; he always treated me like I'd just turned twenty-one. He'd offer me his Guinness, which I'd always turn down, and that would draw forth some other platitude from him.

On one of our last such outings, he seemed happy, almost content. It was wishful thinking on my part that he'd met someone. If he had, he didn't tell me. But I secretly hoped he'd found a woman who'd be waiting for him, someone loyal to him, someone who'd love him and care for him, and perhaps, give him a reason to not return on another mission.

I pour the mixture into a cake tin, then slide it into the oven.

I worried about Ben when he was gone, though I never showed it. I wouldn't have wanted him to feel that I was unhappy with his choice of a career. Serving the country ran in his blood. It's who he was. He thrived on the adrenaline of being on the front line, facing the enemy, and living on a knife's edge. His identity was so tightly bound to that of being a Marine, I couldn't imagine him doing anything else. So, I took a step back. I never showed him how stressful it was for me when he was gone. I never hinted at how lonely it felt without him.

"Do you have some cake mixture left for me?"

I hear his voice behind me and whirl around. "Ben, you came?"

He walks forward and takes my hands in his. "I wasn't going to leave without saying goodbye, was I?"

"Oh, Ben." A tear slides down my cheek. "I miss you so much."

"Me, too, little sis." He pulls me into his arms. "There, there, you're not alone. You have Nate." He pats my head.

"I wish you were here, too." I sniffle.

"But I am."

I lean back and scowl at him. "What do you mean?"

"I'll always be in your heart, sis. I'll always be there for you when you think of me."

"Promise?" I take his hand in mine and kiss his knuckles.

"Promise." He gently extracts his fingers from mine, then leans around, scoops up some of the cake mixture from the side of the mixing bowl, and licks it off. "Hmm…" There's a contemplative expression on his face.

"What's missing?"

"Nothing, it's good," he says in a tone that implies there's definitely *something* missing.

"Ben," I warn.

"No, really, it's good; just not a patch on drinking a pint of stout."

I make a face. "Ugh, I shouldn't have asked you for your opinion."

"But I'd have given it anyway." He grins, then leans down and kisses my forehead. "Take care, sis. And make me one promise."

"Anything."

"Your first born… You'll name him after me?"

"Of course." I laugh. "But we're not going to start a family, not for a few years."

He gives me a knowing smile. "Love you."

"Love you, too, big bro."

He turns and prowls out.

"Starling?" I start out of my reverie to find my husband standing in front of me.

He's watching me with a worried glance. "You okay?"

I sniffle. "Of course. When did you get here?" I blink away the remnants of that vision from my eyes. "I... spoke to Ben again... Only this time, it felt like a goodbye, but... Also... It filled me with so much hope." I look between his eyes. "Is something wrong with me that I speak to my dead brother?"

"Oh, baby." He wraps his arm around my shoulder and pulls me close. "There is no right or wrong here; we all cope with grief in the best way we can."

"H-how do you do it? Don't you miss him? How do you always seem so much in control?"

He laughs. "First, you should know by now, I am never in control around you. As for Ben..." His features grow soft. "A part of me will always regret having stepped out that day, leaving him alone. Even though there's another part that tells me I shouldn't blame myself, that I couldn't have possibly known what he'd do. But we are nothing without hope for the future, and what I know is that I will always carry with me the way he touched my life. How he influenced my love for eating good food—"

"Ben did love that," I muse.

"How he was always optimistic, always believed in doing his best at whatever task was at-hand. How he simultaneously cheered on everyone around him, while also causing them to pause and think about his pithy sayings. We are but amalgams of everyone we meet, and I'll carry Ben's lasting impression on me for the rest of my life."

"You're right." I lean back in the circle of his arms. "Now I know my brother is here with me, always. He survives in my memories of him, in my hopes and dreams for the future."

Still, that mention of a baby? I touch my stomach. *Nah, not possible.*

"You sure you're okay?" Nate glances down at where I've pressed my hand to my stomach.

"Yes, I am." I lower my hand and smile up at him.

"You sure?" He searches my face. I can't hide anything from this man, nor do I want to.

"I'm sure. I was saying goodbye to Ben, is all."

His features soften. "How is he?"

I nod. "I'm glad I got to see him one last time. I feel confident he's happy, wherever he is."

"I owe him so much. If it weren't for him, I'd have never met you." He cups my cheek. "There's something I wanted to tell you."

There's a look in his eyes, something which tightens the band around my chest. My guts churn. "What is it?" I whisper. "Is everything okay?"

"It is." He half smiles. "There's someone I want you to meet." He slides his hand into mine, clasps my fingers, and leads me out into the shop.

There's a young woman sitting at the table nearest the door. Next to her is a pram. I closed up earlier, but Nate has a key to the shop, so he must have let them in. She looks up as we approach. Her dark hair is piled on top of her head in a messy bun. She has dark circles under her eyes, and hollows under her cheeks, but her gaze is clear. She's wearing a coat over her jeans and sweatshirt, and when we reach her, she rises to her feet. She looks from Nate to me. "You must be Skylar," she says in a soft voice.

"And you are?"

"Luna." She glances down at the baby asleep in the pram. "And this is Arrow."

"Arrow. That's a strong name."

"He's a strong boy, like his father."

That churning in my stomach intensifies. "His father?"

She nods. "You knew him."

"I *knew* him?" I clutch at my husband's hand. The hair at the back of my neck rises. *No, it can't be, can it?* "Was his... was his father—"

She nods, a sad smile on her face. "Ben. He's Arrow's father."

My heart threatens to jump out of my ribcage, and my stomach bottoms out. Ben is Arrow's father? I draw in a sharp breath. "But how... Did he know that—"

"That I was pregnant with his child? No. I found out after he left on his mission. I emailed him, messaged him, even wrote him letters, but I don't think he got any of them."

"Once we got to the hospital, he was too injured to stay on top of his communication. And later, after he recovered, he seemed to lose interest in the outside world. The fact he couldn't go on any more missions seemed to drain the life out of him," Nate explains.

"But he had you. He had me. Why couldn't he reach out to one of us?" I turn to Nate. "Why? Why didn't you force him to call one of us."

"I tried." Nate swallows. "I went so far as to dial your number on my phone once, but he grabbed it out of my hand and threw it. He broke down afterward and made me promise I would not do that again. And he—" Nate raises his gaze to Luna's. "He never mentioned you. It was only when I found out he'd put you down with Skylar as his next of kin that I realized he had a girlfriend."

Luna's lips twist. "It was a new relationship. We met a few days before he shipped out. We were instantly attracted to each other and were inseparable until the time he left." Her eyes glitter with unshed tears. "We never got to explore things further. I never got to tell him I loved him. I don't know if he loved me, either, I —"

"Oh, I *know* he loved you." I pull away from Nate and take Luna's hand in mine. "He told me."

"He told you?" Her brow furrows.

I shift my weight from foot to foot. "This is going to sound strange, but the only way I've gotten through the last year is by talking to him."

"You spoke to him?" She blinks. "I don't understand."

"Was it a figment of my imagination? Probably. Did it feel real to me? Very much. It felt like he was communicating with me. Like he was giving me the courage to keep going. And he hinted that he'd met someone special." I laugh. "I thought *that* was definitely me being wishful in my thinking, but meeting you now, I realize he was trying to let me know, in his own way, that life goes on." I look down at the sleeping Arrow, so does she. "And he told me to take care of you, too."

"I wish he'd had a chance to see him —" She swallows. "I should have told him he mattered to me before he left, but I thought... I thought... Maybe it was just a hook-up for him, since he didn't indicate otherwise. And then I found out I was pregnant. When I didn't hear back from Ben, I assumed he didn't want anything to do with me. I was saddened, but my hands were so full with Arrow, it's what kept me going. Later, I received the money from Ben's survivor benefits. It didn't feel right to keep it, but I knew I had to do it for Arrow." She bites the inside of her cheek.

"He put you down as his next of kin, and he'd only just met you. So, he must have felt a connection to you." I swallow. "Do you think" — I turn to Nate — "do you think he had an inkling of what was coming? That he wasn't going to be around much longer, and that Luna would need the money?"

"Perhaps. It's possible his intuition directed him to do so something." Nate turns to Luna, "I also think he may have seen some of your messages, and knew you and the baby would need help, so he left all the benefits from his being a Marine to you."

"But if that's the case, why did he take his own life? Shouldn't he have been motivated to live for his child, if not for me or Luna?" I cry.

Nate squeezes my shoulder. "I think he was so caught up in his own personal hell, he couldn't tell things apart. I think he was so depressed, even the prospect of having a child to return to couldn't penetrate whatever space in his mind he'd retreated to. I don't think he was thinking clearly when he" — he swallows — "when he took his own life."

"I should have reached out to you earlier." Luna's chin trembles. "I should have told you about Arrow's existence, but... I... I wasn't ready. It was all too much for me."

"Understandable. I was shattered to find out about Ben. I couldn't face the reality of it until a few days ago, and I was his sister. I can only imagine how broken-hearted you must have been to lose the father of your child."

She releases my hand and clasps her fingers together. "It... wasn't easy. Nate came to inform me of Ben's death. He tried to keep in touch and help after that, but I didn't want anything to do with him. I knew about you, of course"—she jerks her chin in my direction—"but I wasn't ready to meet anyone from Ben's past. It was all I could do to take one day at a time and focus, first on my pregnancy and then, on the baby. Once Arrow was born, everything changed. As soon as I felt strong enough, I contacted Nate and told him I was ready to meet you."

"I'm sorry I didn't tell you about Luna and Arrow but—"

"She made you promise." I smile at him. "I'm glad you're a man of your word, husband."

His features soften.

He wraps his arm about me. I reach up to kiss him, when Arrow starts crying. Both of us turn toward him.

Luna picks him up. "Hey, baby, did you have a good nap?"

Arrow stares at her with big blue eyes. Eyes so like Ben's. And his features. And that shock of jet black hair. I draw in a sharp breath. "Oh, my god, he looks so much like Ben."

"He does." Luna holds him out. "Would you like to hold him?"

EPILOGUE

A month later

Skylar

I spread the mascarpone mixture evenly over the layer of coffee dipped *Savoiardi* cookies, or ladyfingers, as they're called, then add the biscuit crumbs, before shaving dark chocolate over it. My husband has a sweet tooth… Shouldn't come as a surprise, considering he married me, but I learned about it by accident, when I was experimenting with recipes a few days ago.

He walked in while I was busy putting the finishing touches on a cake, and he licked the mixing-bowl clean. When he caught me watching him, he flushed a little and confessed the coffee-cake mixture was his kryptonite. He acquired a taste for coffee while posted overseas. Combine that with bitter chocolate and cream, and I can get him to do anything… Anything. Which is why I set out to make him the dessert in my home bakery.

Yes, he built me a bakery adjoining the kitchen in our home, so I can stay up as late as I want, messing around with ingredients and trying to create different cakes, and he won't be worried about me.

He also insisted I continue interviewing and hiring more staff. I agreed because he showed me proof of how, as businesses grow, entrepreneurs needed to delegate more of the admin work so they can focus on the creative part... In my case, that's the actual baking process, which is what I enjoy the most. And the focus on the desserts has paid off, along with the additional marketing. Business is going so well, I've already bought space on Primrose High Street, near our home, and will be opening the second location of *The Fearless Kitten*. Yes, we're expanding. In more ways than one.

I smile to myself. I love going to work but I am never happier than when I'm pottering around in my home-bakery, trying out new formulas for my baked goodies, then recording the results in my diary, which I hope to, one day, make into a cookbook.

A few months ago, I barely dreamed about giving shape to my dreams. But then, I hadn't married my soulmate. It's my husband who'd encourage me to aim high. To be confident and go after what I wanted. To believe I could do anything. Somewhere along the way, I'd reined in the possibilities in my life, imposing limitations on what I could achieve. I didn't allow myself to visualize the kind of future I wanted for myself.

Sure, I was audacious enough to start my own bakery in a city as expensive as London, but then, I hit a wall. Probably because I struggled to pay the bills and take care of Hugo and then... Subconsciously, I knew about Ben. I swallow.

It's difficult to think about my brother without tears forming in my eyes. But it's getting better. I'm getting better at dealing with the reality that my brother is no longer around. That he'll never pop into our home or into *The Fearless Kitten* and tell me he's proud of me. After I said goodbye to him that day in my bakery, my visions of him vanished. I don't even dream about him anymore. Which makes me sad, but which also means I'm finally dealing with life. I'm finally facing the fact my brother... Is gone. He gave up his life doing what he loved. Yes, he took his own life, but it was because his service to his country damaged him. That has to count for something.

The compensation Luna has been getting since his death helps her with raising their child, but I realize just how insufficient it is. She needs emotional support with coping. She needs a therapist to help her make sense of what had happened. So do I.

My husband persuaded me to see someone. I agreed, on the condition he got help for his hearing. He agreed to wear hearing aids, which are so discreet, you can't even see them. But it has helped alleviate his stress levels, as well.

I introduced my therapist to Luna, and the two got along. So now, Luna and I meet at the therapist's office weekly. She arrives as I finish my session; I take care of Arrow while she has her session. Then, the two of us get tea and cake while Arrow snoozes in his pram, tired out after our session in the nearby park, which is where I take him while she's in therapy. Nate and I discussed it and decided we wanted to pay for Luna's appointments, but we knew she'd turn us down. To avoid that, we pay the doctor directly, and she tells Luna she qualifies for a discounted rate.

Nate also joined forces with Knight Warren, an ex-Marine who started a charity to help vets cope with PTSD. With Nate's contribution, they've added services to help vets transition to civilian life and jobs. It's funded, not by Davenport money, but from the profits Nate made investing while he was in the military. Quentin also helps out by holding weekly sessions with the vets, to help them figure out what they want to do for the rest of their life. They're still working on getting the other Davenport brothers to help out.

I am so proud of my husband. He's still a strong, silent type, but now I know, beneath that forbidding exterior is a man who cares about his country and his brothers-in-arms. He's also attentive. He insists on waking me up every morning with a cup of my favorite tea. I'm partial to the PG Tips brand, but he insisted on getting me a variety specially-created for me at one of the premier tea estates in the world, and when I tasted it, I had to admit, it's good. Not as good as PG Tips, which I'm not going to tell him, but good enough that I could substitute my morning cuppa with it.

Most days, he also insists on making breakfast, which I can't complain about. It gives me a chance to stalk him as he moves around the kitchen wearing an apron over his suit. with his hair still wet from the shower and combed back from his face. Often, he'll catch me staring and smirk at me.

I have to resist the urge to roll my eyes because, of course, there's a reason the man has such a big ego. Unfortunately, or fortunately for me, his ability to keep me satisfied in bed has more than earned him the right to look so pleased with himself. Not that I'll tell him that—but I don't need to. The way he makes me scream when I come is all the evidence he needs. After breakfast, he'll often drop me off at *The Fearless Kitten*. Today, I woke up feeling exhausted, and he insisted I stay home.

I didn't resist. Instead, I went back to sleep and woke up at 9 a.m.. It's times like this, I'm so thankful I have staff who can open the bakery and keep things going. I called in and was reassured everything's fine. So, I decided to spend the day in my home bakery, testing out some new recipes.

After breaking for lunch, I took a nap, then decided to make a Tiramisu... Mainly because I miss my husband, and also because I want to test his hypothesis that I can make him do anything if I bake him a dessert combining coffee and chocolate… And cream, of course.

I lay down more of the ladyfingers, another layer of the mascarpone, then dust the biscuit crumbs and the chocolate shavings. There, all done. I step back and eye the layered confection. Ooh, it looks so good.

My stomach heaves. I rub at my mid-section. Maybe what I ate at lunch didn't agree with me? I reach for my glass of water and take a sip. That seems to help.

"Is that Tiramisu for me?" His voice rumbles from somewhere behind and over me.

A shiver zips up my spine. On cue, my nipples tighten. Before I can turn around, he wraps his arm about my waist and draws me against his hard chest. I melt against him, lean my head back and close my eyes. "You're home early."

"I missed you."

"I missed you, too." I turn in the circle of his arms, raise my lips, and meet his. The kiss is long and slow, and satisfying, and soo dreamy. I feel like I'm wafting away on a cloud of heat and love, and all the yummy things in this world. "Mmm," I breathe against his lips.

A low growl rumbles up his chest. The sound sinks into my blood and ripples over my nerve-endings. It's followed by a mewl. Huh?

I open one eyelid to find he's staring straight at me. Oh! I widen both eyelids and met his impenetrable gaze. I'm married to this man. I know him better than anyone else alive and yet, I'm never able to decipher what lies behind that heterochromatic gaze of his. Then the skin around his eye softens, one side of his lips lift, and I find myself smiling in reply.

"I love you," he murmurs.

My heart does that stupid skip and jump it always seems to do when I hear those three words.

"I love you." I lick at his lips.

His gaze narrows, and his arm around me tightens. "I'm going to—"

Meow.

"What the— Was that a—"

He sighs.

"Could we finish the kiss before—"

Meeeee-oww— the sound is insistent. Then I hear a scratching sound. I look down to find he's holding a basket in his hand. Only reason I missed it is because, when I see my husband, the rest of the world disappears. And when I smell him, my entire body seems to burst into flames. And when I'm near him, all of my senses are focused on him. But a cat—

"You got me a cat?" I cry out.

"A kitten, actually."

I reach for the basket, then freeze. "Wait, let me put away the Tiramisu."

"Maybe I could get a taste?" He follows me to the island and scoops up some of the chocolate-streaked cream.

"Hey"—I slap at his hand—"this needs to set properly."

"Seems set enough for me." He manages to dip his forefinger in the cream and snatch up another dollop, which he smears on my mouth.

"Nate—" I begin, but he bends and captures my lips with his, and when I part them, he licks into my mouth. A moan bleeds from my lips, followed by a distinctly irate meow.

"Oh, the kitten." I break away from my husband, and he lets me. I cover the Tiramisu, slide it into the refrigerator, and when I turn, I find my husband holding a beautiful brown kitten with the most piercing blue eyes.

"Oh, my gosh." I clasp my hands together. "She's beautiful."

The kitten stares at me balefully, then meows again.

I walk over to them, and stare at her. "Can I... Can I touch her?"

He laughs. "She's yours, baby."

"Aww." I rub my forefinger on her soft downy forehead. She blinks, then looks at me, and meows again.

"I think she wants you to hold her—" Before he can complete the sentence, she wriggles out of his hold, and I catch her.

"She's so tiny," I hold her up. "It is a she, right?"

"It is," he agrees.

I hold her gaze, and she stares back.

"Hey, cutie, where did you come from?"

"Karma and Michael Sovrano's cat Andy fathered them."

"Are they friends of yours?" I continue cuddling the kitten. "Wait, Karma Sovrano?" I look past the kitten. "You mean Karma West Sovrano?"

He nods.

"The famous designer Karma West Sovrano whose wedding dress I wore?"

He nods again.

"You... you... know her?" I squeak.

"I know Michael. And when I found out they had a litter of kittens they were looking to give away, I went over and got you one."

"Thank you." I lean past the kitten, and my husband lowers his head, but before our lips can meet again, the kitten meows, then digs her nails into my hand.

"Ouch! Sorry, baby; I wasn't ignoring you." I straighten and smile down at the irate kitten, who's looking at me with an expectant look on her face.

"Oh, did you want me to kiss you?" I press my lips to her forehead instead.

"Hey, that was my kiss."

I look up to find my husband pouting. No, really. He's pouting. I've never seen Nate pout. But honest to goodness, the expression on his face is so disgruntled now, I laugh. "Oh, my god, you're jealous."

"No, I'm not." He stiffens.

"Of a kitten. You're jealous of the kitty."

Said kitty makes mewling noise and I bring her to my breast and press her into my chest. She curls in and begins to purr.

My husband looks from me to the kitten then back to me. "And that was my hug." His lips turn down.

"Aww, baby." I close the distance between us, and he wraps his big arms about me. I snuggle into him, and the kitten snuggles into me. If I could purr as well, I would. "I'm so happy," I whisper.

"I'm glad you are." He tucks my head under his chin. "I think I'm going to start working from home for half the week."

"I'd like that." My stomach gurgles.

"That way, I could be on a conference call, and you could... you know —"

"What?" I frown.

"Give me a blowjob?"

"What?" I rear back, and when I look up, his eyes gleam.

"Talk about multi-tasking. I could be chewing out executives around the world, and you could be chewing me out... Literally."

"Har, har." I scowl. "That's not funny."

My stomach heaves again, and I taste bile on my tongue. "Oh, no."

"What's wrong?"

I shove the kitten at him, then race out of the bakery and through the kitchen, up the hallway, into the bathroom and to the commode before I'm sick. Everything I ate at lunch and breakfast seems to pour out of me. Then, he lifts my hair up out of the way and presses his palm to my forehead, holding me as I retch. When I'm done, he flushes, then urges me to sit back against the bathroom wall. He wets a washcloth and wipes my mouth. "Better?"

I manage to nod.

"Do you need to rinse out your mouth?"

I nod again. He scoops me up. I don't protest. He walks over to the sink and lowers me to my feet. I open the tap, take a cup and swirl the water around my mouth, then spit it out. Once I've repeated the motion a few times, he scoops me up again in his arms and carries me into the bedroom.

"The kitten?"

"She's in her basket; I'll get her in a second." He lays me down on the bed, then sits down next to me. "I should call the doctor."

"No, not now."

He frowns. "You don't look so good."

"I… I'll be okay." I glance away.

"Baby, you're not okay. Your skin is pale, you have circles under your eyes, and you look exhausted."

"Nothing's wrong with me," I insist.

"Why don't we let the doctor decide that?"

"Why don't you get the kitten first? She must be feeling lonely."

He looks like he's about to refuse.

"Please?" I flutter my eyelashes at him. "Please, baby."

He sighs. "I can't deny you anything when you look at me like that; you know that, right?" He rises to his feet and stalks off, then returns holding the basket. He places it by the side of the bed, opens it and brings out the kitten. It mewls again, and when he places it on my chest, it instantly curls into a ball and begins to purr.

"Aww, she's a cutie-pie."

"Do you have a name for her?"

I nod.

"Is it Cocoa?"

I laugh. "You remembered."

"How could I forget anything you tell me, Starling."

Tears prick the backs of my eyes, and I sniffle.

"Hey, hey, I didn't mean to make you cry."

"It's the hormones."

"Oh, is it that time of the month?" He frowns. "Are you getting a migraine? Is that why you puked?"

"No, and no. In fact, I don't think it's going to be that time of the month, nor am I going to get a migraine for a while longer."

"O-k-a-y?" He seems bemused.

The kitten makes a mewling noise.

"I think she's hungry. Did you buy any food?"

"Of course." He jumps up to his feet and this time, when he returns, he's holding a bowl with her name written on it.

"Whoa, am I so predictable that you knew what I was going to name her?"

"Not predictable, just sentimental, in a good way." He walks over to the side of the room where I spot a cat cave, and next to it, a rubber mat on which he places the bowl.

"You got her a cat cave? How did I miss that?" *Probably because you were hurling your guts out.* I grimace.

He takes the cat from me, and when he places it on the mat in front of the bowl, it instantly begins to lap at the soft food. He strokes Cocoa, who continues to eat.

He rises to his feet, then freezes. Every muscle in his body seems to tense. He slowly turns and prowls toward me. As he approaches me, he picks up speed. He covers the last few steps in almost a lunge and goes down on his knees next to the bed. "Starling," his throat moves as he swallows. "Are you trying to tell me that you're —"

I nod. "I'm pregnant."

"Pregnant?"

I can't stop the smile that curves my features. "After you left for work this morning, I threw up —"

He pales. "You never told me?"

"I thought it was something I ate. But then something inside me insisted I take a pregnancy test, and—"I glance at my bedside drawer.

"It was positive?"

I nod.

"Baby, you're having a baby?" He takes my hand in his, then kisses my knuckles. "We're having a baby."

"We are."

"I... I can't believe it." He presses the back of my palm to his cheek. "I'm so fucking happy."

"Me too."

He lowers my hand, then leans in and kisses my forehead. "I fucking love you so much."

"Me too."

He kisses the tip of my nose, then stiffens. "This changes things."

"What things?"

"It's not safe for you to keep the kitten while you're pregnant."

I blink. "What? No." I stare down at the now sleeping Cocoa, who I'm already attached to. "I'm not letting go of her."

"But it could cause complications for the baby."

"Not if I'm careful."

He firms his lips. Those blue-brown eyes of his have a sheet of ice crusted over them. He looks angry. But if look closely, I can glimpse the worry under that freezing gaze. He's looking out for me, as he's done since the first time I met him. First, as my brother's best friend; then, as the man I had a raging crush on; and then, as my husband and lover. This man has my best interests at heart... And now that I know him better, I think I can find a middle ground that works for both of us.

"I understand how concerned you are for me. I know you want to protect me and our baby."

The expression on his features doesn't change, but his shoulders relax.

"And you're right. It could cause issues with the pregnancy," I concede.

He blinks. "You agree?"

I nod. "I'm aware it could be tricky, but not if I take precautions."

He doesn't reply, but he doesn't outright shut me down, either. It gives me the courage to go on.

"We'll make sure the cat is regularly seen by a vet. I'll make sure to wash my hands thoroughly after playing with her. And I won't handle the litter, at all—"

"We'll make sure to have someone take care of that. And the litter will be in another room, far away from you, as will the cat cave. In fact, I'll give Cocoa her own room, fill it with toys and also, add a scratching post."

I'm about to protest, but then I see the glint of apprehension in his eyes, mixed with the urge to please me, and I nod slowly. "Okay... But I get to play with her."

"Okay." The tension drains from his features. He leans in and presses his mouth to mine. "This baby is going to be so loved. He's so lucky to have you for a mother."

"And you for a father."

His chest rises and falls. He leans back and sits heavily on his heels. "A father"—he blinks—"I'm going to be a father."

"You are." I squeeze his hand. "You are going to be incredible, I know it."

"So are you." Then his gaze shadows. "I wish—"

"Ben." I nod. "I wish he were here to see my child. But he told me, you know."

"Told you what?"

"That last time I saw him—the last time I had a vision about him, I mean—he hinted that I'd be pregnant soon."

"He did?" My husband tilts his head. There's no judgement in his expression.

He gets me. He really does. How lucky does that make me? My therapist confirmed that the visions or dreams were my way of coping with the loss, and the fact I'm not having them anymore shows I've embraced reality.

She also said it was healthy to talk about my feelings with my husband. The more I talk it out, the easier I'll find it to move on. Not that I'll ever be able to move on from the loss of my brother.

"He'll always be a part of me."

"He is." Nate nods and twines his fingers through mine. "You're a mosaic of everyone you ever loved. Ben lives on through you, through Arrow, through his nephew."

"You so sure it's a boy?"

EPILOGUE 2

Nathan

"This Sunday lunch is a tradition?" Quentin looks around the packed table with a mixture of trepidation and awe and a touch of disdain. It's the first one he's attending since he joined the Davenport Group.

"It's something Arthur insists on." I wrap my arm about my wife and pull her closer. In all honesty, the last place I want to be is here in Arthur's house, giving up an afternoon where I could be making love to my wife, in my bed, in our house, and with the prospect of a lazy weekend again. But since I'm sitting next to her, and able to hold her through the next few hours, I'm not complaining.

"The old man thinks this is the best way to foster a sense of family between us." Knox snorts from his other side, "Little does he know; some differences can't be solved by breaking bread together." He's referring to the fact that Ryot is nowhere to be seen since he walked out that day after his run-in with Quentin.

On the other hand, Knox and Quentin are sitting shoulder-to-shoulder at the table, sharing a meal, which goes to show Arthur's idea might have some merit. Of course, it also has something to do with the fact that Knox accepted my offer of becoming the Deputy CEO. It puts him on a level playing ground with Quentin. Besides, it's a short jump to being the CEO, which Knox is keenly aware of. Given how eager he is to take on more responsibilities, it serves me well. I plan to keep reasonable hours and be home for dinner every night so I can see my wife's gorgeous face and support her in every way possible as she builds her business. Which means, Knox can cover for me in instances when I won't be around... Which is going to happen more frequently. Doesn't mean I'm going to shirk my responsibilities, but I'm going to lead a more balanced life. A child's cry splits the air.

Summer begins to rise to her feet to attend to the baby in the pram placed at one side of the table, but Sinclair stops her. He urges her to keep eating, then moves over to take the baby in his arms.

"Why is it such a turn on to see a man in a suit, who runs a billion-dollar business, take his child in his arms to soothe the baby?"

"Hold on, you better not be implying that you're turned on by someone other than me."

She nods, then turns to me. "I mean, I'm not turned on by him, but by the picture he makes." She blushes. "I only have eyes for you, baby."

I look into her eyes, losing myself all over again in those pools of green. Then, because I can't stop myself, I bend and press my lips to hers. She moans, and I deepen the kiss. I pull her closer, slide my arm down to her ample butt and—someone clears their throat.

My wife stiffens, then giggles. "I think we're embarrassing everyone."

"I'm kissing my wife; what's there to be embarrassed about?"

She slaps at my chest. "Everyone is watching us," she hisses.

"Let them." I try to keep kissing her, but she pushes at me.

"Please, Nate."

I sigh, then press my forehead into hers before whispering, "I have a raging hard-on. Maybe you could—"

"—nope."

"Under the cover of the tablecloth."

"No way," she gasps.

"No one will know."

"Everyone will know." She shoves at me again, and I release her.

I look up to find—sure enough—every gaze at the table is on us. Edward and Mira beam at us, Summer laughs, and Sinclair gives me a thumbs-up sign from where he's rocking his kid.

Every gaze, that is, except the rest of the Davenports. Connor looks bemused, Brody is frowning, and Tyler looks bored. When does Tyler not look bored? The exception is Arthur, who looks pleased. To his credit, he doesn't have an I-told-you-so expression on his face. Not that I'd care, even if he did. It doesn't matter that I was pushed to see my wife before either of us were ready. The fact is, I did, and she's mine and I'm hers. End of story.

"Argh" — Knox makes a gagging sound — "get a room, guys."

Quentin rubs his chin. "For once, I second him."

Knox looks at him in surprise.

Quentin notices it and raises his glass. "We might yet find common ground, nephew."

Arthur raps his knife against his water glass, and silence envelopes the room. Even the baby respects Arthur. "I am so happy to have my family in my house today. When I started on this mission of seeing my son and grandsons settled down, I hoped to see them happy. And seeing Edward and Mira, and now, Nate and his beautiful wife Skylar here today, my heart is full." He looks around the faces at the table. "While change is constant, the only other constant is the love of this family. As long as we have each other's love and support, we can weather anything." He raises his glass. "I'm excited to see what traditions we cook up together in this next chapter as a family. I—"

Before he can finish, Otis walks over and whispers something in his ear.

Arthur nods, then lowers his glass. "—we have someone new to the family who will be joining us."

"Another long-lost uncle?" Knox scoffs.

"Or another half-brother, maybe?" I smirk.

A man walks toward the only empty chair in the room, which is next to Arthur. I'd assumed it was because no one wanted to sit next to him, but apparently, this was planned. He's tall, dark-haired, and dressed in a dark suit with a blood red tie which stands out against his crisp white shirt.

On the other side of Nathan, Knox draws in a sharp breath. "Motherfucker," he hisses.

Arthurs shoots him a sharp look. "Language."

"Really, that's all you have to say for inviting a Whittington to the table?" Knox growls.

Toren Whittington looks around the table, then nods in my direction. "Davenport."

"Whittington." I nod back.

"Since our companies are now partners, I thought it would be good to invite Tor here, to join us for our weekly lunch meetings."

"And is he going to weigh in on the future of the Davenport Group?" Knox tilts his head at Arthur.

My grandfather seems to be taken aback by the question. "We are partners, so Tor will attend the board meetings. But Davenports hold the majority stake, so I count on you, Quentin, and Nathan to exercise your veto power as you see fit."

"Can I start with saying I won't dine at the same table as a Whittington?"

Arthur purses his lips. "Tor's our guest."

"And I'm your grandson." Knox juts out his chin.

"Let the boy be." Tor bares his teeth in what should be a smile, but instead, makes him look like a predator scenting his prey.

I frown. For the first time, I realize it might not have been entirely wise to bring the Whittingtons onto the board of our company. Toren is not one to be underestimated. I sensed that when I met him, but I was too focused on finding a way to stave off the Madisons and get my revenge on Arthur. What better way to make the old man pay than by forcing him to work with his mortal enemies?

Although, Arthur may have beaten me at my own game. He seems to be making the most of having to work with the Whittingtons. The old man's a survivor, all right. And more astute than I gave him credit for.

"You thinking what I am?" Quentin says in an aside to me.

"That there's a reason he's trying to present himself as all cordial with the Whittingtons?"

Quentin nods slowly. "Arthur is up to something. I'm just not seeing it yet."

"Me neither."

"Perhaps, it's not to do with business, but something else?" My wife offers.

Quentin and I exchange glances, then he nods. "That's possible."

I kiss the top of my wife's head. "That's brilliant, baby, why didn't I think of that?"

"*Boy*, did you call me *boy*?" Knox rises to his feet.

"You're younger than me, both in age and in business experience, *boy*." Toren's smile widens.

Knox throws down his napkin, pushes back his chair, and begins to round the table, but Quentin jumps up and grabs his arm. "Wanna take a walk with me?"

Knox begins to shake off his arm, but Quentin holds firm.

"My son's getting married; come with me to the wedding."

Knox snorts, "Why would I do that?"

"Because"—Quentin seems to measure his words—"he didn't invite me, and I'm crashing his wedding."

Quentin

"I don't want you at my wedding." My son looks me up and down. He's dressed in a tux and bowtie, and the fuzz on his chin forms dirt-colored patches. He's twenty-three years old. Sure, he's an adult, but he's not yet able to grow a proper beard. Not to mention, the only job he's found so far is that of a pizza delivery boy. Barely enough to support himself, let alone, a wife. And he decides to get married. I shake my head.

"This is a bad idea," I growl.

Felix firms his lips. He sets his jaw, and his face takes on a mutinous expression I'm all too familiar with.

Jesus Christ, did I have to go and lead with a 'no'? I might not have been a good parent to him... and this shows why. I've been able to strategize on military missions and lead my men with tact and diplomacy, but when it comes to my son, all finesse deserts me. I've never managed to handle our discussions with delicacy. I know, if I tell him no, he'll want to do that very thing, and yet, any reading I've done on reverse psychology deserts me when I need it the most. You'd think facing down the enemy and escaping from my last mission would be the most difficult thing I've done. Well, think again. This parenting gig is the one exam I've never passed.

"And who are you to tell me that?" Felix snaps.

"I'm your father." It's out before I can stop myself. How trite I sound. How hackneyed. How banal. I may be his sperm donor, but really, have I done anything to merit the title, *father*?

Felix feels the same, for his eyes narrow. "*Father*," he sneers. Cheeks flushed, he takes a step forward then stabs his finger into my chest. "You gave up the right to call yourself my father, considering you were barely around for me when I needed you."

I wince. "I did what I thought was best for you. I had to find a way to parent, despite being on tours of duty."

"You mean, you barely had time to be a parent because there was hardly a time when you weren't deployed."

I draw myself up to my full height. I know where this argument is going, but I have to try. "I was doing my duty as a Marine."

"You shirked your duty as a father. If it hadn't been for Aunt Margaret—" He looks away, and I follow his gaze to where my aunt is seated. Margaret never approved of my mother marrying Arthur. She broke off all relations, as a result. After I fell out with my father, knowing that'd likely be enough incentive for Margaret to come around, I approached her and asked if she'd be able to help me with Felix. Luckily, she wanted a relationship with her grand-nephew. Her only condition was that she'd never have to see Arthur, which I readily agreed to.

I invited her to stay with us. Tasked her to be his primary caregiver. And to her credit, she stepped up. At an age when she could have been enjoying her retirement, she played the role of mother and father, and friend. It's no wonder Felix looks to her as more of a parent than me.

He finishes, "—I wouldn't have known what a normal home could be."

"I know I made mistakes—"

He laughs. "Mistakes? You call leaving me for months on end while you went off on another assignment a mistake? Why don't we call it what it is? You didn't want me."

My stomach churns. I know I wasn't around much for my son, but I had no idea it resulted in him feeling this abandoned. "I did want you."

"You had a funny way of showing it." His features take on a pitiful look. "You were too busy fighting for the great unwashed—a nameless, faceless mass of people who had no idea what you were sacrificing for them."

"You're right. Most of what I did was undercover. The common populace will never have any idea what I've sacrificed so they can be safe."

"You sacrificed me, Quentin." He takes a step back. "You gave me up, and now, I'm giving you up."

My own son calls me by my first name. He and I both know, he doesn't owe me the respect of calling me Dad.

A ball of emotion chokes my throat. My heart threatens to rip through my ribcage. Every part of my body urges me to tell him how much I love him. How much I miss him. How much I regret not being there for him. I open my mouth, but all that comes out is, "Is that your final decision?"

He merely shakes his head, then pivots on his feet and walks away.

As I stare after him, my aunt walks over. "Couldn't you stop yourself from getting into an argument with him on his wedding day?" She looks at me with reproach. I'm forty-nine years old, and my aunt can still level that look at me and make me squirm.

"I screwed up." I loosen my tie.

"You need to put things right," she says in a quiet voice.

I know, I do. I watch as Felix disappears through the door set to one side of the church, but when I take a step in the direction he's gone in, she grips my arm. "Don't. Give him some time."

"He's getting married, and I need to talk to him before it's too late," I point out.

"You've waited this long. Surely, you can hold off until after the ceremony."

I hesitate, then nod.

Knox, my nephew, who's nearer in age to me than to Felix, and who accompanied me to the wedding, takes in the scene and whistles, "You weren't kidding when you said this wasn't going to be a dull wedding."

It's the only reason he agreed to come with me. Not that I fault him. If it weren't my son getting married, I wouldn't be here. Not when I've had a beef with Knox for a long time.

I look around the space—the soaring columns, the stained glass over the altar, the statue of Christ looking down on the proceedings. The scent of incense is heavy in the air. The very air is still and weighs heavily on my shoulders. I hate churches. I didn't think Felix was religious, but then, I don't know much about my son. *And whose fault is that?*

I follow Knox as he slides into a pew. My aunt walks over to one in the front, where she sits down next to a gaggle of women. All of them are wearing dresses and hats, as befits a wedding, I suppose.

I wouldn't know. I've made it a point never to attend one. It reminds me too much of my own, which thankfully, wasn't in a church. It was before a justice of peace, and then I was called up to serve. The life of a Marine. I returned eight months later, in time to see my wife give birth to Felix. She died the next day.

I didn't have the courage to face Felix after that, which is when my aunt stepped in. Then, it seemed easier not to interfere in the rhythm they had. She and my son formed a bond. The child would be well looked after. I wouldn't have to see the face of my son, who'd remind me of my dead wife and my non-starter of a marriage. I didn't have it in me to be his main caregiver. I was barely keeping it together, myself. I was in no state to take care of a child.

It seemed best to ensure the child had everything, in terms of material needs, and then, let my aunt take on the duties of primary caregiver.

So perhaps, I was lazy. I didn't push myself. I took the easy way out. Or maybe, I was a coward, protecting myself. Either way, my decisions were wrong. I'm watching my son get married, and I don't know who he is.

"You all right, mate?" Knox murmurs.

"Could do with a drink." I roll my shoulders, trying to ease the ache, which seems to have taken up permanent residence there.

He pulls out a flask and hands it over.

I accept it without question; not going to turn my back on small favors. I tilt the flask to my mouth and chug down the alcohol. It leaves a trail of fire down my throat and sets off a bomb in my stomach. I cough, lower the flask, and wipe the back of my hand across my mouth.

"Easy, Tiger." He takes the flask from me, swigs down a few mouthfuls, then caps it and pockets it.

The organist strikes up the chords for 'Here *Comes the Bride*." Could my boy get any more traditional than this? I really don't know him at all, do I? My eyes begin to water. It's from the alcohol, I swear. Around me, people rise to their feet. Knox nudges me, and I push myself to stand. My gaze is trained ahead to where the best man is standing—one of Felix's friends who I don't recognize. Another thing I missed out on. I have no idea who my son hangs out with or who's his best mate. The man glances around, looking worried.

Huh, where's Felix? Is he still outside?

"Maybe I should go get him?" I turn to leave, but Knox grabs my arm. "Stay put, ol' man."

"I think I should find my sh-sh-sh-son?" I'm slurring. *Damn. I didn't have that much to drink, did I?*

"You're not in any condition to go traipsing around by yourself," Knox whispers.

"I'm fine—" I sway, grab hold of the pew in front of me.

"You're not."

I'm not. But I don't care. I—

A shiver runs down my back. The hair on the nape of my neck stands to attention. I turn and see a vision in white gliding past. She's wearing one of those slim-fitting, lace wedding dresses, which clings to her waist and outlines the shape of her hips, before flaring out into a train at her ankles.

The sleeves lovingly cover every part of her arm up to her neck, but her skin glistens through the gaps in the lace. The collar is high, almost Victorian, which makes the contrast to the plunging V-neckline almost disgraceful. Combined with the strategic panels, which cover her nipples, the rest of the embroidered bodice shows off the creamy skin off her breasts. They thrust out proudly, leading the way for the rest of her hourglass-figured body to follow. As she passes me by, a whiff of strawberries, underlaid with something musky, teases my nostrils. I'm instantly hard. Her veil flows over her features, so all I catch is a curve of dark eyelashes over a cheekbone, and then she slides by. Her train flows behind her, a ripple of water in the wake of a yacht with the most sensuous lines I've ever seen. A siren, a temptress, the most beautiful woman I've ever seen.

"Your son's marrying *her*?" Knox hisses. His voice is awed and drips with the half-arousal, half-disbelief I'm feeling. Anger squeezes my chest, and if you ask me why, I couldn't articulate it.

"Keep your eyes off of her," I growl.

Of course, he doesn't listen. He continues to stare at her, until I bury an elbow in his side.

"Ouch, what the — What was that for?"

"Don't look at her like that," I snap. Something hot stabs into my chest. It's like I took a bullet to it. Scratch that, I've taken a bullet to the chest, and it has nothing on this sensation that spears my ribcage. I've swallowed a rock, which weighs me down and threatens to overbalance me. I loosen the buttons on my jacket, then run my fingers under my collar.

Everything within me insists I walk after her. *Don't let her leave. Don't let her marry your son. This is all wrong.* I push a leg out into the aisle, only Knox grabs my shoulder and applies enough pressure that I find my butt hitting the seat.

"What?" I blink.

"What were you going to do?" He looks into my face, suspicion in his gaze.

"Nothing." I shake my head. *What was I going to do? Was I going to march over to her, grab her arm and drag her out of this church, like a scene from* The Graduate, *hop on the next bus and? Hell, no.* That would be all wrong. I'm not the one who gets to decide who my son should marry. *Surely, they must love each other?* That stabbing sensation in my chest intensifies, until it's as if I've had a grenade detonate inside me. Sweat pours down my back. My shirt sticks to my skin. I take off my jacket, then loosen my tie and tear it off.

"You okay?" Knox takes another swig of his drink, but when I reach for his flask, he holds it out of reach. "Not happening, mate. Don't think you're handling that Shochu too well."

"Shochu?" I blink. "You're carrying rice wine with an alcohol content of thirty-five percent?"

"This one's forty-five percent, and it hits quicker than whiskey. It's like having an IV plugged into your vein," Knox says proudly.

No wonder it feels like I've been run over by a tank. And how is Knox knocking back the stuff and staying steady? The man must have a high tolerance to the stuff.

There's commotion ahead, and when I look up, the groomsman is talking to the bride, gesticulating with his hands. The priest has a shocked look on his face. Then the organ stops, and in the silence, the buzz from the gathered crowd is loud.

Knox taps the woman in front of us, and when she turns, he flashes her a smile. "What's happening, darlin'?

She must be fifty, and her dress fit her ten years ago, but looking into Knox's face, even with those scars, her gaze grows dreamy. "The bridegroom is absconding."

"What?" I snap.

"The bridegroom is nowhere to be found."

"What the hell?" I jump up and walk over to where my aunt is seated. She's wringing her hands, and that sinking feeling in my stomach seems to spread to my entire body. "What's happening, Aunt Margaret?"

She shakes her head, a resigned look on her face.

"Felix; where is he?"

Her features crumple. She angles her phone in my direction. The message on the screen from Felix reads:

Tell Vivian I'm sorry. I can't go through with it.

My guts churn. Damn, I shouldn't have drunk that alcohol. I swallow down the bile that laces my throat and hand over her phone. "He's gone."

She nods. "Guess he's following your example."

"That's not fair."

"He never got over you always abandoning him." She shakes her head. "All he knows is how it feels to have no mother and a father who kept leaving. You can't blame him for not stepping up to his responsibilities."

"I stepped up to my responsibility," I say hotly.

"Did you?" Her voice is sad. She pats my shoulder. "In which case, I'm sure you know how to make this right." She nods toward the front of the church.

I follow her line of sight to where the bride is standing. Alone. The groomsman has stepped away, as has the priest. The crowd is beginning to thin. She didn't have any bridesmaids, nor anyone to walk her down the aisle. No one has gone to her to offer comfort. She stands there, spine straight, facing forward, her fingers clasped together in front of her. A ray of light slants down through the stained glass above the altar and haloes her figure.

She's an angel. A vision. A mermaid risen from the depths of the sea, come to save me. She's what I've been waiting for. The woman I've been searching for. The one I've sworn to give my heart to. She's the most beautiful woman I've ever seen, and she is mine. *Mine. Mine. Mine.*

I put one foot in front of the other, until I'm abreast of her. I stare forward at the candles glowing on the altar. The scent of strawberries and that something musky is so strong, my entire being is ablaze. With need. With hope.

With fear. With the certainty that what I'm going to do now is the right thing. With the clarity that this is it. My entire life has led me to this moment, and this time, I will do the right thing.

I turn to her.

My movement must cut through her thoughts, and as if well-rehearsed, she mirrors my stance. She looks up into my eyes, and through the veil, I catch the first glimpse of her eyes. They're not blue, not green, but... violet. The most sublime deep rich shade — more muted than purple, brighter than green, more nuanced than blue. My heart stutters. My pulse seems to pause, then roars back to thud at my temples, my wrists, even in my balls. I am a seething mass of need. Of want. Of a yearning, which fills me so powerfully, it pushes me to reach out and flip up her veil.

Her gaze widens, and her lips part.

Before she can speak, I drop to my knees and look up into her face. "Marry me."

WANT TO FIND OUT WHAT HAPPENS NEXT? READ QUENTIN & VIVIAN'S STORY IN THE IMPERFECT MARRIAGE HERE.

READ AN EXCERPT FROM QUENTIN & VIVIAN'S STORY - THE UNSUITABLE MARRIAGE

Vivian

"Are you sure about this?" My younger sister's worried features look up at me from the screen of my phone.

"Of course I'm sure." I manage to school my features into a smile. My features feel frozen, but I must look convincing because her own relax.

"Vivi, you don't have to do this."

"I am doing this because it's a chance to start afresh. A place of my own, one where you can come and stay on holidays."

"You're getting married so you can give me a place to come home to?" She frowns.

I curse myself. "I mean, it's a fringe benefit, is all I'm saying. That's not the only reason I'm getting married."

"But it is one of the main reasons?" She purses her lips.

I sigh. "Lizzie, it's no big deal."

"My sister decides to get married because she thinks she owes me a stable life. Can you see the problem with that?"

"I'm not doing anything an older sister wouldn't do." I tip up my chin.

"You're young, Vivi; only twenty-two."

"Almost twenty-three, and already, the manager of a pizza-parlor," I remind her.

"You should be going to university and studying for your degree in fine arts."

"Degrees are overrated. Besides, I got to paint the interior of the pizza shop, and the operations director of the company loved it and promised me I can paint the interiors of the other shops, too."

"Not that he's paying you anything extra for it."

"I... Uh... Plan to talk to him about it." I hunch my shoulders. "I promise, I'll find a way to pay for the rest of your term. You don't have to worry about it."

Her features gentle. "I know, you'll never let me down. I wish I wasn't such a burden on you. I think I should leave school and—"

"No, absolutely not. You know how impossible it is to get into the Royal Ballet School. You're talented Lizzie; it's why you made it. And I'm going to make sure you complete it."

"You're a wonderful painter, too. You got admission into the Royal Academy School, and it's just as difficult, if not more so, to pass the entrance exams for it. But you made it."

"With the remainder of the inheritance from Mama, only one of us could pursue an artistic career and—"

"You made the decision it would be me." My sister's expression grows mutinous.

"It had to be you; I wouldn't deprive you of the one thing you were born to do. As for my painting? I can always pursue it another time."

"You're an artist. If you don't get to paint—"

"I do, in my spare time. But as a ballerina, you need to train while your limbs are supple. I can paint my entire life, but for a dancer, her peak years are only until her mid-twenties—mid-thirties, if you're lucky."

She opens her mouth, then shuts it.

"You know I'm right. I did the right thing."

"I hate that you had to sacrifice your career for mine." Her eyes flash. "If only there were a way for both of us to pursue our dreams."

"You become a ballerina and you'll have fulfilled both of our ambitions," I say gently.

She blinks a little, and her eyes look watery. "I don't deserve you."

"I know." I smile, hoping to break the tension, but she doesn't smile back.

"Did you know flamingo chicks are actually born gray or white and get their pink feathers from their shrimp heavy diet?"

"What?" She gapes then cracks a smile.

Success!

"How do you manage to remember these useless facts?" She rolls her eyes.

"Not useless—they made you smile, after all," I point out.

"That it did." She laughs.

"And to answer your question, I don't know how. My brain just happens to have space for these facts. I kind of like knowing about obscure things." I grin.

She grins back. Her features soften. "You look amazing! Did I tell you that?"

I look down at the beautiful lace dress. It's a Karma West Sovrano original. She's one of the leading fashion designers in the country and when I chanced upon this dress in the charity shop, I couldn't believe it. It was just about within my budget, and I snapped it up. I altered it myself and now, it fits like it was tailor-made for me. Of course, it helps that I've been living on instant ramen over the last month. Losing a little weight never hurts, and it definitely makes me appear fashionably thin.

I apply some more color to my cheeks, then look down at the screen. "How's my make-up? Not too much?" I don't normally use foundation. There's no use applying make-up when you spend your days directing the logistics of a pizza parlor, but I'm making a special effort today.

"It's perfect." She scans my features. "You look flushed, which is to be expected. It's normal to be nervous on your wedding day."

"I'm not nervous." *I am nervous.* Though there's no need to be. I admit, when Felix proposed to me, it took me by surprise. I didn't expect to get married. At least, not until Lizzie graduates from ballet school and begins to headline productions. I started dating him, more out of loneliness than anything else. Felix is my age, always polite, and relentless in his pursuit of me. I gave in because he wore me down, and because I was flattered. Considering I share an apartment with three other girls, spend every moment I can at work, and the rest of the time painting in my room, I have no social life.

I began hanging out with Felix because he took me out to dinner and refused to let me pay for it. I'm ashamed to say, those were the only nights I ate. And he must have known my situation because he began slipping me little treats—including chocolate cupcakes from the bakery down the street, which are my absolute favorite, especially because they have names inspired by the owner's love for spicy romance novels. You could say Felix wore me down. And when I made it clear I wasn't ready to sleep with him, he wasn't put off. All the more reason I was shocked when he asked me to marry him.

"You're not marrying him because he's the first person who asked you?"

My sister looks at me with a shrewdness that belies her years. Though I've tried to shield her from the world, when you don't have money, you grow up pretty quickly. She's street smart enough for me to sometimes worry that she's growing up too fast.

"Please give me *some* credit." I roll my eyes. "Do I look like someone who'd go through with this without thinking it through?"

She shakes her head slowly. "You think everything through, Vivi. You're so cautious, I sometimes wish you lived a little more spontaneously. In fact, I wonder if that's why you agreed to marry Felix, because he fits in with whatever plan you have for your life."

"What's that supposed to mean?"

"Just that you were worried you'd never find a man who loves you. And rather than take the risk of waiting and seeing if someone else would come along, you decided to cut your losses and take the plunge with Felix."

I stiffen. "I really don't think you can comment on my relationship with Felix. I love him"—*I'm not sure I do, but I'm not going to let her know that*—"and I intend to marry him."

Her features crumple. "Oh god, I'm sorry Vivi. I didn't mean to hurt you. Of course you love him, and he loves you."

Does he? He never told me that. He asked me to marry him, and I said yes. The next thing I know, I'm here in church. But it's the right thing to do. I'll be settled. Between the two of us, we'll be able to afford a small two-bedroom apartment. With the extra bedroom, Lizzie can come stay with us whenever she has a weekend off. Also, I'll be able to save enough money to help Dad with his medical treatment. Really, I'm making the best of a bad situation. And isn't that what any responsible older sister and daughter would do?

"I'm sorry I'm not there for you today. Actually"—she looks around—"I could leave now and be in time for the reception, at least."

"Don't you dare, Lizzie. Your classes are more important." Also, I'd rather go through this ceremony on my own. If I saw my sister's face, I might lose my nerve.

"I wish you'd allow Dad to walk you down the aisle, at least."

"I don't want to exhaust him. It's enough he's going to be at the ceremony. Really, it's not a big deal." And it's not. To be honest, I want to get it over with. Only because I can't wait to start my new life with Felix. Yes, that's it.

"You sure about this?" She scrutinizes my countenance closely. "It's not too late to back out."

"And let this dress go waste?" I strike a pose. Again, it has the desired effect of making her laugh. One thing I'm good at is deflecting and playing the clown because there is nothing like humor to defuse a situation.

Then she sobers. "Seriously though, sis, if you don't want to go through with it —"

"Hey —" I shake my head. "Don't go there. I'm here because I want to do it. Felix —" I swallow. "Felix will make a great husband."

So what if he hasn't spoken to me in the last week? Sure, he messaged me, but that was only to ask if I'd ironed his tux. And once we decided to get married, we moved in together right away. We've shared a bed for the last month, and except for a chaste kiss, he's made no attempt to touch me. He's doing the right thing. I told him I preferred we postpone the physical aspect of our marriage until after the ceremony. It would make for a memorable wedding night. He accepted my suggestions without protest. *Which is good, right?* It means he respects my wishes. *And isn't that what I want in a marriage? Respect?*

And love and passion and that kind of stomach-bottoming-out-with-a-dizzying-sensation when you see the man you love. That exhilaration of not being able to wait a second before jumping into his arms. Your head spinning as you kiss him, and having him kiss you back like he can't get enough of you, and having him gaze into your eyes like you're the only woman in the world for him…

All of which only happen in my spicy books. I get enough of all the feels in fiction. It never translates over into daily life. No, what I'm going to have with Felix is calm, serene, practical, and a solution that will tide me over until my financial situation improves. It's the right thing to do.

"And you're going to make an amazing wife." She sniffs. Someone calls to her off screen. "I'm so sorry, sis, I —"

"Go." I push away that sinking sensation in my belly. *I'm doing the right thing. I am.* "Love you."

"Love you, too, sis." I disconnect the call, stare at my reflection for a few more seconds, then turn and, raising my skirt, head for the doorway of the small antechamber. I step out, walk up the corridor, and stop at the vestibule which leads into the sanctuary. A buzz reaches me from the small crowd in the pews. Felix's great-aunt Margaret, who raised him, and her friends made sure there's a decent number of people. My father is in his wheelchair at the back of the church. He brought along some of his buddies, so at least he's not lonely.

And me? What about me? I preferred to walk down the aisle on my own; it seemed like the 'done thing.' But now, I wish I hadn't been so foolhardy. Tears prick my eyes, and the scene blurs.

I can do this. I'm doing the right thing.

Why didn't I think of bringing a bouquet? It slipped my mind. A Freudian slip, maybe, considering I don't have any close friends I felt I could ask to be my bridesmaids. My adult life, so far, has been focused on holding down my job and painting whenever I have time off. I lost touch with my schoolmates, and since I never went to university, don't have a friend circle to speak of. Felix is my closest friend, and now I'm marrying him.

My heart leaps up into my throat. My fingers tremble. I lock them together in front of me and take a deep breath. Then, another. Then the organist strikes up the opening chords of 'Here Comes the Bride.'

There. It takes the decision out of my hands. I take a step forward; another. Fix my sight on the altar in the distance. The crowd hushes. I walk down the aisle. As I pass my father, he wipes a tear from his face. My own threaten, but I don't give in. I stifle the ball of emotion that clogs my throat.

Keep moving.

A shiver runs up my spine. The fine hair on the nape of my neck tightens. Beneath the scent of incense, is that of woodsmoke and pine, and something evocative that reminds me of a forest I visited once when I was a young girl. I look to the side, and I meet the gaze of a man I've never seen before. Believe me, I would've remembered him if I had.

Those blue eyes are like sheets of ice. Thick jet-black hair cut in a military style crew cut shows the shape of his skull and lends him a sever appearance. Threads of silver at his temples only add to his distinguished look. Then, there's his hooked nose, and that thin upper lip, which adds to the impression of his spartan nature... And that plush lower lip — I swallow — perfect to bite down on.

Whoa, what am I thinking?

His lips firm, thinning out that upper lip even more. I manage to drag my gaze back to his, to find he's scowling at me. The expression on his face is angry and confused, and yet, there is so much naked need. My nipples tighten, and my toes curl. My steps slow of their own accord. It feels like I've walked into a brick wall.

What is this fluttering sensation in my belly? This shivering that grips me. This hesitation that churns my belly. Who is this guy? Why have I never felt like this before? Then, I pass him.

I force myself to look forward and come to a halt opposite the priest who's going to marry us. There's just one problem. There's no Felix waiting for me.

What does it say about me that I didn't notice my bridegroom is missing until I reached the altar? Maybe he stepped out to sneak a cigarette?

I caught Felix smoking a few times and told him off. He promised he'd quit, but we both knew he was saying it to pacify me.

And how did I miss that he wasn't waiting for me? Had I even looked out for him? I was too focused on gathering my wits, then on putting one foot in front of the other. And when I saw that scowling guy, all other thoughts flew out of my head.

I turn to the groomsman. "Where's Felix?"

"Err..." His Adam's apple bobs. "Err... I... He..." He shakes his head, sweat beading his upper lip.

"What's wrong? Did something happen to him?"

He shakes his head, then nods, then shakes his head again. "Err... He... Uh... He sent me this message." He thrusts his phone under my nose, and I read Felix's message:

Tell Vivian I'm sorry. I can't go through with it.

Vivian

He dumped me. Felix dumped me. My best friend didn't show up for me. My bridegroom didn't even have the courtesy to tell it to me to my face. He messaged his groomsman to convey the message that he'd broken up with me. At the altar.

A headache builds behind my eyes. My stomach heaves. A heavy sensation weighs down my arms and legs. And yet my heart... My heart stays steady. And my brain whispers... *Thank god.*

A giddy sense of relief infiltrates my blood stream. The groomsman steps away; the priest murmurs how sorry he is. Behind me, I sense the crowd whispering, then shuffling footsteps as they begin to leave. I try to move, but my feet don't obey me. My mind, though, is empty. Serene.

I fix my gaze on the flickering flame of the candle on the altar. The same candle that guided me here. You can plan all you want, but life always seems to throw you curve balls. When you least expect it, something happens that teaches you, things were never in your control, after all. I thought I was being smart accepting Felix's proposal. The joke is on me. I thought I was doing the right thing, until... Turns out, I was on the wrong track all along.

It's not that I'm not going to be married that hurts... but this means I'll have to move out of the flat I share with Felix. Back into the accommodation with my three roommates, a shared bathroom, and no space for Lizzie to spend her weekends. I can't save the money I need to help my father with his treatments. Everything is back to square one… Only worse, because now, I'm the woman who was stood up… At the altar.

Hello caricature, meet me. The biggest fool of them all. The headache grows in intensity. My sight blurs. I shake my head to clear it, square my shoulders and straighten my spine. I have my pride. No one can take that away from me. No one.

Footsteps approach me. The murmur and shuffling around me stops. Silence descends. I sense someone stepping up to stand next to me. Woodsmoke, pine, wild open spaces. It's him. I know he's here. He turns to face me, and a cloud of heat leaps off of his body and lassoes around me. I gasp. Goosebumps pop on my skin.

As if in a dream, I turn and am faced with the expanse of a chest so wide, it blocks out the sight of everything else. I tilt my head back, then further back, until I meet those silver-blue eyes. I'm almost not surprised it's him. When our gazes met, I knew… There was something there. I almost stopped in my tracks. Instead, feeling a sense of obligation, I continued forward toward my non-existent bridegroom.

But like this. At the altar after I've been stood up? Like this. Of course, it would have to be like this. A sense of destiny settles around my shoulders. And when the stranger leans in and lifts up my veil, I don't flinch or protest. A gasp runs through the crowd, but I ignore it. My gaze is caught and held by this enigmatic man who something in me recognizes.

It's him. Him. Him. My blood sings in my veins. Electricity fires up my nerve-endings. I've been waiting for him for so long. Only him. There's an answering flash in his eyes. His jaw firms. He seems to come to a decision because he lowers his hand to his side, then drops to one knee. My gaze widens. My pulse rate spikes. *What's he doing? He can't be. No, no. way.* He looks up again and locks his gaze with mine. I see the question in his eyes and know what my answer is even before he growls, "Marry me."

Another gasp runs through the crowd. It fades away, and there's silence. The blood pounds at my temples. My heart seems to swell until I'm one thump from exploding into a ball of smoke—poof—I'll be gone. *No one will know I'm here. No one will pass judgement on me.* I open my mouth to whisper, "It's impossible to hum while holding your nose."

The man blinks slowly.

"Also, most people find it impossible to lick their own elbow." I nod.

"Is that right?" That stern mouth of his twitches.

Did he smile? He *almost* smiled. *What if I could make him smile for real?*

"And it's physically impossible for pigs to look up into the sky," I say in a rush.

One side of his lips lifts. His eyes light up with an amused light. *Yes!* I resist the urge to fist pump.

"And you must be aware, it's impossible for me to say yes to you," I murmur.

"Why?" His gaze grows intense. The silver in his eyes flares. Everything else around me fades. My senses light up as my vision focuses on him. All I can see is his features. *Him.*

"I don't know you," I manage to croak around the ball of emotion in my throat.

"That can be rectified." His voice is confident.

He straightens, and once more, I have to tilt my head back to see his face. Once more, I'm struck by how tall he is. How broad, how big he is. All the air in the room seems to have been sucked out. The voices around us fade. Pinpricks of warning pepper up my spine. My stomach flip-flops. I want to look away from him, but I can't. I feel discombobulated. Like I'm watching this scene unfold from far away. *Is this an out of body experience?*

"This is real. I am here. So are you. And you're going to marry me." His voice rings with conviction.

I shake my head, open my mouth to speak, when—

Footsteps sound and Felix races up the aisle toward us. "Stop, what are you doing?" He comes to a stop between us. Chest heaving, sweat dripping down his temple. "I'm sorry, Vivian. Sorry I sent that message. But I'm here now." He takes a step in my direction, but I throw up my hand.

"Don't come near me."

"Vivian—" He swallows. "Please, listen to me."

"No. You didn't even have the decency to tell me to my face. You were going to break up with me through a text message to your groomsman?"

Said groomsman makes a protesting noise at the back of his throat but doesn't say anything. I'm aware of the rest of the gathered crowd watching the proceedings. I wish they'd leave me to wallow in my self-pity in peace, but there'll be no such luck. Nothing better than a person's fall from grace to hold everyone's attention.

"Why did you return?" I narrow my gaze on Felix. "Did you come to see how your ditching me at the altar has provided fodder for the gossip mill?" I nod toward where a group of girls—Felix's friends, not mine—are busy whispering to each other.

"It's not like that Vivi—" He takes a step forward and I move further away.

"Don't call me Vivi. And don't… Don't try to explain anything."

"But I have to… I … Can't let you go on hating me."

"You know what? I can't waste energy on hating you. I should have realized how immature you are. Hurtful as your actions were, I'm actually relieved. I never should have accepted your proposal in the first place."

"Don't say that." His chin trembles. "Vivi, seriously I… I didn't mean to hurt you." His Adam's apple bobs as he swallows. He blinks, then runs his fingers through his gelled hair, which stands up on end.

He looks so young. We might be the same age, but I've always felt this compulsive need to take care of him. *Is that why I agreed to marry him? So I could be the one in charge?* The one who'd set the tone of the relationship. So I didn't need to have my feelings involved. Because I knew he'd never want to dig behind the facade I was happy to show him. He'd never know about the spicy dreams that often plague my sleep. And how I woke up in a feverish state and often took care of myself. Away from him, in the bathroom, of course. So he wouldn't know, and he never guessed…

Is it because I miss taking care of someone? Was I looking to fill that hollowness inside me with his need for me? And why am I thinking of all this now? Why didn't these thoughts occur to me before I accepted his proposal?

He must see the conflicting emotions on my features, for his own crumple. "I'm so sorry." A tear runs down his cheek.

I bite down on my lower lip. *I will not cry.* I will face this situation head on, like I've done everything else in my life. I shake my head. "I'm not sure what to say? This"—I wave my hand in the air—"is not how I envisioned this day going."

"Me neither. That's the thing. I thought everything was fine, but then I walked into the church and—"

"You had second thoughts?"

He nods.

"I thought it was the usual pre-wedding jitters, but then I saw the crowd… And I knew, I couldn't go through with it."

"Maybe you could have decided that before you proposed to me?"

He hunches his shoulders—so thin in comparison to the stranger. I glance at the man who decided to prolong the mockery of the situation by proposing to me. No doubt, he felt sorry for me. And I must have been too bemused by his actions—reeling from the realization I was not actually going to get married, tinged with that weird sense of relief that still licks at my nerve-endings—to consider agreeing. *Eh? How stupid can I be?* One does not get jilted at the altar and consider marrying a stranger in the same breath.

Felix blinks, then follows my gaze to the stranger, and a strange light flares in his eyes. His hitherto pale cheeks go a pink color that I know only happens when he's angry. It's almost adorable how he resembles a little boy who's been deprived of his favorite treat.

While the stranger—once more my gaze is drawn to him—with the silver threaded through his temples, his cut-glass jaw, his cheekbones that could cut diamonds, that beautiful throat corded with tendons, those shoulders that could fill a doorway, that suit that envelopes his frame like it was tailored for him and which he fills out not because he's fat but because of the layers upon layers of muscles that ripple, even now, with that strange tension radiating from him...

He looks at Felix with those gorgeous blue eyes, so pale they could pass for colorless right now. Silver-blue eyes which are so like—I turn to Felix— like the man I almost married. And the height—they're both about six feet, three inches. Only, Felix is so skinny, he's all arms and legs. But when he fills out and builds up his musculature, and thirty years from now, when there's silver threaded through his temples, he'll look like this man. *What the—?*

I turn on the stranger, the suspicion in my mind beating at my temples. "Who are—"

Felix beats me to it. "What are you doing here?" He glares at the older man. "Didn't I ask you to leave?"

"No way was I going to do that. And I'm especially glad I didn't after you decided to turn into a runway bridegroom," the stranger growls.

Felix winces. His gaze narrows, and he sets his jaw. "I don't have to listen to this from someone who's been an absent father most of my life."

"Father?" I gape at the stranger. "You're his father?" *Of course he is.* My subconscious connected the dots before Felix's big reveal. But still. *He's Felix's father? What the what? Felix's FATHER?*

The man winces. Takes a step in my direction, but I stumble back—"Don't come close to me."

His features take on an agonized expression, then it fades away, leaving behind a mask made of stone. His thick eyebrows draw down, and his lips firm.

I look to where Felix is watching us with a furrowed brow.

"What's happening?" He looks from his father to me, then back to him. "What did you do?"

Quentin

"I'm trying to set right your wrongs," I say in a low voice. Oh, and also, for the first time in my life, I'm following my heart. Letting my gut lead... Which I've done during every situation when I'm on a mission, but this is the first time I've given in to my instinct in my civilian life. The first time I allowed my heart to lead in my personal life. Not since my wife left, have I felt this... overcome by my personal circumstances.

Whatever possessed me to ask her to marry me? Knowing full well that my son, no doubt, has feelings for her. Is that what spurred me on to do the unthinkable? To drop to my knees in front of the avidly watching crowd and ask her to be my wife? I've, no doubt, complicated this situation further. *A father marrying his son's ex-girlfriend? Could anything be more ridiculous?*

And yet... Why not? What's stopping me from marrying her? What's stopping her from saying yes? I've never felt this struck by a woman as I am with her. Never believed in love at first sight, or instalove, as the kids call it. Hey, I'm not completely out of the loop. I've had younger soldiers on my team who've kept me up to date with the lingo. Anyway, I've never believed in it; not until now.

What I felt when I first laid eyes on her earlier today is nothing short of a connection, a soul resonance, two opposite poles of a magnet—all of which is fanciful thinking. But I could swear she felt it, too. Maybe this is my way of adjusting to being back in civilian life—losing my ability to think clearly. One look at her, and every principle I've lived my life by went out of the window. *I'm attracted to a woman much younger than me who almost became my daughter-in-law.*

A wave of disgust squeezes my guts. *What kind of a man asks the woman his son broke up with at the altar to marry him?* One with no scruples. One who is set on consolidating his position within his father's company. I blame the old man for putting the thought of getting married into my head. If he hadn't made it conditional that I find a wife in order to be confirmed as the CEO of the company... Well... Things wouldn't have come to this stage. I wouldn't be this selfish. This... risking the possibility of forever alienating my only son by asking his ex to marry me. *What was I thinking? How could I do this?*

"*'T is some visitor,*" *I muttered, "Tapping at my chamber door, only this and nothing more.*"

"You're quoting Poe?" Her gaze widens.

"Of course you're quoting Poe. Always did have a nonsensical verse when you had no other excuses to offer," my son spits out.

"I didn't mean to hurt you," I murmur. *Am I referring to the distress I caused*

him in the past or what's to come? Am I saying this, knowing full well I'm going to break
his heart? And that I'm not able to stop myself. And that I hate myself for it.

So, step back then. Walk away. Don't let your entire life be marked by this one move;
you don't need to do this. There are other women you can ask to marry you, to fulfill
Arthur's condition. It doesn't have to be her.

It has to be her.

"Are you telling him or me?" Her features grow pinched. "How could you
do this?"

"What did you do?" Felix looks from me to her, then back at me. An
accusatory look comes into his eyes. "What did you say to her?"

How easily my son blames me. And this time, with good reason. I glance
up to my aunt, who has walked over to our little group and is staring at me.
There's a look of trepidation on her face. She, along with everyone else here,
saw me go down to my knees. But likely, she doesn't believe I had the temerity
to do what I did. Likely, she's waiting to give me the benefit of doubt. I shake
my head.

An older man rolls down the aisle in his wheelchair and comes to a halt
next to her. "What's going on?" He scowls at me. "Did you—"

"Propose to your daughter? I did."

"What?" Felix gasps.

My aunt's features turn white. She opens and shuts her mouth as if having
difficulty forming any words. She and I, both.

I turn away from her accusing stare and draw myself to my full height. "It's
true, I asked—uh—Vivian here." I don't even know her name, but given Felix
called her Vivi, I believe it should be Vivian, and going by the lack of surprise,
I know I was right.

"No title defines something so pure.
By any name - the feelings endure," I murmur.

Her forehead furrows. "Shakespeare," she whispers.

"Fucking bard, you always did think you could use a verse to get away
with anything," my son says in a bitter voice.

"Poems have no influence on me." She tips up her chin.

"Then how did you know who I was quoting?" I allow my lips to twitch.

Her features grow mutinous. *Mistake. Jeez, for someone versed in the art of nego-*
tiations, and having talked down enemy soldiers from killing us, I'm unable to keep my
thoughts to myself and complicating this situation further.

"And I'm not trying to excuse my actions." I turn to my son. "I'm not trying to show you up."

Felix scoffs. "I don't believe you. Never have. Never will. You're a selfish bastard. You only think of yourself."

I wince again. "I deserve that, and all your anger. I did not mean for this to happen, believe me. It was… Something beyond my control. I couldn't stop myself."

"Really, that's your excuse?" He levels a look filled with scorn in my direction. "And did you really propose to her?"

"I did."

His jaw drops, then anger suffuses his features. "The one thing I laid claim to. The one thing I wanted to make mine. And you couldn't resist screwing it up."

"Actually, you're the one who screwed it up, when you did a runner on your own wedding."

My son's face grows so red, I'm sure he's going to have a cardiac event.

"Felix, please—"

"Fuck you, Quentin." The next second, he throws himself at me. I see him coming and could step aside but choose not to. I deserve his anger and his hate, and it's better he take it out on me than keep it inside. He slams into my chest. I take his weight without flinching. My son, however, lets out an anguished yell. He grabs his shoulder, and with pain-filled eyes glares at me. "You're an asshole."

"I am."

"I told you not to come. I told you I didn't want you here. I knew you'd send everything tits up."

I open my mouth to point out it was he who, in fact, started the ball rolling in that direction, then wisely rein myself in.

"Did you hurt yourself?" I reach for him, but he steps back.

"Don't touch me. I don't want anything to do with you."

"And I don't want anything to do with either of you." She looks between the two of us. "How dare you, father and son, play with my emotions? How dare you embarrass me like this? It was bad enough what you did." She jerks her chin in Felix's direction. "But then you"—she trains her gaze on me—"make it a thousand times worse. Did you think you could make up for what Felix did by substituting yourself? Did you think I'd be so relieved to be getting married to someone—*anyone*—I'd jump at your offer? I'm not some pawn or possession for you to stake a claim to. I'm not the prize in some twisted competition."

"Vivi— " Felix begins.

"Vivian—" I say at the same time, but she interrupts both of us.

"Neither of you have the right to call me by my name. I don't want anything to do with either of you."

She turns and walks down the aisle. The crowd of people part, and head held high, she glides away. I make to go after her, but the man in the wheelchair glides to a stop in front of me. I pause, torn between stepping around him and wanting to follow her. But then he says, "What are your intentions toward my daughter?"

To find out what happens next read Quentin & Vivian's story in The Unsuitable Marriage

Bonus Scene

Skylar

"You sure you want to do this?"

My husband grabs the basket from near the entrance of The Sp!cy Booktok — an Indie bookshop which had opened recently in Primrose Hill. It was run by Giorgina Mitchell, a friend of Summer's who spent time between LA and London. Her husband, Rick Mitchell, was an ex-NHL player. He now ran coaching camps for teenagers in both cities. I had only met Gio in passing at Summer's place. She'd mentioned she was opening a branch of the store in Primrose Hill and was looking for someone to run it.

It had been a topic of much discussion that we now had a spicy bookshop in Primrose Hill. I had wanted to go there, of course, and my husband had refused to let me. He said I was nine months pregnant, which I am and that I shouldn't be exerting myself. I told him it was because I was nine months pregnant and ready to pop any day I definitely had to go. Once the little mite arrived, there was no telling when I would next be able to go to the bookshop. Not that I am complaining. Since I first kissed Nate when I was eighteen, a part of me had secretly hoped I'd have his child. Is that TMI? Does that make me less of a feminist? Can't you be a feminist and a successful entrepreneur and also want to have the child of the man who makes your ovaries flutter? Do ovaries flutter you ask? Well, you haven't been in Nate's presence then. This tall, dark handsome hunk of a man sends my hormones into a tizzy every time I see him. I wasn't surprised when a month into our marriage I found out

I was pregnant. The man has super sperm after all. He's machoness personified. He's an alphahole with a cinnamon roll heart and the inspiration for a new dessert in my bakery: soft, fluffy pastry with layers of cinnamon swirls and pockets of melted dark chocolate throughout, with a dash of chili. It's called an alpha's heart. It's decadent, sinful and when you bite into it the chocolate oozes onto your tongue, the cinnamon tickles your tongue and the chili heats your palate and other parts of your body. It's both an aphrodisiac and a heart warmer. It's full of contradictions which somehow meld together to form the perfect treat, like my man. Nate scowls at me. "Of course I want to carry your basket while you're shopping for books. You're not allowed to carry anything heavy, nothing more than my child snug in your belly."

"Aww." My heart melts further. In fact, if it swells further, it might cause me to burst my seams. "But don't you have to be at work?"

"Nothing's more important than indulging my wife."

When I'd insisted I absolutely had to come to The Sp!cy Booktok and get enough books to last me through the coming weeks, he'd given in. My husband's mush when it comes to taking care of my needs. He was already so thoughtful but after he discovered I was pregnant, his protectiveness shot up by a thousand fold. I don't think he's let me out of his sight since. Even when I have to go to the bathroom to pee, which I have to do often, he stands outside and waits for me. He insists it's because he wants to make sure I'm okay, that I don't accidentally slip when I'm inside. I've assured him a hundred times, I'm not that clumsy, but he points out I'm still unused to carrying all this extra weight around. I've put on nearly thirty-five pounds during the course of my pregnancy, which the doctor assures is normal, but it feels like I'm lugging around an enormously heavy football. My center of gravity shifted, so I have to be extra careful when I waddle around. In the last month, I've spent most of my time at home except for the short walk to the second branch of *The Fearless Kitten* in Primrose Hill, and sometimes a walk around Primrose Hill in the fresh air. I've carried most of the business related to the bakery on the phone. And since I'm unable to reach over my big belly to bake, I've hired a temporary baker who came recommended through Summer's friend Amelie. By all counts she was doing well, no one could tell the difference in the quality of the pastries on sale. Which was good but also made me feel a little dispensable. Or maybe that's just me being a little wistful that I wasn't missed more in my own shop. On the other hand, the new baker is doing a great job and with my team in place to support her on the front end, I know things are going to be fine with the bakery. Which means for once in my life I have time to focus on myself. And I wanted to spend it by going to the bookshop. Of course, my husband had refused to let me go on my on. When he found he couldn't talk me out of it, he'd insisted on accompanying me. Which is how we'd come to be standing in the aisle of *The Spicy Booktok*. Me running my fingers down the spines of the spicy romance and Nate standing next to me with a basket. A twinge squeezes my back and I rub at it. Nate instantly stiffens. "Are you okay?"

I roll my eyes. "Of course I'm okay." The muscle at the small of my back cramps then begins to tighten toward the front. *I'm not okay.* I'm not in labor though. Am I? Nah, I still have a week to go before the baby is due. I push aside the discomfort and waddle down the aisle. A blue cover catches my gaze. I pull it out and glance at the cover. *The Wrong Wife* by L. Steele. Ooh, the cover is so pretty. And that feather… it's eye catching. Also, it's a marriage of convenience romance, my favorite. I drop it into the basket. Then grab all the other books by the author for good measure. The covers are all sooo pretty. And each book has a different flower on the spine. When I line them up on the bookshelf, they are going to look eye-catching.

Another cramp squeezes down on my lower belly. My breath catches. This one was stronger than the previous one. Or maybe that's my imagination. I love my baby but between being unable to bend over to tie up my own sneakers, and feeling hot and sweaty most of the time, not to mention the heartburn and the farting and having to run to pee every half hour, and I was more than ready to get this little tadpole out of my belly. Of course, the baby was going to come out when they were ready. And it seems they might be ready now? Another jolt of pain tightens the muscle of my lower belly. I manage not to gasp, but move away from Nate and up the aisle. If he sees my face, I have no doubt he'll know something is wrong. He'll whisk me off to the hospital in the ambulance and they'll know the true nature of what is happening. I won't be able to hide that I'm probably in labor. I'd wished for this day over the last month but now that I'm here, I'm in no hurry. A strange calm descends on me. I pull out more books from the next shelf and drop them into the basket. And more. Soon, the basket is full to the brim. Nate doesn't complain. His biceps stretch the sleeves of his sweatshirt, as he carries the basket with ease. I grab a few more books, slide them onto the top of the heap in the basket. He doesn't bat an eyelid. Is there anything more erotic than seeing your man carry the stash of books you want to buy without complaint? Another jolt of pain slices through my middle. My breath catches, a groan I can't stop escapes me. Nate freezes. "What the —!" He swears under his breath. "You're not okay."

I turn to him with a bright smile on my face. "Of course I am, I —" there's a gushing between my legs. I glance down to find water pooling around me on the floor. "Uh, looks like my water broke."

"What?" Nate's voice carries a note of panic. "Your water broke?"

I nod.

"What... what should I do?"

I glance up to find Nate's features have gone pale. Sweat beads his forehead. "Starling, are you—" His throat moves as he swallows. "Are you in labor?"

"It would seem that way."

He sways a little. The sight of my confident, dominant, allphaolic cinnamon-roll of a husband turn nervous is a sight I never thought I'd see. In contrast, I feel calm, collected. A sense of the inevitable grips me.

"Baby, you okay?" I ask.

"Am I okay?" He shakes his head. "Are you okay?"

"No, but I will be."

"What... what should I do?" Nate clutches the handles of the basket with such intensity that the skin on his knuckles stretches white.

I pat his arm. "I think you should take me to the hospital."

He swallows again, then nods, placing the basket on the floor, he moves forward. The next moment he sweeps me up in his arms. "I'll dirty your sweatshirt," I yelp.

"Fuck that." He begins to move toward the exit.

"But my basket of books."

"I'll have it sent home." As he passes the cashier he yells, "Call the ambulance, my wife's having our baby."

Nathan

"Benjamin Arthur Davenport." I peer into my son's features. "You are beautiful." I look over at my wife's face. "Thank you." I lean over and kiss her forehead. "Thank you baby, for the best gift you could have given me."

My wife smiles. Three hours of labor and my son had burst into the world with a gusty cry. He hadn't stopped crying as they'd weighed him, cleaned him, done a quick assessment, then placed him on her chest. With the help of the lactation expert, my wife had coaxed my son to feed and he'd latched on to her teat. His cries had cut out and the next few minutes he'd fed until his body had stilled. He'd dozed off. That's when I'd shed my sweatshirt and placed him against my own chest. Feeling my son's skin against my own with my wife watching on had been the single most monumental moment of my life. The world had shifted at that moment. I had the sense my life would never be the same again. How was it possible to love someone this tiny who had just come into my life with everything I had? "I love you," I whisper into my wife's hair. "I love the both of you."

She sniffles. I glance down to find a tear run down her cheek.

"Don't cry," I say in alarm.

"These are tears of joy." She smiles. "I can't believe he is ours."

"Thanks to you." I continue to stare at her, that sense of awe and shock which had filled me from the moment her water had broken still courses through my veins. The ambulance had arrived in seconds—I'd had the paramedics on standby, and had called ahead to the bookshop to give them all the details of what to do in case of emergency before I took my wife there. You don't think I'd have let her out of the house unprepared, do you? And my caution paid off. For the ambulance arrived and I had her in it and we were racing toward the hospital in seconds. I'd held her hand as the medics had checked her vitals. My heart had felt like it was going to break through my ribcage, every muscle in my body had tensed. I'd felt like I was facing the biggest test of my life. The worst thing? Seeing my wife in pain and not being able to do anything about it. Given a chance, I'd have taken her place but in this case that was not possible. So I had to content myself with holding her hand all through the birthing process. She'd dug her fingernails into my skin until she'd drawn blood but I hand't flinched. I'd faced enemies on the front line, had to navigate diplomatic situations where the lives of hundreds of people were at stake, but when it is the life of the one person you love more than yourself? It's the most vulnerable spot I've found myself in. And when she'd screamed in pain as she pushed, all I could do was mop her brow, feed her ice-chips, talk to her and tell her how much I love her. And when, with a final burst of energy, she'd pushed that last time and my son had been born, my heart had felt so full, joy had flushed my blood, my cells, my very being had felt like this huge infusion of energy, of love, so much love and fear... the fear that I'll not be able to save my son from the world. That I'd give my life to protect his and that of my wife. In that instance my life as I knew it had changed. I had transformed into being a father. I had been protective of my wife this far, but now... it was a primal need in me to ensure she was always taken care of. I had been reduced to my base instincts. Hunter, gatherer, guardian and nurturer. This was my family. A unit carved out in space and time. My little corner of the world which I could call home. For home... was where she was and where my son was. "I am the luckiest man in the world."

Her smile grows brilliant. Her eyes shine. "I am the luckiest woman in the world."

Our son stirs, then begins to cry.

"And he's saying he's lucky to be born to the both of us." She holds out her arms and I carefully place our baby in them.

We had both known it was going to be a boy, which was why we'd agreed we wouldn't find out the gender of the child beforehand. I had an instinct about it and my wife? She wanted a boy so she could call him Ben. She'd hoped this was how her brother would return back to us. As for his middle name? My wife had been insistent we call him after my father. I had resisted but then I realized I did want my son to know his grandfather. He hadn't been a very good father to me, but I had no doubt Arthur would love his first-born grandson and do anything for him. Truthfully, I wanted my son to have his entire family in his corner. I wanted him to start life with the love I never had. I bend my head and kiss my son on his forehead. "I love you. I promise you'll never have to face a moment when you don't feel cherished."

Skylar

I rub Ben's forehead. So soft. So angelic with his dark eyelashes lying close to his cheeks. From certain angles, I am almost sure I can spot glimpses of my brother in him. His eyes, though, they are mismatched like his father's. And he has Nathan's stubborn jaw, his nose is all me, though. Over the last week, Nathan and I have tried to find a routine, only we're fast realizing that the lack of one is the only routine with a newborn. He wakes up thrice every night and demands to be fed. I'd offered to sleep with him in the nursery but Nathan had insisted we put a crib in our bedroom next to me so he could take turns soothing the baby, as well. He'd taken paternity leave and wasn't going back to the office for an entire month. So it was me and him and our son in our little bubble. Now my husband watches me breastfeed the baby. I can't help but laugh at his entranced look. "You're captivated by how he nurses."

Nathan nods. "He drinks like he's imbibing life itself. He *is* life itself." His phone buzzes but he ignores it.

"Why don't you get that?"

"I don't care who it is."

"It might be something important."

"Everything that is important to me is in front of me," he replies.

Happiness blooms in my chest. Every time I think I can't be more content, he says or does something which increases my delight manyfold.

His phone stops then starts again.

"I really think you should get it, darling," I say softly.

He picks up his phone, glances at the screen, then answers, "Quentin, I am on paternity leave."

I hear Quentin's voice on the other side but can't make out the words.

"I'm not sure I want to see your ugly mug right now."

I frown at my husband. He shrugs.

"I think you should meet him," I say in a low voice. "He's rejoined the family after so long and he's also new to the company. He could do with your guidance."

"Hold on, ol' chap." Nathan covers the phone with his palm. "He says he's outside our house."

"He is?"

"He wants to talk with me."

"Why don't you find out what he wants?"

"And leave the two of you on your own?"

I laugh. "Me and Ben are right here, we're not going anywhere. Besides, now that he's asleep, I can take a nap."

Nathan seems undecided.

"I really think you should go."

Nate blows out a breath. "Only because you insist." He leans over, kisses me, then the now-sleeping Ben, before he pushes his legs over the side of the bed and stands up. "I'll be back soon."

As he leaves the room, he speaks into the phone, "On my way to get you."

Nathan

When I open the door to the house, Quentin is running his fingers through his hair. I don't know the guy that well. He's my uncle but given I didn't get to know my birth family until recently I met him first a few weeks ago. Though we'd both served in the Marines I never met him there, either. He and Knox on the other hand, have served on missions together. My recollections of him faded over the years, until he returned home more than a month ago. The last few times I've seen him, he's been dressed like he walked off the pages of GQ. Today he's wearing jeans worn at the knees, a sweatshirt, which has been washed one too many times. He also has a baseball cap on his head. He has a hand stuck in the front pocket of his jeans and a frown on his face.

"The fuck you doing here?" I growl.

His scowl deepens. "I know this isn't a good time—"

"That's putting it mildly."

"I uh, I didn't know who else to speak with." He shuffles his feet and looks embarrassed. In fact—I look closely at his features—he looks like he hasn't slept much.

"You look like shite," I state.

"Thanks." His lips quirk. "Can I come in?"

"Should I let you in?"

"We're not that close but that's the reason you're the best person for me to discuss this little problem I seem to have stumbled into with."

"A little problem?" I tilt my head.

"Okay, it's not little, it has the potential to turn my life into a shit-show unless I get my head around it." He rolls his shoulders. "Look man, you have enough distance to offer some perspective on my situation."

"Hmm."

"Please?" He drags his fingers through his hair again. "I need your help."

I take pity on him and step back. He walks in, I shut the door and follow him into the living room. He begins to pace without taking in his surroundings. I watch him without saying anything. Sometimes silence is best. After a while he turns to me. "Can I get a drink?"

"Juice, milk or water?"

He blinks slowly. "Anything stronger?"

"Chamomile tea?"

He makes a face.

"You look like you could do with Chamomile tea."

"Do I have a choice?"

I head into the kitchen, he follows me. "How's the little one?"

"Good." I find myself beaming from ear to ear. "He has a pair of lungs on him which keeps the neighborhood and me and my wife up at night, but I'm not complaining." I put on the kettle, then head to the refrigerator and pull out two cans of Red Bull. Only reason I have them is because it helps me stay up to watch over Ben. I toss him one.

"Shit, I thought you really were going to pour me a cup of Chamomile tea," Quentin says with relief in his voice.

"I still can, it would settle your nerves." I make to turn toward the kettle which just switched off.

"No, I am good," he says hastily.

I walk toward the sliding doors that lead to the decking and pulling them open and step out. He follows me. I sip from the can, he merely stares at it.

"What's on your mind?"

"I might have done something which I need to make sense of."

"Such as?"

"I might have… uh… asked my son's ex-girlfriend, the woman he stood up at the altar to marry me."

To find out what happens next read Quentin and Vivian's story in *The Imperfect Marriage*

Read Summer & Sinclair Sterling's story **HERE** in *The Billionaire's Fake Wife*

Read an excerpt from Summer & Sinclair's story

Summer

"Slap, slap, kiss, kiss."

"Huh?" I stare up at the bartender.

"Aka, there's a thin line between love and hate." He shakes out the crimson liquid into my glass.

"Nah." I snort. "Why would she allow him to control her, and after he insulted her?"

"It's the chemistry between them." He lowers his head. "You have to admit that, when the man is arrogant and the woman resists, it's a challenge to both of them, to see who blinks first, huh?"

"Why?" I wave my hand in the air. "Because they hate each other?"

"Because," he chuckles, "the girl in school whose braids I pulled and teased mercilessly, is the one who I—"

"Proposed to?" I huff.

His face lights up. "You get it now?"

Yeah. No. A headache begins to pound at my temples. This crash course in pop psychology is not why I came to my favorite bar in Islington, to meet my best friend, who is—I glance at the face of my phone—thirty minutes late.

I inhale the drink, and his eyebrows rise.

"What?" I glower up at the bartender. "I can barely taste the alcohol. Besides, it's free drinks at happy hour for women, right?"

"Which ends in precisely—" he holds up five fingers— "minutes."

"Oh! Yay!" I mock fist pump. "Time enough for one more, at least."

A hiccough swells my throat and I swallow it back, nod.

One has to do what one has to do… when everything else in the world is going to shit.

A hot sensation stabs behind my eyes; my chest tightens. Is this what people call growing up?

The bartender tips his mixing flask, strains out a fresh batch of the ruby red liquid onto the glass in front of me.

"Salut." I nod my thanks, then toss it back. It hits my stomach and tendrils of fire crawl up my spine, I cough.

My head spins. Warmth sears my chest, spreads to my extremities. I can't feel my fingers or toes. Good. Almost there. "Top me up."

"You sure?"

"Yes." I square my shoulders and reach for the drink.

"No. She's had enough."

"What the —?" I pivot on the bar stool.

Indigo eyes bore into me.

Fathomless. Black at the bottom, the intensity in their depths grips me. He swoops out his arm, grabs the glass and holds it up. Thick fingers dwarf the glass. Tapered at the edges. The nails short and buff. *All the better to grab you with.* I gulp.

"Like what you see?"

I flush, peer up into his face.

Hard cheekbones, hollows under them, and a tiny scar that slashes at his left eyebrow. *How did he get that?* Not that I care. My gaze slides to his mouth. Thin upper lip, a lower lip that is full and cushioned. Pouty with a hint of bad boy. *Oh!* My toes curl. My thighs clench.

The corner of his mouth kicks up. *Asshole.*

Bet he thinks life is one big smug-fest. I glower, reach for my glass, and he holds it up and out of my reach.

I scowl. "Gimme that."

He shakes his head.

"That's my drink."

"Not anymore." He shoves my glass at the bartender. "Water for her. Get me a whiskey, neat."

I splutter, then reach for my drink again. The barstool tips in his direction. This is when I fall against him, and my breasts slam into his hard chest, sculpted planes with layers upon layers of muscle that ripple and writhe as he turns aside, flattens himself against the bar. The floor rises up to meet me.

What the actual hell?

I twist my torso at the last second and my butt connects with the surface. *Ow!*

The breath rushes out of me. My hair swirls around my face. I scramble for purchase, and my knee connects with his leg.

"Watch it." He steps around, stands in front of me.

"You stepped aside?" I splutter. "You let me fall?"

"Hmph."

I tilt my chin back, all the way back, look up the expanse of muscled thigh that stretches the silken material of his suit. *What is he wearing? Could any suit fit a man with such precision?* Hand crafted on Saville Row, no doubt. I glance at the bulge that tents the fabric between his legs. *Oh!* I blink.

Look away, look away. I hold out my arm. He'll help me up at least, won't he?

He glances at my palm, then turns away. *No, he didn't do that, no way.*

A glass of amber liquid appears in front of him. He lifts the tumbler to his sculpted mouth.

His throat moves, strong tendons flexing. He tilts his head back, and the column of his neck moves as he swallows. Dark hair covers his chin—it's a discordant chord in that clean-cut profile, I shiver. He would scrape that rough skin down my core. He'd mark my inner thighs, lick my core, thrust his tongue inside my melting channel and drink from my pussy. *Oh! God.* Goosebumps rise on my skin.

No one has the right to look this beautiful, this achingly gorgeous. Too magnificent for his own good. Anger coils in my chest.

"Arrogant wanker."

"I'll take that under advisement."

"You're a jerk, you know that?"

He presses his lips together. The grooves on either side of his mouth deepen. Clearly the man has never laughed a single day in his life. Bet that stick up his arse is uncomfortable. I chuckle.

He runs his gaze down my features, my chest, down to my toes, then yawns.

The hell! I will not let him provoke me. Will not. "Like what you see?" I jut out my chin.

"Sorry, you're not my type." He slides a hand into the pocket of those perfectly cut pants, stretching it across that heavy bulge.

Heat curls low in my belly.

Not fair, that he could afford a wardrobe that clearly shouts his status and what amounts to the economy of a small third-world country. A hot feeling stabs in my chest.

He reeks of privilege, of taking his status in life for granted.

While I've had to fight every inch of the way. Hell, I am still battling to hold onto the last of my equilibrium.

"Last chance—" I wiggle my fingers from where I am sprawled out on the floor at his feet, "—to redeem yourself..."

"You have me there." He places the glass on the counter, then bends and holds out his hand. The hint of discolored steel at his wrist catches my attention. Huh?

He wears a cheap-ass watch?

That's got to bring down the net worth of his presence by more than 1000% percent. Weird.

I reach up and he straightens.

I lurch back.

"Oops, I changed my mind." His lips curl.

A hot burning sensation claws at my stomach. I am not a violent person, honestly. But Smirky Pants here, he needs to be taught a lesson.

I swipe out my legs, kicking his out from under him.

Sinclair

My knees give way, and I hurtle toward the ground.

What the—? I twist around, thrust out my arms. My palms hit the floor. The impact jostles up my elbows. I firm my biceps and come to a halt planked above her.

A huffing sound fills my ear.

I turn to find my whippet, Max, panting with his mouth open. I scowl and he flattens his ears.

All of my businesses are dog-friendly. Before you draw conclusions about me being the caring sort or some such shit—it attracts footfall.

Max scrutinizes the girl, then glances at me. *Huh?* He hates women, but not her, apparently.

I straighten and my nose grazes hers.

My arms are on either side of her head. Her chest heaves. The fabric of her dress stretches across her gorgeous breasts. My fingers tingle; my palms ache to cup those tits, squeeze those hard nipples outlined against the—hold on, what is she wearing? A tunic shirt in a sparkly pink... and are those shoulder pads she has on?

I glance up, and a squeak escapes her lips.

Pink hair surrounds her face. *Pink? Who dyes their hair that color past the age of eighteen?*

I stare at her face. *How old is she?* Un-furrowed forehead, dark eyelashes that flutter against pale cheeks. Tiny nose, and that mouth—luscious, tempting. A whiff of her scent, cherries and caramel, assails my senses. My mouth waters. *What the hell?*

She opens her eyes and our eyelashes brush. Her gaze widens. Green, like the leaves of the evergreens, flickers of gold sparkling in their depths. "What?" She glowers. "You're demonstrating the plank position?"

"Actually," I lower my weight onto her, the ridge of my hardness thrusting into the softness between her legs, "I was thinking of something else, altogether."

She gulps and her pupils dilate. *Ah, so she feels it, too?*

I drop my head toward her, closer, closer.

Color floods the creamy expanse of her neck. Her eyelids flutter down. She tilts her chin up.

I push up and off of her.

"That... Sweetheart, is an emphatic 'no thank you' to whatever you are offering."

Her eyelids spring open and pink stains her cheeks. Adorable. Such a range of emotions across those gorgeous features in a few seconds. What else is hidden under that exquisite exterior of hers?

She scrambles up, eyes blazing.

Ah! The little bird is trying to spread her wings? My dick twitches. My groin hardens, *Why does her anger turn me on so, huh?*

She steps forward, thrusts a finger in my chest.

My heart begins to thud.

She peers up from under those hooded eyelashes. "Wake up and taste the wasabi, asshole."

"What does that even mean?"

She makes a sound deep in her throat. My dick twitches. My pulse speeds up.

She pivots, grabs a half-full beer mug sitting on the bar counter.

I growl, "Oh, no, you don't."

She turns, swings it at me. The smell of hops envelops the space.

I stare down at the beer-splattered shirt, the lapels of my camel colored jacket deepening to a dull brown. Anger squeezes my guts.

I fist my fingers at my side, broaden my stance.

She snickers.

I tip my chin up. "You're going to regret that."

The smile fades from her face. "Umm." She places the now empty mug on the bar.

I take a step forward and she skitters back. "It's only clothes." She gulps. "They'll wash."

I glare at her and she swallows, wiggles her fingers in the air. "I should have known that you wouldn't have a sense of humor."

I thrust out my jaw. "That's a ten-thousand-pound suit you destroyed."

She blanches, then straightens her shoulders. "Must have been some hot date you were trying to impress, huh?"

"Actually," I flick some of the offending liquid from my lapels, "it's you I was after."

"Me?" She frowns.

"We need to speak."

She glances toward the bartender who's on the other side of the bar. "I don't know you." She chews on her lower lip, biting off some of the hot pink. How would she look, with that pouty mouth fastened on my cock?

The blood rushes to my groin so quickly that my head spins. My pulse rate ratchets up. Focus, focus on the task you came here for.

"This will take only a few seconds." I take a step forward.

She moves aside.

I frown. "You want to hear this, I promise."

"Go to hell." She pivots and darts forward.

I let her go, a step, another, because... I can? Besides it's fun to create the illusion of freedom first; makes the hunt so much more entertaining, huh?

I swoop forward, loop an arm around her waist, and yank her toward me.

She yelps. "Release me."

Good thing the bar is not yet full. It's too early for the usual officegoers to stop by. And the staff...? Well they are well aware of who cuts their paychecks.

I spin her around and against the bar, then release her. "You will listen to me."

She swallows; she glances left to right.

Not letting you go yet, little Bird. I move into her space, crowd her.

She tips her chin up. "Whatever you're selling, I'm not interested."

I allow my lips to curl. "You don't fool me."

A flush steals up her throat, sears her cheeks. So tiny, so innocent. Such a good little liar. I narrow my gaze. "Every action has its consequences."

"Are you daft?" She blinks.

"This pretense of yours?" I thrust my face into hers, growling, "It's not working."

She blinks, then color suffuses her cheeks. "You're certifiably mad—"

"Getting tired of your insults."

"It's true, everything I said." She scrapes back the hair from her face.

Her fingernails are painted... You guessed it, pink.

"And here's something else. You are a selfish, egotistical jackass."

I smirk. "You're beginning to repeat your insults and I haven't even kissed you yet."

"Don't you dare." She gulps.

I tilt my head. "Is that a challenge?"

"It's a..." she scans the crowded space, then turns to me. Her lips firm, "...a warning. You're delusional, you jackass." She inhales a deep breath before she speaks, "Your ego is bigger than the size of a black hole." She snickers. "Bet it's to compensate for your lack of balls."

A-n-d, that's it. I've had enough of her mouth that threatens to never stop spewing words. How many insults can one tiny woman hurl my way? Answer: too many to count.

"You—"

I lower my chin, touch my lips to hers.

Heat, sweetness, the honey of her essence explodes on my palate. My dick twitches. I tilt my head, deepen the kiss, reaching for that something more... more... of whatever scent she's wearing on her skin, infused with that breath of hers that crowds my senses, rushes down my spine. My groin hardens; my cock lengthens. I thrust my tongue between those infuriating lips.

She makes a sound deep in her throat and my heart begins to pound.

So innocent, yet so crafty. Beautiful and feisty. The kind of complication I don't need in my life.

I prefer the straight and narrow. Gray and black, that's how I choose to define my world. She, with her flashes of color—pink hair and lips that threaten to drive me to the edge of distraction—is exactly what I hate.

Give me a female who has her priorities set in life. To pleasure me, get me off, then walk away before her emotions engage. Yeah. That's what I prefer.

Not this... this bundle of craziness who flings her arms around my shoulders, thrusts her breasts up and into my chest, tips up her chin, opens her mouth, and invites me to take and take.

Does she have no self-preservation? Does she think I am going to fall for her wide-eyed appeal? She has another thing coming.

I tear my mouth away and she protests.

She twines her leg with mine, pushes up her hips, so that melting softness between her thighs cradles my aching hardness.

I glare into her face and she holds my gaze.

Trains her green eyes on me. Her cheeks flush a bright red. Her lips fall open and a moan bleeds into the air. The blood rushes to my dick, which instantly thickens. *Fuck.*

Time to put distance between myself and the situation.

It's how I prefer to manage things. Stay in control, always. Cut out anything that threatens to impinge on my equilibrium. Shut it down or buy them off. Reduce it to a transaction. That I understand.

The power of money, to be able to buy and sell—numbers, logic. That's what's worked for me so far.

"How much?"

Her forehead furrows.

"Whatever it is, I can afford it."

Her jaw slackens. "You think... you—"

"A million?"

"What?"

"Pounds, dollars... You name the currency, and it will be in your account."

Her jaw slackens. "You're offering me money?"

"For your time, and for you to fall in line with my plan."

She reddens. "You think I am for sale?"

"Everyone is."

"Not me."

Here we go again. "Is that a challenge?"

Color fades from her face. "Get away from me."

"Are you shy, is that what this is?" I frown. "You can write your price down on a piece of paper if you prefer." I glance up, notice the bartender watching us. I jerk my chin toward the napkins. He grabs one, then offers it to her.

She glowers at him. "Did you buy him, too?"

"What do you think?"

She glances around. "I think everyone here is ignoring us."

"It's what I'd expect."

"Why is that?"

I wave the tissue in front of her face. "Why do you think?"

"You own the place?"

"As I am going to own you."

She sets her jaw. "Let me leave and you won't regret this."

A chuckle bubbles up. I swallow it away. This is no laughing matter. I never smile during a transaction. Especially not when I am negotiating a new acquisition. And that's all she is. The final piece in the puzzle I am building.

"No one threatens me."

"You're right."

"Huh?"

"I'd rather act on my instinct."

Her lips twist, her gaze narrows. All of my senses scream a warning.

No, she wouldn't, no way—pain slices through my middle and sparks explode behind my eyes.

READ SINCLAIR AND SUMMER'S ENEMIES TO LOVERS, MARRIAGE OF CONVE-NIENCE ROMANCE IN THE BILLIONAIRE'S FAKE WIFE HERE

READ LIAM AND ISLA'S FAKE RELATIONSHIP ROMANCE IN THE PROPOSAL WHERE TINY FIRST MAKES AN APPEARANCE, CLICK HERE

READ AN EXCERPT FROM THE PROPOSAL

Liam

"Where is she?"

The receptionist gazes at me cow-eyed. Her lips move, but no words emerge. She clears her throat, glances sideways at the door to the side and behind her, then back at me.

"So, I take it she's in there?" I brush past her, and she jumps to her feet. "Sir, y-y-you can't go in there."

"Watch me." I glare at her.

She stammers, then gulps. Sweat beads her forehead. She shuffles back, and I stalk past her.

Really, is there no one who can stand up to me? All of this scraping of chairs and fawning over me? It's enough to drive a man to boredom. I need a challenge. So, when my ex-wife-to-be texted me to say she was calling off our wedding, I was pissed. But when she let it slip that her wedding planner was right—that she needs to marry for love, and not for some family obligation, rage gripped me. I squeezed my phone so hard the screen cracked. I almost hurled the device across the room. When I got a hold of myself, for the first time in a long time, a shiver of something like excitement passed through me. *Finally, fuck.*

That familiar pulse of adrenaline pulses through my veins. It's a sensation I was familiar with in the early days of building my business.

After my father died and I took charge of the group of companies he'd run, I was filled with a sense of purpose; a one-directional focus to prove myself and nurture his legacy. To make my group of companies the leader, in its own right. To make so much money and amass so much power, I'd be a force to be reckoned with.

I tackled each business meeting with a zeal that none of my opponents were able to withstand. But with each passing year—as I crossed the bench-marks I'd set myself, as my bottom line grew healthier, my cash reserves engorged, and the people working for me began treating me with the kind of respect normally reserved for larger-than-life icons—some of that enthusiasm waned. Oh, I still wake up ready to give my best to my job every day, but the zest that once fired me up faded, leaving a sense of purposelessness behind.

The one thing that has kept me going is to lock down my legacy. To ensure the business I've built will finally be transferred to my name. For which my father informed me I would need to marry. Which is why, after much research, I tracked down Lila Kumar, wooed her, and proposed to her. And then, her meddling wedding planner came along and turned all of my plans upside down.

Now, that same sense of purpose grips me. That laser focus I've been lacking envelops me and fills my being. All of my senses sharpen as I shove the door of her office open and stalk in.

The scent envelops me first. The lush notes of violets and peaches. Evoca-tive and fruity. Complex, yet with a core of mystery that begs to be unraveled. Huh? I'm not the kind to be affected by the scent of a woman, but this... Her scent... It's always chafed at my nerve endings. The hair on my forearms straightens.

My guts tie themselves up in knots, and my heart pounds in my chest. It's not comfortable. The kind of feeling I got the first time I went white-water rafting. A combination of nervousness and excitement as I faced my first rapids. A sensation that had since ebbed. One I'd been chasing ever since, pushing myself to take on extreme sports. One I hadn't thought I'd find in the office of a wedding planner.

My feet thud on the wooden floor, and I get a good look at the space which is one-fourth the size of my own office. In the far corner is a bookcase packed with books. On the opposite side is a comfortable settee packed with cushions women seem to like so much. There's a colorful patchwork quilt thrown over it, and behind that, a window that looks onto the back of the adjacent office building. On the coffee table in front of the settee is a bowl with crystal-like objects that reflect the light from the floor lamps. There are paintings on the wall that depict scenes from beaches. No doubt, the kind she'd point to and sell the idea of a honeymoon to gullible brides. I suppose the entire space would appeal to women. With its mood lighting and homey feel, the space invites you to kick back, relax and pour out your problems. A ruse I'm not going to fall for.

"You!" I stab my finger in the direction of the woman seated behind the antique desk straight ahead. "Call Lila, right now, and tell her she needs to go through with the wedding. Tell her she can't back out. Tell her I'm the right choice for her."

She peers up at me from behind large, black horn-rimmed glasses perched on her nose. "No."

I blink. "Excuse me?"

She leans back in her chair. "I'm not going to do that."

"Why the hell not?"

"Are you the right choice for her?"

"Of course, I am." I glare at her.

Some of the color fades from her cheeks. She taps her pen on the table, then juts out her chin. "What makes you think you're the right choice of husband for her?"

"What makes you think I'm not."

"Do you love her?"

"That's no one's problem except mine and hers."

"You don't love her."

"What does that have to do with anything?"

"Excuse me?" She pushes the glasses further up her nose. "Are you seriously asking what loving the woman you're going to marry has to do with actually marrying her?" Her voice pulses with fury.

"Yes, exactly. Why don't you explain it to me?" The sarcasm in my tone is impossible to miss.

She stares at me from behind those large glasses that should make her look owlish and studious, but only add an edge of what I can only describe as quirky-sexiness. The few times I've met her before, she's gotten on my nerves so much, I couldn't wait to get the hell away from her. Now, giving her the full benefit of my attention, I realize, she's actually quite striking. And the addition of those spectacles? Fuck me—I never thought I had a weakness for women wearing glasses. Maybe I was wrong. Or maybe it's specifically this woman wearing glasses... Preferably only glasses and nothing else.

Hmm. Interesting. This reaction to her. It's unwarranted and not something I planned for. I widen my stance, mainly to accommodate the thickness between my legs. An inconvenience... which perhaps I can use to my benefit? I drag my thumb under my lower lip.

Her gaze drops to my mouth, and if I'm not mistaken, her breath hitches. *Very interesting.* Has she always reacted to me like that in the past? Nope, I would've noticed. We've always tried to have as little as possible to do with each other. Like I said, interesting. And unusual.

"First," —she drums her fingers on the table— "are you going to answer my question?"

I tilt my head, the makings of an idea buzzing through my synapses. I need a little time to flesh things out though. It's the only reason I deign to answer her question which, let's face it, I have no obligation to respond to. But for the moment, it's in my interest to humor her and buy myself a little time.

"Lila and I are well-matched in every way. We come from good families—"

"You mean rich families?"

"That, too. Our families move in the same circles."

"Don't you mean boring country clubs?" she says in a voice that drips with distaste.

I frown. "Among other places. We have the pedigree, the bloodline, our backgrounds are congruent, and we'd be able to fold into an arrangement of coexistence with the least amount of disruption on either side."

"Sounds like you're arranging a merger."

"A takeover, but what-fucking-ever." I raise a shoulder.

Her scowl deepens. "This is how you approached the upcoming wedding... And you wonder why Lila left you?"

"I gave her the biggest ring money could buy—"

"You didn't make an appearance at the engagement party."

"I signed off on all the costs related to the upcoming nuptials—"

"Your own engagement party. You didn't come to it. You left her alone to face her family and friends." Her tone rises. Her cheeks are flushed. You'd think she was talking about her own wedding, not that of her friend. In fact, it's more entertaining to talk to her than discuss business matters with my employees. *How interesting.*

"You also didn't show up for most of the rehearsals." She glowers.

"I did show up for the last one."

"Not that it made any difference. You were either checking your watch and indicating that it was time for you to leave, or you were glowering at the plans being discussed."

"I still agreed to that god-awful wedding cake, didn't I?

"On the other hand, it's probably good you didn't come for the previous rehearsals. If you had, Lila and I might have had this conversation earlier—"

"Aha!" I straighten. "So, you confess that it's because of you Lila walked away from this wedding."

She tips her head back. "Hardly. It's because of you."

"So you say, but your guilt is written large on your face."

"Guilt?" Her features flush. The color brings out the dewy hue of her skin, and the blue of her eyes deepens until they remind me of forget-me-nots. No, more like the royal blue of the ink that spilled onto my paper the first time I attempted to write with a fountain pen.

"The only person here who should feel guilty is you, for attempting to coerce an innocent, young woman into an arrangement that would have trapped her for life."

Anger thuds at my temples. My pulse begins to race. "I never have to coerce women. And what you call being trapped is what most women call security. But clearly, you wouldn't know that, considering" — I wave my hand in the air — "you prefer to run your kitchen-table business which, no doubt, barely makes ends meet."

She loosens her grip on her pencil, and it falls to the table with a clatter. Sparks flash deep in her eyes.

You know what I said earlier about the royal blue? Strike that. There are flickers of silver hidden in the depths of her gaze. Flickers that blaze when she's upset. How would it be to push her over the edge? To be at the receiving end of all that passion, that fervor, that ardor... that absolute avidness of existence when she's one with the moment? How would it feel to rein in her spirit, absorb it, drink from it, revel in it, and use it to spark color into my life?

"Kitchen-table business?" She makes a growling sound under her breath. "You dare come into my office and insult my enterprise? The company I have grown all by myself—"

"And outside of your assistant" — I nod toward the door I came through — "you're the sole employee, I take it?"

Her color deepens. "I work with a group of vendors—"

I scoff, "None of whom you could hold accountable when they don't deliver."

"—who have been carefully vetted to ensure that they always deliver," she says at the same time. "Anyway, why do you care, since you don't have a wedding to go to?"

"That's where you're wrong." I peel back my lips. "I'm not going to be labeled as the joke of the century. After all, the media labelled it 'the wedding of the century'." I make air quotes with my fingers.

It was Isla's idea to build up the wedding with the media. She also wanted to invite influencers from all walks of life to attend, but I have no interest in turning my nuptials into a circus. So, I vetoed the idea of journalists attending in person. I have, however, agreed to the event being recorded by professionals and exclusive clips being shared with the media and the influencers.

This way, we'll get the necessary PR coverage, without the media being physically present.

In all fairness, the publicity generated by the upcoming nuptials has already been beneficial. It's not like I'll ever tell her, but Isla was right to feed the public's interest in the upcoming event. Apparently, not even the most hard-nosed investors can resist the warm, fuzzy feelings that a marriage invokes. And this can only help with the IPO I have planned for the most important company in my portfolio. "I have a lot riding on this wedding."

"Too bad you don't have a bride."

"Ah," —I smirk— "but I do."

She scowls. "No, you don't. Lila—"

"I'm not talking about her."

"Then who are you talking about?"

"You."

To find out what happens next read Liam *and* Isla's *fake relationship romance in* The Proposal *where* Tiny *first makes an appearance*

read Michael *and* Karma's *forced marriage romance in* Mafia King

Read an excerpt from Mafia King

Karma

"Morn came and went—and came, and brought no day..."

Tears prick the backs of my eyes. Goddamn Byron. His words creep up on me when I am at my weakest. Not that I am a poetry addict, by any measure, but words are my jam. The one consolation I have is that, when everything else in the world is wrong, I can turn to them, and they'll be there, friendly, steady, waiting with open arms.

And this particular poem had laced my blood, crawled into my gut when I'd first read it. Darkness had folded within me like an insidious snake, that raises its head when I least expect it. Like now, when I look out on the still sleeping city of London, from the grassy slope of Waterlow Park.

Somewhere out there, the Mafia is hunting me, apparently. It's why my sister Summer and her new husband Sinclair Sterling had insisted that I have my own security detail. I had agreed... only to appease them... then given my bodyguard the slip this morning. I had decided to come running here because it's not a place I'd normally go... Not so early in the morning, anyway. They won't think to look for me here. At least, not for a while longer.

I purse my lips, close my eyes. Silence. The rustle of the wind between the leaves. The faint tinkle of the water from the nearby spring.

I could be the last person on this planet, alone, unsung, bound for the grave.

Ugh! Stop. Right there. I drag the back of my hand across my nose. Try it again, focus, get the words out, one after the other, like the steps of my sorry life.

"Morn came and went—and came, and... and..." My voice breaks. "Bloody asinine hell." I dig my fingers into the grass and grab a handful and fling it out. Again. From the top.

"Morn came and went—and came, and—"

"...brought no day."

A gravelly voice completes my sentence.

I whip my head around. His silhouette fills my line of sight. He's sitting on the same knoll as me, yet I have to crane my neck back to see his profile. The sun is at his back, so I can't make out his features. Can't see his eyes... Can only take in his dark hair, combed back by a ruthless hand that brooked no measure.

My throat dries.

Thick dark hair, shot through with grey at the temples. He wears his age like a badge. I don't know why, but I know his years have not been easy. That he's seen more, indulged in more, reveled in the consequences of his actions, however extreme they might have been. He's not a normal, everyday person, this man. Not a nine-to-fiver, not someone who lives an average life. Definitely not a man who returns home to his wife and home at the end of the day. He is...different, unique, evil... Monstrous. Yes, he is a beast, one who sports the face of a man but who harbors the kind of darkness inside that speaks to me. I gulp.

His face boasts a hooked nose, a thin upper lip, a fleshy lower lip. One that hints at hidden desires, Heat. Lust. The sensuous scrape of that whiskered jaw over my innermost places. Across my inner thigh, reaching toward that core of me that throbs, clenches, melts to feel the stab of his tongue, the thrust of his hardness as he impales me, takes me, makes me his. Goosebumps pop on my skin.

I drag my gaze away from his mouth down to the scar that slashes across his throat. A cold sensation coils in my chest. What or who had hurt him in such a cruel fashion?

"Of this their desolation; and all hearts
Were chill'd into a selfish prayer for light..."

He continues in that rasping guttural tone. Is it the wound that caused that scar that makes his voice so... gravelly... So deep... so... so, hot?

Sweat beads my palms and the hairs on my nape rise. "Who are you?"

He stares ahead as his lips move,

"Forests were set on fire—but hour by hour
They fell and faded—and the crackling trunks
Extinguish'd with a crash—and all was black."

I swallow, moisture gathers in my core. How can I be wet by the mere cadence of this stranger's voice?

I spring up to my feet.

"Sit down," he commands.

His voice is unhurried, lazy even, his spine erect. The cut of his black jacket stretches across the width of his massive shoulders. His hair... I was mistaken—there are threads of dark gold woven between the darkness that pours down to brush the nape of his neck. A strand of hair falls over his brow. As I watch, he raises his hand and brushes it away. Somehow, the gesture lends an air of vulnerability to him. Something so at odds with the rest of his persona that, surely, I am mistaken?

My scalp itches. I take in a breath and my lungs burn. This man... He's sucked up all the oxygen in this open space as if he owns it, the master of all he surveys. The master of me. My death. My life. A shiver ladders along my spine. *Get away, get away now, while you still can.*

I angle my body, ready to spring away from him.

"I won't ask again."

Ask. Command. Force me to do as he wants. He'll have me on my back, bent over, on my side, on my knees, over him, under him. He'll surround me, overwhelm me, pin me down with the force of his personality. His charisma, his larger-than-life essence will crush everything else out of me and I... I'll love it.

"No."

"Yes."

A fact. A statement of intent, spoken aloud. So true. So real. Too real. Too much. Too fast. All of my nightmares... my dreams come to life. Everything I've wanted is here in front of me. I'll die a thousand deaths before he'll be done with me... And then? Will I be reborn? For him. For me. For myself.

I live, first and foremost, to be the woman I was... am meant to be.

"You want to run?"

No.

No.

I nod my head.

He turns his, and all the breath leaves my lungs. Blue eyes—cerulean, dark like the morning skies, deep like the nighttime...hidden corners, secrets that I don't dare uncover. He'll destroy me, have my heart, and break it so casually.

My throat burns and a boiling sensation squeezes my chest.

"Go then, my beauty, fly. You have until I count to five. If I catch you, you are mine."

"If you don't?"

"Then I'll come after you, stalk your every living moment, possess your nightmares, and steal you away in the dead of night, and then..."

I draw in a shuddering breath as liquid heat drips from between my legs. "Then?" I whisper.

"Then, I'll ensure you'll never belong to anyone else, you'll never see the light of day again, for your every breath, your every waking second, your thoughts, your actions... and all your words, every single last one, will belong to me." He peels back his lips, and his teeth glint in the first rays of the morning light. "Only me." He straightens to his feet and rises, and rises.

This man... He is massive. A monster who always gets his way. My guts churn. My toes curl. Something primeval inside of me insists I hold my own. I cannot give in to him. Cannot let him win whatever this is. I need to stake my ground, in some form. *Say something. Anything. Show him you're not afraid of this.*

"Why?" I tilt my head back, all the way back. "Why are you doing this?"

He tilts his head, his ears almost canine in the way they are silhouetted against his profile.

"Is it because you can? Is it a... a," I blink, "a debt of some kind?"

He stills.

"My father, this is about how he betrayed the Mafia, right? You're one of them?"

"Lucky guess." His lips twist, "It is about your father, and how he promised you to me. He reneged on his promise, and now, I am here to collect."

"No." I swallow... *No, no, no.*

"Yes." His jaw hardens.

All expression is wiped clean of his face, and I know then, that he speaks the truth. It's always about the past. My sorry shambles of a past... Why does it always catch up with me? *You can run, but you can never hide.*

"Tick-tock, Beauty." He angles his body and his shoulders shut out the sight of the sun, the dawn skies, the horizon, the city in the distance, the rustle of the grass, the trees, the rustle of the leaves. All of it fades and leaves just me and him. Us. *Run.*

"Five." He jerks his chin, straightens the cuffs of his sleeves.

My knees wobble.

"Four."

My pulse rate spikes. I should go. Leave. But my feet are planted in this earth. This piece of land where we first met. What am I, but a speck in the larger scheme of things? To be hurt. To be forgotten. To be taken without an ounce of retribution. To be punished... by him.

"Three." He thrusts out his chest, widens his stance, every muscle in his body relaxed. "Two."

I swallow. The pulse beats at my temples. My blood thrums.

"One."

Michael

"Go."

She pivots and races down the slope. Her dark hair streams behind her. Her scent, sexy femininity and silver moonflowers, clings to my nose, then recedes. It's so familiar, that scent.

I had smelled it before, had reveled in it. Had drawn in it into my lungs as she had peeked up at me from under her thick eyelashes. Her green gaze had fixed on mine, her lips parted as she welcomed my kiss. As she had wound her arms about my neck, pushed up those sweet breasts and flattened them against my chest. As she had parted her legs when I had planted my thigh between them. I had seen her before... in my dreams. I stiffen. She can't be the same girl, though, can she?

I reach forward, thrust out my chin and sniff the air, but there's only the damp scent of dawn, mixed with the foul tang of exhaust fumes, as she races away from me.

She stumbles and I jump forward, pause when she straightens. Wait. Wait. Give her a lead. Let her think she has almost escaped, that she's gotten the better of me... As if.

I clench my fists at my sides, force myself to relax. Wait. Wait. She reaches the bottom of the incline, turns. I surge forward. One foot in front of the other. My heels dig into the grassy surface and mud flies up, clings to the hem of my £4000 Italian pants. Like I care? Plenty more where that came from. An entire walk-in closet, full of clothes made to measure, to suit every occasion, with every possible accessory needed by a man in my position to impress...

Everything... Except the one thing that I had coveted from the moment I had laid eyes on her. Sitting there on the grassy slope, unshed tears in her eyes, and reciting... Byron? For hell's sake. Of all the poets in the world, she had to choose the Lord of Darkness.

I huff. All a ploy. Clearly, she knew I was sitting next to her... No, not possible. I had walked toward her and she hadn't stirred. Hadn't been aware. Yeah, I am that good. I've been known to slit a man's throat from ear-to-ear while he was awake and in his full senses. Alive one second, dead the next. That's how it is in my world. You want it, you take it. And I... I want her.

I increase my pace, eat up the distance between myself and the girl... That's all she is. A slip of a thing, a slim blur of motion. Beauty in hiding. A diamond, waiting for me to get my hands on her, polish her, show her what it means to be...

Dead. She is dead. That's why I am here.

A flash of skin, a creamy length of thigh. My groin hardens and my legs wobble. I lurch over a bump in the ground. The hell? I right myself, leap forward, inching closer, closer. She reaches a curve in the path, disappears out of sight.

My heart hammers in my chest. I will not lose her, will not. *Here, Beauty, come to Daddy.* The wind whistles past my ears. I pump my legs, lengthen my strides, turn the corner. There's no one there. Huh?

My heart hammers and the blood pounds at my wrists, my temples; adrenaline thrums in my veins. I slow down, come to a stop. Scan the clearing.

The hairs on my forearms prickle. She's here. Not far, but where? Where is she? I prowl across to the edge of the clearing, under the tree with its spreading branches.

When I get my hands on you, Beauty, I'll spread your legs like the pages of a poem. Dip into your honeyed sweetness, like a quill pen in ink. Drag my aching shaft across that melting, weeping entrance. My balls throb. My groin tightens. The crack of a branch above shivers across my stretched nerve endings. I swoop forward, hold out my arms, and close my grasp around the trembling, squirming mass of precious humanity. I cradle her close to my chest, heart beating thud-thud-thud, overwhelming any other thought.

Mine. All mine. The hell is wrong with me? She wriggles her little body, and her curves slide across my forearms. My shoulders bunch and my fingers tingle. She kicks out with her legs and arches her back, thrusting her breasts up so her nipples are outlined against the fabric of her sports bra. She dared to come out dressed like that? In that scrap of fabric that barely covers her luscious flesh?

"Let me go." She whips her head toward me and her hair flows around her shoulders, across her face. She blows it out of the way. "You monster, get away from me."

Anger drums at the backs of my eyes and desire tugs at my groin. The scent of her is sheer torture, something I had dreamed of in the wee hours of twilight when dusk turned into night.

She's not real. She's not the woman I think she is. She is my downfall. My sweet poison. The bitter medicine I must partake of to cure the ills that plague my company.

"Fine." I lower my arms and she tumbles to the grass, hits the ground butt first.

"How dare you." She huffs out a breath, her hair messily arranged across her face.

I shove my hands into the pockets of my fitted pants, knees slightly bent, legs apart. Tip my chin down and watch her as she sprawls at my feet.

"You... dropped me?" She makes a sound deep in her throat.

So damn adorable.

"Your wish is my command." I quirk my lips.

"You don't mean it."

"You're right." I lean my weight forward on the balls of my feet and she flinches.

"What... what do you want?"

"You."

She pales. "You want to... to rob me? I have nothing of consequence.

"Oh, but you do, Beauty."

I lean in and every muscle in her body tenses. Good. She's wary. She should be. She should have been alert enough to have run as soon as she sensed my presence. But she hadn't.

I should spare her because she's the woman from my dreams... but I won't. She's a debt I intend to collect. She owes me, and I've delayed what was meant to happen long enough.

I pull the gun from my holster, point it at her.

Her gaze widens and her breath hitches. I expect her to plead with me for her life, but she doesn't. She stares back at me with her huge dilated pupils. She licks her lips and the blood drains to my groin. *Che cazzo!* Why does her lack of fear turn me on so?

"Your phone," I murmur, "take out your phone."

She draws in a breath, then reaches into her pocket and pulls out her phone.

"Call your sister."

"What?"

"Dial your sister, Beauty. Tell her you are going away on a long trip to Sicily with your new male friend."

"What?"

"You heard me." I curl my lips. "Do it, now!'

She blinks, looks like she is about to protest, then her fingers fly over the phone.

Damn, and I had been looking forward to coaxing her into doing my bidding.

She holds her phone to her ear. I can hear the phone ring on the other side, before it goes to voicemail. She glances at me and I jerk my chin. She looks away, takes a deep breath, then speaks in a cheerful voice, "Hi Summer, it's me, Karma. I, ah, have to go away for a bit. This new... ah, friend of mine... He has an extra ticket and he has invited me to Sicily to spend some time with him. I... ah, I don't know when, exactly, I'll be back, but I'll message you and let you know. Take care. Love ya sis, I—"

I snatch the phone from her, disconnect the call, then hold the gun to her temple, "Goodbye, Beauty."

To FIND OUT WHAT HAPPENS NEXT READ MICHAEL AND KARMA'S FORCED MARRIAGE STORY IN MAFIA KING

READ JJ AND LENA'S EX-BOYFRIEND'S FATHER, AGE-GAP ROMANCE IN MAFIA LUST

READ KNIGHT AND PENNY'S, BEST FRIEND'S BROTHER ROMANCE IN THE WRONG WIFE

READ DR. WESTON KINCAID AND AMELIE'S FORCED PROXIMITY, ONE-BED CHRISTMAS ROMANCE IN THE BILLIONAIRE'S FAKE WIFE

DOWNLOAD YOUR EXCLUSIVE L. STEELE READING ORDER BINGO CARD ON HER WEBSITE

DID YOU KNOW ALL THE CHARACTERS YOU READ ABOUT HAVE THEIR OWN BOOK? CROSS OFF THEIR STORIES AS YOU READ AND SHARE YOUR BINGO CARD IN L. STEELE'S READER GROUP

WANT TO BE THE FIRST TO FIND OUT WHEN L. STEELE'S NEXT BOOK IS OUT? SIGN UP FOR HER NEWSLETTER ON HER WEBSITE

FROM THE AUTHOR

Hello, I'm L. Steele. I write romance stories with strong powerful men who meet their match in sassy, curvy, spitfire women.

I love to push myself with each book on both the spice and the angst so I can deliver well rounded, multidimensional characters.

I enjoy trading trivia with my filmmaker husband, watching lots and lots of movies, and walking nature trails. I live in London

FOLLOW ME:
On Amazon
on BookBub
on Goodreads
on Audible
On TikTok
On Threads
on Pinterest
My YouTube channel
Join my secret Facebook Reader Group
Read ALL my books

SKYLAR'S RECIPES

Skylar's The Movin' On Macarons

Ingredients:
  Macaron Shells:

- 2 egg whites
- 1 cup powdered sugar
- 1 cup almond flour
- 1/4 cup cacao powder
- 1/4 cup honey Zest from 2 lemons
- Chamomile flowers from 3 tea bags

Instructions:

1. Whip egg whites until foamy.
2. Gradually add powdered sugar while whipping to stiff, glossy peaks.
3. Fold almond flour, cacao powder, honey, lemon zest and chamomile flowers gently into egg white mixture.
4. Pipe batter onto baking sheets lined with parchment.
5. Tap trays firmly on the counter to release air bubbles.
6. Let shells rest for 30 minutes before baking.

7. Bake at 300°F for 18-20 minutes until set.

Chocolate Honey Lemon Buttercream:

Ingredients:

- 1 cup unsalted butter, softened
- 3 cups powdered sugar
- 1/4 cup cacao powder
- 3 Tbsps honey
- 1 Tbsp lemon juice
- 1 tsp lemon zest
- Pinch of salt

Instructions:

Cream butter until smooth. Add powdered sugar, cacao powder, honey, lemon juice & zest, and pinch of salt. Beat on medium until light and fluffy.

Assembly:

1. Pair macaron shells by size.
2. Spread buttercream on flat side of one cookie.
3. Top with another shell, twisting gently to adhere.

As you enjoy these bittersweet yet soothing macarons, taste the emotions of relationships past and the hopeful sweetness of fresh starts ahead. Each complex flavor brings to mind that when something ends, there are still joys to be found as we move forward with courage.

Skylar's Chocolate Cinnamon Hero

Ingredients:

- 2 cups (500ml) milk of your choice
- 3 tablespoons (21g) cocoa powder
- 2 tablespoons (30g) brown sugar
- 1 teaspoon (5ml) vanilla extract
- 1/4 teaspoon cinnamon, plus extra for garnish
- Pinch of cayenne pepper (optional)
- Whipped cream (optional)

Instructions:

1. Add the milk, cocoa powder, brown sugar, vanilla and cinnamon to a small saucepan. Whisk well until there are no lumps from the cocoa powder.
2. Place the saucepan over medium heat and warm the mixture, while continuing to whisk, for about 5-7 minutes until hot with steam rising. Be careful not to allow it to boil.
3. Pour the hot chocolate into mugs. Top with an additional dash of cinnamon and/or a dollop of whipped cream if desired.
4. For a spicy kick, add a small pinch of cayenne pepper.
5. Drink up and enjoy this rich, chocolatey, cinnamon-kissed and warming hero of drink! It's sure to save your day.

Skylar's Crab and Asparagus Omelet

Ingredients:
- 2eggs
- 1⁄4 cup lump crab meat, picked over forshells
- 4 asparagus spears, trimmed and cut into 1-inchpieces
- 1 tablespoon unsaltedbutter
- 2 tablespoons freshly gratedParmesan
- Salt and pepper totaste
- 6 cherry tomatoes,halved
- 2 cups rocketleaves
- 1-2 tablespoons good quality balsamicglaze

Instructions:

1 Beat the eggs lightly in a small bowl with a fork. Stir in the crab meat and asparagus pieces. Season with salt and pepper.

2 In a small nonstick skillet over medium heat, melt the butter. Pour in the eggs and cook, lifting the edges to allow uncooked egg to flow to the bottom of the pan, until the bottom is set but the top is still moist, about 2 minutes.

3 Sprinkle the Parmesan over half of the omelet. Using a spatula, fold the plain half over the cheese half. Cook for 1 minute more.

4 Make a salad by tossing the cherry tomato halves and rocket leaves together. Drizzle with balsamic glaze.

5 Carefully slide omelet onto plate. Serve with salad on the side.Enjoy!

Skylar's Tiramisu

Ingredients:

- 6 large egg yolks
- 3/4 cup granulated sugar
- 1 cup mascarpone cheese, at room temperature
- 1 1/2 cups heavy cream
- 2 cups strong brewed coffee or espresso, cooled to room temperature
- 1/2 cup coffee liqueur (optional)
- 2 packages ladyfinger cookies (savoiardi)
- Cocoa powder, for dusting
- Dark chocolate shavings or cocoa powder for garnish (optional)

Instructions:

1. In a heatproof bowl, whisk together the egg yolks and sugar until well combined and pale yellow in color.
2. Place the bowl over a pot of simmering water (double boiler) and whisk constantly until the mixture thickens slightly, about 5-7 minutes. Remove from heat and let cool slightly.
3. Add the mascarpone cheese to the egg yolk mixture and whisk until smooth and well combined. Set aside.
4. In a separate bowl, whip the heavy cream until stiff peaks form.
5. Gently fold the whipped cream into the mascarpone mixture until well incorporated. Be careful not to deflate the whipped cream.
6. In a shallow dish, combine the brewed coffee and coffee liqueur (if using).
7. Quickly dip each ladyfinger into the coffee mixture, ensuring they are soaked but not overly soggy.
8. Arrange a layer of soaked ladyfingers in the bottom of a 9x13 inch dish or a similarly sized serving dish.
9. Spread half of the mascarpone mixture over the ladyfingers, smoothing it out with a spatula.
10. Repeat the layers with the remaining soaked ladyfingers and mascarpone mixture.
11. Cover the tiramisu with plastic wrap and refrigerate for at least 4 hours, or preferably overnight, to allow the flavors to meld and the dessert to set.

12. Before serving, dust the top of the tiramisu with cocoa powder and garnish with chocolate shavings or additional cocoa powder, if desired.
13. Slice and serve chilled. Enjoy your homemade tiramisu!

Note: Tiramisu can also be served in individual glasses or cups for a more elegant presentation. Simply layer the soaked ladyfingers and mascarpone mixture in each glass and refrigerate as directed.

NATE AND SKYLAR'S INTIMATE WEDDING DINNER MENU

Created by Chef James Hamilton

Appetizers:

- Burrata cheese with heirloom tomatoes, basil pesto and balsamic reduction
- Seared scallops with cauliflower puree
- Beef or vegetable carpaccio

Salads:

- Mixed baby greens with shaved fennel, crispy prosciutto and lemon vinaigrette
- Endive and pear salad with gorgonzola and candied walnuts

Entrees:

- Filet mignon with herb butter, grilled asparagus and roasted fingerling potatoes
- Salmon en croute stuffed with spinach and ricotta in beurre blanc sauce

- Chicken saltimbocca with sage, prosciutto, and madeira wine sauce over risotto

Sides:

- Sautéed wild mushrooms
- Roasted brussels sprouts with pancetta
- Parmesan risotto

Dessert:

- Chocolate molten lava cakes
- Fresh berries with sweet ricotta and honey

MARRIAGE OF CONVENIENCE BILLIONAIRE ROMANCE FROM L. STEELE

The Billionaire's Fake Wife - Sinclair and Summer's story that started this universe... with a plot twist you won't see coming!

The Billionaire's Secret - Victoria and Saint's story. Saint is maybe the most alphahole of them all!

Marrying the Billionaire Single Dad - Damian and Julia's story, watch out for the plot twist!

The Proposal - Liam and Isla's story. What's a wedding planner to do when you tell the bride not to go through with the wedding and the groom demands you take her place and give him a heir? And yes plot twist!

CHRISTMAS ROMANCE BOOKS BY L. STEELE FOR YOU

Want to find out how Dr. Weston Kincaid and Amelie met? Read The Billionaire's Christmas Bride

Want even more Christmas Romance books? *Read A very Mafia Christmas, Christian and Aurora's story*

Read a marriage of convenience billionaire Christmas romance, Hunter and Zara's story - *The Christmas One Night Stand*

FORBIDDEN BILLIONAIRE ROMANCE BY L. STEELE FOR YOU

Read Daddy JJ's, age-gap romance in Mafia Lust HERE

Read Edward, Baron and Ava's story starting with Billionaire's Sins HERE

ABOUT THE AUTHOR

Hello, I'm L. Steele.

I write romance stories with strong powerful men who meet their match in sassy, curvy, spitfire women.

I love to push myself with each book on both the spice and the angst so I can deliver well rounded, multidimensional characters.

I enjoy trading trivia with my husband, watching lots and lots of movies, and walking nature trails. I live in London.

Follow me:
On Amazon
on BookBub
on Goodreads
on Audible
On TikTok
Join my secret Facebook Reader Group
on Pinterest
My YouTube channel
Read ALL my books
Spotify

Milton Keynes UK
Ingram Content Group UK Ltd.
UKHW021124270524
443319UK00019B/1242